Murder
by Another Name

Jo Stone

ISBN 978-1-957220-77-2 (paperback)
ISBN 978-1-957220-78-9 (hardcover)
ISBN 978-1-957220-79-6 (digital)

Rushmore Press LLC
1 800 460 9188
www.rushmorepress.com

Printed in the United States of America

They laughed as they held hands and tripped down the exit stairs from the darkened medical suite. Dr. Daniel MacNamara, handsome plastic surgeon and president of the Colorado organization of plastic surgeons, opened the heavy exit door from the fire stairs into the dimly lit parking lot behind his building, briefly surveyed the nearly empty parking lot, then held the door open as his pretty, blonde companion stepped out ahead of him. The door closed with a definitive bang.

"Oh damn, I forgot my bag," he said. Dan MacNamara stood there for a moment, grimacing in thought.

"Do you need it if you're just stopping by the hospital?" the young woman asked, suddenly very serious.

"No, I guess not. It's just that Sally will think it is strange if I come home without it. That's all."

"How will she know you didn't leave it in the car?" Sherrie Barker asked, all semblance of the laughter of a few moments ago now missing from her concerned voice.

"I always leave my bag on a table by the front door. I always have, ever since Suzanna was little and lost it for me when I was on my way to an emergency call. She'll know I don't have it. It's more likely that she would leave her purse somewhere, than that I would come home without my bag—one of my many peculiarities." He smiled at her wrinkled brow.

"Oh, come on, let's go. First time for everything—especially when you're about to turn forty-five," he said as he took her elbow and guided her toward the sole car in the parking lot, past his own jade green Jaguar parked directly in front of the exit door.

They stopped at the door of Sherrie Barker's blue Mustang, and he waited as she unlocked the door and slid into the driver's seat. She looked up at Dan and smiled.

"We'll make it through all of this, Dan if you help me think it through and we decide what to do together. Just keep those documents safe until I get back in town and we have a chance to talk all this over again."

He bent down and gave her a soft kiss on the lips and brushed a wisp of hair out of her eyes with the back of his hand.

"The stuff is okay locked away in my safe. No one even knows that safe is there except Sal, and she thinks I never use it anymore since we moved our things to the safe in the new house. I'll wait until you're back and we can go through it together. In the meantime, I'm going to ask some people some careful questions on my own. Have a safe trip home, angel."

"I love you, Dan," she whispered.

He kissed her again and shut the car door. Dan MacNamara stepped back a few steps so that she could back out. Sherrie waved to him again with her left hand as she turned the ignition key with her right. The explosion blew him into the air and flung him backwards nearly to the bumper of his Jaguar, where he lay unconscious in the light of the flames.

Pamela Lawson hardly noticed the siren of another ambulance arriving at the Emergency Entrance three floors below her room. She turned her head on her pillow to watch her husband stare out the window at the fire engines and their flashing lights in the parking lot of the medical building across the street from the hospital. She could just make out the flickering of the lights and the fire reflected on the ceiling.

"Is there a building on fire?" she asked.

"I can't tell what's burning, but it looks like it's behind the building across the street," he answered, craning his neck as though that might help him see over the four-story building. "Sure is causing a lot of commotion, whatever it is. There are four fire trucks and an ambulance and three police cars still there. That ambulance we just heard came tearing across the street from there."

"Well, maybe you'll get a better look when you leave," Pamela said wearily, as she closed her eyes and sighed.

"I'm sorry, honey," Larry Lawson said, turning sheepishly from the window. He sat down in the chair by her head and gently touched her tousled hair. She looked thin and pale in the hospital gown. He could see his wife's shoulder blades through the well-worn and often washed cotton. Her hand showed the marks of two weeks of intravenous needles, and he wondered if they could find a place to put a new one in the morning. Her beautiful blue eyes were dull and sunken and he knew she needed to sleep.

Pamela said it first. "Go home, Larry. You need to sleep and I need to sleep. Besides, I feel like things are lots better for the kids if you put them to bed. Sara's going to stay awake until someone tells her a story. Go now. I'll be fine."

Larry leaned down and kissed her forehead. Her skin felt clammy and cool to his lips, and she suddenly shivered.

"Are you okay? Shall I call the nurse?"

"No, sweetheart," she said keeping her eyes shut. "Just get that extra blanket on the chair and put it over me. I guess I'm just a little cold. Then go. I'll see you in the morning." She opened her great blue eyes and smiled at him.

Larry Lawson got the blanket and spread it tenderly over her tiny frame, tucking it gently around her bare-looking shoulders and carefully around her IV and hand. She smiled again and closed her eyes. "I really love you," she said.

He kissed her as she smiled and said, "Bye, darlin', I'll be back at the crack of dawn."

"I know you will," she said, still smiling with her eyes closed, "Bye."

"Bye," Larry said and quietly left the room, pulling the door almost shut behind him. He stopped for a moment to try and remember if her call button was in easy reach, then continued down the hall as he remembered it was pinned just an inch or so from her hand with the IV.

"Good night, Mr. Lawson," the large nurse behind the nurses' station said as he approached.

"I covered her with another blanket, but she seems cold. Could you check on her in a little bit and make sure she's okay?" he asked.

"Sure. I'll be going in a minute to check her IV and blood pressure, so I'll make sure she's fine. You just get some rest. You look really beat."

"I'm a little tired," he confessed. "I'll leave her to you and her angels for the night. I've got to go see about our kids."

"You go right along. We'll be fine until morning," the nurse said warmly as she came around the counter and gave him a pat on the arm. "Go get some dinner and some sleep. Good night."

"Good night," Larry said and hurried through the double doors to the elevators. He needed to see David and Sara. He needed to hug them and hear their laughter.

Inside the elevator, he was lost in thought and missed his floor. Larry snapped back to reality as the doors opened in the basement, just outside the cafeteria, and two nurses in operating room garb got on with coffee to go and a bag of what smelled like hamburgers. Larry's stomach growled and he realized that he had not eaten since the granola bar he ate in the car on the way to the office that morning. He had come to the hospital to help Pam eat lunch and had no time to eat himself before he went back to work. At five o'clock, he had hurried back to the hospital so that he would be there to help her with her dinner tray. He kept believing that if he could get her to eat and gain some weight that she would start to get well. In the process, he had lost nearly fifteen pounds himself. Larry Lawson drove home, immersed in thoughts of Pamela, and once more forgot that he was hungry.

He was deep in thought as he passed the parking lot to the medical office building across from the hospital where the fire trucks were still surrounding the smoldering ruins of the blue Mustang. The car of the County Coroner and one ambulance were parked beside the fire trucks obscuring the view from the street where Larry Lawson passed in his minivan.

About thirty minutes later, Larry pulled into the driveway of their cozy ranch-style house in the Beaver Valley subdivision and hurried inside. As he opened the door, he smelled the dinner his mother had fixed for the children. She was sitting on the living room couch with a freshly bathed child in pajamas under each arm. She was reading "Winnie the Pooh and Tigger Too!"

"Hi, Daddy!" Sara and David squealed as they ran across the room and into his waiting arms. He hugged them close and smelled the baby shampoo smell of their damp hair. His eyes filled with tears of weariness and joy.

"Hey, it's Sara-jara and David-snavid!" He laughed.

"Daddy," they both said and hugged him again as he laughed at their chagrin at being called his silly made-up names.

"Let Daddy go and eat, and we'll finish our story." His mother smiled at him from the couch. "Dinner is waiting for you in the oven, Larry. I'm sure you haven't eaten a bite all day," she guessed.

"I'm starved," he said. "I'll get my plate and come hear the story, too."

The children ran back to the couch and under Emma Lawson's arms and Larry went into the kitchen, following the delicious smell of his waiting dinner. He opened the oven and found his welcome plate of meatloaf, mashed potatoes, corn and hot rolls."

"There's a Jello salad in a bowl for you in the fridge," his mother called, hardly missing a beat in the story. He found the salad and poured himself a large glass of milk. Instead of going back into the living room, Larry sat his hot plate on the table in the kitchen and sat down absentmindedly in front of the window, listening to his mother's voice as she read to his children just as she had read to him many years ago. The children giggled as she changed her voice to sound like Pooh and Tigger and Piglet. He smiled as she did her gloomy rendition of Eeyore. That had been his favorite.

Heading back to the living room, he paused at the door with the bowl of Jello. Larry noticed the notes by the telephone. He sat the bowl down and shuffled through them. Then his eye caught the last one—time: eight o'clock. It was from Janet Stephenson, their lawyer. "Call back tonight—no matter how late. Urgent."

"Mom, what's this message from Janet Stephenson about? What's urgent?" he interrupted.

Grandma Lawson looked up smiling from her book, and suddenly got a puzzled look on her face? "I don't know, dear. I asked her if it could wait until morning, but she said she thought you would want to talk to her tonight. She sounded upset."

Larry returned to the kitchen and picked up the receiver on the wall phone, then put it down and went up down the stairs to the lower-level master bedroom to make the call.

"Hello," she answered quickly, as though she were waiting by the phone.

"Janet? Larry Lawson. What's up?"

"Larry, bad news. Dr. MacNamara was hurt tonight when a car exploded in the parking lot where he had his car parked. He's in the hospital—the floor above Pam. It wasn't his car; he was apparently just in the parking lot of his office at the same time the other car exploded."

"Is he okay? When did this happen?" Larry's mind leaped back to the blazing fire in the lot next to Dr. MacNamara's building across from Pam's hospital room.

"Just this evening—some time after seven. I called you from the hospital. I was on my way up to see Pam when they brought him into emergency. I just happened to hear a nurse screaming his name - and I just poked my nose where it didn't belong, I suppose. I sort of hung around to try and see what was going on, but I'm still not sure what happened. I wanted you to know before someone tells Pam that he won't be coming to see her. I thought that might be more than she could take at this point. She is really counting on him to bring her through this crisis."

"I think it may be more than just a crisis, Janet. I'm not seeing any improvement. She just seems to be slipping away, and she doesn't seem to really care anymore. I was really afraid to leave her tonight, but she ordered me out of there. She said she needed to sleep I know she's dreading surgery tomorrow."

"What shall we do, Larry. Do you want me to tell her, or do you want to do it?"

Larry Lawson sat on their bed with his head in his hands, feeling numb. "Why don't you do it," he said. "Maybe you can find out more about what happened before you tell her. Maybe he isn't hurt that bad. What do you think?"

"I'll see what I can find out," Janet said, deep in thought. "I'll go by the police department and see what I can find out and then I'll go to see Pam before Dr. MacNamara would normally make his morning rounds."

"Are you sure, Janet? It's already so late!"

"No sweat," she said gently. "I don't have anything else to do and you need to spend some time with your kids. I'm sure they'll need you first thing in the morning - and you sound beat."

"Thanks," he said wearily. "I'll try to be at the hospital by seven-thirty. Is that soon enough?"

"That will be fine. I should be there by six-thirty or so. See you then. Bye, Larry."

"Bye," he said and quietly hung up the phone. That was the fire I saw, he thought to himself. I wonder what happened.

"Daddy?" Sara stood in his doorway in her long nightgown, with the light from the hall shining through her golden hair.

"Come here, sweetheart!" he opened his arms as she flew across the room and hugged him tight.

"Grandma said I should ask you if you want to tuck us in."

"Sure, I do. Come on, where's David? It's long past your bedtime." He swooped her up and carried her, giggling up the stairs and calling, "David-snavid, let's hit the sack. Come on, I'll tuck you in and do prayers. Hurry. Hurry."

David came running down the hall from the living room, and he swooped him up under his arm and carried them both off to bed.

"**S**on of a gun! Son of a gun! Why don't they go off together tonight? Every other Wednesday for the last two months, and tonight, they don't do it! Son of a gun!" The angry dark-haired man pounded the dashboard of the van which began creeping slowly down the street next to Dan MacNamara's office building just as the ambulance and fire trucks screamed around the corner. "Hey man, we sure blew her to kingdom come, though! There couldn't be much left of him. He was too close. Hey man, he was flyin' through the air and landed on his friggin' head. He's gotta be dead. No way, man, he's dead."

The driver, a tall Ichabod Crane kind of man in his early twenties, with greasy brown hair hanging below his baseball cap, shook his head in glee. He looked at his small dark companion in the Peter Falk raincoat and Sherlock Holmes hat, slumped angrily in the passenger seat of the van, and continued. "It looked like the friggin' Fourth of July! Did you see that explosion? It was one of my best. Better than even that three-tiered explosion in the Pelican Brief. Hey man, awesome. We can finish the friggin' doc later. Hey, man, just relish the moment! It was great. He was extra anyhow. Wasn't it her you really wanted to be wasted?"

"Yeah, asshole, I wanted her. But it would've been so much better if we had gotten them both - with one shot. I hate loose ends. The boss hates loose ends even more. Shit! Take me to the airport."

"Yes, sir!" the greasy driver responded, mocking the other man's French-Canadian accent. "Your wish is my friggin' command."

They turned on the freeway and drove in silence to the airport exit. At the terminal, the Canadian got out and handed Tom Slade an envelope.

"Don't spend it all in one place, Tommy, and lie low so that I can use you if I'm sent back to finish the job. You know how my people hate any kind of publicity. Drive carefully - stay away from coppers and keep your mouth shut. I'll call you in a few days." Raoul Lecroix grabbed his bag from behind his seat and closed the door. Tom Slade watched as the automatic doors opened and Raoul disappeared. Then he drove slowly away, chuckling to himself.

He couldn't keep himself from driving back by the hospital and the parking lot across the street. Slade was stopped, momentarily, by a policeman who was directing traffic to allow the coroner's hearse to leave the parking lot. He smiled as the policeman looked directly at him through the windshield. Then he drove to the Horny Toad Lounge for some beers and some laughs.

"I done good! Damn, it was the best explosion I ever did!" he repeated to himself.

The parking lot of the Horny Toad was full, as usual. Slade had to circle through it a few times and wait for a tipsy customer and his date to back their pickup truck out of a spot near the corner of the building before he could go in. He saw Charlie's old junker and Ben's Jeep parked in front by the street. But it was Lorraine who caught his eye as he walked in. She had her back to him, leaning over to deliver drinks at a long table. Her frayed leg denim short shorts and bandana halter uniform left little to the imagination. Slade, the owner and most of the customers liked it that way.

Tom Slade pinched her thigh playfully as he slid by her and sat down backwards on a chair at the next table. "Hey, bud, that chair's taken. He's just in the can," the guy at the table yelled over the loud country band.

Slade waved his hand at him and yelled, "I'm not stayin', man. I just got to say a word or two to Rainey, here. Hi, babe."

Lorraine Wilson shook her head at him and turned away. He grabbed her arm as she started off with her tray of dirty glasses and ash trays.

"Wait a minute, chickie," he said.

"Let go of me, scum," she growled at him, her green eyes flashing. "You smell."

"We'll see who smells, slut." He flung her arm at her, almost making her lose her balance. The tray tipped precariously, but Ben appeared behind her and kept it from falling. Lorraine turned and headed toward the kitchen without speaking to Ben.

"Hey man, come on over, Tom, we got a table and a pitcher." The tall, tan, blond man in a red plaid western shirt without sleeves, tight Levis, and a toothpick in his mouth smiled and gestured toward the corner where four or five guys were sitting around a round table, laughing. Tom and Ben made their way through the crowded room and snagged an empty chair for Tom on the way.

Charlie was clearly drunk and entertaining the group with an obscene story. Tom soon forgot the waitress and was drinking and laughing with his friends. Ben winked at Lorraine as she passed. She smiled a grateful smile, relieved that she was not assigned their table.

"That Tom Slade really gives me the creeps," she told Susan Sampson, the waitress who had the misfortune of being charged with keeping the rowdy group in the corner in pitchers of beer, chips, and salsa and clean ash trays. Susan was unloading her tray of dirty dishes and baskets in the kitchen trash.

"Yuck, me too." Susan shuddered as she emptied the trash off her tray into the huge plastic garbage can. "I wonder why those other guys hang out with him. Ben and Charlie really aren't half bad. But Slade's really a bottom dweller. He's always touching me. Makes me want to puke. He looks like he dips himself in Crisco. I never saw a grown man with so many disgusting zits." She shuddered again.

"Charlie said he's really some kind of genius. He knows all kinds of chemistry and science and stuff. He said Slade was in college. He just got kicked out because he got high and blew up a million-dollar lab or something. He got hurt in the explosion and was in a rehab place for a long time for the drugs. But it didn't help - he's really a slug - and crazy as a bat. Did you ever look at his eyes?"

"Rainey, I try not to look anywhere at his person, let alone his eyes!" Susan loaded up six mugs of strong black coffee and headed through the swinging doors of the kitchen.

The coffee was wasted. The rowdy bunch from the corner were already heading out the door. The band was packing up. It was fifteen minutes until closing time.

"What a relief," sighed Susan. She sat down the tray and went back to the table to see if they left her a tip. Fifty dollars in ten dollar bills were under Ben's glass, along with a note scrawled on a napkin. "Thanks, sugar," was all it said. She picked up the money and the napkin and put them in her pocket.

"Ben's okay," she thought.

Lorraine returned her last load of dirty glasses to the kitchen and was taking off her apron as Susan came in with her last tray. "Bob, picking you up?" she asked Susan.

"No, I'm going to stop by the hospital and peek in at my sister on my way home. She has surgery in the morning," Susan said.

"Will they let you in?" Lorraine asked

"They always let family in when someone is on the critical list. All transplant patients are considered critical," Susan said, suddenly overwhelmed with sadness. Her eyes filled with tears. Lorraine saw the tears and put her arms around her friend. Susan began to sob.

"It's not fair, Rainey, it's not fair. Pam always did everything right. Good grades, good boyfriend, good husband, good kids. First, she gets cancer, and now this. It's not fair."

"Hey, kid, life's not fair." Lorraine held her back at arm's length and wiped the mascara and tears from her face with a napkin. "Hell if life was fair, we'd both be married to millionaires instead of holding on by a shoestring and being single parents because the guys we got kept going. Nobody works harder than you and me and all we get is guys like slimy Slade and tips if we're lucky."

Susan looked gratefully at her friend, gave her a hug, and said, "At least we got our health. My Gramma says, 'if you got your health, you got everything.' I guess we have everything."

They left the bar together as the last customer's car left the parking lot. The burly bartender, Al, stood at the door and watched them, then locked the door and left himself.

Janet Stephenson hung up the telephone with Larry Lawson's exhausted voice still in her mind. She had just called her friend at the police precinct near the hospital to see where the police would be processing the information about Dr. MacNamara and the explosion. Her eight years as a prosecutor had given her some invaluable contacts and access to police personnel. The fact that she was attractive and looked nothing like the stereotyped lawyer didn't hurt either. But, Janet was smart enough to be humble. She had been humbled first by growing up a skinny kid with dishwater blond hair and thick glasses. Now she was still slender, with too-long legs, but her glasses had disappeared with the miracle of contact lenses, and the dishwater had been transformed into the sparkling gold available in a box from Payless Drugs to anyone with $6.95. Even though she was no longer young, her thick tresses, smooth skin, and long legs, a genetic gift from her Dutch ancestors, gave her a timeless beauty. She had also discovered that, in her profession, with age comes credibility, particularly for a woman.

Janet had also been humbled by her inability, when she was a young prosecutor, to right the obvious wrongs in the world. She had been horrified as her first jury refused to convict a fat defendant who had terribly abused a three-year-old child, and further horrified as he committed a similar crime three months after he was acquitted. She knew and feared the capricious nature of the system of justice which she had sworn to uphold. Judges and juries didn't always share her clear view of right and wrong. Procedure often obscured truth. Finally, she resigned and left the world of criminal law.

Janet was married to her college sweetheart, a fighter pilot turned airline pilot and writer. They had two children, Brad, Jr. and Hannah, before she went to law school. When she opened her own office as a civil trial lawyer, she started her quest for justice and truth again, on her own turf. After ten years, she had her own building, two associates, three paralegals, and overhead costs which made her work sixteen-hour days. But she also had her own benevolent dictatorship and sometimes she even liked it.

That was how she met Larry and Pamela Lawson. They were the second couple with PSS implants to seek her help in suing the manufacturer of the silicone gel breast implants which were killing Pam. She didn't really want the case, but here she was at two in the morning, up to her ears in tragedy and problems without solutions. Now, Dr. MacNamara.

"What is going on?" she thought.

As she sat at the desk in their book-filled study, the phone rang. Startled, she picked it up.

"Hello?"

"Hi, sweetums."

"Oh, Brad, you scared me to death. Is something wrong?" she asked relieved to hear her husband's voice.

"No. I told you I'd give you a call when we landed in Paris. Here I am, giving you a call. I tried to call from the air but the line was busy. What's going on? Something wrong with the kids?"

"No, they're fine, I think. I was on the phone because Dr. Dan MacNamara was hurt tonight when a car exploded in the parking lot of his office - not his car. He's still alive."

"My God, wasn't he supposed to be deposed in a couple of days in Pam Lawson's case?

"Yep, day after tomorrow—well, tomorrow now. But worse yet, I have to tell Pam he won't be one of the surgeons who will be operating on her today. I'm going to the hospital to talk to her in a few hours - before the doctors do rounds. I've been up all night trying to get some information about the explosion from the police. I just found out where the report was made, and I'm going down about five o'clock in the morning as soon as it's filed. I want to read it and talk to the guys on duty before I go see Pam. When are you coming home?"

"I have to sleep. Then I'm scheduled to fly the hop from Paris to Vienna, and back home from there. I only fly into Dulles, where we have a crew change. Then I'll catch a hop home - the next one out of Dulles. So that should be late afternoon, day after tomorrow if I don't get stuck with delays in Vienna. They've been going through a lot of security crap because of some terrorist threats there out of Bosnia. If we're held up, I'll be over my hours and I'll have to sleep over in Vienna. Sorry, I think I need to be there."

"I'm fine, honey. There's no crisis, at least that I can do anything about. Just call me on my cell if things change. I'll take it with me. Bradley is supposed to call and tell me how he did on his history test and if he's coming home this weekend. Hannah called. The baby is better. She's been giving her nebulizer treatments at home. I just hoped the baby wouldn't have asthma, but so far it doesn't look like she'll escape. Otherwise, things are fine. I just have to work through this MacNamara thing with Pam and Larry."

"You'll be fine, Janet. You just sound like you need some sleep. I'll get off the phone so you can go to bed for a few hours."

"Call me from Vienna," she said.

"I will. Sleep tight. I love you."

"I love you, too."

"Bye," he said.

Janet hung up the phone, and went upstairs to take out her contacts. As she crawled into bed weariness engulfed her. She set her alarm for four o'clock in the morning, and she was asleep.

Raoul LeCroix got off the plane in Toronto in a driving rainstorm. The weather matched his mood. It was nearly morning. His plane had been delayed for four hours in Chicago because of thunderstorms. LeCroix was late and the man sent to pick him up was silent and belligerent. He drove Lecroix to the Marriott hotel and deposited him without ceremony at the front door.

"Someone will call you at nine o'clock. Be up," was all he said.

Jennifer Fordham and Jerry Carson were in the California offices of PolySurgical Specialties at 6:30 in the morning. Jerry followed Jennifer's red Porsche off the freeway, through the sleepy streets, and pulled his silver Rolls up beside her. He smiled. Jennifer leaned over to retrieve the cardboard cups of coffee and a sack of donuts from the floor. Jerry opened the door for her and took the coffee. The reception area and the stairway were deserted. They took the elevator to the fourth-floor penthouse office suite. The waves were just beginning to turn pink and silver with the sunrise. Jennifer opened the drapes to expose the wall of windows which overlooked the ocean. They sat down at her small conference table with the coffee, the telephone between them.

"Two bits says he's not there," Jerry said as Jennifer picked up the phone.

Jennifer Fordham smiled and shook her long black hair away from her ear, holding the phone with her shoulder as she punched out the number, asked for Mr. Lester, smiled again, and pushed the button marked "Speaker."

"Yeah," a gruff voice responded. Lecroix was still having a bad day.

Jennifer nodded her head at Jerry.

"Raoul?" he asked.

"It's me," he responded.

"How was your trip?"

"I completed the sale, but I didn't make the bonus," he replied. "The products were not in the same container, so we couldn't deliver them to the customer at the same time. I'd like to go back and make the delivery sometime next week if possible."

Jerry scowled and hit the table with the palm of his hand, spilling the coffee. Jennifer wrinkled her brow and silently wiped up the coffee with napkins from the donut sack.

"Well, we'll have to confirm the reports from your territory and see if we can sponsor another trip to that region. When will your sales reports be available?" Jerry asked clenching his teeth.

"I'm sure there is something on the wire this morning. I'll send you a report."

Jerry's face was red with rage. "Listen, Lecroix, we were counting on you. I think you better plan a trip real soon to the home office to discuss this - at your expense."

"I'll be there Friday noon," Raoul said and hung up the phone. Jennifer punched the button.

"Sure am glad you filled in his last name, for whoever might be interested," Jennifer snapped.

"I had a feeling he would screw it up," Carson growled.

"He didn't screw it up. He said she was dead; he just didn't get MacNamara too. Let's see if there is anything on the news."

There was nothing on the news in Santa Barbara and nothing on the news in Denver. The only report was of the unexplained explosion of a rental car across from St. Anthony Hospital, and the incidental injury of a pedestrian in the parking lot. But by ten in the morning, Jennifer Fordham and Jerry Carson were notified by the Santa Barbara police of the death of Sherrie Barker, their Sales Manager for the Rocky Mountain states. The police had tracked the rental car to her charge card and confirmed that she did not appear for her flight home to California. Her mother had been called to officially identify the remains and make the arrangements.

Before noon, Jennifer and Jerry met with the stunned sales staff in the large conference room. Sherrie's secretary, Ann Lowe, ordered flowers for Sherrie's mother and asked to be allowed to go home.

Later that day, Jerry Carson called his wife to explain that he would be late because of the chaos at the office and then drove to meet Jennifer at the Embassy Suites in Goleta. She met him, as he closed the door, in her red silk robe, and handed him a glass of champagne. They drank to the events of the day, as they had done many times before,

Around ten o'clock, as Jerry was pulling himself together to go home, Jennifer propped herself up on her elbow and said, "You know, we probably celebrated a bit too soon. We still don't know where the documents are or which ones she even had. And, we still have the problem of Guilliot and Sonier. They're much more troublesome than Sherrie would have been a year from now."

"I know." Jerry Carson was sitting on the side of the bed pulling on his socks. "I found out today from the PSAA that Guilliot and Sonier are going to be on Emily O'Brien's network news magazine sometime in September blasting our implants. The Lawson case is about to go to trial in Denver in September and they want to showcase the fact that Pamela Lawson is dying from liver cancer and scleroderma after having polyurethane-coated silicone implants. Both of them are experts in that case. MacNamara's her doctor. Jesus! This is still a real mess."

"I was afraid of that. Why doesn't that woman just die?! We have to see how badly MacNamara is hurt. Another 'accident' at this juncture would be just too much. More important, we've got to find out about Sherrie's documents. God, I hate copy machines. It's impossible to tell which ones she has. I hope she didn't get the Aegis labs stuff. Why couldn't she pick a lover in Albuquerque? Why MacNamara?"

"Maybe they all burned with her."

"I hope so. Raoul should know."

"Or maybe she gave them to the good Dr. MacNamara, as she planned to do. I wonder who knew that they were lovers."

"We need to really think about this. I don't want any major screw-ups now. Our sales figures for the last quarter are up 62%. But Guilloit and Sonier could put us in the toilet. Why can't they just stay in Canada where they belong? Shit, Sonier is such a little scorpion!"

Jerry was putting on his jacket. "Are you staying here?"

"For a while, maybe all night. I fed my cat extra this morning. I don't feel like driving. See you tomorrow."

He leaned down and kissed her lips. "Ciao," he said and closed the door quietly behind him.

Jennifer lit a cigarette and leaned back against the pillows. If only Raoul had earned his bonus.

She finished her cigarette, mashed it out in the ash tray next to the bed, picked up the phone, and dialed.

"It's me," she said. "Raoul is coming in on Friday. What's next?"

"What does Carson know?" the man on the other end asked.

"Nothing. And if he knows which documents she took, he sure doesn't act like he knows. I don't think he's keeping anything from me. He thinks I'm the brains behind the deal."

"I'll make it worth your while. Call me tomorrow night," the man said and hung up without saying goodbye.

Jennifer hung up the phone, leaned back in the pillows, lit another cigarette, and smiled to herself. "It isn't perfect," she thought, "but it isn't that bad a plan. Sherrie Barker was just a detour we hadn't planned on. Just another day's work for Raoul."

When Janet Stephenson arrived at the police station, she met Joel Steiner, the detective who had been assigned to the explosion. She had known Joel for many years. He had graduated from the police academy and started as a traffic cop, but was soon assigned to juvenile crime about three years before she left the prosecutor's office. He had moved quickly up the ranks and was now a lieutenant in homicide. He smiled as Janet came into the room in her hooded sweatshirt and jeans. He offered her a cup of coffee in a purple mug. She accepted gratefully.

"Hey, Jan, I thought you were out of this kind of thing. What on earth are you doing here at five o'clock in the morning Are you doing criminal again?"

"No, Joel, the other guy who was injured in the explosion is a doctor—plastic surgeon for one of my clients who is in the hospital. He was supposed to assist in a serious surgery she has scheduled for today. Also, he was supposed to be deposed in my case tomorrow. I just came to see what I can find out before I go to the hospital to break the news to Pam that her favorite doctor isn't going to be there today - or maybe ever. What can you tell me? Who was in the other car - another doctor?"

"Nope, we just got the I.D. from forensics. The car was a rental from the airport. Rented two days ago by Sherrie R. Barker, Santa

Barbara, California. She rented the car with a corporate American Express card from PolySurgical Specialties. Ever heard of them?"

Janet's ears started to ring and she felt faint. This could not have been a coincidence. Janet slid off the desk top into a chair.

"Oh, my Gosh," she said.

"Okay, clue me in. Who was this chick?" Joel wasn't expecting any reaction from Janet, let alone this reaction.

"Joel, this woman is the regional sales manager for the company which manufactured the polyurethane-coated silicone gel implants which were placed in my client, Pam Lawson. I'm supposed to depose her three weeks from now."

"What's she doing blowing up in MacNamara's parking lot last night?"

"I don't know. Five years ago she was the detail person, salesman, who sold the implants to Dr. MacNamara. She sold all of the PSS products to physicians in Colorado, New Mexico, Wyoming, and Utah. She was made sales manager for the region and moved to the home office in Santa Barbara about a year ago. I don't know why she would be here now. But I'm sure going to find out, especially because Dr. MacNamara's deposition was scheduled for tomorrow."

For a moment she had forgotten about Dan MacNamara.

"Oh my God, how is MacNamara?" she asked looking up at Joel Steiner's shocked face.

"Don't know yet. He was found behind his Jag, unconscious, but it looks from the burns on his face and hands that he was pretty close to the other car when it exploded. He has a major head injury and the last I heard he was in surgery. They expected him out of surgery around seven o'clock in the morning - skull fracture. Doesn't look good." He ground out a cigarette in the half-full ash tray. "You've given me more information than I've been able to find anywhere. Can I talk to you again when I get a few more of the pieces?"

"Sure. Here's my card. I've got to get over to Pam's room before rounds. She'll be expecting to see MacNamara."

"What kind of surgery is she having, Jan?"

"Liver transplant, we hope. The donor's liver was supposed to arrive around four-thirty in the morning. She's dying of cancer of the liver and an autoimmune disorder caused by TDA from her disintegrating polyurethane implants. The trick will be whether her body will keep the liver, if they can get it in. She's really weak and I'm worried. See you, Joel. Call me if you hear anything I should know - and thanks." She stood up and gave him a peck on his stubbled cheek.

"See you, Janet," he said. "Geez, even in jeans she smells like Shalimar," he thought. He watched her leave, her blond ponytail bouncing as she slung her briefcase-sized purse over her shoulder. She ran down the hall, through security, and out the door to her car.

"I hope I get there before they start prepping her," she thought.

Susan Sampson had slipped into her sister's room at three in the morning. and sat a long time watching Pamela sleep before weariness overcame her and she, too, fell asleep in the chair beside the bed. She was still sleeping there when Janet Stephenson cracked open the door and crept into the room. She looked down at the thin young woman with her teased blond hair, no makeup, and torn blue jeans. She looks like Pam, Janet thought. Like Pam should look. Just then Pam stirred and coughed and Susan's eyes popped open.

"Hi, Mrs. Stephenson," she said, embarrassed. "I just came by for a few minutes after work. I got off at two-thirty. I guess I fell asleep. I wanted to see Pam before she went to surgery."

"It's okay, Sue, I'm glad you're here," Janet whispered, as she leaned over and patted Susan's shoulder. "I've got some bad news for Pam. Let's go outside for a second."

They left the room quietly and Janet told Susan about Dr. MacNamara. They were still in the hall when Larry Lawson arrived, his hair still damp from his shower. Janet told Larry what she had learned at the police station, and they all went into Pam's room. Pam had wakened and was looking out the window as the sun began to rise.

"Hey, it's the whole congregation." She smiled a big smile and held out her hand. Janet lightly kissed her forehead and said, "Pam,

Dr. MacNamara isn't going to be able to assist in your surgery today because he was injured in an accident last night. In fact, he's in surgery himself right now."

Pam gasped and put her hand over her mouth. "What happened?" she asked.

"Hon, it was the fire we saw before I left last night. A car blew up in the parking lot of his building and he was in the parking lot. He was injured in the explosion. Those were the sirens we heard last night. They were from the accident."

"Was he blown up?" Pam asked, horrified.

"No. He wasn't in the car. They found him on the pavement by his car, which was parked behind his office building. He has a head injury and some burns, and that's all we know right now," Janet told her gently. "I'm sure he'll be fine. We just need to think about you now. You've got to get through today. I spoke to Dr. Emanuel, your transplant surgeon, a few minutes ago, and he already has someone lined up to fill in for Dr. MacNamara. He thought the surgery should go just fine. Your new liver is here - right on schedule. They are going to throw us all out soon so they can get you ready. But we'll be here waiting for you."

"Janet, you're so busy. You don't have to stay." Janet put her hand over her fragile client's lips.

"Hush. Of course, I'll be here. I have nothing else on my calendar. Just you. I'm going to go out now so that you can spend some time with Larry and Sue before they come in to prep you. Just remember there are at least ten thousand angels standing by. You'll be just fine." Janet leaned over and gently kissed her head. "I'll be praying for you," she said and slipped out the door.

Janet went from Pamela's room to the Pathology Laboratory where she found Dr. McBride, white-haired and arrogant. She handed him the consent form and instructions which Pamela had signed the day before.

"What's this?" he scowled at the paper through his bifocals.

"Pamela Lawson is having a liver transplant today. These are special instructions about what Pamela wants done with her liver and any pathology samples from the surgery after you are through with them. I gave another set, just like this, to Dr. Emanuel who is doing the surgery. He asked me to bring a duplicate set to you so that there would be no mistake about how the specimens were to be handled. They're to be sent to LeVeer University as part of a research project. Perhaps you've read the recent work of Dr. Guilliot and Dr. Sonier? Their phone numbers are on the instructions so that you can give them a call if you have any questions."

"And just who are you, young woman?" Dr. McBride inquired, peering at her over his glasses with disdain.

"I'm Janet Stephenson, Pamela Lawson's lawyer." Janet smiled her sweetest smile, reserved only for recalcitrant judges and arrogant doctors over sixty.

Dr. McBride read the documents carefully, then looked up at her and said. "No, I think we can handle this. We're always happy to participate in research, my dear."

"When will you have your pathology report, Dr. McBride."

"Always have it to the surgeon in 48 hours," he said a little cross.

"Could I come by and pick up a copy, too?" Janet asked.

"Do you have a release?"

"Right here." Janet took the document from her briefcase-purse.

"Then you may come by and pick up a copy," he said, taking the release. "Saves me the postage."

He watched her as she left. Then smiled and placed the documents carefully in the "in" tray on his desk. Then he picked up the forms again, glanced at the clock on the wall opposite his desk and picked up the telephone.

D r. Richard Guilliot just happened to be meeting in his office at LeVeer University with Jean Sonier, Ph.D. when Dr. McBride called him. He took the call because the secretary said McBride was calling about Pamela Lawson. Sonier and Guilloit were meeting that morning to prepare for their depositions in her case. Both of them had been named as expert witnesses and they were to travel to Denver to be deposed by the defense attorneys, Rex Montague and Terry Napoli, who represented PolySurgical Specialties and the silicone supplier, Conway Chemical. Guilloit knew that Pam Lawson was scheduled for a liver transplant if they could find a donor before her condition worsened.

"Allo, Guilloit here," he said into the phone, in his thick French accent.

"Dr. Guilloit, my name is Kevin McBride. I'm the chief of pathology at St. Anthony's Hospital in Denver. I'm calling because I have a release and letter of instruction directing me to send all specimens from a liver transplant patient to you. Do you know about it?"

"Is the patient Mrs. Pamela Lawson, doctor?"

"Yes, it is. What do you know about this?"

"I know, doctor, that we are to receive the liver and related tissue blocks and slides here in our laboratory after you have done the required routine pathology at your lab. We are conducting a special study under a grant from the Canadian government to analyze such specimens as this for the presence of changes, and for the TDA, TDI, and the silicone in women who have had silicone gel or polyurethane implants. We have already done the analysis on the tissue and the explanted polyurethane implants for this patient, some time ago already. Perhaps you have seen the report on those implants, eh? Also, we recently published the results of our recent study in this area in the journal."

"When was your study published?" Now McBride remembered that he had reviewed the paperwork of the implants that were sent to LeVeer University while he was on vacation last year, but he hadn't put it together until now.

"The article was just published last month in the Journal of Biomaterials. Shall I send to you the reprint copy? I have some of them here."

"Yes, please do. If it's not too long, could you fax it to me as well?"

"Of course, I shall have you give my secretary the fax number. When do you think we can expect the specimens?"

"Assuming the surgery goes as planned, I can get them out of here by courier tomorrow. We'll work on them overnight so that they are not in formalin too long before you get them."

"That's perfect. Thank you, doctor. If you hold on, I'll transfer you to my secretary for the fax."

Dr. Jean Sonier, a small man with thick glasses and thinning hair, sat forward in his chair with his chin on his palm, watching Guilloit intently as he spoke on the phone,

"So Pamela Lawson is getting her liver? That's super," he said. "Just maybe she'll have a chance and we'll have evidence for her case as well. Just checking up on us were they, eh?"

"Yes, he is checking up on us. The good Doctor McBride wanted to know who would be so stupid as to want a worn-out liver in formalin. He hadn't read the papers, of course."

"It appears that he also does not read the newspapers."

"Maybe he does, and just wants to know which is the safest side to be on when the storm breaks in the Rocky Mountains." Guilloit laughed, his bright blue eyes twinkling in his round, slightly flushed face. The sun shone in little streams through the Venetian blinds behind his desk through his white hair, making him look like Santa Claus in a white jacket. He leaned back in his chair, folded his hands, and rested them on his stomach.

"So, Jean, what is it we must do to prepare? Or, should we put off preparing until we have had the chance to see the liver and do some work on it, first, eh?"

"If we go to the depositions and then do the work on the liver specimens, we will likely have to be deposed again. But our friends at PSS will most probably endeavor to block the evidence if we can't give opinions about the specimens the first time around. They will likely squeal "foul" and try and hit Janet Stephenson for costs for a second depo. I'd say we work like the devil to get the work done before we go to Denver this time and then hit them between the eyes with what we find as the punch line. Can we get all the lab work done if you get the specimens by Friday?"

"Even if they come on the weekend, we shall work on them. I think I have some graduate students who will be willing to come in and help. The only problem is the report. I will have to write the report in French and then it must be translated so that it is the most accurate that it can be."

"I can write the report in English if you dictate it to me in French, Richard. And I can't get back to Quebec until Sunday, so that should work out. I will bring my laptop with me. How long will it take to get the slides and photographs of the samples?"

"Oh, that is no problem; that is not a problem at all. I have just had delivered to my lab yesterday the new electron microscope which has the camera right on it and the pictures come out developed. It is like the old Polaroid, Jean, only better—they are in, how do you say, the living color, stains and all. It is wonderful. You will love it."

"Let's meet on Sunday then. I have to fly to Washington for a meeting with a Support Group of Silicone Survivors who are preparing to testify at the hearings the FDA is planning in June on requiring testing for the silicone gel breast implants. I have also been asked to testify, and I wanted to meet with these ladies to make sure that their points are grounded in science and not hysteria. I must go to Denver for the first stage of my deposition, but I can be back here by eight o'clock in the morning Sunday. Will that work?"

"I think so—if the specimens from Denver get through customs without any problems so that we don't lose any time. I think I will go to the customs office myself, just to make sure."

Both Jean Sonier and Richard Guilloit were looking forward to the trial of Pamela Lawson's case. It would be the first opportunity to bring to the public eye all of the worst damages from the use of polyurethane-coated silicone gel breast implants. The two men were brilliant scientists who had quietly uncovered the dangers of the implants in their daily work ten years before. In Pamela Lawson's case, the effects of the disintegration of the polyurethane coating into a carcinogen, which attacks the liver, and the effects of the silicone which adversely affects the autoimmune system were combined in the tragedy of a young mother, who had been an early breast cancer victim, and who was now fighting for her life because her breasts were reconstructed with an untested, deadly implant.

Jean Sonier, a biomaterials scientist and chemist, had been the Chief of Research for the Canadian Health Services for fifteen years. He met Richard Guilloit when Guilloit's laboratory at LeVeers University had applied for a published grant to establish a nationwide implant retrieval program to study the condition of explanted medical devices, based on criteria of biocompatibility, biodurability, chemical and mechanical degradation and safety. Guilloit's laboratory at LeVeer University received the grant and for twelve years had been collecting artificial joints, heart valves, intrauterine devices, hydrocephalic shunts, silicone gel breast implants, and all manner of other implantable devices from the medical profession and the community.

Guilloit's studies on these implants began to collect increasing data on silicone gel breast implants, and silicone gel breast implants coated with polyurethane. The studies revealed that although silicone is chemically inert and is not dissolved by inorganic chemicals or acids, it is not biologically inert. When placed in the human body, the silicone shell around the implant begins to disintegrate. Further, they discovered that whether or not the shell is disintegrated, the liquid component of the silicone gel inside the implant regularly and consistently "bleeds" through the shell and is transported by white blood cells throughout the body of the patient. Because the human body has no way to dispose of the silicone, it is stored in the liver, the spleen, and other body organs. The presence of millions of micro-droplets of silicone then confuses the body's autoimmune system and the body creates anti-bodies to silicone in various of its body organs, resulting in silicone-associated diseases. These diseases have symptoms similar to the symptoms of rheumatoid arthritis, lupus, scleroderma, and fibromyalgia.

To add insult to injury, Guilloit and Sonier discovered that one particular brand and design of silicone implants, those coated with a thin coat of polyurethane foam were even more dangerous. The foam covering was actually discovered by Sonier to be made from industrial handi-wipes, glued to the outside of a poor-quality silicone gel implant with a silicone adhesive. Neither the foam nor the adhesive was designed or tested to be used in the human body. Once in the body, the polyurethane degraded into one of the components of its manufacturing process, tolulene diamine, or TDA. TDA had already been proven to be a carcinogen and had been banned by the FDA from uses which required bodily contact, such as hair sprays.

Only one company manufactured the polyurethane-coated implants, PolySurgical Specialties, and the foam coated implants were taking over the market. Because the body tissues grow into the foam, the coating prevents the formation of the troublesome scar tissue shell which the body produces around any foreign body. Cosmetically, the polyurethane implanted breast remained soft and supple while breasts with smooth-skinned silicone implants often became hard and painful. Not knowing what Sonier and Guilloit knew, many plastic surgeons believed the PSS marketing and were choosing the deadly polyurethane implant for their patients in increasing numbers.

In Canada, Jean Sonier, Chief Scientist for the government, and Richard Guilloit, Chief Scientist for one of the major medical research universities, had mounted a campaign to have the polyurethane implants banned. PolySurgical Specialties' parent corporation was largely owned by Canadian investors and when the political pressure was placed on the right people, Sonier was ordered to destroy the results of the research provided to him by Guilloit. When he would not and went to the curious press instead, he was fired. Sonier filed suit against the government, and he was reinstated and compensated as a part of a secret settlement. Then Sonier resigned and started his own independent biomaterials research laboratory with the proceeds.

In the meantime, he had gathered many enemies, one of whom was Raoul Lecroix, who had owned the medical distributor with the exclusive contract to distribute the fast-selling polyurethane implants for PolySurgical Specialties in Canada. Sonier's attacks in the press had pushed Lecroix into bankruptcy and into disgrace because Sonier also uncovered the kickback method by which he cornered the plastic surgery market. Although Lecroix was placed on probation when criminal charges were filed, he hated Sonier. When Jerry Carson contacted him in a pub, where he hung out in Ottawa, and outlined the plans others had for the future of Sonier and Guilliot, he was delighted to be involved. He would have done it for free, but the pay would make him a very rich man again.

The attention of the press was nothing new to Jean Sonier, Ph.D. He was a brilliant man who knew as well how to manipulate the press for positive ends. He had thought about those processes very carefully when he was an unknown scientist in the Canadian government. Jean realized one night as he walked their dog in the fog near his cozy home in Ottawa, that he must use the press to get the polyurethane implant off the market in his country. Words were his forte'. Unlike most scientists, Jean Sonier was a true renaissance man. His curiosity about life and learning ran the gamut from ancient Anglo-Saxon manuscripts to the latest formulation for rocket fuels. He knew more medicine than most physicians and more law than most lawyers, but at his roots, he was a gentle, humble man who never turned away from an intellectual fight or championed a cause that was not just and right.

Jean had grown up as the son of a Canadian journalist and newspaper publisher of French Huguenot descent. His grandfather was a man of some wealth, and being of a frugal nature, had passed it on to his only son. Jean had spent many hours as a boy in the wonderful library of his grandfather's country home.

But Jean had gone to public schools and to colleges on academic scholarships. Learning had come easy to him and he excelled in everything he studied. As a Ph.D. student in Chemistry on a post-graduate fellowship, he met his Lorna, the witty challenge who became his wife, his partner, and the mother of their two children. She was his best friend, and perhaps the only person who truly understood his amazing mind as hers was very similar. Each of them loved solitude as much as conversations, and neither considered their personality traits to be an odd match. She managed the home front with tolerance and humor and left her laboratory supervisor position to run their company when Jean left the government. As a result, he was free to travel, leaving umbrellas, and other miscellanies about the country as he gathered more business than they could accomplish or properly bill from his scrawled memos. That was why she got him a laptop computer as soon as the smallest computers were available. Miraculously, he did not lose it, and it became his friend. The first thing Lorna did when Jean returned home from a consulting trip was to copy all of his disks. She wasn't confident he would not lose his disks.

Jean Sonier hated arrogance and ignorance and he was not intimidated by position or power. He lived his own life with vigor, seldom sleeping and without pretense or fear of any man. His only major problems were that he could not remember directions and he regularly lost things. Sometimes he was accused of being absentminded, but he explained that fault by saying that he was often preoccupied.

Jean Sonier was preoccupied as he waited for the elevator outside Richard Guilloit's lab. Suddenly, just as the elevator came, he turned and hurried back to Guilloit's office. He stuck his head through the door, which stood partly ajar, and said, "Oh, Richard, I forgot to discuss something with you."

Dr. Guilloit looked up from his work with an amused smile.

"Yes, Jean, I know. The American T.V. show. I thought you would return, but if you did not, we could talk about it on Sunday."

"You knew already, eh? What do you think? Should we do it just before the Lawson trial and the FDA hearings?"

"Miss Emily O'Brien called me at the home last night. Bridgette answered the phone and was very excited. Apparently, she likes this, "Eye on the World" show very much. What do you think? I have not ever seen this show."

"Well, I think it may be a particularly good opportunity to do some jury education in the United States and to counteract some of the power of the industry over the media in America. Most Americans don't know anything about what goes on in Canada. Not one in two hundred know who the prime minister is or even that we have a prime minister. I know most, no, none of the people in Denver know anything at all about our fight with PolySurgical Specialties over the safety of these implants here."

"Then we should do it, eh? Do you agree? Perhaps we should call Janet Stephenson and see what she has to say on the matter. Although, I cannot imagine that any true information on the television would not help Pamela Lawson's case."

"Emily O'Brien and her co-host, Patrick Kennedy, wanted to meet me tomorrow in Washington to discuss the content and where they would film the show. Shall I just tell them that it's a go then?"

"Sure, Jean, tell them it's a go. You had better go or you shall miss your plane once more. It is a long drive to Washington." Richard Guilloit laughed and waved to his friend to be on his way.

Jean waved one hand at him as he disappeared out the door again.

At the airport, Dr. Sonier bought two newspapers, a USA Today and a New York Times. As he opened the paper on the plane, he noticed the "Colorado" blurb in the USA Today. It reported the injury of the prominent Denver plastic surgeon, Dr. Daniel MacNamara, as incidental to the explosion of another automobile in the parking lot of Dr. MacNamara's office building. A chill went down Jean Sonier's spine as he recalled the explosion of another car bomb outside his wife's laboratory just before he had resigned from the Canadian Health Service.

"So it begins again," he thought to himself. Somehow he doubted this one was meant as a warning. He made a mental note to call Janet Stephenson as soon as he got to Washington.

In the New York Times, he found an article entitled "Irate Women descend on FDA Demanding Silicone Hearings." It quoted at length the women he was to see. "I should have come a day sooner," he said aloud.

Sally MacNamara waited anxiously in the surgical waiting room with her children. Suzanna, Madeline, and Brian—fourteen, twelve, and eleven years old respectively—were dressed in sweats and had disheveled hair from sleeping on the waiting room couches. They had insisted on coming with Sally to the hospital after the policemen had come to the house and told them of their father's injury. Sally had just gone to the store to pick up some cucumbers for the salad and had returned to a driveway full of official vehicles and a living room full of weeping children. They had been at the hospital all night. Even though every physician in the hospital had stopped by to talk to her, there was no news yet on how Dan's surgery was going. Sally had been afraid to even leave to get coffee from the cafeteria, but Brian had been more than willing to make several trips to pass the time.

When Susan Sampson and Larry Lawson came in at seven-thirty, Dan's surgeon had just come in and beckoned the MacNamara family into a counseling room. Sally had forgotten all of her medical training, and for this moment, she was not a physician, just a wife with a critically injured husband. Moreover, their last conversation was an angry disagreement which she had caused and allowed to simmer. She'd gladly have taken it all back now. Both of them had been on call for the last two days. She really hadn't spoken to Dan since Sunday night. She felt miserable and so afraid.

"How is he, Al? What's going on?"

"Just relax, Sal. We're through with surgery for now, although we may have to go back in later if we get any swelling. He was thrown backward by the explosion so he has burns on his hands and face and the back of his skull was fractured when he hit. Luckily his head hit the bumper of his car before he hit the pavement or we might not be having this conversation."

Madeline began to cry, and Suzanna cradled her in her arms. Brian was snuggled under his mother's armpit, motionless and wide-eyed.

"We put some plates in to hold the repairs to the skull. Now, all we can do is wait and pray. I think prayer will be our best hope. It may be days before he regains consciousness. We haven't done a complete x-ray work-up yet because we were too worried about moving his head at all. If he needs any orthopedic work, it won't hurt to wait a few days."

"Can I see him?" Sally asked.

"Not a good idea now, Sal. He wouldn't know you were there and we have him on every machine known to man. Just wait a while, huh? I don't think you need the stress of Monday morning quarterbacking, and I don't think you'd be able to avoid it. Just be a wife - just pray - just be with the kids. We're taking special care of Dan."

Sally began to weep, her shoulders shaking.

"Come on back to the physician's lounge. It's more private there and everyone wants to see you. Besides, the kids can crawl in a bunk and get some sleep. I know there's no chance of getting any of you to go home, so I won't suggest it until Dan is out of recovery and we know what's what."

"Okay," was all she could say. Dr. Al Matthews, surgeon, took the family of his medical school chum and colleague through the door on the other side of the counseling room to wait, just as Pamela Lawson was taken into surgery through the adjacent hall.

Amy Larabee, FBI, had been tracking the activities of Raoul Lecroix ever since the bomb had exploded outside Lorna Sonier's laboratory in Ottawa. Although the bomb did not hurt Lorna or her staff, it did injure an elderly woman, mother of Hugh Mason, Solicitor for the City of Ottawa. She later died from complications, and only a small story appeared in the local papers. Hugh Mason asked the cooperative local press to limit their coverage to aid the investigation. The investigation turned up a bank surveillance camera on the corner which showed Lecroix's car and Lecroix with the parcel which Mason was sure was the bomb. Shortly thereafter, Lecroix moved to Chicago, and Mason and the Canadian authorities called the FBI.

For Amy Larabee, it had been a dull assignment for two years until Lecroix started traveling - to Santa Barbara, to Detroit, to Washington, D.C., to Denver, where he stayed for three weeks. Amy could not stay in Denver for three weeks, so she contacted the FBI in Denver, where she met Special Agent Ben Smith, who took up the Denver surveillance.

Ben Smith began to follow the surly, but sophisticated Lecroix from his digs at the Brown Palace or the Westin Hotel, the Lo Do nightlife, and to his surprise visits to the suburbs and the Horny Toad Lounge.

Ben, who was tall, blond, clean-cut, and handsome, and preferred to dress in jeans and cowboy boots, fit right in at the Horny Toad. Before long he was accepted as a regular and had befriended the waitresses, the band, and the regular customers, including Charlie and Tom Slade. He sometimes sat in with the band and played guitar or keyboards or sang because he loved to sing. He was always surprised if the crowds applauded. No one knew that he became a regular because he saw Raoul Lecroix talking with Tom Slade in the parking lot.

"Now, there's a real odd couple," he said out loud to himself as he watched from his rented car mirror as Raoul and Tom went inside. Ben had on a suit and tie and didn't follow. He only waited, and pulled his car into the space which opened up between Raoul's Lincoln Town Car and Slade's pickup truck. While they were inside, he slipped a bug in each vehicle, carefully relocking the doors. No one expected high-tech surveillance in suburban Arapahoe county and he was not noticed.

Raoul's bug was useful only until he turned in his Lincoln for a Cadillac. The bug in the pickup had a constant competition with the country music Slade played at full volume at all times. But, it was enough to convince Ben Smith to become a regular at the Horny Toad Lounge. It wasn't long before he met Tom Slade.

"He's one of the scariest dudes I've ever met!" he had reported to Amy Larabee in one of their phone conversations.

"Then he's a perfect match for Lecroix," she said. "I only hope we can find out what they're up to before it comes down. Lecroix is a cold-blooded killer, who will do anything for money. Just keep a close eye on them."

Ben heard the news report about the bombing across from St. Anthony's Hospital but he hadn't heard enough to link it to Slade. "That's something Slade could have done," he said to himself as he got in the shower, "but he was hanging out at the Horny Toad last night."

When Ben Smith got to his office at ten in the morning, there was already an urgent message from Amy Larabee in Washington on his voice mail.

Before he called her, Ben called the Westin Hotel to see if Lecroix was still registered. His stomach sank as he heard that Lecroix had checked out yesterday before noon.

"Hi, boss," he said to Amy when she answered the phone.

"Ben, where have you been? I've been trying to find you."

"Been right here. What's up?"

"Do you know who died in that car bomb in Denver last night?"

"No, they haven't released the victim's name yet. I just heard it this morning on the news."

"It was Sherrie Barker, a sales manager for PolySurgical Specialties from Santa Barbara."

Ben's head hurt. He sat down and felt even sicker. "Did she have anything to do with Lecroix's contact, Carson?" he asked.

"He was her immediate superior."

"Oh my god, it had to be Lecroix and Slade. How did I miss it?"

"Where is Lecroix, Ben? Isn't he there in Denver?"

"I don't know if he's here or not. I just found out that he checked out of the Westin yesterday before noon. I should have tailed him yesterday myself. Let me see what Derrick has on him. I gave him day duty and I took the night at the Horny Toad. Slade was at the Horny Toad last night, though, just being his slimy self."

"When did he get there?"

"After eight thirty, his normal time."

"The bombing was before seven."

Ben felt like throwing up. He wasn't really sure that Slade had been at his job before he came to the Horny Toad. His pickup truck was already gone when Ben drove by the parking lot outside the asphalt plant where he worked, at ten minutes before six in the evening. Maybe Derrick knew more.

"I'll check with Derrick and get back to you right away, Amy."

"I have a one o'clock afternoon flight to Denver, Ben. I'll rent a car and come to your office when I get there. It'll be about five o'clock your time. Will you be there?"

"With bells on," Ben replied.

"Good. See you then."

"Bye."

By the time Amy Larabee arrived that afternoon, Ben Smith knew that Lecroix had left Denver for Toronto on a seven-forty flight on United Airlines. But, his whereabouts between the eleven-thirty in the morning checkout and the flight was unknown. He had given Derrick the slip and left his Cadillac in the Westin parking garage to be picked up, along with its new bug, by the rental company. No cab driver who had been covering the Westin remembered giving Lecroix a ride. He had vanished for the entire afternoon.

Ben and Derrick had also discovered that Tom Slade had left his job at the asphalt plant at eleven-seventeen, claiming he was sick. No one had seen him between the time he left work and when he appeared at the Horny Toad later that night.

Amy listened thoughtfully to Ben's report. She leaned forward, cupped her chin in her hands, her elbows on the table in the small executive suite conference room for the small geophysical engineering company that served as Ben's cover. She pursed her lips and then shook her head.

"It's got to be them," Amy said emphatically. "There are no coincidences here. I've got to go and see what the local police have found out, but you need to stay here. We still need you and I don't want to blow your cover. When I get back maybe we can get a bite to eat and sort out what we have."

"I'm really sorry, Amy. Nothing happened to indicate to either me or Derrick that yesterday was a special day. Raoul was acting just like he does every time he comes into Denver and hangs out for a while. He just spends money, parties at the breweries, catches a Rockies game or a Broncos game, depending on the season, and looks for women. He's like the playboy of the western world, and he was no different this time. He always hangs out a little with Slade at the Horny Toad, but he didn't even do that this time."

"Don't beat yourself up about it Ben. We'll just have to take it from here. I want to nail this guy, especially if he killed Sherrie Barker. But, more important, this isn't the end. There is more going on here than we understand, and we have to get ahead of this game now. No more mistakes."

"Yep."

She patted his arm, gathered her briefcase and her beige silk jacket, and ran her fingers quickly through her shiny short black hair.

"I'll be back soon. Think of some Chinese place to eat. I'm already starved."

"I know just the place already."

"Good." She flashed him a quick smile and closed the door behind her. He could hear the quick steps of her small high heels down the hall. When they stopped, Ben could see her through the conference room windows, with her petite frame and her head tilted as she looked up impatiently at the elevator lights. The elevator came and she was gone.

Ben Smith sat down at the table and put his head in his big athletic hands. He couldn't forget the pictures of the burning car he had seen on T.V. that morning or Tom Slade's sleazy face.

"How could I have missed it?" he asked himself again.

At five thirty-two in the evening, Pamela Lawson left the operating room and was transferred to recovery in intensive care. A few minutes later, Dr. Levi Emanuel called Larry Lawson, Janet Stephenson, and Susan Sampson into the family counseling room adjacent to the surgical waiting room.

Dr. Emanuel closed the door and untied his surgical mask from around his neck.

"Well, Larry, I think it all went very well. She tolerated the surgery fairly well. We only had a little trouble with her respiration until we got the ventilator organized. But, she's going into recovery in the intensive care unit and there will be three nurses and a resident with her all of the time for the next four hours, at least.

The donor's liver was a little smaller because it actually came from a thirteen-year-old child, but that is good because it is young and it will grow. Pamela is not much larger than a child herself."

Larry Lawson had tears streaming down his face, and he reached out for Dr. Emanuel's hand.

"Thank you, Dr. Emanuel, thank you," he said.

"It was my pleasure. Pamela is a delightful lady, and I hope that we have secured a long life for her."

"When can we see her?" Larry asked. Susan could only nod.

"Well, I'd rather she be undisturbed for at least the next five hours, maybe six. I suggest that you all go home and get something to eat and some sleep. She is fine. I'm sure the folks at home need a report. At your attorney's request, we have had an information ban on her case so that if anyone calls, they will not find out anything you don't know first."

Janet Stephenson reached out and shook Dr. Emanuel's hand. "Thank you, Dr. Emanuel," she said.

"Well, I'm no fan of the press, and they can wait as long as you want them to, as far as I'm concerned. We really shouldn't say much about the surgery until we know how the new liver is going to be accepted. As you know, the hardest hours and days are still ahead. Pamela's immune system isn't normal so we may have a higher-than-normal danger of rejection here. Right now, her color is good. But, she's just off of the machines, so we'll just have to be patient and bide our time. I suggest you slip out the physician's elevator and out the back. The press is currently laboring under the misunderstanding that there will be a press conference. But, I, too, intend to go home for some sleep as soon as I look in on Dan MacNamara."

"How is Dr. MacNamara?" Janet and Larry spoke in unison.

"Don't know. He was just going into recovery as we were going into Pamela's surgery. I'm anxious to know myself, but I'll let you know. I'll give you a call. After all, he is Pam's primary physician on this case But for now, go see the children and get some sleep."

He gave Larry and Susan a brief hug, shook Janet's hand again, and disappeared through the swinging door on the back of the room, as Larry and Susan collapsed into tears on the couch. Janet looked after the elderly surgeon and noticed that he walked as one weary with exhaustion and worry. She said a prayer for Levi Emanuel, M.D., good doctor, good friend.

"Thank you, God," Larry said softly with his eyes still tightly shut and tears streaming out the corners. "It's all in your hands. Bless my precious Pam."

They sat there together for a long time, and when they slipped through the swinging doors and down the physician's elevator, they could see all of the television vans in the parking lot in front of the hospital. They said goodbye outside the door and hurried silently and separately to their cars.

Inside, Levi Emanuel sat in intensive care by the bed of his unconscious friend, Dan MacNamara, holding his hand.

When he arrived in Washington, Jean Sonier hurried to his hotel to call his wife, Lorna, and Richard Guilloit before he met with the Silicone Sisters Association members. He wanted to tell Lorna about the Denver bombing and warn her of the uneasy feelings he was having.

Loretta Ross, who headed the Denver branch of the Silicone Sisters, had wanted to meet him at the airport, but Sonier always tried to travel incognito and stay where he could not be reached unless he chose to be. But, Sonier was anxious to talk to Loretta today because she always had the scoop on the silicone news before it even showed up on the Internet. Just in case, he plugged in his laptop and searched the Internet as soon as he got to the hotel. There was only a wire story about the bombing without specifics.

Jean tried to telephone Lorna, but all he could reach was her voice mail. He left a message with the name and phone number of his hotel and told her he would try again after his meeting.

Late again, Jean Sonier rushed down to the lobby and took a cab to the Mayflower Hotel, where he was to meet with Loretta Ross and Cynthia Rich, head of the California Silicone Sisters, to review their statements and coordinate the testimony they would give at the FDA hearings tomorrow.

Cynthia and Loretta were waiting in the lounge with their usual glasses of white zinfandel. They waved at him excitedly when he appeared at the door, peering into the dim room. He saw their waves and hurried over.

"Perrier, please," he told the waiting cocktail hostess as he sat down across from the ladies.

"Oh, Jean." Loretta's face was flushed with the excitement of a school girl who had just learned a terrible secret about the most popular girl in the class. "Did you hear who was killed in Denver?"

Bingo, thought Sonier. "I heard about the incident, but that's all," he said to Loretta.

"Sherrie Barker, the western regional sales manager for PolySurgical Specialties."

Jean Sonier felt dizzy. "Are you certain?" he asked.

"The police just announced it and April gave me a call before I came down. What's more, Dr. Dan MacNamara was with her."

"Was he killed?" Sonier asked. He had just spoken to MacNamara not three days ago. They were both to be deposed in the Pamela Lawson case.

"No, but he's in critical condition. The police said he just happened to be in the parking lot. He was found behind his car unconscious and burned. It happened just behind MacNamara's office building."

"What do you think, Loretta?" Sonier asked.

"We know!!!" she said excitedly looking at Cynthia and nodding, her jaw set with determination. Cynthia was nodding as well.

"What?" asked Sonier.

"All the girls in Denver think that MacNamara was having an affair with Sherrie Barker. They gave a seminar at the Tech Center Marriott about the polyurethane implants, and some of the girls who stayed for a drink saw them go up the elevator together. She was staying at the Marriott."

"That's pretty thin evidence of an affair, don't you think, Loretta?"

"Oh, there's lots more. Anyway, what was Sherrie Barker doing at night in the parking lot behind MacNamara's office building? She was moved to the home office of PSS in Santa Barbara over a year ago."

Cynthia chimed in. "Six months ago, MacNamara did a traveling road show all over California with Jennifer Fordham and Sherrie Barker, trying to sell the safety of PSS polyurethane implants to the plastic surgeons and their patients. They spent days together. Why MacNamara, all the way from Denver when California is crawling with plastic surgeons and PSS is headquartered in Santa Barbara?"

Loretta answered the rhetorical question posed by her friend. "It's because they were having an affair when she was the PSS detail person for Colorado, and those seminars gave them a chance to travel together after she was transferred to Santa Barbara, without suspicion."

Sonier laughed, "But you suspected, didn't you, Loretta?" he teased.

"I didn't suspect. I knew," she said, with another definitive nod.

Sonier knew that she was probably right. But why kill Sherrie Barker? Why not MacNamara? He was the one who was going to be an expert witness in Pam Lawson's case. However, although he was Pam's surgeon, and he clearly was fond of her, MacNamara had always taken the position that there was no causal relationship between Pam's disintegrated polyurethane implants and her liver cancer. He did not appear to be a threat to PSS.

"I think she was killed by a jealous wife!" Loretta was saying, as Jean tuned back in from his momentary reverie. "He was married to a doctor, Sally MacNamara, a well-known pediatrician. She was supposed to have quite a temper, even though she is a baby doctor."

"Doesn't that seem unlikely," said Sonier softly, drifting back into his own thoughts.

Cynthia and Loretta did not know all of the dangerous and sinister past which haunted Sonier. They traveled, with most of the public, in the world of the National Enquirer. The sex and intrigue of a love triangle resulting in murder was just too enticing for Cynthia and Loretta to ignore. They despised Dr. Daniel MacNamara because he had actively supported silicone implants and been hostile to their cause. He appeared to them to have jumped at the chance to travel and do seminars for the manufacturers in support of silicone implants, just as the first set of FDA hearings began and silicone started to get adverse publicity. He continued to put in implants, ignoring what to Loretta and Cynthia appeared to be overwhelming evidence of the danger. They were sure that his motive was greed and greed alone. Such a man could easily be guilty of infidelity and the victim of a justifiably jealous and angry wife in their minds.

"Isn't it unbelievable that he is Pamela Lawson's surgeon? Why does she keep him?" Cynthia asked.

"He took her implants out, and I don't think he charged her," Loretta said. "But April told me that Dr. MacNamara was even going to assist in Pamela's liver transplant if she got a liver."

"I think it is arranged," Jean Sonier told them. "I think her transplant will be very soon if not this week."

"Isn't her case against PSS set for trial, Jean?" Cynthia asked.

Loretta answered before Jean could open his mouth. Loretta prided herself on having full information regarding all of the silicone litigation information around the country. She spent her days on the telephone with contacts everywhere, and she published a newsletter for "silicone survivors" from her kitchen netting her a nice income, which she didn't report lest she loses her $1140 per month social security disability. "Her trial is supposed to start on September 25 - in about 120 days."

"I'm to go to Denver from here for my first deposition in her case. It will be taken in two stages, thus two trips" Jean Sonier added.

"Wow, isn't it too much. Sherrie Barker getting killed, Dr. MacNamara getting hurt, and Pam, the first woman with a silicone-related liver cancer, getting a new liver, all in Denver," said Cynthia. "I thought California was the center of the universe."

"California may be the center of the universe," said Loretta, "but today it looks like Denver is the center of Hades itself. Let's get to work." She began pulling yellow legal pads out of her briefcase. "Tomorrow's the big day."

Jean Sonier looked at the pushy, portly women and wished the FDA Committee could see and hear from Pamela Lawson instead.

In her room in intensive care, Pamela held on to life only by the thinnest of threads and vigilant angels.

S ally MacNamara stared in wide-eyed disbelief at Detective Joel Steiner as he sat across from her in her living room.

"What do you mean?" she demanded.

"Didn't you know Sherrie Barker, Dr. MacNamara?"

"Yes, I know her by name," she responded. "She worked for the manufacturer from whom Dan gets some of his implant materials. But, I think she's been gone from Denver for quite a while."

"Has your husband seen her since she left, Dr. MacNamara?"

"Well, he did do a series of seminars for physicians about the breast implants he used. The travel, his expenses, and honoraria were paid by PSS, the company she worked for. But that was after she was already gone, and someone else took the Denver region. The seminars were arranged by PSS management—a Jerry Carson, I believe, from Santa Barbara."

"Do you know if your husband was meeting or seeing Sherrie Barker last night, Dr. MacNamara?"

"No, he wasn't. He was seeing patients, completing paper work and going to the hospital to check on a patient who was having a liver transplant in the morning. He was supposed to assist in the surgery."

Sally MacNamara could not hold back the tears. She had just come from the hospital where her husband was still in intensive care. She had not been prepared to have to deal with Joel Steiner or anyone else from the police. They were the furthest thing from her mind.

"I'm sorry, Dr. MacNamara. This is a bad time. We'll be back in touch later on. I apologize for this intrusion, but we do have a murder on our hands. We'll let ourselves out."

All Sally could do is nod, as she continued to sob in her chair. Joel Steiner backed to the door of the living room and he and the uniformed officer left quietly through the front door.

When Joel Steiner got back to his office, Amy Larabee was waiting for him in his office. As he walked in, she stood up and extended her hand.

"Detective Steiner, I'm Amy Larabee, from Washington, FBI." Amy reached in her purse and pulled out her identification badge.

"Please, call me Joel. To what do we owe the honor of this visit?"

"There is a confidential fax on your desk. I understand you are investigating the car bombing last night that killed a Sherrie Barker, from Santa Barbara"

"That's me - Why is that of interest to the FBI?"

"In conjunction with the Canadian government, we have been tracking the travels of a Canadian suspected of setting off a car bomb in Ottawa a couple of years ago. The target in Ottawa was a biomaterials research lab. The only fatality was a nearby elderly lady who was a pedestrian. She just happened to be the mother of Ottawa's D.A. - "solicitor" there."

"Okay. But what does Canada have to do with Denver? You think the mad Canadian bomber may be responsible for this bomb?"

"In a nutshell, yes. We have had this guy under surveillance on and off in Denver for the past year. A local special agent has been tailing him when he is in town, and his local contacts are also being tracked."

"Is he in town now?

"No, but he was here until last evening when he took the 7:50 United Flight to Toronto."

"The bomb went off just before seven apparently when Sherrie Baker turned the key to start her car. But it could have been planted anytime. We don't know yet how long her car had been in the parking lot. What's his motive - if he's the one?"

"We're not sure. Those pieces don't exactly fit. We think his target in Canada was a chemist and biomaterials scientist named, Jean Sonier, or his wife. But, an employee of PSS is on the other side, so I don't know?" Amy shook her head pensively.

"Wait a minute, you lost me on that turn. What 'other side?'"

"Jean Sonier used to work for the Canadian equivalent of the FDA, and he had the job of approving or disapproving drugs and medical devices for marketing in Canada. PSS, PolySurgical Specialties, manufactures a polyurethane-coated silicone gel breast implant which it was marketing in Canada. Sonier and his colleagues at LeVeer University ran some tests on the implant that were not done by the manufacturer, or at least not disclosed by PSS. These tests showed that the implant disintegrated after it was placed in the human body, and that, worse yet, the polyurethane broke down in the body into TDA, which causes liver cancer in laboratory animals. Sonier saw to it that the implant was removed from the market in Canada."

"So?" said Joel with a frown, "I still don't get it."

"Our mad bomber, Raoul Lecroix, owned the exclusive distributorship with PolySurgical Specialties for the implants in Canada - a multi-million dollar operation. Sonier shut him down and he was ruined financially. To add insult to injury, Sonier's investigation also uncovered an illegal kickback scheme that was making Lecroix even richer. When all was said and done, Lecroix, and some prominent plastic surgeons were indicted and ruined financially, and Sonier was a national hero."

"But why would he target a regional sales manager for his old employer, PSS, especially in Denver?"

"That I don't know. But it's all too weird to be a coincidence. What do you have so far?" Amy asked, taking a notepad out of her bag.

"Not much. The car she was driving, a new blue Ford Mustang, was rented on her corporate card at Denver International Airport. Her mother has been asked to come to identify the body, and I haven't spoken with her yet. We are just about to go over and go through the dead girl's room at the Brown Palace Hotel. Her mom is staying at the Brown too.

Also, a doctor, who offices in the building adjacent to the parking lot were also injured - Dr. Dan MacNamara, We're not sure why he happened to be in the parking lot at the same time as the explosion, I just spoke to his wife, Dr. Sally MacNamara. She told me that her husband used to know Sherrie Barker when she worked in this region as a salesperson for implant materials. But, she was transferred to the home office of PSS in Santa Barbara over a year ago.

The wife denies any hanky panky between the decedent and the injured doc - but he is a plastic surgeon. We can't talk to him yet. He was pretty seriously injured and is still in intensive care. The injured doc and his pediatrician wife are very prominent and I expect the medical community to close ranks around them. But, as an interesting side note, early this morning, I talked to the attorney for one of Dan MacNamara's patients who was to have a liver transplant operation this morning. She is suing PSS because she believes that the PSS implant caused her client to have liver cancer."

Amy Larabee's eyes sparkled and she stopped writing.

"No, kidding?" she blurted excitedly.

"Yep."

"What's this attorney's name?"

"Her name is Janet Stephenson. I have her card with her home number, I've known her since she was a prosecutor years ago. Now she is a plaintiff's lawyer and she has a bunch of breast implant cases. Pamela Lawson, MacNamara's patient, is one of them. Janet was on her way to the hospital when I saw her around six o'clock a,m to tell her client abcut Dr. MacNamara's injury."

Amy Larabee took Janet Stephenson's card with her home number scrawled on the back. She didn't know how it would fit together but Janet Stephenson might be a key.

"Thanks," she said, shaking Joel Steiner's hand. "I'm staying at the Embassy Suites downtown. Can we talk again tomorrow?"

"Anytime. My time is your time. I need all the help I can get. Right now I'm just trying to stall the press."

"I understand. I'll call you tomorrow." Amy handed him her card with the Embassy Suites number written on the back.

Amy's stomach growled and she was reminded that Ben was waiting back at the office to go out to dinner. Later as they ate sesame chicken at the Imperial Chinese Restaurant, Amy filled Ben in on what she had learned.

As they left, Amy said, "How about a night cap at the Horny Toad."

Ben laughed. "They don't know anything about "night caps" at the Horny Toad. It's a beer and salsa joint with a country band. If you really want to go there, you'll have to put on some stompin' duds!"

"Stompin' duds—what's that?"

"Jeans, tennies, or boots. No high heels, no silk suits. Let's just stop in at Miller Stockman at the Mall on our way and you'll be all set. You need some Colorado clothes anyhow."

An hour later, dressed in her Levi's, boots and shirt, Amy Larabee was introduced to the crowd at the Horny Toad. Not by name, only as "Chickie" and Amy got her first look at Tom Slade. Chills ran down her spine as she watched him spit tobacco juice in an empty beer can, and leer at the waitress everyone called "Rainey."

Lorraine wondered if the pretty petite dark-haired "Chickie" with her striking blue eyes was someone special to Ben. He seemed to like her, but he didn't hug her or treat her like a girlfriend. Lorraine wondered if she was Ben's sister.

"He treats her like a sister," she thought. Even so, Lorraine was glad that Susan was not there to see Ben with a girl. She knew that secretly Susan wanted to be Ben's girl, and Ben had never come in with a girl before. He always seemed to be content to hang out with the guys or the band. She hoped he was just a gentleman. She didn't know he was on duty.

Susan Sampson had the night off. When she called to tell Lorraine that Pamela had made it through the surgery, Lorraine told her that she would cover her shift. Susan went home to sleep for the first time in twenty-four hours.

Dr. Dan MacNamara woke up in intensive care with his wife's eyes staring into his.

"Hi, you." She smiled and kissed his cheek. Sally MacNamara's eyes were full of tears and her voice was soft and filled with emotion.

Dan MacNamara looked at her, smiling weakly, and trying frantically inside his troubled brain to remember what had happened. A vague feeling of dread overwhelmed him suddenly, and Sherrie Barker's smiling face flashed before his confused eyes. He shut his eyes, trying to remember and trying not to ask about Sherrie. Sally didn't know that he was meeting Sherrie, and he remembered that, perhaps only instinctively if not precisely.

Suddenly his friend, Dr. Levi Emanuel, was there, touching his hand and his face. "Hey, Dan," he said softly, "Welcome, back."

"Where have I been?" Dan MacNamara was overwhelmed with relief at being able to ask that question.

"You were apparently just going to your car in the parking lot behind your office when another car in the parking lot blew up. You were found by your car. Your keys were in your hand. You have a serious skull fracture, among other things. But, your being conscious enough to ask where you have been is the best news I have had in seven days."

"Seven days?" was all he said before the darkness overwhelmed him again.

Dr. Emanuel saw that he had gone back to sleep. He wanted him to sleep and not move and had given him sedatives to insure that he would remain still enough to allow his skull to begin to heal. But Sally MacNamara was filled with dread again.

"Do we have to keep him so sedated?" she asked, trying to sound completely professional.

"Sal, we don't want to have to drill more holes and put in metal if we can help it. He's a healthy guy and if we can just keep him still and let him sleep, we may get enough healing to avoid that further surgery"

"I know," Sally sat down by Dan's bed. "I'm just so anxious to hear his voice again and hear him laugh again. He looks as though he is somewhere else, lying there."

Dr. Emanuel smiled. "He is," he said.

Sally smiled, resigned to continue waiting.

"Why don't you go home to the kids?" suggested Dr. Levi Emanuel.

"They're fine with our nanny. My parents are also staying at our house, so they have lots to do. I just need to be here, I can't leave Dan alone. He wouldn't leave if it were me."

Emanuel patted her shoulder and said gently, "Sally, I know. I know."

Dr. Emanuel took the chart and went outside the hospital room to the nurse's station. He sat down and was soon absorbed in writing the voluminous record of Dan's recovery of consciousness and making very specific instructions for his continued care and medications.

Dan MacNamara remained in an alternating drug-induced coma and a dream-like state for another ten days. Dr. Sally MacNamara was by his side most of the time. Her mother brought her a suitcase of clothes and toiletries and she showered and napped in the physician's lounge. The nurses brought her food from the cafeteria, including the obligatory Starbuck's mocha that she loved. She also took time to visit all of her patients in the pediatric ward, nursery, and intensive care nursery, but all of her office appointments were rescheduled or handled by the partners in her practice.

In his dream states, Dan found himself with Sherrie, reliving their time together. The first day he saw her, an unsure, but obviously well-prepared and intelligent drug salesperson, or "detailmen" as they are known in the pharmaceutical industry. Sherrie had come to his office suite, in the building across the street from St. Anthony hospital and had waited patiently until he could see her. He saw her from behind the glass in the reception area—the slim, blond young woman, patiently reading, as she waited more than an hour for him to have a break between patients.

When she was ushered into his office, she thrust out her hand to him and smiled that fabulous smile that made him melt.

"Hi, Dr. MacNamara, I'm Sherri Barker, the new detail person from PSS. Thank you for seeing me."

"Hi," he said intrigued by her dimples. "Have a seat. What's new with PSS, today."

Sherrie opened her case and put two polyurethane-coated breast implants on his desk. "These," she said.

"What are they?" Dan MacNamara picked one up. It felt soft, almost like a child's toy.

"As you know, Dr. MacNamara, capsular contracture is a serious complication with silicone gel breast implants. These implants are designed to prevent capsular contracture altogether. I know that is a serious concern of yours because I have read your articles about it in the Journal of Plastic Surgery. These implants solve the problem. The foam coating prevents the formation of scar tissue around the implant," she stated with enthusiasm and emphasis.

"How does the foam do that?" he asked.

"We're not exactly sure," she said, "but in the animal studies and the clinical studies, none of the foam coated implanted patients had a single case of capsular contracture."

Dan MacNamara was intrigued. Sherrie Barker was right. He had implanted scores of patients with silicone gel breast implants as well as saline-filled implants and the major problem was that in many patients if not most, a hard layer of scar tissue formed around the implant within the first year after the implantation surgery. The condition was known as capsular contracture. In addition to being painful, the scar tissue caused the breasts to become deformed and very hard. Instead of making the breasts of his patients more beautiful, their breasts often became grotesque.

He and other plastic surgeons had worked on devising treatments to break up the scar tissue, both with and without surgery. One technique was called the "nutcracker" among plastic surgeons. This procedure required the surgeon to grasp the hardened breast in both his hands and squeeze and twist the breast to break up the scar tissue. The danger was that the procedure would also, unbeknownst to the patient or her doctor, also rupture the implant. Another surgical procedure required the surgeon to actually reopen the breast and release the scar tissue by cutting it surgically. This procedure also presented a risk of nicking or damaging the implant within the scar capsule. So, to finally have a breast implant, which prevented capsular contracture in the first place, would be a huge benefit to his practice.

"Sounds too good to be true. What's the catch?" he queried the pretty, salesperson, looking at him intently with her bright blue eyes. She was perfectly dressed in a navy-blue suit, with matching heels and a hint of a lace camisole. She wore a single string of pearls and pearl earrings peaked out from below her perfectly coiffed short blond hair.

"No catch," she smiled. "It is just PSS's new product. Of course, we're trying to make sure we are the only manufacturer with it and we're trying to build our market share as fast as possible so that we can stay ahead of the other manufacturers. Right now, we are the only company that has it. And, PSS is prepared to make you and your practice some special offers if you will try it with your patients."

"Okay, what offers?"

"First, we will give you a 25% discount on your first fifty implants. Also, after you have tried it with a few patients, PSS would like to offer you a generous honorarium if you will travel, all expenses paid, first-class, of course, to give a few presentations around the country about how the implant solves the problem of capsular contracture. PSS obviously has chosen you for this offer because of your prominence as a plastic surgeon and because of the widely published and circulated articles that you have written on the problem of capsular contracture." She titled her head and smiled that smile again.

"Almost a deal I can hardly refuse, isn't it?" Dr. Dan MacNamara was smitten by the message and the messenger. "Can you meet me for dinner and give me the safety and FDA rundown on this implant? I have to finish seeing my patients right now."

"You bet," she stood up and gathered together her implant samples, and put them in the case. "Where would you like me to meet you?"

"Where are you staying?" he asked.

"A little hotel downtown, called Il Teatro Hotel, near the Denver Center Theater complex."

"That hotel has a fabulous restaurant called *Chaplin's*. I'll get reservations and meet you there at seven-thirty; does that work for you?"

"That will be perfect. I'll see you then." Sherrie Barker was thrilled at her unexpected success with Dr. MacNamara. He wasn't committed yet, but she was sure she could convince him.

They shook hands and Sherrie Barker left his office.

That night, Sherrie decided to leave her sample case and information about the implant's specifications, in her room when she went down to dinner. "I can come back up after dinner and get the case," she thought to herself. But after wine at dinner and after dinner drinks instead of coffee, the two of them decided to just go to her room to look at the information on the testing. From that evening until her death, Dr. Dan MacNamara and Sherrie Barker saw each other as often as they could. He began using the PSS implant and became a popular presenter on the medical and pharmaceutical trade show circuit, with his presentation on the elimination of the problem of capsular contracture from his practice. Neither of them knew that the PSS polyurethane implant, known and marketed under the ironic name, Mammselle, was, in fact, just murder by another name.

P amela Lawson was the second patient to receive a Mammselle from Dr. MacNamara. Pamela was trying to rebuild her life and regain her confidence after she had had three pregnancies and two children in six years. Her first child had been still born, which drove her to want another pregnancy as soon as possible. One morning she looked at herself after she got out of the shower. Her tummy was flat again but she burst into tears, alone in her bathroom.

"I look like Granny!" she said out loud. "Look, even if I push them up, they look 80 years old!"

Pamela secretly made an appointment with Dr. Dan MacNamara. Brenda, a beautiful, busty, girl who played tennis with her friend Linda Oakes, confessed that Dr. MacNamara had made her breasts look young again after her husband has divorced her and left her with two rambunctious little boys.

Pam rescheduled her appointment twice before she had the courage to go. But approximately ten showers later, she sat in Dr. MacNamara's examining room in her paper gown.

"Hi, there. It's Pam, is it?" Dr. MacNamara smiled as he came into the room.

"Yes, Pam." She said, nervously as she sat helplessly before the handsome, kind-looking doctor in his white coat.

"Your questionnaire says that you want to have breast implants because of sagging. Is that right?"

"Yes." Pam's eyes filled with tears. "I'm only thirty and my body looks like my grandmother. I want my breasts to look young again," she said.

"Let's take a look." Dr. MacNamara examined her and looked at the photographs of her that the technician had taken two days before in her preparatory consultation.

"I have some good news for you." He said with a smile. "There is a new breast implant, called the Mammselle, stupid name, but I didn't pick it. It is very soft and made of silicone gel covered with a soft foam, which, I think, will make you as good as new. Would you like to see one?"

Pam nodded. Dr. MacNamara went to the cabinet behind his desk and took out a plastic box that held a Mammselle implant. He took it out of the box to show it to Pam, and silently noticed that it was slightly stuck to the box on the bottom. Pam took the soft foam implant from his hand and listened as he described how the implantation surgery would be done so that the scars would be nearly invisible. A rush of joy and excitement caused her eyes to fill with tears as she listened.

"How soon can I have the surgery?" she asked.

"Let's get Anna, to see when you can be scheduled." He smiled and gave her arm a reassuring pat. The surgery was scheduled in two weeks and Pam went home to tell Larry that she was spending $5,000 of her inheritance from Granny on surgery to prevent herself from looking like Granny before her time.

Larry looked at her in amazement. "Good Lord, Pam, you don't have to do this. I think that you look just fine! We could all go to Disney World for two weeks on $5,000!"

"And when we got back, I would still look just like this," Pam said emphatically.

"You look just fine. Just fine." Larry was shaking his head. "But, it's your money so if it makes you feel better, you should just do it." And she did.

Pam loved her new figure and she loved being able to go to the pool and feel good about how she looked. She told a few friends about her surgery and they all made appointments with the famous Dr. Dan MacNamara. One of her friends, Gail, saw Dr. MacNamara on Oprah. He was explaining that there had been a tremendous improvement in breast implants and that his major concern about capsular contracture had been solved by the new Mammselle implant. Pam's beloved doctor was becoming a famous spokesman for PSS and the Mammselle. She felt so pleased with herself and her decision to take control of her life and claim her youth again.

Sherrie Barker was also pleased. She had arranged to make sure that all of Dr. MacNamara's speaking engagements and television appearances were made by her office assistant. Those arrangements usually meant that Sherrie accompanied him as a personal assistant. Those arrangements usually meant that she accompanied him as his personal assistant. Her bosses at PSS, Jennifer Fordham and Jerry Carson, were more than pleased to pay the costs of the publicity and the honorariums because their sales were nearly outstripping their ability to supply the Mammselle and their profits were growing dramatically with every appearance and publication by the charming Dr. Dan MacNamara. Forrest Winchester, the CEO of Conway Chemical, was also extremely pleased. He had just closed the deal to make PSS the newest acquisition of the Conway Chemical family. Jennifer Fordham and Jerry Carson had agreed to stay on and run the subsidiary, PolySurgical Specialties, for generous salaries in addition to the price of the buy out. PSS had other products, but none of them came close to producing the profits being projected for the sales of Mammselle implants.

It came on Pamela slowly. At first, she noticed that she was never hungry and that she felt nauseous when she ate foods she normally loved. Pizza and lasagna made her violently ill. Then she noticed that she was more and more tired. She could barely finish the laundry and she canceled tennis matches and runs around the park with her friends.

Pam went to see her primary care physician, Dr. Carol Simon, who did some blood tests, including a scan for autoimmune disorders,

"Pam, your ANA titer, a marker in your blood for autoimmune disorders is high. I would like you to go to see a specialist at the University of Colorado Medical School. His name is Dr. Hanson Bricker. He is doing a study on autoimmune diseases in patients who have breast implants and people who do not. He is trying to find some cures for autoimmune disorders such as lupus, rheumatoid arthritis, and the like."

"Do you think that I have lupus?" Pam was terrified. She had heard that lupus was not curable.

"No, I don't think that you have any of those diseases. I would just like you to go through the tests that Dr. Bricker is doing. They aren't readily available tests, except in his study, and I think that we might learn something interesting about why you are feeling this way."

"Okay. I'll do whatever you say." Pam was ready for answers about her fatigue and undifferentiated pain.

The next week, Pamela Lawson went to the Rheumatology department at the University of Colorado Medical School. There she met Dr. Hanson Bricker, a small man with glasses, in a white coat and with his brown hair combed to one side.

"He's really nice," she thought to herself, "But he does look a bit like a mad scientist."

Dr. Bricker took more blood for additional laboratory tests and put her in a small room to fill out a twenty-four-page questionnaire about her health and habits. The questionnaire asked for specific information about her implants, including the manufacturer, the lot number, and the style number of the implants. Luckily, Pam had a card in her purse with the information about her specific implants.

After filling out the questionnaire, Pam was interviewed by a medical student assistant who worked for Dr. Bricker and placed in an examining room, where she removed her clothes and put on a paper gown. After a long wait, Dr. Bricker appeared with a nurse.

"Good morning, Mrs. Lawson," he bowed slightly but did not shake her hand.

"Hi, Dr. Bricker," Pam said

"I have reviewed all of your answers to our multitude of questions and your written answers to the questionnaire, but I still need to examine you if you will be so kind."

"That's fine," Pam said.

Dr. Bricker listened to her heart and lungs and examined her breasts and the scars where the implants were placed. He also tested her reflexes with a little rubber hammer and scrupulously examined the joints of her fingers, toes, and knees. He peered inside her nose and ears with his instrument and looked deep in her throat while she said, "Ahhh."

Then he looked again at her chart, and pulled his glasses down to the tip of his nose, looking over them at her.

"You say that you have fatigue and pain, but no difficulty with your joints. Have you noticed any pain in your joints at all?"

"No, I haven't," said Pam. "I am stiff as a board when I get up in the morning and I generally hurt everywhere. Mostly, I am so tired and nauseous. And I can't sleep, which makes it all worse."

"The reason I ask is that in addition to an elevated titer of antinuclear antibodies, ANA, you also have an elevated rheumatoid factor in your blood work. That usually accompanies pain in the joints and changes in the joint structure. Do you have rheumatoid arthritis in your family? Your questionnaire indicates that you do not."

"I don't think so," Pam said.

"I don't know quite what to make of your blood work, Mrs. Lawson. I'll be frank. I want to get some opinions from other colleagues and then I would like you to come back again," he said.

"What does that mean, doctor? Can you do anything to help how I feel? I am barely able to function." Pam said in desperation.

"I don't want to give you a diagnosis or prescribe anything just yet," Dr. Bricker said. "I'll give you a call in about a week if that is all right with you."

"I guess," she said. "I was just hoping for some relief or treatment."

Dr. Bricker smiled at her and finally took her hand. "Look, we don't want to start treating you until we know what we are treating. If you just take some ibuprofen, to help you deal with the pain issues, I'll get back to you as soon as I can."

"Okay," she said. Dr. Bricker left the room with his nurse. Pam dressed and drove home, feeling worse than ever.

One beautiful Saturday morning, she and Larry had tickets to take the kids to Elitch's with the neighborhood friends, and she told Larry that she was too tired to go.

"You need to go see your doctor, Pam. Something is wrong with you."

"I know." Pam sat at the kitchen table with her head in her hands. "I am so tired, and I feel so sick that I can hardly move."

Larry took the kids to Elitchs and Pam slept the entire beautiful summer Saturday, with the drapes closed tight.

Larry Lawson took Pamela to see Dr. Carol Simon, the next Monday. Dr. Simon sent Pam to the lab for blood work as well as urine samples. She called Pam the next day.

"Pam, this is Dr. Simon. Can you come in about one o'clock this afternoon?"

"Sure," Pam said.

"Do you suppose that your husband could bring you?" Dr. Simon asked.

"Why? What's wrong?" Pam felt a knot in her stomach as she asked.

"We may want to do some other tests and you may not feel up to driving," her doctor said.

Larry and Pam sat in Dr. Simon's office after Pam had more tests, including an ultra-sound and x-rays. "What do you think is going on here," Pam asked her silent husband.

Just then, the door opened and Dr. Simon came into the office. She smiled slightly, then sat down behind her desk. "We have some serious things to discuss," she said with her brow furrowed. "I won't sugar coat it. It will not be helpful to do that. Pam, it appears that you have a malignancy on your liver. Your auto-immune system is also showing signs of being severely compromised, and I don't know if that is related to the liver issues or not."

Pam was stunned. Hadn't she just gotten her life back with her new breast implants? How could this be happening? Larry looked at her as though he had been hit with an iron. "Oh, no!" was all he said.

"What do we do?" Pam finally asked, softly.

"The first thing that we do is get you the best oncologist possible. That would be Dr. Barber at the Rocky Mountain Cancer Center. I have already sent him all of your tests and he can see you on Friday at two o'clock. He will tell us the stage of cancer and design the treatment. They call it a treatment 'cocktail' I will send him all of your records. You also need to have Dr. MacNamara send him your records from your breast implant surgery."

"From my implant surgery? What does that have to do with this?"

"I don't know if it has any relevance or not," shrugged Dr. Simon. "But, there are reports in the literature, although mostly anecdotal, linking breast implants to autoimmune disease and even cancer. But we don't know if they are statistically significant or if they are accurate about implants posing any medical risk—particularly for cancer. But, here is a release for you to sign. I will have it delivered to Dr. MacNamara so that Dr. Barber can have everything when he sees you."

Pam signed the paper. She was numb from head to toe and she was not sure that she could walk out of the office.

"We'll be at Dr. Barber's office on Friday," Larry told Dr. Simon. He helped Pam to her feet.

"Good luck. I'll be checking with Dr. Barber, Pam. Your follow-up will be with both of us. I will be with you through whatever the treatment turns out to be. You must just have faith and hang in there. Your attitude, faith, and courage are the key to recovery here." Dr. Sampson gave her a hug. Pam could only manage a nod and a weak smile.

On Friday, Pam and Larry drove to downtown Denver to the Rocky Mountain Cancer Center. Dr. Barber saw Pam immediately. Larry was grateful that they didn't have to wait in the waiting room, where cancer patients were waiting for treatments or appointments. Many had lost their hair and were wearing scarves or hats. Some braver patients simply waited with fashionably bald heads and no eyebrows. Pam didn't seem to notice. She was still feeling very weak and ill and had all she could do to make it from the parking lot to Dr. Barber's office.

Dr. Barber was a kindly physician, with white hair and a gentle smile. He came himself, to the waiting room and guided Pamela and

Larry to a small office, with a round table, where he motioned for them to sit. He also sat down at the table.

"Nice to meet both of you," he said with a smile. "I know that this is not easy for you. I have read all of the reports and studied the results of the tests that Pam has had so far, so it's time to discuss where we go from here."

Pam looked at him and only nodded. Larry smiled a little.

"Pam," Dr. Barber continued "You have been referred to me to give you a diagnosis, a prognosis, and a treatment plan, by Dr. Sampson. She broke the news of cancer to you, I know. What I have to add is that the cancer is at Stage 3. What that means is that we have reason to believe that it involves more than the tumor that we can see and possibly the entire liver. It has not spread to other organs as far as we can tell at this time. But, we can't take out the liver unless we can do a liver transplant. I have already put you on the transplant list. If we can keep cancer from spreading until we get a new liver, you may be as good as new. In the meantime, we need to get you into some treatment to prevent spread and eliminate cancer."

"Does that mean chemotherapy?" Larry asked.

"Yes, in a specific kind of program that is different for each patient. Dr. Sampson sent your case to me to figure out your prescription or "treatment cocktail.""

"That sounds so funny. To call a medical treatment a cocktail!" Pam actually laughed.

"It just means a combination of medicines, administered in a specific method and time sequence. Yours will be a complicated procedure, but we need to get started right away. Your treatment is also complicated by the unusual results from some of your autoimmune tests. But, I think we have a good plan. I'd like you to start on Monday if possible."

"Whatever you say. I'll do whatever it takes. Will I lose my hair?"

Dr. Barber smiled kindly. "Unfortunately, you probably will. However, not until we start the second phase of your treatments.

For the first month you'll be safe, and have some time to order some beautiful wigs. I can also get you information about support groups that will help you think about all of this. There are also some good support groups for women who have had problems with silicone gel breast implants. I encourage you to share with others who have faced these same challenges. There is no need to go through this, either of you, without the help of others who have gone before and prevailed. It's about becoming a cancer survivor, you know."

Pam tried not to cry, but her blue eyes filled with tears. So much for trying to be young and beautiful again.

19

Janet Stephenson had been involved in silicone gel breast implants for three years, against her will at first. As a young lawyer, she had been enthusiastically involved in the product liability cases involving IUDs, intrauterine devices, used for contraception. Several of those devices had escaped the scrutiny if you can call it that, of the FDA because they were classified as devices rather than drugs. After she had tried many of those cases against huge manufacturers and finally, settled all of those cases, she had decided not to take any more contingent fee products liability cases involving medical devices. She changed her mind when she encountered a client, who demonstrated to her that the same legal problems with grandfathering of defective medical devices also applied to silicone gel breast implants. She decided to take one case, which touched her heart, and soon was the local and regional expert on silicone gel breast implants. Janet started out her academic life planning to be a research chemist and she was always fascinated with chemistry. She did not find it difficult to understand the medicine or the science surrounding the issues relating to silicone gel breast implants. In fact, the intellectual challenge of the cases made them increasingly interesting to her. Janet had the skill to explain difficult and complex science to the women who had been injured by the silicone gel implants. As a result, she was a sought out speaker at support groups for women who had been injured by the implants.

Pamela Lawson heard Janet Stephenson speak at the Silicone Sisters Support Group meeting that she attended, at the suggestion of Dr. Barber. It was love at first sight. Pamela Lawson knew that she had to have Janet Stephenson and that she had to fight PSS. For the first time, Pam understood that there were people who knew what Dr. MacNamara did not know, or did not tell her, that polyurethane silicone gel breast implants cause cancer. Janet Stephenson's case against the PSS implants was based on the research of two amazing scientists, Jean Sonier and Richard Guilliot, who forced the PSS implants off the market in Canada. It was not smoke and mirrors. Janet Stephenson had facts, research, and science which explained why she, Pamela Lawson, had liver cancer. At the meeting, Pamela asked Janet Stephenson for her business card. The next day, she called Janet Stephenson's office and made an appointment to see her.

Janet's office was on Wadsworth Boulevard, near the mountains, and very near Pam's home in the Beaver Valley subdivision. Her building was a sprawling converted ranch-style mansion surrounded by several acres of beautiful trees and landscaping. Janet's office was in the back corner, with a window looking out on the grounds.

Janet came to the reception area to meet Pam and they went back to Janet's office, where they sat at an octagonal table by the window. Pam was shocked to see two deer, calmly grazing near a big locust tree just twenty feet outside.

"Isn't it amazing," Janet said. "I guess they feel safe here. Sometimes they come and actually look in the window. I'm always afraid I will come to work one day and see one of them hit by a car on Wadsworth."

Pam looked at Janet Stephenson, thinking that she didn't seem tough enough to be the trial lawyer that she had heard about from her friends in the silicone support group. She was tall and blond, with shoulder-length hair, which she wore pulled back behind her ears. Her grey-blue eyes were fringed by long black lashes and she had the slightest hint of smile lines at the corner of her eyes. Janet seemed more like a gentle and kind friend than a tough trial lawyer.

"Tell me about you," Janet was smiling at her.

"I have breast implants and I have liver cancer," Pam said simply. "I guess that pretty much sums up why I am here. I went to the meeting because Dr. Barber, my oncologist, suggested that I find some support groups to help me through this."

"What kind of implants do you have," Janet wasn't smiling now and she looked deadly serious.

"Mammselle," Pam said.

"How long have you had them?" Janet asked.

"About two and a half years," Pam said, "And I have loved them. I had no idea they might be making me sick. I got them because I was completely saggy after my last baby and I hated the way I looked."

"Who is your plastic surgeon?" Janet asked.

"Dan MacNamara." Pam smiled. "I just love him and I thought that he told me everything about the implants. He said they were the newest thing and I wouldn't have to worry about the complications of hard breasts or pain with the Mammselle implants because of the foam cover. He actually showed me an implant and let me hold it."

Janet Stephenson sat back in her chair and took a deep breath.

"Pam, it is probably true that Dr. MacNamara did tell you everything that he knew about the implant. The problem is that he didn't know and probably still doesn't know what PSS knew about their implants. They knew that the implants were never tested in humans, but they did not tell that to the doctors. They got their implant on the market based on Conway Chemical's studies on silicone. A loophole in our antiquated law allows them to piggyback on studies that have been previously approved by the FDA. They cited the Conway Chemical studies on silicone. Those studies claim and supposedly prove that silicone is chemically inert and therefore not harmful. The problem is that silicone in a biological environment, such as a live human body, triggers all kinds of biological reactions. The capsular contracture problem results when the body attempts to wall off the intruder foreign object. The body just surrounds it with scar tissue, so that the foreign object cannot cause problems.

The autoimmune system also kicks into high gear and tries to rid the body of the tiny micro-droplets of liquid silicone which seep through the silicone shell of the implant. Giant macrophages, or white blood cells, gobble up the droplets and try to carry them to organs in the lymphatic system which would normally excrete the foreign substance. The problem is that the droplets get deposited in the spleen, the lymph nodes, the liver, even the brain and stay there. This causes atypical autoimmune diseases with the symptoms of lupus, scleroderma, thrombocytopenia, fibromyalgia, rheumatoid arthritis, to name a few."

"But, I have cancer," Pam said. "How is that related to my implants. I have been examined and tested by Dr. Bricker at CU Medical school and he says I have weird blood work, but he has never diagnosed me with an autoimmune disease. Maybe he will, but he hasn't so far and he hasn't given me any treatment. He also never said that my illness is related to my implants."

"Your implants are coated with polyurethane foam," Janet explained. "That foam has never been tested in the human body. However, in animal tests done by Dr. Jean Sonier and Dr. Richard Guilliot, two Canadian biomaterials scientists, that foam totally degraded in the animals and dissolved into a compound called tolulene diamine, or TDA. If left undisturbed in the test animals, it caused cancer in all of them. TDA is such an aggressive carcinogen that it has been banned by the FDA in the United States from being used even in external products such as hair spray and hair color."

"How could this happen?" Pam was horrified. "Do you think that the foam covering my implants has dissolved into TDA ?"

"I don't know," Janet said. "There is only one way to find out. You will have to have the implants removed. You should probably have them removed anyway. Have any of your doctors suggested that you remove them?"

"None of my doctors have said anything about my implants. The only thing that Dr. Sampson said was that Dr. Barber, the oncologist, would have to have Dr. MacNamara's records before he could fully diagnose and treat my cancer. So we got his records about my implant surgery and they were sent to Dr. Barber." Pam replied.

"I would love to review all of your medical records, including reports on all of your lab work. I would also like to send your records to Dr. Sonier and Dr. Guilliot for their analysis, particularly of the lab and blood work."

"Will you take my case, Janet? Will you sue PSS for me?" Pam asked, her eyes filling with tears.

"Of course I will," Janet said "If your medical records show what I think they will, I think you may have the very case which will prove what charlatans Jennifer Fordham, Jerry Carson, and all of the greedy folks at PSS really are."

"Do you know them, Janet?"

"Yes, I do." Janet became very serious. "I have taken the depositions of each of them, but I am still battling in the court to get their records. So far, they have not had to disclose all of the records about the development of the Mammselle implant. However, with the facts of your case, they can't hide them anymore. Everything becomes relevant and discoverable."

"Let's do it," Pam said.

"There is one more thing. I think you should contact Dr. MacNamara immediately and tell him that you want to have the implants removed. I know that causes you a lot of anxiety, but honestly Pam, they are killing you. I can't put it more clearly. We will arrange for your implants to be sent directly to Dr. Sonier and Dr. Guilliot directly from the hospital lab, to be examined. The condition of those implants is a critical part of our case at trial. If your implants are smooth, we know the foam has gone somewhere. We also have to make sure that Dr. MacNamara removes the entire capsule if there is one, around the implants. We must have all of that tissue tested for TDA, and that is not a test that is normally run by a hospital after implant removal surgery. We have to talk Dr. MacNamara into ordering that test. If he won't, we may have to ask your oncologist to intervene and order the test."

"Can I do all of that?" Pam asked.

"They will be a lot less suspicious if your doctor orders it, than if your attorney intervenes." Janet was thinking out loud. "I would really like to have Dr. MacNamara and Dr. Barber on our side. But all doctors hate attorneys and see us as a threat to them. However, you should know that it is not my practice to sue doctors. I think they were sold the same bill of goods by PSS. I want to see if we can work it out so that Dr. MacNamara will testify for you."

"I doubt it," Pam said. "He thinks that PSS and the Mammselle are wonderful because they made an implant that stays soft. I don't know if I can even talk him into taking my implants out. I am sure that he will not think they have anything to do with my liver cancer."

"Where are you in your chemotherapy, Pam?"

"I have just started. As you can see, I haven't lost my hair yet. That comes with my second cocktail. I start those treatments next month. I have two more treatments with the first cocktail, as Dr. Barber calls it."

"I think you should call Dr. MacNamara right away. You need those implants out. It might even help your cancer treatments."

"I'll call him today. I agree. I want these implants out of me." Pam stiffened. "But, I don't think Dr. MacNamara knows about them. If I need you, will you talk to him or even go with me to my appointment with him."

"I'll do whatever you need me to do." Janet reached over and touched Pam's arm. "We're going to be in this together for a long time."

"I hope I have long enough," Pam said.

Janet met with Pam and Larry again the next day. Pam brought copies of all of her medical records and told Janet that she had an appointment with Dr. MacNamara on Thursday, the day following that. The three of them decided that Pam and Larry would go to the appointment without Janet. Larry was ready to advocate for the removal of the implants, no matter what Dr. MacNamara said to

Pam about the safety and effectiveness. Janet Stephenson was sure that she could not be a better advocate than this husband who loved his wife and was sad to the point of distraction that the implants might play a part in taking her from him.

20

Dan MacNamara sat back in his chair, behind his large mahogany desk. He couldn't believe it was true. The Mammselle implant had changed his life. His practice was booming. He was becoming a famous plastic surgeon throughout the country because of his tour with Sherrie Barker, promoting the implant at medical meetings. He had the additional income of the PSS honorariums and, certainly not least, he had Sherrie. His time with her added a special vitality to his life and their association appeared to all the world, including Sally, to be above reproach. Sherrie Barker was extraordinary. She never pressed him about leaving his wife or his life with his children. She was smart, fun, and captivatingly beautiful. She loved him, but she didn't demand that he sacrifice his life for her. It seemed too good to be true. In addition, she was a person of ethics and integrity in her profession. He couldn't believe that she would have lied to him about the testing of the Mammselle implant. Perhaps it seemed too good to be true—because it was.

Pam and Larry Lawson had just left his office. He had agreed, reluctantly to remove her implants, but he still did not believe that there was any relationship between the Mammselle and her liver cancer.

"It's just coincidental!" he said out loud to no one. "There is not one shred of truth to this. There can't be."

He picked up the phone and dialed Sherrie's number. She should be in her office in Santa Barbara today. It rang twice and she answered.

"Sherrie Barker," she said.

"Sher?"

"Dan! What's up?" her voice sparkled.

"Sherrie, I just saw a patient who has the Mammselle. My second implanted patient, Pam Lawson. She now has liver cancer and wants her implants removed immediately. She has a lawyer, a certain Janet Stephenson. Do you know her, or do you know anything about this?"

"I have heard of Janet Stephenson. She is a sort of thorn in the side of Jennifer and Jerry and has taken their depositions. I know that she wants internal documents that PSS doesn't want to give her and so far she has not succeeded in getting them. That's all I know and it is only hearsay"

"What internal documents does she want? Have you seen them?"

"I have no idea. I have always been told that it is just part of a witch hunt that started with two kooks in Canada, who prevented the sale of our products there."

"Is the Mammselle one of the products, or do you know?"

"I honestly don't know. I don't usually meet with the R&D or International side. I'm strictly involved with U.S. marketing. We hardly see each other actually because the marketing offices are in a completely different building about a mile from the plant. And, as you know, I'm usually on the road. My office is really at the airport." She laughed.

"Well, it looks as though I am going to have to remove these implants as a part of her cancer treatment. When I objected to removing them, I got a call from the patient's oncologist, who convinced me that it couldn't hurt and might even help with the cancer treatment."

"So, what's the problem? Lots of people get cancer."

"The problem is that now I have a direction from the patient and Janet Stephenson, to do additional tests on tissue, for a substance called TDA, and what's more, the implants are being sent to some outside laboratory after we are through with them, for analysis."

"Why is Janet Stephenson involved?"

"I thought you might know."

"I know that she has sued PSS in the past, but I haven't heard anything about a lawsuit involving the Mammselle and any of your patients. Do you know if there is a lawsuit?"

"No. I only assume that if there is a lawyer involved, a lawsuit is coming right up. Just what I need."

"I wouldn't worry about it. I'll see what I can find out, without asking directly. I'm sure it will come to nothing. You know how hysterical people become when they are diagnosed with cancer. I'm sure it has nothing to do with the implant or with you." Sherrie tried to sound reassuring, but her mind was putting together bits and pieces of things she had picked up around the plant. She was afraid there might be something more going on.

"Well, I just have to do the doctor thing and remove the implants. I will be assisted by the oncologist, of course. Cancer creates strange bedfellows."

"Don't worry, Dan. I'll see what I can find out and let you know."

"Will you call me?"

"I'll be in Denver on Tuesday for a regional meeting. I'll be in touch."

"Good. See ya."

"Bye."

The following Tuesday, Dr. Dan MacNamara and Dr. Arthur Barber scrubbed together in preparation for the surgery to remove Pam Lawson's implants. They laughed and shared stories about their families and renewed their acquaintance and friendship. Dr. MacNamara had done an oncology rotation under Dr. Barber during his residency. Dr. Barber had just come from the Cleveland Clinic to Rocky Mountain Cancer Institute and its related hospitals, including St. Anthony when Dan MacNamara first met him. They had remained friends and colleagues since then and Dan respected his prudent and successful approach to treating cancers. He referred every suspected cancer case to Dr. Barber and always had. This was their first surgery together, however, since Dr. MacNamara's residency.

"The question will be, Art, whether the foam coating around this implant is there."

"Why is that a concern?" asked Dr. Barber.

"Because there is a lawyer, who thinks she is a doctor, who told my patient that it will have dissolved and that the implant will be smooth, instead. She also told her that there will not be a scar capsule around the implant, only atypical liquefied tissue."

"And how does a lawyer know that?" asked the older physician.

"Because lawyers are smarter than God." Dan MacNamara laughed.

Dr. Barber furrowed his brow. Lawyers may not be as smart as God, but he has learned over the years that they were not usually entirely wrong and sometimes knew about medical problems before the problems were recognized by the more conservative medical establishment. He hoped that was not the case here.

Thirty minutes later, Dr. Dan MacNamara, assisted by his friend and a surgical resident, made the incision to reopen Pam Lawson's right breast along the same scar line as the implant surgery. He carefully moved the tissue to expose the implant.

"Oh my God," he exclaimed. "Look at this! There is no scar capsule."

He carefully removed the liquefied tissue surrounding the perfectly smooth Mammselle implant and placed it in a stainless steel tray for the hospital laboratory.

"And there does not appear to be a trace of foam on the implant," Dr. Barber added calmly.

"I don't believe it!" said MacNamara. "Let's be very careful in removing this implant. The shell may be really fragile and I don't want silicone gel spilling out everywhere."

The surgeons worked silently and carefully removing the implant and placing it in a laboratory tray. Then they irrigated the site and carefully closed the incision. They found the implant on the left side in a collection of liquefied tissue and totally without its foam covering. The implant and the tissue were also collected and sent to the laboratory.

"There are special instructions for additional tests and for retention and treatment of those implants." Dr. MacNamara told the lab technician, who retrieved the specimens from the operating room. "Be sure all of the special instructions are followed to the letter. I don't want any missing or accidentally destroyed tissue or implants in this case. Do you understand?"

"Yes, Dr. MacNamara. I have read all of the special instructions and I have made arrangements for the implants to be preserved as instructed and shipped already." The laboratory technician was a tall

African American girl with a quick smile and intelligent eyes. "We'll make sure it's all good." She smiled as she pushed the cart with all of the specimens of tissue and the implants out of the operating room. She knew that her supervisor had specifically assigned her to handle the laboratory work in this case because there were "lawyer instructions." Secretly she hoped that she would be able to stay involved in this case.

Dr. Barber's main concern throughout the surgery and after was for Pamela. He carefully monitored all of the anesthetic procedures and her breathing. He sat with her in the recovery room until she became conscious and could answer his questions.

"Hi, there," he said to his sleepy patient.

"Is it okay?" Pamela asked.

"You did well, my child." Dr. Barber patted her hand. "I think it was a very good idea to remove the implants and you came through it just fine—with flying colors."

"Were they smooth?" Pam asked.

"Yes, they were smooth," he said. "We'll leave it at that for now. At least they are out."

"Yes, at least that," she said.

Later in the physicians' lounge, Dr. MacNamara and Dr. Barber met again.

"What do you think, Art?" Dr. MacNamara asked his friend.

"Well, I hate to admit that a lawyer is right, but I sure am interested in those lab reports. How long will it take?"

"We won't have the TDA test results until tomorrow, probably late."

"Let's talk as soon as we get them." Dr. Barber said

"Yep." Dr. MacNamara had a lot of thinking to do if the tests came out as he feared they would. He still was not convinced that TDA in a confined area of the breast could be the cause of liver cancer. He needed some answers about the testing of the implants. Surely PSS had cleared that hurdle before the Mammselle was put on the market.

Forrest Winchester had always wanted to be rich. He had married his current fortune when he married Leslie Conway. Her family had built Conway Chemical into a huge part of the military-industrial complex in World War II as a supplier of liquid silicone to aircraft and other manufacturers. After the war, Conway continued its expansion of the use of silicone into other industrial and medical applications, such as artificial joints and implants. Silicone gel implants were developed after the FDA banned injections of silicone liquid into the breasts of women following WWII. It had become common for Asian women, especially the Japanese, to seek to enhance their figures to attract American soldiers. However, the silicone injections caused many serious complications including breast deformity, granulomas, little hard tumors, in the area of the injection. No attention was paid by the FDA to the systemic effect of silicone on the health of the women who had the injections. As a result, once the liquid was exchanged for silicone gel and enclosed in an implant, silicone gel breast implants went on the market as medical devices, virtually unregulated by the FDA. Conway and other manufacturers had made a fortune marketing them to women in America, Asia, and Europe. When Winchester married Leslie Conway, he became the CEO in charge of marketing and acquisition for Conway Chemical. It was her dowry from her aging father, who was anxious to retire with his new trophy wife to the South Pacific.

Now, with the acquisition of PolySurgical Specialties as a subsidiary of Conway Chemical, Winchester had cornered the market on the implant which solved the most serious complaint of plastic surgeons—capsular contracture. Soon, he believed, every surgeon in America and, quite possibly, the world, would be using the Mammselle implant.

Forrest Winchester had negotiated the purchase of PSS with Jennifer Fordham and her sidekick, Jerry Carson. Jennifer's father had owned the small pharmaceutical supplier since the Korean war, and he had turned the company over to Jennifer when he developed Alzheimer's disease ten years ago. Jennifer was a smart and ruthless woman, with a degree in marketing from UCLA. She, too, was determined to be rich. Jerry Carson had been a detail man who worked for her father. He was a gifted salesman, who had made a name for himself marketing their line of silicone gel breast implants, manufactured with Conway Chemical components, to California plastic surgeons. He was a bright and energetic man who tired of the complaints of his physician customers about capsular contracture in their patients with implants. He had begun going to pharmaceutical meetings regarding all kinds of implants and he heard a presentation by a German scientist regarding the use of foam-covered sutures to prevent scarring.

"Why not put foam on these breast implants?" he thought. "Capsular contracture is just a mass of scar tissue."

Jerry discussed the idea with Jennifer Fordham, who was intrigued. She contacted the laboratory which the R&D department used in testing new products and the lab designed a set of tests implanting polyurethane foam into mice. No scar tissue developed. Next, the lab was instructed to implant a series of silicone objects covered with foam. No scar tissue. Finally, the laboratory designed and implanted a tiny gel-filled implant. No scar tissue formed around the implant.

"Eureka, Jerry!" Jennifer had exclaimed as they read the last report together in her office. "We've got it. We can just put a polyurethane coating on our existing silicone gel implants and we can be in production almost immediately. We have the supplier for the foam. It is the same material used by the US military for cleanroom handi-wipes. We'll just order it by the roll."

"Wait a minute," Jerry said. "What about the FDA. Don't we have to get it approved before we market it?"

"Of course, we do. But that is a cinch. We already have our implant approved for sale. All we do is an application for an improving modification. We have the animal tests proving there is no scarring."

"That's all we need to do?" Jerry thought it sounded too good to be true. But it wasn't.

Jennifer and her revered father, Josiah Fordham, knew everybody in the pharmaceutical world, especially the political appointees to the FDA. Within six months, Jennifer had the approval of her amended application. In a year, the Mammselle was on the market.

As in all filings with the FDA, the FDA relies on the manufacturer to produce the tests, including the protocol for the tests, which prove that a product is safe and efficacious. Medical devices are governed by much less stringent requirements than drugs. There was no requirement that the Mammselle, as a device, be tested to determine if the process by which the foam prevented scar tissue was dangerous in itself.

Unfortunately, for Jennifer Fordham and Jerry Carson, the official report prepared by the Aegis laboratory scientists included the information that the scar tissue did not develop because the body tissue essentially grew into the foam, preventing a scar. Thereafter, the foam degraded into a substance known as tolulene diamine, which continued the process indefinitely. TDA, as it is known, is also a well-known carcinogen. But the FDA didn't ask that question and PSS didn't tell them. The reports from the testing laboratories were kept in locked file cabinets inside a locked closet in Jennifer's office. Only Jennifer, Jerry, and their hired laboratory knew that every one of the rats and mice into which the polyurethane-covered implants were placed, as well as all of the others into which foam was implanted, developed liver cancer.

When Forrest Winchester approached Jennifer Fordham about purchasing PSS and making it an operating subsidiary of Conway Chemical, Jennifer kept the information in the closet. It was not until the deal was fully signed, sealed, delivered and Jennifer's share was in her Swiss bank account that she opened the closet. Winchester's assistant, charged with the due diligence on all of the PSS products, finally uncovered the study results several months after the sale was accomplished and Jennifer Fordham and Jerry Carson were installed as CEO and President of PSS, a subsidiary of Conway Chemical. But, he decided to continue his search for the golden fleece, rather than to seek to undo the sale. After all, the Mammselle was approved for marketing by the FDA. What more did he or the shareholders of Conway Chemical need to know? What more indeed.

But, he did have a meeting with Fordham and Carson, where he established the plan they would follow to ensure they all became rich. That plan included the demise of Dr. Jean Sonier and Dr, Richard Guilliot, who had caused the banning of PSS Mammselle sales in Canada, with their research on polyurethane-coated implants.

On the thirty-third floor of the Tyrex building in downtown Chicago, Terrence Ray Napoli, said "Yes, sir." into a dark purple phone, held it out from his ear for a moment, studying it with disdain, then hung it up with a resounding thump.

Just that moment, a crisp-looking middle-aged woman, dressed in a dark gray suit, opened the door and entered carrying a large tray covered with a burgundy napkin. Napoli did not turn around. He continued to stare at the skyline and the setting sun.

"The dinner you ordered is here, Mr. Napoli. Should I set it up on your conference table or coffee table?"

"Just set it down, Mildred," he snapped. "I'll take care of it."

She set the tray down on the coffee table and turned to leave without saying a word.

"Did they send my wine?" he asked without turning.

"No, sir," she replied, putting her hands together as though she were at prayer, and lowering her head.

"No scotch either?"

"No, sir, I'm afraid not."

"Damn." was all he said. She left, silently closing the door behind her.

Terry Napoli, born with a platinum spoon in his mouth, was also born small in stature. His slight build and his five-foot-four-inch height were contrasted to his louder than average baritone voice, his keen intelligence, and his arrogance. His arrogance was born of an aristocratic birth as an only child of middle-aged parents and hardened by a life of exclusive boarding schools and colleges, where his classmates didn't care if he was rich and smart. They knew he couldn't run fast, throw far or play football. He became the class orator and verbal bully. He was suited to be a trial lawyer from birth.

Terry's expensive tastes and his upper-class heritage required that he be a defense lawyer. He couldn't represent the un-moneyed riff-raff who require a contingent fee for access to the legal system. He was destined to protect the fortunes of corporate America and the world, where his bread had always been buttered.

Terry Napoli was a good trial lawyer, and while he was very young, he won often enough to be offered a partnership, after only five years, at Black and Blocker, P.C., Chicago's premier defense firm, representing everybody who's anybody in the businesses of medical products, pharmaceuticals and plastics. That's how he came to represent Conway Chemical International and PolySurgical Specialties.

Terry had the obligatory wife, Carolyn, and one son, Jason, age six, a six-bedroom house in suburban Deerfield, and a penthouse apartment in downtown Chicago for nights when he worked too late or did not want to go home. Mostly he had his career. He also had Mildred, who had been widowed five years ago, and who was dedicated to him, no matter how badly he treated her. He genuinely liked Mildred - almost as much as his mother and more than his wife. He just treated her badly because he treated all those who worked for him badly because he thought that was the way you did it. He had never had the sense that he worked for anyone until he worked for Forrest Winchester, who treated him as badly as he treated others.

Terry sat down on his couch and started to uncover the tray. Then he got up and opened the door. Mildred sat dutifully at her desk outside peering at her computer screen over her half glasses.

"You can go now, Mildred," he said. "I won't need anything else. I'll leave you what I do tonight on the network." He turned to shut the door.

"If I leave, don't forget to put your tray in the kitchen, Mr. Napoli." Then, she added hurriedly, "I'll be glad to stay until you finish so you won't be bothered,".

"I'll do it. You may go," he said, and he shut the door.

He listened until he heard the door to his suite close, then he went to his desk, opened the bottom drawer, pulled it all the way out, and removed a bottle of Chevas Regal from the door over a false bottom.

Napoli took a water glass from his credenza, poured the remaining water in the plant by the window, and filled the glass a quarter full with scotch. He returned to his couch, peeked under the burgundy napkin covering the tray, and settled back with his drink. The last rays of the setting sun sparkled on the glass covering his desk.

Terry Napoli had been personally chosen by the firm's biggest client, Conway Chemical to defend Conway Chemical and PolySurgical Specialties, under the indemnification agreement between the companies, in the pending suit brought by Pamela Lawson. Conway Chemical supplied all of the silicone products used in the manufacture of the PSS polyurethane-coated silicone gel breast implant. Conway and PSS could easily have settled the Lawson lawsuit as they had many others, even with Janet Stephenson, but they chose to take this one to trial, in order to quash once and for all the building assertions that the polyurethane implants caused cancer. Conway and PSS knew that they had to try a cancer case now before all of the pending research being conducted by Sonier and Guilliot in Canada was completed. They were experts in this case, but they would be precluded from testifying about research that was not complete, and from which no formal scientific conclusions could be drawn.

Forrest Winchester was the CEO of Conway Chemical. Terry Napoli was awed by Winchester's money but despised his athletic build and mature good looks and his arrogant way of treating Napoli as though he were a servant.

Even Mildred had betrayed him and was attempting to enforce Winchester's memo that no attorney who worked for him was allowed to have alcohol in the office, or while he was on the clock for Winchester. Hence no wine with the dinner Terry had ordered because he had to work late. He was preparing for the depositions of Dr. Dan MacNamara, treating plastic surgeon, and experts, Jean Sonier, Ph.D.. and Richard Guilliot, M.D, Ph.D. He had to fly to Denver to meet with local council tomorrow.

He reflected on his lack of courage in not hanging up on Winchester just now. All he said to him was "Yes, sir." The guy's not even a lawyer, Napoli thought, boiling with rage, but he thinks he can teach me how to take a deposition. He was too upset to eat the crab salad he had ordered. It was no good without a glass of chardonnay anyhow.

The phone rang, interrupting his thoughts and his scotch sipping. At first, he was not going to answer it, then he remembered that he had left his cellular phone in his car and it might be Carolyn. He wasn't up to the silent treatment if his wife couldn't get hold of him. He reached for the extension phone on the table beside the couch.

"Napoli," he said into the receiver.

"Terry?" It was Janet Stephenson. "I can't believe I got straight through to you, I was going to be content with your voice mail."

"Hi, Janet," he replied deepening his tone just a little. "What's up?"

"Bad news about our depositions. Have you heard that Dr. MacNamara was injured in an accident?"

"No, what kind of accident?"

"Actually, he happened to be getting into his car in the parking lot of his building when a car bomb blew up another car. I was sure you would have heard by now."

"Sorry, I haven't seen any news."

"I thought sure you'd hear by now from your client." Janet was fishing. She was sure Napoli knew and was being coy.

"Why my client?" he asked, sipping his scotch.

"Because the person killed in the car bomb was Sherrie Barker, the Western regional manager for PolySurgical Specialties."

Napoli swallowed too much scotch and almost choked. He was silent.

"Terry. You there?"

Napoli wiped his mouth with the back of his hand and regained his composure.

"Yes, I'm here. I've been in meetings all day, and I haven't gotten to my messages," he lied. "So, how's MacNamara?"

"He's pretty badly hurt and he's still in intensive care. He was in surgery nearly all day for a skull fracture. We really don't know much yet. There have been no medical releases to the press or anyone. But, obviously, his deposition is off for now."

"I plan to be in Denver tomorrow anyway." Napoli tried to regain control of the conversation. He liked to be in control.

"Well, you probably don't need to come," Janet said, "We can adjust our schedules by telephone if you like."

"I have a meeting with our local counsel anyway, so I'll call you while I'm there so we can revise our discovery schedules."

"I don't think they need revision," Janet was persistent. "We can go ahead with the depositions of Sonier and Guilliot, and just reschedule MacNamara for later. I don't want to proceed as though MacNamara's injury will require a delay of the trial date. By the way, Pam had her liver transplant today too. If all goes well, she'll be fine to testify by the trial date."

"Well, Janet, I'll have the review all of this with my client and get back to you. For now, I plan to be in Denver tomorrow. I'll call you then,"

"Okay. If I'm not in, leave a message, and I'll get back to you."

"Sure, bye." Terry Napoli hung up the phone. *'I wonder when Winchester was going to fill me in,'* he thought. *'The arrogant SOB knew all this when he called not an hour ago.'*

Napoli had the uncomfortable feeling that he was being manipulated and he didn't like it. He went to his desk, found Winchester's private number, and dialed it. There was no answer. He didn't leave a message. He just sat down at his massive desk, turned his chair toward the glass wall of windows behind him, and looked out at the evening skyline."

After a few moments, he turned around and pushed the autodial number for local counsel in Denver, Rex Montague. Montague answered the phone.

"Rex, Napoli here."

"Hello, Terry. Well, you're probably up to your ears in it. What's the story about Sherrie Barker?"

"I'm calling to ask you, Rex. Was she in Denver to do trial preparation with you? Wasn't she the detail person who sold the implant to MacNamara that ended up in Pamela Lawson?"

"Yep. But we didn't have any meetings scheduled with her. She's on our witness list, but we didn't even know she was in town. I have to call Jennifer Fordham and Jerry Carson to see why she was here."

"What happened to her?"

"Don't know. All we know is that her car blew up. The police identified her because the car was a rental. They called PSS in Santa Barbara, and Ann Lowe, Sherrie Barker's secretary called me after Jennifer and Jerry met with the employees. Sherrie's mom was on her way to Denver, and Ann Lowe asked us to make her reservations at the Brown Palace and sort of look after her."

"Where was Sherrie staying?"

"Also at the Brown, but the police have taken control and cordoned off her room until they can search it carefully for clues."

"What about Dr. MacNamara?"

"There's a freeze on all information about Dr. MacNamara's condition and, by the way, on Pamela Lawson's condition. The donor's liver came last night, as I understand it and the transplant took place today. This place has been a zoo today. A few savvy members of the press have picked up that Sherrie worked for PSS and that Pam, who's suing PSS, had her liver transplant today, and it smells a little too coincidental not to have a story in there somewhere. Is it coincidental, Terry?"

"Hey, guy, I'm sitting here in Chicago in an information vacuum. Why didn't you fill me in on this when you found out?"

"Listen, be cool, Terry. I only know what I find out from the media. I understand some network types like Emily O'Brien and Patrick Kennedy are even interested and are beginning an investigation. I thought you were the one with the information and that you were deliberately not sharing it with me. After all, you're the one with the connections to Winchester. I've never met the guy. I'm lowly local counsel assigned to carry your briefcase and get you in the local court. You've been designated as the P.R. guy charged with charming the media and the jury in the Pamela Lawson case for all the world to see."

"Sorry, Rex. I've been in meetings all day," he lied again, "and so I've been a little incommunicado. I'm still planning to come tomorrow, so we can talk then."

"Good. See you, Terry. Oh, by the way, do you want someone to pick you up, or are you planning to rent a car?"

"That's not funny, Rex. Have someone at the airport. I have reservations at the Westin."

Rex Montague hung up the phone, still smiling slightly because he did think it was funny. He hadn't met Sherrie Barker, but he felt sorry for her. He didn't feel sorry for Napoli. Twenty years Napoli's senior, Rex Montague was known in the Denver legal community as a fine trial lawyer. It galled him to walk two steps behind and one step to the left of cocky little Terry Napoli. But, money talks and the enormous check which his firm received from Conway Chemical/ PSS convinced him to cater to the client and its chosen hired gun. He knew Terry Napoli was a flash in the pan. He also knew he was a little too fond of scotch.

Forrest Winchester replaced the airfone into its place after talking to Terry Napoli and leaned back in his first-class seat. He stretched his long legs toward the bulkhead and ran his fingers through the hair of his graying temples.

"Another scotch, Mr. Winchester?" the pretty flight attendant asked.

"Yes, thank you," he replied returning her smile.

She took his empty glass. Two scotches were his limit, even though he could probably have at least two more without anyone knowing.

'That's the only problem with Napoli,' he thought. *'He likes scotch as much as I do. He just isn't old enough to know what it can do to him. Still in the invincible thirties.'*

Forrest Winchester picked up the phone again. He took out his credit card and ran it through the phone, listened, and dialed. Voice messaging answered.

"Hello, Leslie. I'm just checking in from the plane. I had to fly off to Phoenix. I'll be at the Biltmore if you need me. Just give me a call."

He had carefully waited until he knew his wife would not be home. She was so predictable, and it made life and its little deceptions very easy for him. He was off to Phoenix to give a thirty-minute speech, standing in for the Director of Scientific Research at Conway

Chemical, on silicone technology in aerospace for a convention of engineers at the Biltmore Hotel. That thirty-minute speech gave him two days incognito.

If Napoli and the curious press went into orbit about Sherrie Barker, he would simply be unavailable. Jennifer and Jerry had been fending off the media well so far.

Forrest Winchester checked in at the Biltmore and settled into his secluded cottage suite, the last one on the garden path. He changed into his formal clothes and had another scotch from the bar in the living room before he went through the gardens of the Biltmore to the convention center and the banquet where he would be announced as one of the speakers for tomorrows seminars. He was not easily recognized, and for that he was grateful.

When he returned to his cottage, she was standing in the living room in a swimsuit and white lace cover-up, holding a glass of champagne.

"Jennifer, will you never acquire a taste for scotch?" he said before he took her into his arms and kissed her waiting mouth. She did not answer.

At their country home outside Woodland, Michigan, Leslie Winchester listened to her husband's message when she returned from her tennis match. She poured herself a glass of iced tea and turned on the speakerphone in the kitchen to listen to the messages reminding her of meetings and from her children. The last message was from Forrest.

"Well, no need to fix dinner tonight, Meg," she said to the housekeeper who stepped into the kitchen from the French doors leading to her beautiful rose garden. "Forrest had to go out of town. I'll just have some fruit and cottage cheese so you might as well take advantage of having a night off."

"Thank you, mum," Meg said in her thick Irish accent. "There is a new movie a playin' at the mall that I'd like to see if I could."

"Go. Go," said Leslie waving her hand as she looked over the mail. "Have a good time. I'm fine. Just take your key because I'm going to have a long bath and go to bed early. I'm so tired that I can hardly wiggle. I'm going to have to give up tennis. I just can't do it anymore."

Leslie took her iced tea, went to the den, and switched on the TV with the remote as she sank into her favorite chair. The story about Sherrie Barker's murder was just on the evening news.

Leslie paid little attention until the newscaster said. "Police have disclosed that Ms. Barker was a regional manager for PolySurgical

Specialties who lived in Santa Barbara, California. She was apparently in Denver on business."

That story was followed by the story of Pamela Lawson's liver transplant and her pending lawsuit against PSS, manufacturer of her polyurethane-coated silicone gel breast implants. At the end of the story was an interview with Janet Stephenson, attorney at law.

"Mrs. Stephenson, do you see any connection with the death of Sherrie Barker, a PSS employee, the simultaneous injury of Dr. Dan MacNamara, and Pamela Lawson's lawsuit against PSS?"

"I don't know of any connection," Janet Stephenson said. "It appears to be just a tragic coincidence."

"Isn't Dr. MacNamara your client's physician?"

"Yes, Dr. MacNamara is Pamela's plastic surgeon. Another surgeon, Dr. Levi Emanuel, actually performed her liver transplant surgery."

"What was Dr. MacNamara doing in the parking lot?"

"It is the parking lot of the building where his offices are located. He was apparently just leaving his office and getting in his car when the bomb went off elsewhere in the lot."

"Elsewhere being in Sherrie Barker's car?"

"Yes."

"By the way, how is Mrs. Lawson?"

"At this time there is no news, but no news is good news for now."

"And Dr. MacNamara?"

"Nothing has been released about his condition yet."

"Thank you. That was Janet Stephenson, attorney for Pamela Lawson, whose claims against the breast implant manufacturing company which employs the bombing victim is set for trial soon here in Denver. ABC's Emily O'Brien and Patrick Kennedy are en route to Denver and will be providing us with breaking news and upcoming reports as this story develops. It is interesting to note that the FDA is also holding hearings in Washington this week on the safety of those same silicone gel implants. Emily O'Brien and Patrick

Kennedy have been covering that story as well. We'll have more on those hearings tonight at ten o'clock and tomorrow at five o'clock. This is Don Dennis reporting live from Denver."

Leslie Winchester sat transfixed in front of the T.V. not hearing the remaining news. Then she went to the desk, took a pad, and wrote, "Denver, Pamela Lawson, attorney: Janet Stephenson. plastic surgeon: Dan MacNamara. PSS: Sherrie Barker - DEAD -Emily O'Brien - Patrick Kennedy - FDA hearings" She might need that information and she knew that if she didn't write it down, she'd never remember. Her memory wasn't what it used to be. She left the pad on the desk and went upstairs to run a hot bath, still pondering the news she had seen.

As she got into the sunken marble tub, Leslie settled into the bubbles and leaned back. Her curly, strawberry blond hair was graying just a little and silver wisps fell around her face as she gathered the rest on top of her head and secured it with a large barrette. She was thin and athletic, and her breasts were slightly asymmetrical but those of a twenty-five-year-old. Her nose was small and freckled and her green eyes were fringed with dark red eyelashes. At forty-five years old, she rarely wore makeup, except on formal occasions and when Forrest insisted.

"I look okay," she said out loud to herself, "until you touch me."

With a slight look of disgust and sadness, she touched her nipples and her breasts. *'Nothing,'* she thought. *'They have lost all sensation except pain.'*

Her breasts were hard, and when they were subjected to the heat of the bathwater, they became discolored and more painful.

"I should never have let him talk me into it," she said to no one. Forrest Winchester hadn't touched his wife or made love to her since he convinced her to have breast augmentation surgery with the state-of-the-art silicone implants made by PSS.

"Nobody would want to touch me," she said sadly, sank deeper into the bubbles, and thought, *'I wish I were Sherrie Barker.'*

As he walked out of the hearing room, Jean Sonier was met by Emily O'Brien and her camera crews. Loretta and Cynthia were trailing behind, besieged by ladies who wanted to get the information about silicone-related diseases and sympathetic physicians which they had promised to anyone who wanted it during their presentations to the FDA panel.

"Dr. Sonier, could I have a moment?" Emily O'Brien asked. The cameras were not yet rolling.

"Hello there, Miss O'Brien, I'm sorry I haven't had the opportunity to respond to your telephone communication since I spoke with Dr. Guilloit. We are agreeable to do your show."

"That's great. We'll get it all worked out, but right now I'd like to talk to you about what's going on in Denver, and perhaps an exclusive on the breaking news in the Pamela Lawson case."

"Oh, I see. What exactly do you mean about what's going on in Denver?" he asked innocently.

"Sherrie Barker from PolySurgical Specialties was killed in a car bomb, and coincidentally, Pamela Lawson's plastic surgeon happened to be in the same parking lot at the same time and is in intensive care. Smells like a story to me. What do you think?"

"Possibly, just possibly," he rubbed his chin and took off his glasses. "I'm just headed to Denver, and I will be going to Quebec from there at the end of next week, but right now I haven't spoken to anyone in the know there."

"Who would be 'in the know' there, Dr. Sonier."

"I'm quite sure you might know better than I about that. I perhaps would only speak with Janet Stephenson, as she is the attorney for Pam, and I have agreed to offer expert testimony in her case. Have you spoken to Mrs. Stephenson?"

"No, not yet, although she was interviewed locally for the news. Could we tag along on your flight to Denver? We'll be happy to upgrade your tickets to first-class if we can tag along with you to Denver and talk on the way."

"How do you know I am in need of an upgrade?" his eyes twinkled.

"Dr. Sonier, you are well known for your small suitcase and your frugal style of travel. But I'm willing to stand corrected."

Emily laughed her infectious laugh and patted him on the arm. She was a full head taller than Dr. Sonier, and her beautifully coiffed but bountiful auburn hair made her seem taller yet. Her hazel eyes sparkled with good humor and affection for the diminutive scientist. She, like Sonier, had a good sense of humor and she was enchanted by his charming use of the English language. She looked forward to this difficult assignment partly because she would be able to interview Dr. Jean Sonier.

Emily was in college in Ottawa when the PSS scandal broke in Canada, and she had first seen Sonier on television and at news conferences when he was dogged by the Canadian press. "A gentleman and a scholar" was what she called him in her report on the travesty of his discharge and rehiring by the National Health Service as its Chief Scientist, over the PSS implants, for the Ottawa College Clarion.

He laughed and replied, "I shall happily accept your offer if you give me a receipt for the upgrade so that it can be properly reported. I'm sure some solicitor somewhere will likely accuse me of not reporting it during some upcoming cross-examination if it is not completely documented."

She handed him a ticket. "I was hoping you'd agree. Here's your first-class ticket. See you at the airport."

The cameraman was taking pictures of Loretta, Cynthia, and the other Silicone Sisters, who never turned down a photo opportunity. A local newswoman was asking them questions until Emily O'Brien was free. Dr. Jean Sonier scurried away in the chaos and returned to his hotel to try and call Janet Stephenson before he had to leave for Dulles and his upgraded flight.

When Dr. Sonier got to the hotel, there was a waiting message from his wife. He returned her call and forgot all about Janet Stephenson for the moment.

"Lorna? Are you all right?"

"Yes, my dear," she replied, her voice warm and soft.

"Did you hear about the bombing in Denver?"

"Yes, it was on the news. It sounds a little too familiar, doesn't it? But unless they are turning on their own, it can't be related, can it Jean?"

"That all depends on the agenda and activities of Miss Sherrie Barker, I think. Janet Stephenson, the plaintiff's lawyer, may know something because the plastic surgeon who was injured is the plaintiff's physician, and also a witness in the case."

"I don't understand, Jean," she said.

"Well, well, let's just let the sleeping dogs snooze on for now, Lorna. But be extra careful, these kinds of tragic coincidences usually travel in threes."

"I understand, even though you've not only mixed metaphors but proverbs, Jean." She laughed. He made her laugh, that's why she loved him.

"I'll call you from Denver to fill you in on the punch line. Got to run. Love you."

She laughed again, "Goodbye, dear. Hang on to your laptop."

He grabbed his suitcase and backpack and raced for the door, his mind already on Quebec, the implants, and Denver. In the hall, he suddenly stopped, rummaged in his pockets for his key, with his ticket in his teeth, re-entered his room and retrieved his laptop computer from the desk where he had plugged it in.

"Don't laugh," he said to the bedside table phone.

On the way to Denver on the plane, Jean Sonier filled in the two reporters about the FDA hearings on the safety of the implants. Emily knew most of what he said already from her own research. Patrick Kennedy was all ears, especially when Dr. Sonier disclosed all of the mysterious events which followed the removal of the PSS breast implants from the market in Canada.

"And then, of course, there was the bombing," he added matter of factly.

"What bombing?" Kennedy asked.

"A bomb exploded outside our newly established laboratory in Ottawa and killed a pedestrian. No one from the lab was hurt, but we know that it was related to the demise of one Raoul Lecroix."

"What do you mean? Who is Raoul Lecroix?"

"Is this off the record?" Sonier asked, knowing that nothing is really "off the record," but that sources are protected - usually, anyway.

"Of course. Of course "Patrick Kennedy was nodding and leaning toward Sonier. Emily sat across the aisle.

"Raoul Lecroix owned the medical distributorship which had the exclusive right to market PSS breast implants in Canada. When the implants were taken off the Canadian market, Lecroix was ruined financially. He and his family blamed me, and we started getting death threats in the mail and by phone. Once, a phone call was traced to a payphone in the lobby of the apartment building where Lecroix's son lived. Ironically, that boy died in an automobile collision a week later, while he was being tailed by police. He just drove off a road into a tree. The police saw the entire catastrophe."

"Where is Lecroix now?"

"Somewhere in the U.S. I lost track of him when he moved to Chicago shortly after his son died." Sonier knew that the FBI knew because he had had many conversations with the City Solicitor who had contacted the FBI, but he thought that the reporters had enough information for now to develop their own investigation. He watched Patrick Kennedy's eyes widen in interest and fascination as he adroitly fed him just the right facts to peak his interest.

Patrick Kennedy had already decided to call his sources in the FBI and was formulating a plan to put into action as soon as they landed in Quebec.

'There may be a Pulitzer Prize in this one,' he thought to himself.

my Larabee, FBI, called Janet Stephenson the next morning after she got her business card from Lieutenant Joel Steiner at the Denver Police Department. Amy wanted to know what Janet knew about Sherrie Barker, the PSS regional manager killed by the bomb.

"Mrs. Stephenson, you don't know me, but I got your card from Lt. Steiner at the police department. I'd like to make an appointment to discuss some things with you."

"What can I do for you?" Janet asked, "Joel Steiner should have told you that I don't do criminal law anymore." Joel had a habit of referring her kids and nearly indigents who couldn't qualify for legal aid, but couldn't pay her either. Janet was never really enthusiastic about Joel's referrals because they always broke her heart and her pocketbook.

"I'm not looking for an attorney," Amy said quickly. "I'd just like to meet with you to discuss a matter of mutual interest to us both."

Janet was intrigued! This sounded really mysterious.

"Sure," she said. "How about coming over to my office about ten o'clock."

"I'll be there," Amy said.

"Need the address?"

"No, I have your card," Amy said.

By the time Amy arrived Janet had imagined all kinds of interesting things, but she was not prepared for Amy's questions nor for the information she shared. Just to be sure, Janet asked to see Amy's FBI identification. This petite young woman didn't look like an FBI agent. She looked like somebody's secretary. Janet Stephenson, the lady lawyer, was embarrassed by her own first impression and chastised herself secretly for being chauvinist.

Amy Larabee asked Janet what she knew about Sherrie Barker. Janet explained that Sherrie was the detail person or salesman from PSS who serviced the Denver plastic surgeons and supplied them with PSS medical products for about five years, ending a year ago when Sherrie was transferred to the home office of PSS in Santa Barbara. Sherrie was the salesman who sold Dr. MacNamara the PSS implant which had been placed in Pamela Lawson, Janet's client. Janet had secured a list of all of the detailed persons at PSS when she finally got the production history, which included the "lot" numbers and production testing for Pamela's breast implant. It had been a real battle but the court had finally ordered PSS to a partial document production, which included all of the production records for the PSS implants which were implanted in Pamela Lawson. The discovery process in preparing Pam's lawsuit for trial was a battle that was continuing.

"But why is the FBI interested in Sherrie Barker?" Janet asked.

"She appears to be the latest victim of a Canadian bomber we've been tailing here in Colorado. We're just trying to figure out why he killed her—if he killed her," Amy replied.

Janet's mind was whirling. Why would anyone want to kill Sherrie Barker?

"Who did he bomb in Canada?" Janet asked

"We suspect him in the bombing of the laboratory of a biomaterials scientist named Jean Sonier." Amy was looking at her notes and did not see Janet's mouth drop open.

"I know Jean Sonier well; he's due in Denver tonight to meet with me. He's a major expert in a case I have going to trial."

Amy looked up. Janet was staring at her in disbelief.

"There has to be a connection, and the connection has to be PSS," Janet exclaimed.

"What do you mean?" Amy asked quickly.

"Sonier drove PSS implants off the market in Canada with his research and his government reports which were gobbled up by the media. Sherrie Barker sold Dr. MacNamara the PSS implant that my client had, and MacNamara was almost killed as well. Suppose Sherrie Barker and MacNamara were on to something and were both the targets."

"It could be," Amy added. "The guy we suspect of masterminding the bombings is Raoul Lecroix, a man who used to own the exclusive distributorship for PSS implants in Canada."

"Did he do it?"

"No, we don't think so. We've been tailing a low life named Tom Slade who lives here in Denver. We think that Lecroix hired him because Lecroix has made several recent trips to Denver - as recently as this week."

"Do you know when Sonier is getting in or where he is staying?"

Janet laughed, "Of course. Nothing but the best for Dr. Sonier. He always insists on the Holiday Inn by my office because he knows the staff and he hates the waste of expensive hotels. He always rents his own car because he likes the freedom to travel about incognito. But I don't think he will get in until very late. I'm supposed to meet him for breakfast at seven in the morning. Want to come?"

"You bet," said Amy. "Where is this hotel?"

"Somehow, I thought the FBI knew everything!" Janet laughed as she wrote down the address and handed it to Amy. Amy looked at it, the stuck it in the side pocket of her purse. She stood up and extended her hand to Janet.

"If we knew more lawyers like you, maybe we would," she smiled. "I'll meet you at six fifty-five in the lobby."

Janet shook her hand. "Great," she said. "See you then."

Amy was on time, and so was Janet. Jean Sonier was early and was sitting at a table in the coffee shop with his glasses on his head, peering at the newspaper when they found him.

"Jean," Janet said. Dr. Sonier started to stand and extended his hand.

"Good to see you, Janet." he pumped her hand vigorously, then looked at Amy Larabee.

"Amy Larabee, meet Dr. Jean Sonier."

"Pleased," said Sonier gently and quizzically.

"Shall we sit?" Janet motioned to the chairs, and they all sat down.

"Let me explain, Jean. Amy is from the FBI. She came to see me last night about the bombing of Sherrie Barker's car."

Jean Sonier immediately started nodding sadly. "It is so sad. What bastards these guys really are!" he said emphatically.

"What do you mean, Dr. Sonier?" Amy asked.

"The FBI knows, or you wouldn't be here, would you? You know it's Lecroix and his henchmen. I'm probably next."

"Have you had any threats, or other contacts recently," Amy asked.

Suddenly Janet understood why Sonier always preferred to be "incognito" as she called it. It wasn't that he was shy; he was being cautious. But he never seemed afraid, even now.

"No. No, I haven't—but it is more likely that they would threaten my wife."

"Why your wife?" Janet asked.

"She is alone with our son most of the time, and she is more vulnerable than I am. I have quite a thick skin, you know." Sonier smiled, but his voice betrayed a slight concern.

"I'll just check and ensure that she has protection. At least until we have a little more information here." Amy was reaching in her bag for her cell phone. "It all seems a little too coincidental for me. Another bombing, just as you are about to present Dr. Sonier for depositions in your PSS case."

"Dr. Sonier, did you know Sherrie Barker?"

"No, no I did not. But I know her bosses, Jennifer Fordham and Jerry Carson."

"How well do you know them?" Amy asked.

"Very well. Jennifer is the brains behind the addition of the polyurethane foam to the outside of the implant. She and Carson are, no doubt, lovers. He always travels with her. They came to Ottawa together to try and convince the Canadian government not to recall their implants when I was Deputy Minister of Health," Sonier said matter-of-factly.

"How involved were they with Raoul Lecroix?"

"He was handpicked by them to be the exclusive distributor in Canada before their implant line was bought out by Forrest Winchester and Conway Chemical. I dare say if they hadn't stalled the governmental recall, Conway would never have purchased their implants line and secured their future employment."

"So they did stall the recall for a time?" Janet Stephenson was amazed. She learned something new every time she talked to Dr. Sonier.

"Only a year or so. Meanwhile, they set about attempting to destroy me. And, I might add, they nearly succeeded -- were it not for my stubborn Huguenot ancestry."

Janet was stunned. "Do you want to reschedule your deposition, Dr. Sonier? Would you feel more comfortable if you were back with your wife?"

"No, no, no." He was shaking his head emphatically. "We must go forward. Pamela may not live, and we cannot let these bastards win her case by intimidation."

"Well," said Amy, "It's a little more than intimidation. They've nearly succeeded in killing Dr. MacNamara, who, I understand was to be deposed in Pam Lawson's case just after you."

"Nevertheless, I am here. We must act as if the two events are unrelated. Put on our most naive face and march ahead," he insisted. "We must keep them off guard. They expect us to cancel."

Amy looked at him in amazement, then dialed her cell phone. In a moment, she said, "Hi, Ben, good morning. Have I got a deal for you!"

Dr. Sonier smiled and looked intently at his menu. Janet felt her stomach tighten. *'How can he eat?'* she thought.

Ben Smith hung up the phone after speaking with Amy Larabee and immediately dialed a number in Washington. After a few minutes of conversation, he was transferred directly to the Canadian consulate, and the protection for Dr. Sonier's family was on the way. Lorna Sonier noticed the car almost immediately. "Friend or foe?" she asked herself.

Terry Napoli and Rex Montague also met for breakfast, catered into the conference room looking toward the mountains off the main lobby of Montague's law firm. They were both on edge, and neither wanted to do the deposition of Dr. Sonier that day.

"Sherrie Barker's mother is in town." Montague disclosed.

"I hope you have a keeper for her." snapped Napoli.

"Why should she need a keeper?" Montague inquired tersely. "Do you know something I should know?"

"Unfortunately—I know nothing. Nothing! Winchester tells me nothing. I don't know why I put with the S.O.B?"

"I do," said Montague, rubbing his thumb and forefinger together in front of Napoli's nose.

Napoli slapped at it. "You should know," he said.

Napoli went to the sidebar and poured a cup of coffee. He looked out the window as the mountains glowed pink in the sunrise.

"We'd better bury the hatchet, Rex," he said still looking out the window.

"It's your hatchet, Terry. Where do you want to bury it."

"I'm serious. Why can't we find a way to be friends since we are on the same team."

"I just can't carry your briefcase, Napoli. You weren't even out of college when I took the bar. The only thing I'm missing is the parental connection." Montague smiled condescendingly.

"You don't have to carry my briefcase. And, I'd be obliged if you would take Sonier's deposition today. I'm really not up to it."

Rex Montague looked at him in disbelief. Then panic spread over him. He wasn't prepared to take Sonier's deposition. He didn't know biomaterials science well enough to depose a world-class biomaterials expert like Sonier. Napoli was calling his bluff.

"I'm not prepared to do Sonier's deposition, and you know it, Napoli."

"Then I guess you'll just have to carry my briefcase," Napoli said. He turned on his heel and left the conference room. "I'll be at my hotel until nine fifteen," he told the receptionist.

Montague stared after him seething with anger and outright hatred.

At nine thirty when Janet Stephenson and Dr. Jean Sonier arrived, Terry Napoli was sitting on the mountainside of the table coolly reviewing a stack of documents. Rex Montague was in his office on the phone with Forrest Winchester's assistant.

"Good morning, Janet. Dr. Sonier." Terry Napoli beamed and thrust out his hand toward them.

"Good morning, Terry," Janet said. Dr. Sonier nodded and shook his hand briskly.

Dr. Sonier's deposition continued through a catered lunch of Subway tuna sandwiches and finally concluded at 5:15 in the evening so that Dr. Sonier could catch his seven o'clock plane. Janet rushed him to Denver International Airport. Despite the fact that he had answered Napoli's arrogant questions all day, Dr. Sonier talked all the way to the airport giving Janet instructions about Pamela's case. The time was too short. Janet stopped in the parking lane, furiously writing notes after she dropped him off lest she forgets any of the precious information he had heaped on her as she drove.

'He didn't mention the danger he's in once!' she thought as she drove back to her office.

Patrick Kennedy and Emily O'Brien were energized by their meeting with Dr. Sonier. He had given their story a new angle. He was determined to see what the Denver Police knew and to get the special scheduled before the pending trial in Denver of Pamela Lawson's case. When he and Emily O'Brien landed in Denver, they shared a rental car and set out for downtown and the Marriot Hotel on California Street. After they checked in to their rooms, they met in the hotel bar. Patrick was there first and ordered calamari for them to munch on. He was sipping a glass of red wine when Emily appeared in jeans with her hair in a ponytail.

"Hi, there. Can I buy you a drink?" he joked.

The waiter appeared and Emily ordered a glass of white wine.

"Red is healthier." Patrick smiled at the weary Emily.

"I'm beat," she said. "I feel as though I've been up for days."

"We're on to something here, Em." Patrick's brain was buzzing with ideas about their planned television special. He loved Dr. Jean Sonier and his disarming and intelligent way of explaining the most difficult scientific questions.

"I think that we should use Dr. Sonier as much as possible in telling our story because he just makes so much sense. I am afraid that our audience may have their eyes glaze over when we start talking about dimethylpolysiloxane and tolulene diamine if we don't have him explain that it's only silicone and TDA that comes from handi-wipes wrapped around and glued on to a silicone breast implant. Even I can get that and I don't understand why the FDA hasn't gotten it a long time ago."

"I love him too," Emily said. "But he may sound a bit like a sour grapes whistleblower if we disclose the entire complicated history about his experiences with the Health Ministry in Canada. I think we have to do that. We should meet Janet Stephenson, Dr. MacNamara, and Pamela Lawson, first."

"Frankly, I wasn't much impressed with the Silicone Sisters," Patrick said. "I hope that Pamela Lawson is a little more sympathetic. They are hard to listen to."

Emily laughed. "Middle-aged ladies with a cause are always a hard sell."

"I have Janet Stephenson's number. Let's give her a call and see if she can arrange for us to see Pamela Lawson. She's got to be pleased that our story is going to air the week before the Lawson trial is supposed to start."

Emily frowned. "Are you suggesting that it is a sure thing that our investigation and story are going to work in her favor? What if we aren't convinced by the evidence that TDA results from the breakdown of the polyurethane?"

"You're joking, right?" Patrick said and then she burst into laughter.

"Patrick, I've seen enough and learned enough to make me love being flat-chested, forever!" she said, her eyes still twinkling with laughter. "I just hope we don't have to rely on the Silicone Sisters to tell the story. If that is our only choice, Dr. Sonier gets the gig, hands down."

They outlined their Denver interviews over another glass of wine and more appetizers. Patrick called Janet Stephenson's cell phone and left a message, asking to meet with her and possibly Pamela Lawson, as soon as possible. Then they set off for the Denver police department on Cherokee street, with all their credentials, to see what they could learn about the bombing and the death of Sherri Barker.

When they returned to their rooms, they each had a message from the Silicone Sisters with a list of other silicone survivors to interview, along with their phone numbers.

"I may have to get a short-term lease on a Denver apartment," she joked to Patrick, "if we are going to cover all of the angles of this story and get it on the air before Pam Lawson's trial."

"Maybe I can get the FDA to chip in . . . Naw." Patrick laughed.

Janet Stephenson listened to the voice mail from Patrick Kennedy. *'What a great name,'* she thought. She called back and made an appointment to have Patrick and Emily O'Brien come to her office the next day. She told them she would check on Pam Lawson's condition, but she doubted that she would be recovered enough from her liver transplant surgery to give any sort of interview.

Patrick Kennedy and Emily O'Brien came to Janet Stephenson's office with the full camera and sound crew, which had taken the red-eye from New York. They had arrived only two hours before and seemed remarkably ready for a full day of work.

"We just want to take a few shots of you and your office if it's okay," Emily said.

"We are in the middle of trial preparation, so we're not ready for company," Janet told her.

"The story is about the trial and about Pamela Lawson's struggle, as well as the implants, and how they slipped through the FDA approval process," Patrick urged. "Your office is perfect, just as it is."

Janet was not convinced, but she was always prepared to talk about the implants and the problems they posed for patients who were implanted with them. She could talk about all of these things in her sleep—in fact, she felt as though she often did.

Janet did a general interview, scrupulously avoiding any discussion of the facts of Pamela Lawson's case. She talked about the science of the disintegration of polyurethane into the carcinogen TDA and the removal of all other products, such as hairspray, which contain TDA because TDA causes cancer. How much more dangerous would TDA inside the breast be? She spoke in her most mellow voice, knowing the peril of a screeching image, and was convincingly intelligent, professional, and perhaps, even beautiful. Emily was more convinced than ever that this special program must air before the Pamela Lawson trial.

Janet Stephenson called the hospital and talked to Larry Lawson, who was holding his vigil in Pamela's room.

"She's really much better today," he said. "I think that she is stronger and is no longer on morphine drips. All of her pain meds are oral now."

"What do you think are the chances that she would be able to do an interview with the press anytime soon?" Janet asked tentatively.

"I know that she wants to do it, Janet, but not unless she has her wits about her and not unless she can have her hair done. She won't do it otherwise and I wouldn't let her."

"Nor, would I. I just told the television crew that I would ask about how she is doing. Perhaps we can see if they can come back in the next week or so."

"What's the rush?" Larry asked.

"Well," Janet said carefully, "If we are going to do this, it would be terrific if it could air before our trial starts."

There was a silence on the other end of the phone. Then Larry Lawson replied. "Janet. Why don't you call me tomorrow? I will talk to Pam. I agree that it is important for this to work for us too. What a crime it would be if her interview only helped cases which came after hers."

"I agree," said Janet softly "I'll call you tomorrow morning."

"How'd that go?" asked Emily O'Brien as Janet hung up the telephone.

"I think I will be able to give you an answer tomorrow. She's actually feeling lots better."

Patrick Kennedy and Emily O'Brien both smiled. Tomorrow or even any time in the next three days would be fine. If they could interview her then, they could still meet the deadlines to air the show before the trial.

Two days later, the camera crew, with Emily O'Brien and Patrick Kennedy went to St. Anthony hospital. Pam's room was filled with flowers and she was sitting up in bed, either beautifully coiffed or with a very expensive wig. She had on lipstick. The television crew had a makeup member, who gently asked Pam if she could touch up her makeup. Pam gratefully nodded. Emily asked her questions softly and respectfully and Pam answered, with candor and grace, telling her story innocently and convincingly to the two reporters. She was without anger but seemed profoundly sad. Larry sat on the side of her bed, with noticeable tears in his eyes.

Later that evening, the crew went to the Lawsons' home and interviewed Larry's mother and took shots of the children in their jammies, with their stuffed animals. Grandma Lawson also got some help from the makeup artist. She told them bluntly that she "didn't fix up much." She had on her Sunday dress, even though she was just putting the children to bed. Larry arrived from the hospital while the crew was there and they filmed the arrival scene with all the hugs and kisses.

Later that night, Emily and Patrick met for a drink in the bar of their hotel to recap the progress of the production of their special report.

"That couldn't have been more touching if it were scripted," Emily said, taking a sip of her wine.

"I sure hope she makes it," Patrick replied. "That has got to be the all-American family, right down to the Aunt Bea grandmother."

"I hope that Pam doesn't look too well. She went to great lengths not to appear sickly."

"But did you see her eyes? They were sunken and sad. It will be obvious that she is in big trouble. I'm not sure she looks as though she will even make it."

Emily suddenly became very serious. "Of course she'll make it! Modern medicine can do wonders and she has a new healthy liver."

"And a severely compromised immune system." Patrick reminded her.

"Well, at least we are on track to put the show on the air by September 15. That will be a little more than a week before the trial and it gives some time for slippage in the schedule." Emily said looking at her notebook.

"Are we ready to finish up with the Silicone Sisters tomorrow?" Patrick asked. "That should be a trip!"

"Loretta is inviting all the ladies with the best stories to her house for coffee in the morning at ten o'clock. It would be great if we could finish up all of their interviews tomorrow at that gathering. Then I'd like to get to Chicago to interview Terry Napoli, the lead trial lawyer for PSS. He handles all litigation for them all over the country. What do you think?"

Patrick was looking at his notes. "What about Rex Montague, the local Colorado attorney for PSS. We're showing Janet Stephenson, shouldn't he have equal time if we are presenting a fair and balanced story?"

"I think we pick one lawyer for the women and one for PSS. So we should choose between Napoli and Montague. But, perhaps we should interview them both and then decide."

"Good plan. I'll call Montague's office in the morning and see if we can see him tomorrow. Do you think we can shoot the Silicone Sisters in the morning and Montague in the early afternoon and still get to Chicago tomorrow night?"

"Let's take one more day and fly in the daylight," suggested Emily. "I am so done with these red-eye flights and arriving in the middle of the night.

"Suits me," said Patrick.

They finished their drinks, talking of the Colorado weather and telling each other stories about their ski adventures at Vail and Keystone.

Loretta was ready for them in the morning. All of the women who had been chosen by her to participate in the interviews were primed and ready to tell their stories of problems with silicone breast implants. Unfortunately, only two of them had Mammselle implants, so the interviews finished up with dispatch.

Rex Montague was scheduled to be in depositions, but he assigned an associate to take his place so that he could meet with Emily O'Brien and Patrick Kennedy at two thirty in the afternoon in his office. The office was buzzing with excitement that a network news crew with such celebrity reporters was coming to interview Mr. Montague. Several secretaries had on new outfits from their quick lunchtime shopping trips. Rex Montague, himself, had sent his secretary out to purchase a light blue shirt and a new tie. His wife had advised him when he called to tell her the news, that light blue shirts look much better on television than white shirts. Of course, he always wore white shirts.

Rex Montague tried to call Terry Napoli to advise him of the interview, but Mr. Napoli was not in the office. He called back at 2:15, just before the television crew arrived.

"Be careful as hell about how much information you give them," Napoli ordered.

"What would you like me to say, Terry?"

"I don't know what they will ask, and they have probably read the pleadings in the Colorado court file. That's a guideline."

"I won't admit that the Mammselle causes cancer if that's what you mean," laughed Montague.

"I should have cleared this with Winchester, but there's no time. And—we can't have them saying that we declined their request for an interview. Just be careful.

"It isn't the first time I've talked to the press, Terry," Montague reminded him. Montague had been interviewed by every newspaper and TV station in Denver when the Lawson case was filed.

"Oh, crap, my secretary just handed me a note that they want to come here and interview me tomorrow afternoon. Call me as soon as you are finished, and tell me what they ask. I don't see why they need to interview us both."

"It's because you are the national celebrity. I'm just the local yokel."

"Goodbye, Rex." Napoli could hardly stand Rex Montague and didn't understand why he had to work with him. The feeling was entirely mutual.

Ben Smith, Amy Larabee, and Joel Steiner finally concluded that they should bring Tom Slade in for questioning in the bombing. The questioning was all done by Joel Steiner at the direction of Rick Plume, the District Attorney, and an undercover cop, Derrick Nelson. Ben still needed his cover at the Horny Toad and Amy had been with him there. They were closing the trap because they had found some wire and pieces of steel, which may have been linked to the bomb in Slade's truck and in his basement.

They had no real proof, but Slade had even less patience. He didn't like police, and he didn't like the pressure. But he was recalcitrant and sullen and said nothing except obscenities. Then suddenly, one day, on his fourth trip to the police station for "questioning" he said.

"I wanna see the D.A."

"Who?" Joel Steiner asked.

"I wanna see Plume. Rick Plume. He's behind this, and I wanna talk to the man."

An hour later, Rick Plume walked into the examination room.

"What's up Slade?" Plume asked.

"I'm just sick of this shit. I wanna deal. You wanna deal?"

"Depends on what the deal is, Slade. We got you going down the tracks to the Big House, and nobody else is on the train."

"You wanna know who's on the train bad enough, I figure you'll deal. I know who's on the train, and I want off. But I want off clean and in the witness protection program."

Rick Plume drew his breath. He hadn't expected this. They had figured another six months of working on Slade. Plume and Amy Larabee and Ben Smith knew that Slade was the key to Lecroix. Was he going to give them to Lecroix?

"What kind of deal?"

"You heard me. I walk, and I get some cover—a new life in the witness protection program."

"We don't have a witness protection program in Colorado for murderers."

"The FBI has one for big hits and big gigs. This, my man, is no random bombing. I'm about to give you the big gig."

"Tell me what you know, and then we'll see."

Behind the glass, Amy Larabee and Ben Smith were transfixed with anticipation.

"Here goes, dude." and Slade told them how he had been hired by Lecroix to kill both Sherrie Barker and Dan MacNamara and destroy whatever documents Barker was giving to MacNamara. He told them that Lecroix was only the messenger. The people sending the message were much bigger. He told them that Dr. Jean Sonier and Dr. Richard Guilliot were the next targets to be hit by the Colorado mad bomber when they came to Denver to testify in Pamela Lawson's trial against PSS. He had already been given the commission. He was just waiting for final instructions.

"Did you get the documents?" Plume asked.

"My only mistake. They came out of the building empty-handed."

"What were the documents?"

"Dunno. Only know that the big guys will kill for them whatever they are."

"Where are they?"

"Dunno. I'm not on the document trail now. They was gravy. I'm only on the scientist trail. No experts, no win for Pam Lawson and her lawyer."

"How do we know it won't be just your word against Lecroix? Do you have any evidence? Any hard proof?"

"I got all you need, my man. You and the FBI can make a case outta what I got. Do we have a deal?"

An hour later, Larabee, Smith, Plume, and Steiner decided they had a deal, but Slade would have to be released to go about his business until they could get his "evidence," so as to not raise suspicion. But Ben still had his cover and could tail him. He'd head right for the Horny Toad anyway.

Joel Steiner slowly entered the interrogation room, stroking his chin. He closed the door softly behind him and stood, for a moment, looking down at Slade. Slade looked up at him with a blank expression, but there was anticipation in his eyes.

"Okay, Slade. It's a deal. We're going to let you walk out of here, just like normal tonight while we work out the details. This deal is contingent on our picking you up again at your place tomorrow with the "evidence" you promised. What is it?"

"Oh, dude, now you'll have to wait on me."

Against their better judgment, Slade left the police station. Ben Smith would be waiting for him at the Horny Toad. Amy would work out the details with headquarters. Then he would be taken into full protective custody.

In the parking lot of the Horny Toad Bar and grill, a dark figure slipped up behind Tom Slade and put a bullet in his head just as he was getting out of his pickup truck and was stepping on his cigarette. He fell between the cars in a puddle of blood and no one noticed the dark blue car leave the parking lot and disappear into the night.

Slade had parked his pickup next to Susan Sampson's car. She and Ben Smith discovered the body at the end of Susan's shift. Ben was walking her through the dark parking lot on the pretense of being neighborly when he noticed Slade's pickup.

"Tom Slade wasn't in tonight, was he?" he asked Susan.

"Didn't see him," Susan replied.

"Well, I think that's his truck," Ben walked around the bed and almost stepped on Slade's hand. Susan gasped, then screamed and began crying hysterically.

Ben grabbed her to him, holding her tight. "Hush, hush" he whispered. By then the parking lot was filling with people, and before they knew it an ambulance and police car appeared.

Ben sent Susan inside. Then quietly showed his FBI badge to the Littleton police officer. Quickly they put yellow tape around Slade's truck and Susan's car and a nearby tree at the edge of the parking lot. The officer sent the crowd back inside the Horny Toad.

From Slade's jacket pocket, Ben quietly removed the envelope with the Westin Hotel return in the corner with his gloved fingers. Inside there was a bank deposit receipt. Ben Smith put the envelope inside the manila envelope in the leather folder he always carried.

'*This is Lecroix's only mistake,*' he thought.

Ben went to his car and called Amy Larabee on his car phone.

"What's up?" Amy asked?

"They whacked Slade," Ben replied. "Shot him in the head in the parking lot of the Horny Toad. I found him lying by his truck. Looks like he's been here a while. The local police are here. I think you ought to come on over."

"Be right there" She hung up, pulled on a jacket, and raced out the door.

'*This is like a T.V. show—not real life.*' she thought and for a moment imagined herself as one of Charlie's Angels, before the awful intrigue of what was going on hit her again. '*Who's next?*'

Throughout the summer, Janet Stephenson battled with Rex Montague and Terry Napoli on pretrial issues, not the least of which was whether or not the trial should be continued because of the scheduled airing of the Emily O'Brien and Patrick Kennedy special on the PSS implants and silicone implants in general. It had finally been scheduled to air on September 20, just before the beginning of the trial on September 25. Patrick Kennedy had left the FDA investigative unit and had become a full-fledged reporter, teaming up with Emily on this project.

Rex Montague and Terry Napoli filed a motion to continue the trial, arguing that the scheduled television program would unduly prejudice the jury pool. Judge Parsons held a hearing on the motion and then took it under advisement. Both sides waited in anguish until he finally issued his written order denying the motion on the grounds that the scheduled television show was too remote in time, that there is no evidence that it would be watched by a substantial Denver audience, and that there was no evidence that it would actually affect the jury pool from which jurors would be selected. The trial would go forward as scheduled, with a formal pre-trial conference scheduled for August 20 and the exchange of all exhibits and witness lists set for September 5.

Dr. Dan MacNamara was listed as a witness for both the plaintiff and the defendant. He was listed as an expert by PSS and as a treating physician/expert for Pamela Lawson. However, neither side had been able to schedule his deposition because of his injury. He was still in the hospital under the close supervision of Dr. Levi Emanuel, who was still limiting visitors to immediate family.

Janet Stephenson was not as concerned about this problem as was Terry Napoli. The parties had already stipulated to the admissibility of Pam's medical records, including the detailed narrative of the removal of the implants and the laboratory tests which showed the presence of TDA in the liquefied tissue surrounding the implant. She also had the expert reports of Dr. Guilloit and Dr. Sonier regarding the implants and the tissue because the implants and tissue had been couriered to them by Dr. McBride, head of the St. Anthony hospital laboratory, immediately after Pam's implant removal surgery.

Terry Napoli and Rex Montague, on the other hand, needed Dr. Dan MacNamara to testify about his opinions regarding the safety and efficacy of the implants. MacNamara had been a major force in marketing the implants to the plastic surgeons and the Plastic Surgery Association members, of which he was the president of the Colorado Chapter. They expected that he would say that the implant was a great improvement over other implants because it prevented capsular contracture.

Despite the need for Dr. MacNamara to offer live testimony at trial, Forrest Winchester secretly just wanted him dead. However, there did not appear to be a way to get at Dan MacNamara, so long as he was under the watchful eye of Dr. Levi Emanuel at St Anthony hospital

All of the Silicone Sisters waited for the television special "What Price Beauty" with Emily O'Brien and Patrick Kennedy to be aired. Loretta and the Silicone Sisters had a potluck dinner and planned to watch it on Loretta's big-screen TV. They were pleased that they all were included in one way or another. Only the women, who had PSS implants, had their interviews included, but they hoped there would be pictures of all of them. Everyone agreed that Dr. Jean

Sonier would be the most important interview on the show and they expected him to be his articulate and charming self.

"He was made to be on TV," said Cynthia Rich. "He's the smartest man I have ever met!"

"How can PSS expect to win the Lawson case after he has explained on TV how the rats who had their implant developed liver cancer?" asked one of the sisters.

"Because television isn't trial evidence," answered Loretta confidently. "He's a witness in the trial, but the judge has to rule that his tests or studies are relevant in this case. But you're right, he is very smart and so is Janet Stephenson. They will find a way to get that into evidence."

Dr. Sonier had been extensively questioned about his testing and his opinions about Pamela Lawson's implants when he was deposed by Montague and Napoli. They had been aware of his opinions and the basis for them for months. He was entitled to rely on his own research in forming opinions about Pamela Lawson's medical status and the condition of her implants and tissue.

Nothing appeared in the national news about Slade's murder. Lecriox was sure it was the end of Tom Slade, leaving him with only the problem of finding a new Denver connection. It took him months and months to find Slade. He needed a loner. Someone no one would miss when he was gone. The dark figure who flew in from Chicago to meet Slade at the Horny Toad was a possibility, but only a remote possibility. He was no good at accidents. Sonier and Guilliot were supposed to be accidents.

Lecroix was going to find himself a latte and croissant when the Chicago FBI took him into custody on the street outside his hotel. He acted surprised and outraged, and totally innocent. He had left no trail and he was confident.

Inside, he was only the slightest bit concerned that he did not have a lawyer. He hated lawyers but he needed a good one now. While he sat in his cell considering the matter, the guard came, unlocked his cell, and announced, "Your lawyer's here to see you."

In an examination room sat a grizzled elderly man in a brown tweed coat, impatiently thumping his pen on a yellow legal pad. When Lecroix came in the room, the lawyer stood, stuck out his hand, and said, "Raoul, nice to see you again."

After the guard left and locked the door, Raoul asked, "Who the hell are you?"

"Wally Girton. I don't know you, but a note from an old friend and a fat envelope encouraged me to make your acquaintance."

"Who sent you?"

"It doesn't matter, but we have an extradition hearing in one hour, so we had better talk."

"Extradition to where?"

Girton looked at him in dismay. "Colorado," was all he said. In a few moments, they were joined by a crisp-looking young man in a blue pinstripe suit."

"This is local counsel, John O'Hara, he'll get me admitted for the purposes of this hearing. We'll lose it of course, but if we win, he's your lawyer."

"Why?" asked Lecroix.

"Because I don't intend to move to Chicago just for you, my friend. I like the Rocky Mountains."

They lost the hearing.

Before the deputies took Lecroix out of the courtroom, Girton said, "I'll see you when you get to Denver."

———— ··◆·· ————

Janet Stephenson hung up the phone and told her husband. "Well, they got Lecroix in Chicago and they are bringing him back here. Amy and Ben think the FBI has enough on him with his fingerprints, and saliva DNA on the envelope they found in Slade's pocket. The airline records also confirm that Lecroix was here on the day Sherrie Barker was killed, but not on the day that Slade was killed."

Brad looked up from his newspaper, "What do you think?" he asked.

"It seems a little thin to me. I think they need more. But, perhaps it will be safer for Dr. Guilloit and Dr. Sonier to come here to testify in Pamela's case if Lecroix is in jail."

"Why? You don't think that Lecroix is behind all this, do you? I thought Slade indicated there was someone giving Lecroix orders."

"He did. He called it giving up the 'big gig,' whatever that means."

"Well, you probably are going to have to leave Lecroix to the police and FBI, since your trial starts tomorrow. Are you going to the office?"

"I'm on my way. You want to come down around dinner time and have a bite with me?"

"Sure if you have time."

"I'll make time for you, my love." She kissed him, gathered her overfull briefcase, and blew him a kiss as she went out the front door."

"I'll be there around seven," he called after her.

"Great," she called back, hurrying to her car in the driveway.

A few moments after Janet arrived at her office she had a call from Jean Sonier and Richard Guilloit.

"Janet, we're calling you from the plane. We'll be landing in thirty minutes or so. Shall we come to your office straightaway?"

"Yes," she said. "Do you need a ride?"

"No, no. We'll pick up a rental. See you in a bit," Sonier concluded cheerfully.

"Goodbye," she said and absentmindedly hung up the receiver.

She looked at the conference room table. All of the trial notebooks were finished. All of the boxes and boxes of exhibits were prepared, numbered, and neatly organized in their folders. Her trial notebook, with the materials for jury selection, opening statement, and the direct testimony for the first two days lay on her desk. She went into her office, sat down at her desk, and flipped the pages to Sonier's testimony. "We are ready," she told herself out loud.

At the police station, Wally Girton was meeting that Sunday afternoon with his angry client, Raoul Lecroix.

"I'm not going down for these bastards, even if they are paying your bill, Girton. Let's make a deal with the D.A. and with the woman's lawyer. Slade was willing to sell me and he ended up dead. What do you think my chances are, even if I'm silent as a stone?

"What do you propose, Lecroix?"

34

Janet Stephenson was deep in meditation over her opening statement and was startled when her phone rang.

"I thought he was renting a car," she said out loud as she picked up the receiver.

"Janet Stephenson," she said into the phone.

"Janet, Wally Girton here. Could we have a talk?"

"Today? I've got a trial starting tomorrow, and worlds of witness prep, Wally. What's up."

"Nothing important, just some little details I don't want coming out in the press in your trial."

"What details. Lecroix has already said he won't testify in my trial, and he's taking the fifth on the stand surely won't help Pamela. It will only confuse the jury, even if I get a conscious jury."

"Five minutes, Janet. Meet me for a quick cup of coffee. Perkins on Wadsworth, in fifteen minutes."

Janet looked at her watch. "Okay. Five minutes." She hung up the phone, and scribbled out a note to stick on the door for Sonier and Guilliot, just in case they got there before she got back.

When Janet got to Perkins Restaurant, both Rick Plume and Wally Girton were waiting for her.

"What's going on?" She frowned.

Rick Plume grinned his little boy grin at her and said, "Janet, what would make all your dreams come true."

"Well, I guess if Jennifer Fordham and Forrest Winchester came to Pam's trial and admitted to PSS's fraud under oath." she said flippantly and pulled out a chair. "that would make all of my current dreams come true."

Rick Plume smiled at her and said, "Well, let's see what we can do. We are prepared to allow you to call Raoul Lecroix as a witness in your trial."

"Thanks a lot, Rick," Janet said. "But, you must know, that under the rules, the only way I can add a witness at this late date is to endorse him as a rebuttal witness. I will need to do that immediately and that will disclose him to the Defendants and their attorneys right now. Are you prepared to have me do that?"

"We don't have a problem with that," Plume said "We are prepared to cut him a deal if he will give us the real people who wanted Sherri Barker dead. He hasn't done that yet. For some reason, he has told us that he wants to testify in your trial to 'even some scores' as he says."

"What will he testify about in my trial? I don't see what he has to offer unless I can put in the evidence about him killing people to keep the information about the implants disintegrating and causing cancer from becoming public. Is he prepared to do that?"

"We don't know yet, but perhaps you should disclose him as a rebuttal witness, just in case. You have to be close to the deadline for disclosure of rebuttals."

Janet nodded. "It's tomorrow," she said. "Okay, I'll do it. Just keep me posted."

She went back to her office, drafted the supplemental designation of rebuttal witnesses, and filed it electronically with the Court.

When his secretary brought him the copy of the filing, Terry Napoli felt strangely troubled. He had never heard of Raoul Lecroix and he couldn't imagine what testimony this unknown person with a strange name could contradict or impeach, as a rebuttal witness.

That night Terry Napoli called Forrest Winchester at PSS headquarters in Santa Barabara. He was in Jennifer Fordham's office, with Jerry Carson, waiting for the call.

"Hey, Terry, how goes the war. Have you beaten down that little Colorado bitch yet?" Jerry Carson practically shouted into the phone.

"We're on the way. Is Mr. Winchester there?"

"Yep, as ordered."

"Put him on."

"Can we put you on speaker?"

"I need a few words with Mr. Winchester first."

Jerry handed the phone to Forrest Winchester. "Winchester here," he said, almost stiffly in his reserved for lawyers tone.

"Forrest. Nice to talk to you. Before I talk to all of you generally, do you know how I can get in touch with someone named Raoul Lecroix?"

Winchester stiffened noticeably, "Never heard of him," he said.

"I hope that's true, sir. I really do, but I must remind you how important it is to tell your attorney everything. I don't need any surprises here."

"No surprises, son. Never heard of him."

"All right. Put me on the speaker."

Without mentioning Lecroix again, Terry Napoli gave a brief report to his clients about the status of the pretrial maneuvers by both sides in the case. It did not appear to him that there had been much negative effect as a result of the Television expose' by Emily O'Brien and Patrick Kennedy, but they wouldn't know for sure until jury selection began. The judge had not ruled on the Motion in Limine to exclude the testimony and evidence of Dr. Jean Sonier's tests on foam.

At the end of his report, he asked into the speakerphone, "Oh, by the way, Jennifer and Jerry, have either of you ever heard of a Canadian by the name of Rauol Lecroix?"

He noted, with interest, the substantial silence on the other end of the phone conversation. ·

"Don't think so. Should I?" Carson asked.

"I don't know. How about you, Jennifer?"

"No," was all she said.

"Well, that's all for now. I'll talk to you tomorrow. I understand that all of you will be here for the beginning of the trial."

"We're flying in tomorrow night," answered Jennifer.

"Good, see you then," said Napoli and pushed the button on his phone. "Damn, they know who he is. What aren't they telling me!" Napoli thought.

When Napoli was off the line, Winchester slammed his fist on the desk and shouted," What the hell is going on? Didn't you take care of Lecroix?"

"Yeah, we got him a great criminal lawyer!" Carson beamed.

"You did what? What did you say? Don't tell me he is still alive."

"I thought you wanted me to get him a lawyer who wouldn't let him talk." Carson looked confused.

Winchester was so furious that he could not speak. He looked at Carson and then left the room abruptly.

"What's with him?" Jerry Carson looked at Jennifer. She stared after Winchester, and then followed him quickly.

Amy Larabee found Sandra Barker and Ann Lowe at the Brown Palace Hotel. Sandra had finally come to collect Sherrie's things left there when she was killed. She had not been able to force herself to come until now. They were sitting in the hall on an upholstered bench outside the room that had been Sherrie's. She introduced herself and Sandra Barker's eyes filled with tears.

"Why is the FBI involved?" she asked.

"I can't answer that question just yet, Mrs. Barker. All I can tell you is that we think there may be more to Sherrie's death than meets the eye. Do you know why she came to Denver? She hasn't been the sales rep for this area since she was transferred to California, has she?"

"She came to see me," her mother said quietly. "I don't know why she was at the medical plaza. I know that she still knew lots of doctors here, and many of them are still her friends. Dr. MacNamara was one of her old clients."

Ann Lowe was sitting silently, looking Amy Larabee over carefully. She patted Mrs. Barker's hand and handed her a tissue from her purse.

"Ann, how long have you worked for Sherrie?"

"Almost eight years," Nancy said.

"So, you worked for her while she was in Denver?"

"Yes, I transferred with her when she got her promotion to the home office. We were very close."

"Do you know what she was doing at Dr. MacNamara's office building? Did she have business with him?"

"I know that she and Dr. MacNamara kept in touch and that she often sent him promotional materials about our products. I know that she took some documents when she came to Denver because she took two briefcases."

"Why would she do that if she were on a pleasure trip to see her mom."

Sandra Barker did not like the curiosity in Amy's voice.

"I live on a farm outside of Loveland," she interjected. "Sherrie often brought work to do in the quiet of the country when she came to visit."

"Did she work this time?" Amy asked.

"I didn't expect her for a couple of days. In fact, I was actually in California at my son's house when she was killed." Sandra sobbed. "I didn't even know that she was here."

Amy looked at Ann Lowe, who immediately looked down at her lap. She knew that she would have to wait to ask her remaining questions if she really wanted answers.

"Ann, are you planning to stay in Denver for a while?"

"Yes, I've taken some vacation time. I'm staying at the Adams Mark. I thought I might like to see some of the PSS trial at the Denver District Court."

"I have some other things to clear up right now, but do you suppose I could have another chat with you before you go back to California?"

Their eyes knew what the questions would be.

"Sure," she said.

"Just give me a call," Amy handed her a business card. "I have voice mail, so just leave me a message any time it's convenient for you."

Ann took the card and nodded.

The next day, Ann called and arranged to meet Amy in the Irish pub on the ground floor of the hotel at three o'clock in the afternoon. She had gone to the courthouse that morning and discovered that they were in the middle of hearings, and that jury selection had not yet begun. The pub was nearly empty when Nancy arrived.

"Thanks for seeing me," Amy said.

Ann just smiled and nodded.

"I have a feeling that you know what I want to talk to you about."

"I'm not entirely sure," said Ann, "but I know what I would ask if I were you."

"I see why you were invaluable to Sherrie," Amy smiled in admiration at the pretty, serious face across the table. Ann didn't respond.

"Were they involved?" Amy didn't waste any time on preliminaries.

"I'm not sure there was anything intimate," Ann said, "But I do know that Dr. MacNamara called her regularly, and he sent her flowers on her birthday. But, they had known each other for years. Nobody thought anything about it."

"Did you?" Amy queried.

"I know that he is married and that Sherrie respected and liked his wife. If she had a special relationship with Dr. MacNamara, I thought it was probably about business things and the documents that she brought with her to Denver."

"What documents? What are you talking about?"

"They were internal documents about testing that PSS had done on the polyurethane breast implants, showing that the polyurethane degraded in the body into a carcinogen. The tests PSS did were secret, and they showed that the animals used in the tests developed liver cancer. All of them. The documents were all stamped 'CONFIDENTIAL—PROPRIETARY INFORMATION.' But Sherrie had sold Dr. MacNamara, and other doctors hundreds of the implants, and she felt terrible about PSS not telling the doctors what they knew."

"Didn't PSS tell the FDA or anybody?"

Ann shook her head. "PSS doesn't even know that Sherrie knew, or that I know. They assume that all of their detail persons and clerical staff are too ignorant to understand medicine or science. Dr. MacNamara's patient, Pam Lawson, is suing PSS because she is dying of liver cancer. It's her trial that is starting in the Denver District Court. Dr. MacNamara was supposed to be a witness."

"Did Sherrie give the documents to anyone?"

"I think she may have brought them to Dr. MacNamara so that he would have them before his deposition in Pam Lawson's case, but I can't be sure. After she died, I looked all through the office for them, and they were gone. Sherrie had the originals."

"Have you told anyone what you just told me?" Amy asked quickly.

"Not a soul," Ann said.

"We have to see if we can find those documents. How well do you know Dr. MacNamara's wife?"

"I have been in her office. She's a really nice lady." Ann said.

"Let's go see what she knows. Can you come?"

"Sure," Ann said, "I'll do whatever I can. I'm sure my job is gone as soon as my vacation time is used up anyway."

Amy Larabee transferred her call to Sally MacNamara's cell phone, as she was driving home with her kids. Sally listened to her briefly, then said. "Sure, come on over, I've just got to order the kids a pizza."

She hung up and felt a twinge of concern in her stomach.

"Who was that, Mom?"

"Just a lady who needs to talk to me. She's coming over while you guys eat pizza."

When they arrived about forty minutes later, Sally ushered Amy and Nancy into the living room, while the kids ate pizza to the noise of "Rug Rats" on Nickelodeon on the TV in the kitchen.

"What can I do for you ladies, "Sally MacNamara asked.

"I don't want to waste your time, Dr. MacNamara," said Amy Larabee. "But can you tell us how your husband is doing?"

"He's better, but it's going very slowly. He'll be in isolation for some time because of the high risk of infection with the burns. But, I'm sure you didn't come here just to check on his medical status."

Anne Lowe felt very uncomfortable as she looked at pretty Amy Larabee. She was every inch a lady, as was Sherrie Barker.

"We're looking for some documents which might explain the death of Sherrie Barker," Amy said. "I'd like Ann to explain it to you."

Sally MacNamara looked silently at Ann, who cleared her throat.

"Dr. MacNamara, Sherrie Barker was my boss at PSS. She used to be the detail person who serviced your husband's plastic surgery practice for PSS."

"I know who she was." Sally MacNamara cut her off coldly. "What documents?"

Nancy continued, wishing she were anywhere but here. "I think Sherrie may have brought Dr. MacNamara some internal memos and studies on the breast implants to help him prepare for his testimony in the Pamela Lawson case. At least, I think the documents are missing."

"Why would they help him prepare?" Sally demanded.

"They were documents which showed that PSS knew that the polyurethane on the implants was linked to liver cancer. Pam Lawson has liver cancer."

"Oh, my God!" Sally MacNamara put her hands over her face. Then she straightened and said," But I haven't seen any such documents, and he didn't have anything in his briefcase when he was hurt."

Amy suggested, "How about at his office. Could he have left them there? Sherrie was killed just outside his office building."

Sally looked pensive for a moment, then said, "We did take our old safe down to his office. I doubt that he would leave documents like that lying around—if he even had them in the first place."

Amy quickly asked," Do you suppose we could take a look in that safe?"

"Let me see if I can get someone to come over a watch the kids. If I can, I'll meet you there in an hour. If I can't, I'll bring them with me."

Amy and Ann stood up. "Thanks so much," said Amy, extending her hand. Sally MacNamara stood up and took her hand, holding it briefly. "I hope you are wrong." was all she said.

An hour later in the darkened office, they found the documents that Sherrie Barker and Dan MacNamara had placed in the safe on their last night together. Amy Larabee was ready to place them in her briefcase when Ann held out her hand for them.

"Those documents should go to Janet Stephenson. They were intended for her, and for Dr. MacNamara. They will make Pamela Lawson's case, and that is what Sherrie wanted."

Amy Larabee stopped, then said, "I'm sorry, this is a criminal investigation."

Ann stiffened, and Dr. Sally MacNamara said coolly, "Where's your warrant, Miss Larabee."

Amy stopped. Clearly she would have to compromise here, particularly if the two of them ganged up on her. She couldn't take the chance that the documents would be excluded, and if they became a part of the civil trial they would be a part of the public record.

"Let's give Janet Stephenson a call." she said.

anet Stephenson was up to her ears in alligators. She was out of money and out of time. The trial was beginning and her bank had turned down her request for a short-term loan to front the costs of the trial. The Lawson's had no money, and her first witness had to be on the stand in two days. Jean Sonier was first, and he would not be a problem. He would come without being paid first, Harry Jensen, M.D., retired plastic surgeon and former insider who had warned PSS of the dangers of silicone and polyurethane, was another story. He wanted ten thousand dollars to get on the plane. To top it all off, she had received a call from the IRS who advised her that they wanted to send a field auditor to her office to audit her tax returns for the past three years, while she was in trial. Janet knew that the call was not accidental. PSS was behind the scenes somewhere. PSS was skilled at just this sort of manipulation of governmental agencies. PSS had manipulated governmental contacts in Canada against Jean Sonier in order to get him fired as Deputy Minister of Health just as he was about to have the polyurethane-coated implants banned from the Canadian market. It would be a simple matter to get the IRS to insist on a field audit of the financial records of a plaintiff's attorney, who made most of her living from contingent fee cases.

Brad was gone on his third, unscheduled intercontinental flight in two weeks. Surely they couldn't have gotten to the airline too! Her only hope was that Brad could borrow some money from his pension plan so that she would have the funds to pay the costs associated with Pamela Lawson's trial, but she couldn't even talk to him about it, and she wasn't sure he could go through all the red tape to get the loan in time to help her anyway.

Janet was sitting at her desk, deep in thought when the phone rang. She was startled and only said, "Hello."

"Janet?"

"Yes?"

"It's Amy Larabee. Do you suppose we could meet somewhere and talk for a few minutes?"

Janet looked at her watch. It was almost nine o'clock. "Where?" she asked.

"Could we come to your office?"

"Who's 'we'?"

"Me, Dr. Sally MacNamara, and Ann Lowe. Ann is Sherrie Barker's assistant from PSS."

Janet's heart jumped. Why would this interesting combination of people want to talk to her in the middle of the night? "Sure," she said. "I'll make sure the main door is open."

Less than an hour later, Janet heard them enter her office and she hurried out of her office and met them in her reception room.

"Come on into my office," Janet said with a smile. "Our conference room is full of trial notebooks and stuff for the trial."

Amy Larabee, Dr. Sally MacNamara, and Ann Lowe followed her and sat down around her octagonal table by the window in her office. Amy placed a fat briefcase on the table.

"Okay, what's up?" Janet asked, without more pleasantries.

Amy Larabee opened the briefcase and put a large stack of documents on the table.

"Sherrie Barker brought these documents to Dr. MacNamara on the day she was killed,"

"What are they?" Janet asked.

"She thought they would prove your case. She wanted Dr. MacNamara to have them before you took his deposition in Pamela Lawson's case," Ann Lowe said.

Janet Stephenson's heart began to race. She felt the blood rush to her head. "This is like a movie," she thought to herself. "May I look at them?" she asked.

"Help yourself," said Amy Larabee, "You will probably understand them better than any of us, except Dr. MacNamara." She smiled at Sally MacNamara.

Janet slid the documents toward her and began to read them. She was so fascinated at what she saw that she read for a long time before she realized that the other women were sitting in silence, intently watching her, but not saying a word.

"This is incredible!" Janet exclaimed. "These are the original narratives of the studies and all of the backup data which demonstrate that every animal which had the polyurethane implants in these studies developed cancerous liver tumors—everyone, 100%!"

"You will note that each document is stamped 'CONFIDENTIAL— PROPRIETARY INFORMATION,'" Ann Lowe pointed out. "Sherrie actually took these documents from the files of Jennifer Fordham. I don't think that she and Jerry Carson knew for a long time that these documents are missing."

"That's not all," said Amy Larabee. "Here is the text of a telephone conversation on speakerphone, between Jennifer Fordham, Jerry Carson, and Forrest Winchester. They are discussing their decision not to disclose this information to the FDA nor to you, in the Pamela Lawson case."

"Forrest Winchester?" Janet questioned.

"Apparently Conway Chemical was not thrilled to find out about these documents, especially after Conway had just purchased PSS for a ton of money," Amy added.

"But, he obviously doesn't back out of the deal or sue PSS," Janet laughed, "The publicity about that would win every Plaintiff's case in the land."

"I think you call that a rock and a hard place," Sally MacNamara added, as she smiled for the first time. All of the women in the room, bonded by their secret knowledge, laughed together and the tension in the room instantly disappeared.

"I wish I had known about these," Janet frowned. "How will I get them into evidence at this late date, and without any witness to lay a foundation?"

"I'm no expert on civil procedure," said Amy, "But, I hear you are really a tough litigator and I'm sure you'll find a way. In the meantime, would you agree to make us some copies? These originals are the only ones in the world, as far as we know."

"We must keep these documents a secret!" said Sally MacNamara frantically. "I think that Dan is still in danger and until I can get him out of the hospital and home, I don't think we can make sure he is safe from these people. I think that they killed Sherrie and planned to kill Dan, too. None of you have said that, but you have to know that it is true."

"It's true," Amy said softly. "We all have to join together to make sure that you, Dan, and the children are all safe."

"What will you do?" Sally asked, suddenly looking very alarmed.

"We have a cast of thousands." Amy smiled and patted her arm. "They moved into place before we even left your house. Both the FBI and the local police are on it and they are everywhere, especially at the hospital, protecting Dr. MacNamara. However, it is important that you go about your normal routine so that they can remain completely undercover. We don't have everyone involved in this yet. And, we don't know who all the players are. They hired Slade and we don't know who else is out there or what they look like."

"We do have one thing on our side, so far." Ann Lowe added, "I don't think that anyone at PSS knows that the documents were not blown up with Sherrie. But, that doesn't mean that they won't take every possible step to make sure that they aren't in Dr. MacNamara's office or home."

Amy Larabee looked pensively at the table. "I would think that they would have attempted to retrieve those documents before now if they thought they had survived the fire. There haven't been any break-ins or burglaries at the office or your house, have there?"

Sally shook her head, looking increasingly concerned.

"Janet, the point is, you have to get these documents in evidence in your trial, or we'll never get them into evidence in any criminal prosecution of these bastards because we didn't have a warrant and they were meant to be disclosed to you and not to the FBI or Denver police," Amy said, suddenly very serious.

"Cool, no pressure!" Janet smiled. "It will be a real trick to do that, but there must be a way. All of the deadlines have passed and Napoli would love a mistrial at this point."

"Well, it's late. Can we just make some copies for my file? You will obviously need the originals," Amy asked. Janet nodded and motioned them all toward the copy/war room.

Janet made a packet of copies for Amy. She made three copies for her trial materials and put them, with the originals in her briefcase, with her trial notebook and personal memos.

"Goodbye. Thanks for this, I think" Janet joked.

The women all exchanged business cards and gave each other hugs, as bonded women do.

"I'll be in close touch. Call me!!" Janet waved at them as they headed for the lobby. Then she went into her office and collapsed in her chair. "Oh, my God," she said to herself, "Nothing is ever easy."

Pamela Lawson and Larry Lawson came to court early and met Janet in the basement coffee shop.

"Are Dr. Sonier and Dr. Guilloit ready to go on the stand?" Larry asked.

"Yes," Janet nodded. "They got here yesterday and will hang out at the office until we finish jury selection and opening statements. I'm sorry you have to sit through all of this Pam, but it is important that the jury see you at least today. If you can't make it through the rest of the trial, I will explain it to the jury and to the judge."

Pamela was incredibly thin and she had dark circles under her eyes. Her blond hair looked thin and dry and all of the veins in the backs of her skeletal hands stood out. She wore a light blue suit, which matched her enormous eyes, and an embroidered white blouse. She and Janet had spent many hours discussing her courtroom decorum and all of the clothes she and Larry would wear throughout the trial. She was perfect. Larry had on a dark blue blazer and gray pants. Larry helped Pamela stand up and supported her as they walked slowly down the long marble halls to Courtroom One.

Terry Napoli and Rex Montague and their cast of a thousand paralegals and backup lawyers were already there, bustling about and hauling in boxes of exhibits on dollies. In the corner of the courtroom, by the jury box, a crew was installing an enormous TV/VCR combination, with monitors for the jury, the judge, the court reporter, and the defense counsel table—none for the plaintiff's table, however.

"Quite a dog and pony show, Terry, but have you cleared it with the court. I intend to object. Ordinarily, Judge Parsons doesn't let us have all this junk and boxes in his courtroom. He likes to focus on its turn of the century beauty, especially since it was remodeled as a set for Perry Mason."

"How can he object, counsel? This is our trial. Our trial depends upon the proper presentation of technological evidence."

"I'm the one who objects, Terry," Janet said. "I've asked his clerk for a hearing on trial presentation before we do jury selection. There was no disclosure that you intended to use all this electronic razz-ma-tazz. What's wrong with simple overheads and slides? It's the same information you have converted to videotape so that you can clutter the courtroom with all this equipment. None of this so-called demonstrative evidence was supplied to us for review before trial."

"Yes, it was counsel" Napoli slapped a two-inch stack of xerox copies with tiny print on the table by Janet. "All of our exhibits are in his disclosure."

Janet had already reviewed the "disclosure."

"We'll let the court decide," was all she said, looking straight into his eyes. With his characteristic turn on his heel, Napoli walked away, just as the Bailiff came in a said, "All rise, this court is in session."

"Good morning, counsel. I understand that we have some preliminary matters before we begin. Will Counsel enter their appearances please?"

"Good morning, Your Honor, Janet Stephenson, 8621, present with the Plaintiffs, Pamela and Larry Lawson.

"Good morning, Judge. Rex Montague, 7342, here with Mr. Terry Napoli, who is admitted to the bar in Illinois, and whom I am recommending for admission pro hac vice for the purposes of this trial."

"I assume you represent the Defendants, PolySurgical Specialties, counsel. Is that correct?"

Embarrassed, Montague said, "Yes, Judge Parsons."

"Have you filed the appropriate affidavits in support of your motion to admit Mr. Napoli?"

"They will be filed this afternoon, Your Honor."

"Very well. I'll look at them when they are filed. In the interim, the court will expect you to speak for the Defendant."

Napoli sprang to his feet, "But Your Honor, we have a very important motion to be heard this morning."

"I'm sure Mr. Montague can handle it. I've considered him to be a very competent lawyer for many years. Please be seated." Judge Parsons, calmly replied. "Now, Mrs. Stephenson, you have a Motion?"

"Yes, Your Honor. We have filed a motion objecting to the presence of all of this electronic equipment and scores of banker's boxes in the courtroom throughout the trial. It is our position that all of this paraphernalia is merely stage dressing and meant for purposes of inappropriately influencing the jury as to the weight of the Defendant's case."

The judge turned to Rex Montague. "Just why do you need all of this stuff in my courtroom for jury selection, Mr. Montague. You don't propose to use it until the Defendant's case, which could be days or weeks away, do you? Why do you think this clutter is necessary now?"

"It's in the nature of voir dire, your honor. A method of determining whether potential jurors will be attentive throughout a long, complicated case. If they will be intimidated by technology and science."

"Well if they are not—I am. We won't be using that level of complex psychology on our jurors. I've already agreed to your joint jury questionnaire, and you may submit questions. I don't intend to have anyone suffer from claustrophobia in this courtroom. Have your staff remove this stuff. One box and two briefcases are all the evidence any lawyer can deal with in one day, and that's all you'll have each day in this courtroom.

Napoli was on his feet, face red, hands shaking. "But your honor, we will need electronic demonstrative aids."

"Use your lawyering skill, not flim-flam, Mr. Napoli. And please let Mr. Montague share your views with the court until I rule on your admission. We'll be in recess until the courtroom is restored to its original condition." The judge banged his gavel and left through the door behind the bench.

"That was too easy," thought Janet. Now she would be waiting for the next shoe to drop. Napoli, on the other hand, was furious. It was as though he had lost a major strategy battle. Montague was directing the removal of equipment and boxes and ignoring Terry Napoli.

As they were packing, Judge Parson's clerk came into the courtroom and announced that the proceedings would be in recess until the next morning at nine o'clock.

"Thank goodness," Janet thought. So much had happened in the last forty-eight hours that she needed some time to modify her strategy and talk to her clients about her plans for the trial.

"Do you feel well enough to chat for a few minutes?" she asked Pamela and Larry.

"Sure," Pam answered, "I was prepared to have to be here for the entire day, anyway. "Pamela smiled at her, but Janet noted that the circles under her eyes were darker, and she had trouble standing up. Larry helped her gently and she took his arm."

"If you go on ahead to the cafeteria in the basement," Janet said, "I'll meet you there in a few minutes, and we can have a coke and talk a little bit."

"Sounds, good," smiled Larry, and they slowly left the courtroom.

The meeting with Dr. Sally MacNamara and Amy Larabee and Ann Lowe had created new challenges and opportunities for Janet. She had the original PSS documents, but it was too late to designate them as exhibits in her case. The rules of civil procedure and the local rules of the Denver District Court required that all documents must be disclosed and included in the exhibit lists according to the Case Management Order and Trial Management Order. The days of "trial by ambush" made popular by television shows like Perry Mason, were long gone. Of course, these documents, unknown to her until last night, were not on those lists and had not been disclosed by Janet in any of the discovery procedures which are a part of all trial preparation.

"I have to use them as rebuttal documents or in the process of cross-examination of witnesses," she thought.

Janet had spent the night thinking and re-thinking the strategy of the trial and how to get the documents into evidence, without causing a mistrial, or worse yet, having the documents excluded and losing the trial because of the lack of substantial proof that PSS knew that their polyurethane-coated implant caused liver cancer. If she bungled the use of the documents in her trial, they would likely not be admissible in the criminal action against Lecroix, his underlings, and bosses because the documents were not obtained with a warrant. The only hope for Pamela Lawson and for the criminal case against

Lecroix and company was to have the records become a part of the public record in Pamela Lawson's civil trial.

Amy Larabee had to give her the documents because Ann Lowe and Dr. Sally MacNamara would have it no other way. Rick Plume was offering the testimony of Lecroix in her trial as a rebuttal witness, to contradict the testimony of Jerry Carson and Jennifer Fordham that the PSS breast implants were inert in the body system. But, Lecroix knew nothing about the documents and she could not lay a foundation to admit the documents through him. Lecroix was not a physician or scientist and he was useless to offer any opinions about the implants at all. Only Dr. Dan MacNamara or Sherrie Barker could lay the foundation to admit the documents. Sherrie was dead and Dr. MacNamara was not sufficiently recovered to testify, even under a subpoena. The last thing she wanted to do was confuse the jury with the testimony, under subpoena, of the plastic surgeon who told her client that the implants were safe.

It seemed clear. The only way to get the critical documents in at this stage was to use them in cross-examination of Jennifer Fordham and Jerry Carson. Documents used for cross-examination did not have to be disclosed in advance, under the rules of civil procedure. But, it was also important that Fordham, Carson, and their attorneys remain totally unaware that the documents were in the hands of Dr. MacNamara or Janet Stephenson. Only Dr. MacNamara's testimony could help her in the presentation of the Plaintiff's case and there was no chance that he would be well enough to testify anytime soon. She also knew that those who sought to kill him were still out there even with the arrest of Lecroix and that Dr. MacNamara and his family were not out of danger.

Without the testimony of Dr. MacNamara, the only way for Janet Stephenson to get the documents into evidence would be in the Defendants' case as cross-examination documents, or to successfully call Jennifer Fordham and Jerry Carson as hostile witnesses in her case and ask for leave to cross-examine them. She had listed "any witness designated by the Defendants" on her trial management certificate, and both of them had been designated by Terry Napoli and Rex Montague as defense witnesses. Further, she had deposed both of them and only learned that they were arrogant and well prepped by their attorneys.

She decided to call them hostile witnesses at the end of her case. If she did not take this unorthodox action, she would risk not proving her case and not surviving the inevitable motion, from Napoli, for a directed verdict at the end of the presentation of all of her witnesses. If Judge Parsons granted a motion for a directed verdict, the trial would end, Pamela Lawson would lose, and the Defendants would not be required to put a single witness on the stand.

When Janet walked into the caféteria, in the dungeon-like basement of the courthouse, she was still pondering the trial strategy. Janet's paralegal assistants, James Olson and Adam Knotts, were with Pamela and Larry, keeping them company until she arrived.

"Hi, guys," she smiled at James and Adam. "We just need to talk a little bit. Could you go up and pack up our things in the courtroom and take the boxes to the car. We have some work to do tonight. I'll be right there."

"Sure," James smiled and the two young men hurried off, taking their cokes with them.

Janet slid into the booth across from Pam and Larry. "How are you doing?" she asked Pam, gently.

"It is harder than I thought it would be," Pam answered. "I thought that just sitting in the courtroom would be easy. It's not easy. I don't see how you take this every day."

"I don't do it every day." Janet laughed. "It would kill me off if I did."

"How do you think it is going?" Larry asked the inevitable and constant question of litigants.

"Today was good!" Janet said. "I was glad that we got all of their junk out of the courtroom. Judge Parsons was wonderful on that issue. I didn't expect to win that motion so easily."

Janet noticed that Pamela looked very relieved. She knew that her clients didn't understand the subtleties of the courtroom and that not understanding exactly what was happening caused them stress.

"I have had some interesting developments in the past two days. They are very good for our case, but I can't really discuss them with you right now." Janet began.

"What, Janet, we need to know," Larry said excitedly.

That was exactly why Janet knew that she had to keep the information about the new documents and witness to herself until just the right time.

"I have designated a rebuttal witness before the deadline passed, that I may need to use. But, I can't really talk about it yet because I haven't met with him and I don't know how useful he will be to us. He may contradict some of the PSS witnesses, which will help us."

"What documents? Can we see them?" Larry insisted.

"No, I can't disclose the documents to anyone yet."

"Then how can you use them? I thought we had to show them everything already?" Larry looked very worried and skeptical.

"Larry, you will just have to trust me on this one. Sometimes you will just have to do that." Janet wished that she had just let them go home, but she always shared what was going on. This time she felt she should have kept her own counsel. Larry looked almost angry. He wanted to know everything about everything. It had driven her crazy during the preparation of the case for trial.

She continued. "I do not have to disclose documents that I am going to use for cross-examination of their witnesses. I have come across some documents that I think will be very good for cross-examination. Let's just leave it at that for now. Please don't discuss this with anyone. I have good reasons for asking for your confidence and that you keep all of this to yourselves. Don't share it with anyone."

"Share what?" Larry asked angrily. "Janet, we're the ones on the stove here. You need to tell us what you are up to."

"When the time is right, I'll tell you about everything we are going to do. I still haven't made some of the important decisions about how to proceed just yet. You'll know. I won't keep anything from you. Please trust me on this."

Pamela put her hand gently on Larry's mouth. "We trust you, Janet" was all she said.

"Thanks." Janet was relieved. "Shall we go? Tomorrow is another day."

Larry was looking at Pam. Then, he turned toward Janet and smiled.

"I'm cool with it—whatever it is," he said.

They got up together and walked out of the cafeteria to the elevators.

Janet Stephenson hurried back to the courtroom and met James and Adam, each with a banker's box of documents, which they had packed. Her faithful law clerks were laughing together as they came down the hall toward her.

"Hey, Mrs. Stephenson," James hailed her. "Missing anything?" Janet was baffled.

"It's your cellphone," Adam explained as he stopped, put down his box and dug into his pocket. He handed it to her, "It's been ringing it's little heart out. We didn't answer because we thought it would be better for you to get a voice mail.

Janet Stephenson looked at her phone. "Missed calls," it said, and, "new messages."

Janet didn't recognize the number, so she punched in "new messages." It was Terry Napoli and he sounded furious.

"So, I'm sure you're not surprised." He was almost shouting. "The Emily O'Brien and Patrick Kennedy special on the implants is airing tonight! A little too coincidental, don't you think?"

Janet's heart leaped. She thought that it had been delayed or canceled and had not thought about it for weeks. The last she had heard from the Silicone Sisters, it had been held up until after Thanksgiving. "It's not going to happen, lady!" Napoli said angrily. "This is notice that I am asking the judge for a forthwith hearing to postpone the trial. We've filed our motion to be heard at seven o'clock in the morning—be there."

Janet had another message from Dr. Jean Sonier telling her about the show and the fact that advertisements for it had been running for the last 24 hours. Janet, of course, hadn't been watching television. Sonier advised that the corporate defendant PSS had filed a motion in the New York and California courts to block the show. "The bad guys are attempting to get an after-hours hearing, I understand." Dr. Sonier added a little chuckle. "I'll see what I can turn up and let you know." He hung up without a number, but it was on Janet Stephenson's cell phone.

"What's up?" James asked.

Janet was already dialing Pamela and Larry Lawson. She had Pam's cell phone listed on her phone. "Hello."

"Pam? Janet." Janet could hardly speak. "When you get home, check the television listings. It seems that Emily O'Brien and Patrick Kennedy's special on the implants is going to air tonight. Just FYI, Terry Napoli has asked the judge for a seven o'clock in the morning hearing on his motion to continue the trial because of it."

"Oh, dear! Is that good or bad?"

Janet could hear Larry asking what's wrong in the background.

"It's all good. I don't think the trial will be continued. But it sure makes it interesting. I'll call you at home later. I'm still just leaving the courthouse."

James and Adam were standing in the hall, with their boxes at their feet listening intently to her conversation. "Oh, my God," Adam said excitedly. "This is great! -- Don't you think it's great for our case?"

"We'll see," Janet replied gathering up her briefcase and purse. "It will either be really good or really bad. Let's get back to the office and figure out what is going on. I have some research to do and you guys need to make sure we get this program recorded. That's your mission. I haven't figured out that DVD thing yet." James and Adam looked at each other and laughed.

"We're all over that mission." James smiled. "We'll each record it on different TVs just to be safe." Adam nodded and picked up his box. "Let's get out of here," he said.

When they arrived at the office, there were messages from at least six people telling Janet about the program, which was to air at seven o'clock in the evening on Channel 9. It was nearly six o'clock in the evening when Adam and James and Janet arrived, so they had very little time to make sure that all of the equipment to record the program was in place on both of the television sets in the office. James was monitoring the TV in Janet's office and Adam was in charge of the set in the conference room. Charlene, Janet's secretary, was still at the office and had ordered pizza for the weary courthouse crew. She also decided to stay and watch the show with them. The only person waiting at her condo was her little fluffy dog, Sam, and she had gone home to feed him at lunch. He was likely still sleeping. They decided to watch it together in the conference room. Charlene brought some paper towels and paper plates. The pizza came just five minutes before seven.

The hour-long show was a careful and balanced investigation of the dangers of the polyurethane-coated silicone gel implants. Dr. Jean Sonier was careful, articulate, and scholarly. But he stole the show and he was as convincing as could be. Forrest Winchester, pompous and too well dressed, seemed slick and ignorant. The Silicone Sisters would have been accused of hyperbole, but for the careful editing of O'Brien and Kennedy. Pamela Lawson looked frail, but was gracious and articulate. They had edited all of Larry Lawson's interview by voice-overs that moved the show along. Janet Stephenson was professional and concise, The editing gave a lot more time to Terry Napoli and Forrest Winchester, but their longer speeches didn't help their cause, Pam thought. Napoli and Winchester also were given the opportunity to blast Dr. Sonier on camera and their inarticulate expert was given equal time. Because Emily O'Brien and Patrick Kennedy had done a masterful job in putting the program together, they would make it very difficult for Napoli to argue that it was prejudicial to the case or biased against PSS. Yet, Janet reflected, she was delighted at the timing and was so grateful that no one had advised her ahead of time about when it was going to air. She could say truthfully, as an officer of the court, that she had no idea that it would air on the night before jury selection. Emily O'Brien and Patrick Kennedy had played their cards well and had done nothing to put Janet's case at risk.

"It's the work of angels," Janet thought as she sat back and took one last bite of pizza.

"I thought it was great for us!" James said.

"It sure won't hurt," was all she said. "Let's see what happens at seven o'clock. We need to take our DVD player and small TV from the kitchen, as well as the disc of the show when we go to court tomorrow. Can you guys handle showing it to the judge if we have to?"

"Is the Pope Catholic?" Adam said as he shrugged and smiled. "We'll take care of it."

Janet went back into her office to do some more research on cases about pre-trial publicity and other issues that she was sure that Napoli and Montague would be arguing in the morning.

"It's a good thing that we haven't actually begun voir dire," she thought to herself. She would argue that the attorneys could explore any issues of prejudice as they questioned potential jurors. But she knew that all of the attorneys were well aware that in our current society people are clever and not so intimidated by the oath to tell the truth. Janet, as well as Napoli and Montague knew that it is difficult to find a jury where all of the members make decisions based on a common moral belief. Jurors lie to get on juries. Jurors lie to stay off of juries. But, more important is the fact that many people choose to be on juries to promote a personal hidden agenda. Such a juror is almost impossible to detect in voir dire questioning.

While she was deep in thought, Charlene came in to tell her that she had had a call from Judge Parson's clerk advising that there would be a forthwith hearing on Napoli's motion to continue at seven o'clock in the morning She also handed Janet the motion, which had just been delivered by fax.

It was just what Janet anticipated. "We're ready for you, Terry Napoli," she said to no one. "We're ready."

41

Leslie Winchester had just settled into the comfy orchid bedecked cushions of the large chaise lounge in the sunroom, with her martini, and had turned on the TV when her husband appeared at the door, leading to the family room.

"Forrest!" she exclaimed. "I thought you were going to be in Denver at the big trial."

"No, Darling," he said gently and with a slight smile. "I decided to be low profile and let our legions of lawyers handle the beginning motions hearings and jury selection. They don't need me there and I was anxious to be home for a change."

"It is a change, for sure." Leslie sipped her martini and intently flipped through the channels with the remote.

"Want to go out to dinner?" Forrest asked.

"I've already had a crab salad," Leslie said, still intent on the television. "Besides, I want to see this special TV show with Emily O'Brien. It is on the breast implant case and I think you're on it. Didn't they interview you in California at PSS a while back? I saw a clip this afternoon and you were on it—although not talking."

Forrest Winchester suddenly looked grim. "Oh, is it finally on?" he said softly.

"Didn't you know? I was sure that your lawyers would have told you." Leslie said.

"No," was all he said. "I think I'll have a scotch."

"Here it is. It's about to start." Leslie settled back into the chaise lounge and sipped her martini.

Forrest Winchester went into the family room to the well-stocked bar and poured himself a large scotch and returned to the sunroom, where he sat down on the couch. He looked at the TV and frowned.

"Could you turn up the sound a little?" he asked his wife.

Leslie automatically adjusted the sound with the remote. Emily O'Brien was holding up a PSS polyurethane-coated implant and indicating on a cross-section diagram how it was made.

Then Dr. Jean Sonier described the chemistry of the degradation of the foam into the carcinogen TDA. Suddenly a bunch of laboratory rats, some missing hair and others with grotesque tumors were on the screen. Dr. Sonier's voice was describing his research which seemed to prove that every rat implanted with the foam material developed cancer.

Leslie Winchester wrinkled her forehead and grimaced at the television. Forrest Winchester sipped his scotch without speaking. Then suddenly there he was on the screen, in his expensive suit with his Rolex watch clearly visible on his wrist as he gestured. Using his most melodious tones, he was describing how the Mammselle implant complied with all of the government requirements of a medical device and that it was perfectly safe. Moreover, he explained, it was of great benefit to women because it prevented capsular contracture—a wonderful idea. Then Patrick Kennedy introduced Dr. Dan MacNamara, in an old interview, explaining the problem of capsular contracture to reporters after one of his speaking tours to medical meetings with Sherrie Barker. Sherrie Barker was also in the room, but not introduced. Then Emily O'Brien introduced his patient, Pamela Lawson—in her hospital room—after her liver transplant. Pam explained why she had the Mammselle and what Dr. MacNamara had told her. Then she explained her current illness and mentioned her lawsuit. However, the lawsuit was explained carefully, but briefly by Janet Stephenson, her attorney, who revealed that experts, including Dr. Sonier, would be testifying as a biomaterials expert about the implant and that the case was based upon the fact that the Mammselle was marketed, even though it was known that polyurethane in the body, causes cancer. After a commercial break, Terry Napoli, Rex Montague, and Forrest Winchester, described at great length how the case of Pamela Lawson was based on lies and that the women of the world would be greatly harmed if they were denied the wonderful Mammselle, which had solved the terrible side effect of capsular contracture for implant patients. Then there were brief interviews with the Silicone Sisters, who were asked questions about capsular contracture, which made them appear to be testifying for Terry Napoli and PSS. But the show ended with more shots of the rats and a gentle and precise explanation by Dr. Jean Sonier and Dr. Richard Guilliot, who presented the medical dangers of putting an implant on the market, which has not been tested for all of the possible side effects, after there is scientific proof of the degradation of the implant materials after implantation in the animal studies. Emily O'Brien mentioned, as the show concluded, that jurors in a Denver courtroom would get the chance to address these issues in Pamela Lawson's case very soon. There was no mention that the trial was technically underway.

"Well, that wasn't so bad." Forrest Winchester said calmly, actually feeling good that he looked so suave and sophisticated on camera.

"Not so bad if you're Pamela Lawson," Leslie said softly.

"What do you mean?" her husband was almost shouting at her. "This case is based on an outrageous pack of lies put together by a greedy lawyer."

"Janet Stephenson does not look like a greedy lawyer to me," she replied. "I, for one, believed every word that she and that Canadian scientist said. I'll bet the jury will too."

"Nonsense! Napoli is twice the lawyer and a bearcat in the courtroom."

"I hope so, for our sake," was all she said. "I'm going to bed."

Forrest Winchester watched her go. He was shaking with anger and went to pour himself another drink. Then he went to his study, just on the other side of the family room bar, and called Terry Napoli's cell phone.

"Napoli—did you see the O'Brien-Kennedy piece?"

"Yes, Mr. Winchester, we're on it. We're already drafting a motion for a continuance of the trial and I've asked the court for a forthwith hearing at seven o'clock in the morning."

"Will he grant a continuance?"

"He will have to." Napoli sounded confident. He, too, was sipping on a glass of scotch. Rex Montague, sitting at the end of the conference room table was not confident. He knew Judge Parsons and he knew that he would not see the same threats in the broadcast that PSS feared. If only they had declined to be interviewed. That would have made the piece seem as though it were a plaintiff lawyer's plant. But, Janet Stephenson was only on camera half as long as Winchester and Napoli. It looked like their attempt to influence a jury. If only Sonier had not had films of those rats.

"Make it happen," said Winchester and he hung up the phone.

"God, this is a mess," Napoli said. "Any more scotch?"

Jennifer Fordham and Jerry Carson watched the program from their motel suite hideaway. Jennifer had brought a bottle of wine and some submarine sandwiches. They sat on the couch, with the sun setting behind them over the California oceanfront. Neither said a word until it was over.

"Winchester sounds and looks like a shyster racketeer!" Carson sneered.

"You're just jealous of the flashy Rolex," Jennifer mused.

"Like hell. You, or even I, should have been the spokesperson for PSS. How did Winchester get that gig?"

"He's got the pocketbook that keeps us rolling on." Jennifer was nibbling at her sandwich.

"Sonier has got to go! I can't believe we can't get that guy." Jerry Carson was pacing around the room, waving his cigarette. Jennifer sat calmly, holding her wine glass in one hand and her half-eaten sandwich in the other.

"What time do we have to be at the airport, Jerry? I told Napoli that we'd be at the courthouse in Denver in the morning at nine."

"Our flight is at 10:20 in the evening I've got to go back to the office for my suitcase. Do you want to come with me?"

"No, I have to stop by my house and check on my cat." Jennifer was getting her things together. "I've got to go, right now."

"You go first, Jen. I'll finish my cigarette and my wine and meet you at the airport."

Jennifer was opening the door.

"Wait," Carson said, "Let me give you your ticket so you can clear security. I'll see you at the gate."

He reached in his jacket pocket and handed her the ticket. "Later, Beautiful." He kissed her.

Jennifer smiled and quickly went out the door and down the steps to the parking lot. Just as she started her car, her cell phone rang. It was Forrest Winchester.

"Did you see the O'Brien thing on TV?" he asked.

"Yes," she said, without further explanation.

"What did you think?" he asked, hoping for a good review of his performance.

"I think we are in deep doo doo," Jennifer responded as she drove out of the parking lot and headed toward the freeway.

"I didn't think it was that bad. I thought we sounded like we knew what we were talking about and that Sonier is just a little creepy egg head."

"You'd be wrong," Jennifer said coolly.

"Well, I just talked to Napoli and they are already filing a motion to continue the trial that they believe the judge will hear at seven o'clock. He agrees with you, apparently. Are you going to Denver."

"I'm on my way to the airport," Jennifer replied. "Are you coming to the trial tomorrow?"

"No, but, I'm flying in tomorrow morning. We need to make some plans for Sonier and Guilloit. I've been thinking about them and I don't think we can allow them to testify."

"Sonier is close to the Plaintiff's first witness," Jennifer said, "There is no time."

"They haven't picked the jury—that will take at least one day, assuming the case is not continued. Then they have motions and all that preliminary crap. Sonier won't get on the stand until about the third day. We have time."

"It sounds as though you have a plan already," Jennifer said quietly.

"I do. I'll work on it some more and explain it to you tomorrow night in Denver. Are you at the Hyatt Regency?"

"Yes."

"I'll catch up with you there," Winchester said cheerfully.

"Okay—see ya" Jennifer hung up. She exited the highway at the next exit and drove down the street and finally through the gates to her exclusive beach side townhome. Her beautiful Himalayan, Jekkyl, was waiting inside the front door and rubbed against her leg with a soft purr as she opened it and went in.

"Hi, sweet baby," she picked up the cat and snuggled him to her face. "Sorry I have to go."

She fed the cat in the sparkling white kitchen, grabbed her suitcase from the entry hall closet and went out the front door to her car in less than ten minutes. An hour later, she was seated beside Jerry Carson in first class on United flight 354, headed for Denver and the chaos that she secretly feared.

At the Denver Police station, Investigations Unit, Amy Larabee, FBI, and Joel Steiner, DPD watched the O'Brien-Kennedy breast implant expose' in the employee lounge on the second floor of the main Cherokee Street station. They could see the Denver City and County Building from the window. They had been pooling their efforts to put together the case against Raoul Lecroix, whose attorney, the famous Wally Girton, was resisting and making their job very difficult. Girton was demanding a bail hearing for his client, who was being held in the Denver jail.

"Wow," exclaimed Joel Steiner, "What do you think of that Winchester dude? What do you know about him?"

"Not much," said Amy Larabee. "His wife's family has owned Conway Chemical forever, and Conway recently bought PolySurgical Specialties, which makes the Mammselle implant. I wouldn't think he would be the expert. His company didn't develop the implant they are talking about. PSS was started by Harry Fordham, a Stanford University scientist, as a medical research and development company. Harry Fordham is dead and the company is run by his daughter, Jennifer."

"How do you know all of that?"

"From talking to Dr. Jean Sonier. The man is a walking fount of all knowledge. But he has been doing battle with PSS and their implant in Canada for years. Enter Raoul Lecroix, who had the exclusive marketing distributorship for the Mammselle in Canada, until Sonier got the Canadian government to ban it, based on the rat and rabbit studies we just saw on TV."

"Ah, ha, it all becomes a little clearer, don't you think?"

"I guess I don't follow."

"Amy, who would have the most to lose, other than Lecroix if the PSS implant goes down the tubes in the United States, as well?"

"Conway Chemical," they both said to each other simultaneously.

"Yep, let's find out how much Conway Chemical paid for PSS—and how it was paid," said Amy. "Forrest Winchester doesn't look as though he is trusting the PR about this implant to the people who developed it at PSS. I wonder why?"

"We need to know more about Mr. Winchester. Ten bucks says he knows our man Raoul and knows him well." Joel said to Amy, as she sat down in front of her trusty laptop computer.

"I'm going to call Wally Girton. We need to ask his client some more questions."

"Check with Rick Plume first," said Amy. "I think the questions should really come from the D.A. and not from us—unless Plume gives us the go ahead. I think he is talking directly to Wally Girton."

"Can't you pull rank as the FBI," teased Joel.

"Murder is a state offense." Amy was concentrating on her computer. "But we all need to be on the same page because this one should go to a Grand Jury. However, we may not be able to get jurisdiction over Forrest Winchester . . . unless, by chance, he is coming to Denver for this Lawson trial. We've got to work with the D.A. so we don't screw it up. If Winchester is going to be arrested, detained, questioned the best way to do it is while he is here in Denver. I don't think we could extradite or even question him outside Colorado at this point. We don't have enough of anything on him. And Raoul is certainly not inclined to rat on anybody at this point."

"Janet Stephenson might know if Winchester is coming to Denver. I'll see what she knows."

Joel Steiner pulled out his cell phone and began scrolling for Janet Stephenson's cell phone number. He knew that he had entered it from her business card. When he found it, he pushed the button and called.

"Hey Janet? Joel Steiner. Got a minute?"

Janet Stephenson was at her office, with James and Adam. They had just turned off the television sets and were preparing for the next day in court. Janet was at her desk computer researching cases for the continuance hearing.

"Joel, what's up?" Janet answered brightly.

"Not much. I was just wondering who is coming into town to represent PSS in the trial?"

"I'm sure it will be Jennifer Fordham," Janet said, "Although Napoli did mention that Forrest Winchester might be coming. After watching him on TV tonight, I'd say there is a better than good chance that we will see Forrest Winchester in the courtroom before the week is out. Provided we don't get continued at our hearing in the morning."

"What do you mean?"

"Predictably, Napoli has filed a motion for a continuance because he thinks the Emily O'Brien piece will unduly influence prospective jurors against PSS." Janet shared.

"No way," said Joel. "If anything it looked like a PSS plant, although Sonier and Pam Lawson carried the day when all was said and done. You did pretty well, yourself, Jan."

"Thanks. But why the interest in their corporate reps?"

"Nothing certain. But we just might like to talk to Winchester, after hearing him on TV tonight. I'd appreciate your keeping that to yourself. Do you suppose you could give me a jingle, or have someone on your staff call me if you find he is going to be at trial or in town?"

"Sure, but it all sounds very mysterious!" Janet teased her old friend.

"Nothing really at this point. I'd just like your help if it's no trouble."

"No trouble at all. Just call you on your cell phone?"

"Yep. Do you have my number?"

"Yes, I think so. Let me check." Janet flipped open her cell phone and scrolled to Steiner. "Is it 303-221-7778?"

"That's it."

"Okay, we'll do it. Anything I should know, Joel." Janet sounded somber.

"I'll let you know if there is, Jan. Just stay in touch."

"Will do. Bye Joel."

"Bye" Joel flipped his phone shut. "He is coming, sure enough." He said to Amy Larabee.

Amy looked up from her laptop at the serious face on her new friend and colleague.

"I think this is about to get a lot more interesting, very quickly." she said. "Let's think about this a little bit. Somehow if there is a Winchester/Lecroix connection, was Sherrie Barker the target or someone else? And, why aren't they really concentrating on Dr. Sonier and the number he is continuing to do on their business? Or if Winchester is, hypothetically, at the source of this killing, is he going to be thwarted just because Raoul Lecroix is out of commission in the Denver City Jail? Put on your criminal's hat, Joel, and let's do some brainstorming. It may be that Sherrie Barker was really small potatoes and not the target at all—at least not the only target."

D r. Sally MacNamara and her husband, Dr. Dan MacNamara, watched the O'Brien- Kennedy expose' on the Mammselle implant on the television set in his private hospital suite, where he was still recovering from the burns and fractured skull he suffered on the night of Sherrie Barker's death. Sally had seen the ad promoting the special in the physician's lounge the day before. Dan MacNamara had been in isolation to prevent any infection while he healed and had plastic surgery to repair the damage from his burns. The suite was one of three of the VIP accommodations which every hospital has for visiting presidents, kings and beloved staff, who need privacy and special care. There was no question about the need for Dr. MacNamara to be treated as a king. He was doing better each and every day. But, the program clearly set him back. He watched in horrified silence. So did Sally.

"Sal, this is worse than I thought." He finally said.

"Dan, I have to be honest with you, now that you have seen this program. I know that Sherrie Barker brought you secret documents from PSS on the day that she was killed. I know that she was in your office. Her secretary secretly told an FBI investigator and they came to see me about the documents. We went to the office and found them in the safe."

"Oh, my God, Sally. Where are they now?"

"Janet Stephenson has them. We surmised that Sherrie Barker brought them to you because you were named as a witness for PSS in Pam Lawson's case, even though you are also a witness for Pam, as her treating physician."

"Yes," was all he said.

"Did you read them, Dan?"

"No, I didn't have time. I just put them in the safe, but I know that they were the reports of secret animal studies that were bad for PSS, according to Sherrie. She was a very honest person and she didn't want me to go on the stand without knowing what she knew."

"After seeing Dr. Sonier's rats, you can only imagine that the PSS studies are similar."

"So why didn't the FBI keep the documents?"

"Because they are secret internal documents that were obtained without a search warrant. They would be precluded from use in a criminal case unless they become public record somehow in Pamela Lawson's civil trial."

"I am the person who could testify that they came from PSS," Dan said, stunned.

"Yes, my dear, but you can't testify. The trial is about to start any day. It may have already begun at least with preliminary things. I don't think they have started to pick a jury yet, however."

"I was never deposed, so I probably can't testify anyway," Dan said.

"I don't know the rules or any of that. I just know that you can't testify. You are still in isolation."

"What is Janet Stephenson going to do. This evidence wins her case and vindicates Pamela Lawson, whom everyone has been saying is a money-grubbing, typical plaintiff."

"Janet is a smart lawyer. I'll bet she has it all figured out." Sally said, patting his hand. "In any case, it is not your worry. It will all go on without you. You just have to get well."

"It isn't that easy. You know that there is a criminal investigation into Sherrie's death or the FBI wouldn't be involved. Have you been contacted by the police or anything."

"Yes. A detective, Joel Steiner, from the Denver Police came to see me. I know there is an ongoing investigation, but I have no idea where it stands at this point. It hasn't been on the news at all. It is as though it never happened and that you are not in the hospital trying to regain your former life." Sally's eyes filled with tears, which spilled down her cheeks. She wiped them with the back of her hand. Dan looked at her and suddenly remembered why he had loved her so much all of these years. He had talked about Sherrie with Sally, and it had seemed okay. But Dan MacNamara was still overcome with remorse and guilt and sadness when he was alone.

"I have to think about this. There must be something I can do to put things right.

I talked Pam Lawson into having these implants, which are killing her, just as they killed those rats in Dr. Sonier's lab. There must be something...."

"Not tonight, Dan. Just go to sleep now. I'll have the nurse bring you something to help you sleep." She looked at her husband, at his scarred and healing, yet handsome face, deep in contemplation, his brow furrowed with sadness.

Dan looked at her and returned to the present. "I'll be okay. I don't need any medication. You should go home to the kids and I'm going to bed." he said, gently.

Sally came to his chair and kissed him lightly on the top of the head. "I love you, my sweet." she said.

"I love you, Sally. I couldn't make it without you. Thank you for loving me." Dan had tears in his eyes.

"It will all be good." Sally said. "Good night, sweet prince."

"Good night." Dan said and she closed the door quietly behind her.

Sally MacNamara went to talk to the nurse about Dan's sedatives. She did not notice the police officer whom Joel Steiner had just ordered to guard Dr. Dan MacNamara's door.

At the Holiday Inn at Hampden and Wadsworth, Dr. Jean Sonier and Dr. Richard Guilliot had adjoining rooms, with a door conveniently in between. They ordered in Chinese food from Mu Lon Landing, a restaurant next door, and each of them stretched out on a bed in Sonier's room to watch the Emily O'Brien television program about the PSS Mammselle implant. They hurried to the hotel from the airport so that they would not miss the special. They watched the show in silence. During the commercials they ate without speaking and sat transfixed to the screen when the program began again. When each of their interviews were on, each reacted with distaste at how they appeared on camera. Dr. Guilloit was embarrassed that his English was not more clear. Dr. Sonier expressed his distress at the portions were edited from his interview. But they both agreed that the expose' was not going to help PSS.

"Jean, I have the concern, more serious," said Richard Guilloit solemnly.

"What would that be, my dear friend?" queried Sonier.

"The Winchester fellow, he seems most sinister, as you would say."

"I know, I know," said Jean Sonier, nodding his head. "I have the concern myself, especially with my dear Lorna at home, far away. We have had a taste of the danger posed by PSS when their pockets are picked by the likes of you and me. I am continually vigilant because I know they are likely to be plotting my demise."

"The death of poor Miss Barker, she was not an accident, I think." Said Guilloit "Further to the point, we may be a trouble to them that they cannot repair."

"That is why I skulk about like a shadow, dear Richard. I never publish my whereabouts, even to the most friendly of our employing attorneys. With my laptop, I often change my flight plans on the way to the airport. The satellite computer connection is usually invaluable to me, though costly. Even thrifty Lorna does not complain."

"It would seem that we may be in the hot bed of the trouble here in Denver, eh, Jean?"

"We must be most vigilant ever watching for danger. That is not easily done, I fear."

"This Winchester, could he be behind these dangers?" asked Richard Guilliot.

"I have had that unspoken opinion for some time—though I have no direct proof. The likes of Raoul Lecroix would need money and encouragement to carry out these deadly activities. Winchester, at least his wife, has the wherewithal, as they say. Also, I think, the inclination to wipe me, at the very least, from the face of the earth."

"I have chosen my friends well, I see." laughed Guilloit.

"We should lie low and drive our own car to the court when it is time for us to go."

Jean Sonier was solemn and his face looked tired and drawn. Dr. Guilliot, whose face was round and usually ruddy, looked a little pale. He patted his friend's arm and stood up from the bed with some effort. His round tummy made it difficult to move quickly.

"I shall now retire. We can leave the door open, should you like."

"Good, that's fine." answered the absent minded Dr. Sonier. He was already thinking about something else, making other plans. He was typing rapidly on his laptop computer.

Sometime later, Jean Sonier noticed that his friend was gone. He looked around the room and then noted the light in the room next door through the crack that Guilloit had left. He felt somehow safer knowing that his friend was in the next room.

"A good friend, one should always keep." Sonier said to himself as he went into the bathroom to brush his teeth. A few minutes later, he was sound asleep in bed. Guilliot noted his soft snoring as he set the alarm for six o'clock in the morning and switched off the lamp by his bed.

Brad Stephenson landed at JFK in New York and thirty minutes later was in the Sheraton Hotel by the airport. He had heard that the Emily O'Brien-Patrick Kennedy special was going to air at nine o'clock and he arrived at the hotel just in time to check in and order a chicken salad sandwich and a glass of milk from room service before it started. He sat at the small table in his room and watched the entire program, interrupted only by the delivery of his food. At the end of the program, he called Janet, but her cell phone was busy.

"She's probably at the office," he said out loud to no one, then dialed her office number.

"Janet Stephenson's office," answered James.

"Hi, is this James or Adam?" he asked.

"James. Hello, Mr. Stephenson," the young man replied with a smile. "Mrs. Stephenson is talking on her cell phone. Did you see the program on the implant?"

"Yes, I saw it in my hotel room. I just got in to JFK from France in time. What did Janet think of it?"

"Well, sir, you should ask her, but I think she thought it was good for us. Shall I interrupt her?"

"No, no—just tell her that I called. She can call me back if she has time"

"We will probably be here for a while, Mr. Stephenson. Adam just showed me a fax that we received this minute, telling us that the other side is trying to get the trial continued. I'm sure that means more work for us tonight."

"Oh, no!" Brad knew that Janet desperately needed this trial to go forward or be settled.

"Mrs. Stephenson hasn't seen it yet. I'm sure she'll call you."

"Okay," Brad felt sick. "Have her give me a call on my cell if she has a minute."

"Okay, bye," said James.

Brad Stephenson looked at his sandwich and the glass of milk. He didn't want either one of them now. He picked up the sandwich and took a bite, but his mind was half a continent away in Denver. He ate the sandwich and drank the milk mechanically, deep in thought. Suddenly his cell phone rang.

"Hey, you." His wife's cheery voice made him smile.

"Hi, sweets," he said.

"Well, we're still up to our ears in alligators," Janet said. "James said you saw the special."

"Yes, what did you think of it, Jan?"

"I think it was okay. I'm glad I stuck to facts and understatement in my interview. It turned out to be a good contrast to Napoli and Winchester. I thought that Pam was great—and I was glad that they voiced over most of the shots of the Silicone Sisters. They tend to really get off task.

The best parts were that Dr. Sonier was so credible and that Winchester and Napoli just talked and talked."

"James said that you got a fax that they want to continue the trial."

"Yes, and since then, the judge's clerk called and said the judge will hear their motion at seven in the morning. We're working on the response and the guys recorded the program so that we can make sure that the judge sees it. I doubt Judge Parsons follows this kind of news, but I could be wrong."

"What do you have to do to prepare, other than taking a recording of the program?"

Janet sighed and said, "Well, I have to find a couple of cases, and then I am going home to bed. I am really tired. I sent James and Adam to get something for us to eat. I think I can finish up in about an hour or so."

Brad could hear her cell phone ringing in the background.

"Sorry, Brad, this is Joel Steiner from the Denver Police. I'll call you in the morning."

"Okay, sweets, bye," and she was gone. Brad flipped his cell phone shut.

Brad Stephenson could picture Janet in her office. They had purchased two buildings on the west side of a steep hill on South Wadsworth Boulevard years before when he was discharged from the Air Force. The buildings were sprawling ranch-style homes, surrounded by three acres of beautiful grass and trees and shrubs. They converted both of the buildings into the campus of Gingerbread House, a progressive child development center. During the Viet Nam war, Brad was a fighter pilot stationed, ultimately, with the Fourth TAC Fighter Wing at Seymour Johnson AFB in Goldsboro, North Carolina. His squadron, the 335th, known as the Chiefs, and the other two squadrons which made up the wing were the emergency responders at the beck and call of the President. As a result, Brad's squadron often went TDY, or on temporary duty, to such glamorous places as Kunsan, Korea, and Spangdahlem, Germany or Norway, where they flew public relations missions with NATO flyers from other countries. The 4th TAC Fighter Wing also flew the firepower demonstrations for members of Congress, VIP events to encourage military appropriations. The wing also provided the flybys for important national events. Brad had been one of the pilots who did the missing man fly by for the funeral of President Dwight D. Eisenhower in Washington, D.C. All during these five years of their young lives, Janet had been teaching English literature at East

Carolina University and Wayne Community College and raising their two small children.

But a tour in Viet Nam was looming on the horizon for Brad, who was actually a reserve officer, having been commissioned out of the ROTC program at the University of Colorado before going to pilot training at Vance AFB in Enid, Oklahoma. Because he was a reserve officer, Brad would have to volunteer to be sent to Vietnam and he steadfastly refused to volunteer, despite the pressure from his fighter pilot peers, most of whom were graduates of the Air Force Academy.

However, as time went on, it became increasingly more difficult to avoid a tour in Viet Nam and Brad decided to leave the Air Force. Janet and Brad had always secretly opposed the war in Viet Nam and neither of them could even consider Brad volunteering to go. They wanted to do something that was a "positive good" and so they decided to develop a revolutionary kind of child development program designed to meet all of the child care and development needs of a young family. They designed Gingerbread House to be open seven days a week from six o'clock am to midnight and to take children from ten months old to twelve years old. Janet went back to school and earned her Certification in Early Childhood Education and became a certified Director of early childhood programs. Then they put together the idea of Gingerbread House, with their Air Force friends as the initial investors. Their first school was the campus on South Wadsworth where Janet's office was now located.

Brad found a flying job as soon as he could, to provide family cash flow and Janet went to law school, to gather the information and education they needed to run their schools. She never really intended to practice law, but as way led on to way, after eight years of working for another firm, she left and started her own practice.

After twenty years when their own children were raised, Janet and Brad moved the school to a nearby church facility and sold it, eventually to the church. They kept the houses and the land and converted both into office buildings. Janet moved her office from downtown Denver to the building that was originally the main school. They rented the offices in the former infant and toddler house. Now she was involved in the fight of her life with one of the biggest corporations in the country. But Janet Stephenson was never one to back off when circumstances seemed the most difficult. She was a survivor and a fighter.

"You'll be fine, Jan." Brad Stephenson said to his telephone. "You'll be fine. I just wish I could have gotten home sooner."

Brad went to his briefcase and took out the pad of paper he always carried with him and began to write. The words came easily as they do sometimes for poets, who only fly for fun.

A Brief in Time

Just a moment,
Then we're gone.
A little flicker,
Then we're done,
But never mind,
What is must be.
You and I are so much
More when we're together

Yesterday is but a dream.
Today is what we have,
Today and all our dreams,
Our hopes and plans.
Together, so much more,
Apart, apart, another word for pain,
Let's be together

Children come like wind.
They warm us like a fire,
We have our today;

They own tomorrow.
We'll travel with them there.
They take the love we give them there.
They know of dreams, of hope and plans,
Like us, they borrow,
Based on love, the love of those
Who loved them.

One day soon we'll be alone
The wind and fire will move away,
And, too, the chaos.
Just a moment, then we're gone.
A little flicker, then it's done.
Never mind, my Love, we are together.

F orrest Winchester was a man on a mission. The more he thought about the Dr. Jean Sonier, the angrier he became. The Mammselle was his ticket to bona fide wealth that did not come from his wife, Leslie, and now Sonier and his rats were destroying his dreams. If he testified and showed the photos of those rats to the jury, PSS would lose the trial, he was sure of it. Only Sonier could testify about the rats and draw scientific opinions from the Canadian rat studies. Only the researcher who did the work could adequately explain and interpret the data from the rat studies for the jury. Winchester's mission was to make sure that Sonier did not testify.

Winchester was just leaving the first-class cabin and walking through the causeway to the terminal at Denver International Airport when his cell phone rang. It was Raoul Lecroix.

"Hello," he answered

"Winchester?"

"Yes, who is this?"

"Your friend from Canada, Lecroix."

"I thought you were in jail. Why are you calling me?"

"I'm out on bond," he lied. "I still owe services to you for what you paid me."

"And just what do you have in mind?"

"An accident, eh? How does that sound to you, eh?"

"Accidents are good, sometimes, especially now. But how can you do it?" said Winchester.

"To me, you must leave the details. The payment is your part, eh?"

"Cash?"

"Yes, cash."

"How?"

"UPS Store, Colfax and Clarkson, Box 235, Manila Envelope"

"Wait a minute, let me write that down." Winchester opened his briefcase in the boarding area and took out a small notebook. "Say again?"

"UPS Store, East Colfax and Clarkson, on the corner. Box 235, addressed to John Smith in a manila envelope."

"Okay. I'll leave the half the remainder due until confirmation."

"I'll let you know. "Lecroix hung up.

Forrest Winchester put his cell phone in the pocket of his Pierre Cardin suit, replaced his notebook in his briefcase and headed for baggage claim. Suddenly his heart felt lighter. He might get out of this after all.

Winchester collected his bags and took a taxi to the Hyatt Regency hotel in downtown Denver. He registered, went to his elegant penthouse suite and noted that he could see the City and County Building from his window.

At police headquarters, Amy Larabee and Joel Steiner were with Raoul Lecroix as he talked to Forrest Winchester on the speakerphone. Both were silent as mice writing notes to Lecroix, as he talked, on a yellow pad, passed between them.

"Okay, Lecroix, back to your cell until we get a confirmation of the drop."

Raoul Lecroix gave them a surly look as he left the room with the officer. He looked more like a derelict than a successful businessman in his orange jumpsuit and unshaven face.

When he left, Amy Larabee leaned back in her chair, tilted her head, and smiled at Joel Steiner.

"I told you that Dr. Sonier is a genius." She laughed as she picked up her empty coffee container and threw it toward the trash can. Amy was dressed in a gray striped pantsuit with a pink silk blouse, which complimented her shiny black hair and blue eyes perfectly.

"I can't believe that Sonier figured out when Winchester was arriving and gave you this entire scheme by email." Joel Steiner was enjoying working with this intelligent and beautiful agent both because she was so much fun, but also because she was so smart and so unassuming.

"He's always emailing me. I tell you, his mental wheels never stop turning" said Amy.

"This one recorded telephone conversation if it is followed up by Winchester delivering the money to the UPS Store, will give us probable cause to arrest Winchester and put him before the Grand Jury." Joel Steiner leaned back in his chair and put his hands behind his head. He was wearing a leather jacket and jeans, with his perennial cowboy boots.

"Do you think we need to do more to clinch the charge on Winchester?"

"You mean like staging a real accident, and inviting Winchester to observe or participate in some way?"

"Yeah, or something like that. I'm just afraid he will weasel out of this if it is only a shady telephone conversation and an envelope full of money addressed to a fictitious person. I'd like to find a way to catch him red-handed."

Amy Larabee was sitting across the table from Joel, looking at him intently. "I think we might just be able to do that if we can get Sonier's help. I'll send him an email and see what he thinks. You can never talk to the man because he moves in the world of shifting shadows, but he always reads his email."

"Let's give it a shot." Said Joel.

"Okay—let's talk about this a little more."

The two talked in the conference room for a long time and then Amy Larabee took out her laptop computer and wrote an email to Dr. Jean Sonier.

Janet left her darkened and silent office at one o'clock in the morning She drove home, still deep in thought and mechanically brushed her teeth and climbed into bed.

"I wish you were here, Brad." She said to his empty pillow. "Maybe you'll get home before the weekend." Instantly, she fell into a deep sleep.

The next morning, Janet Stephenson met Adam and James at the office at 5:45 in the morning They loaded their boxes and the television/VCR gear in the car and went through a drive through Starbucks on the way downtown. Janet had black coffee and a cinnamon roll. James and Adam had giant coffee drinks with exotic names and two scones each.

Napoli and Montague and their cast of thousands arrived ten minutes after Janet and her clerks. James and Adam had already set up their TV and VCR for the judge. The PSS attorney team came in with a dolly and a much bigger TV, but they were too late. Adam and James smiled at each other in satisfaction.

At seven ten in the morning, the bailiff came in and announced, "All rise. This honorable court is in session. The Honorable Jameson Parsons, presiding." Judge Parsons swept into the room and sat down behind the bench.

"Mr. Napoli, Mr. Montague, it is your motion which gets us here at this ungodly hour. What's this about?"

Terry Napoli stepped briskly to the podium and pulled the microphone down to his height. "Your Honor, as we stated in our motion, a program aired on NBC last night about this case and we have filed this motion because PSS believes that it will so prejudice the jury pool that our client will not be able to obtain a fair trial at this time."

"Well, I was watching football and I missed it, "Judge Parsons responded. "But, I see that I am not going to be able to miss it—from the looks of the equipment set up for my viewing at the bench. I guess I'll have to see it. But, I don't want to watch it here. Whose equipment is this?"

Janet stood up, "It is ours, Your Honor."

"Well, let's move it to my chambers. At least I can sit in a comfortable chair and have a cup of coffee. How long is it?"

"Almost an hour," Janet responded "without the commercials, which we have removed."

"Mercifully!" Judge Parsons smiled at her. "Well, can you move this?"

James and Adam were already on the move. "Yes, Sir," James responded.

"We'll reconvene at eight fifteen or so. Go have a cup of coffee." Judge Parsons said as he stood up and went through the door behind the bench.

The judge's clerk came out and ushered James and Adam and the equipment into chambers. In a few minutes, they emerged, smiling and talking softly to each other.

"Let's go have some real breakfast," Janet said.

"Let's go to Dozens," Adam said.

"Sounds great," smiled Janet. They left through the side door of the City and County Building and walked the short block to Dozens, a popular breakfast and lunch café situated in a remodeled Victorian house. They all had eggs and English muffins with fruit and coffee. At 8:13 in the morning they entered the courtroom and found Napoli and Montague, and about six other attorneys huddled together at counsel table, furiously making notes and talking. They fell silent when Janet opened the door.

"Guess they missed their chance for breakfast," said Janet to Adam and James. James and Adam sat behind Janet, along the bar, and she took her place at the plaintiff's table. A minute later the bailiff came in and said "All rise."

Judge Parsons sat down and looked up with a quizzical expression. "Well, Mr. Napoli, there doesn't seem to be much prejudice to either side to me. I watched the entire program and listened carefully to everything. It was a balanced piece of journalism, which doesn't appear to favor either side. You certainly had your fair share of time to present the position of your client on the air. What is the problem?"

"Your Honor, it is just inappropriate for the potential jurors to have this kind of information about the subject matter of this case before they hear it in the courtroom. It is just prejudicial. It makes picking an impartial jury all but impossible at this time."

"And when will be a better time, Mr. Napoli? As I see it, you got a really good crack at explaining your case on TV last night and you took it. Are you taking a different position in this trial than you expressed to the television reporters?"

"No, Your Honor, certainly not. But our client is not responsible for the injuries to this Plaintiff."

"And so you said in the interview, Mr. Napoli. I don't see where the prejudice is?"

"We cannot anticipate the effect that this kind of publicity will have on the expectations and understanding of the jurors, Your Honor."

"Did anyone know that this program was going to air last night?" the judge asked.

"We did not know until after court yesterday," answered Napoli.

"Mrs. Stephenson, how about you?" the judge looked at Janet.

"No, Your Honor. I found out when I got back to my office after being in court—less than an hour before the show. I would say that I did have a voice mail on my cell phone from Mr. Napoli advising me of the show and that he would be filing this motion."

"Did either of you have anything to do with the timing of this broadcast? You both obviously participated in giving interviews to the reporters, but I assume that was some time ago."

"I have had no contact with anyone since the interview, weeks ago." Said Janet

"Nor have I" said Napoli.

"How about you, Mr. Montague."

Rex Montague stood up, looking startled. "No, Your Honor. I will say that I have had a paralegal attempting to find out what happened to the show and when it was going to air. However, she was unable to find out and we received no advance notice of the airing."

"Mrs. Stephenson, did you make attempts to discover when it would air?"

"No, none at all." Janet answered truthfully.

"Well, I'm sure that you both have lots of case law to cite to me. You can submit that in the form of a brief for the record, due in the morning. But, I know the law with respect to pre-trial publicity pretty well and I don't see how this broadcast militates for or against any party to this litigation. You all had an equal chance to state your positions to the reporters and each of you took the opportunity. If anything, the editors gave more time on camera to the counsel and representatives for the defendants than the plaintiff, but the plaintiff doesn't appear to wish to have a continuance. We will continue with jury selection after we have disposed of all of the pretrial motions. I understand that there are some motions in limine. We will take those up tomorrow morning. I have already advised the jury pool that they can come back tomorrow morning. We will begin at eight o'clock in the morning with motions. I told the jurors to report by ten o'clock in the morning That gives me the rest of today to dispose of other pending matters before this trial goes into full swing. I'll see you in the morning. We will be in recess."

Janet Stephenson, Terry Napoli and Rex Montague were all standing. They all continued to stand as the judge left the bench and entered his chambers through the door behind him.

"Is that it?" Napoli snapped at Rex Montague.

"Guess so." Rex Montague shrugged.

Just then Pamela and Larry Lawson came into the courtroom. "What's going on, Janet?" Larry asked.

"The judge just ruled that the trial goes on. He denied their motion for a continuance."

Pamela sat down at the table and put her head in her hands. "Thank God," she said softly.

"However, we're done for today. He said we'll start again tomorrow, with motions and then proceed with jury selection at about ten o'clock in the morning You can really take a break until then, unless you want to be here for the motions hearing part."

Just then the judge's clerk came out and beckoned to James and Adam to come into chambers to remove the TV/VCR gear. They hurried to follow her.

"What are those motions," Larry asked.

"I listed a rebuttal witness that they want to strike," Janet said. "I'm sure that the judge will probably reserve judgment until and if I call him."

"Who is the witness?" Larry asked.

"I can't explain that now, Larry." Janet smiled.

"Then we'll be here to hear what you tell the judge." Larry looked stern.

"Okay." Janet smiled at him and patted Pam's arm "but I suggest you rest for the rest of today." Pam smiled at her and nodded. Larry helped her up and they left the courtroom.

"Let's go, guys," she said to her waiting clerks. "I have a ton of work before tomorrow."

Napoli, Montague and the cast of a thousand lawyers had already left the courtroom.

When Janet Stephenson returned to her office that she found a new motion in limine. It was a motion to preclude the evidence regarding the rat studies from Dr. Sonier's testimony. Janet had been anticipating the motion and had already done the research and a draft response. She spent about an hour revising her response and then sent it by courier to the Court, so that it could be heard the next day in the pre-trial motion hearing. She faxed her response to Montague and Napoli.

Janet also emailed the Motion and her Response to Dr. Sonier. She wanted him to be thinking about how to restructure his testimony, just in case Judge Parsons excluded any reference to his animal tests from Jean Sonier's testimony. She felt certain that her brilliant expert would find a way to support his opinions. The results of his studies had been published in the Journal of Biomaterials as well as in the Canadian newspapers. Janet also believed that she could convince the judge that Dr. Sonier's studies were relevant and admissible, but she had to be prepared for the worst case scenario. The biggest problem she had was linking the degradation of the implants into TDA in the breast with cancer of the liver. All the little rats with liver cancer were her link.

Janet had traveled many months earlier to Santa Barbara, California, to PSS headquarters and spent a full week going through all of the internal documents relating to the Mammselle and other implants sold by PSS. She had to fight for the disclosure of the documents and finally got an order from Judge Parsons, directing Jennifer Fordham and Jerry Carson to produce all of the documents at their headquarters. They were also ordered to make copies of any documents chosen by Janet in her review at the PSS headquarters in Santa Barbara.

She arrived at PSS offices and the warehouse where the documents were produced for her at nine o'clock each day. She spent the entire day reading documents and putting sticky notes on the documents she wanted PSS to copy. Each day she had a "keeper" who noted everything she did, including when she went to the bathroom. At twelve o'clock, she was ushered out so that the keeper could go to lunch. At one o'clock, she was readmitted to the warehouse and she was ushered out again at five o'clock.

Although Janet was a speed reader, the process was exhausting. Her bad vision and hard contact lenses made it even more difficult to accomplish the task of reviewing a room full of bankers' boxes full of documents in the time she was allotted.

At five o'clock every day, Janet went to the beach, which was deserted at that time of year. She sat in a trance and watched the magnificent Santa Barbara sunset. Each day the sunset was different, sometimes all pink and orange. On other days the ocean was a deep purple, then a light purple, then pink and silver as the sun disappeared and darkness crept over the sand and the beach creatures, including the weary lawyer, whose contact lenses were cloudy and painful. Janet would stop and get fast food and go to her hotel room to take out her contacts and collapse before the TV, without seeing or hearing it at all. In the morning, she would grab an egg McMuffin and coffee and return to the warehouse dungeon.

While Janet found many interesting documents which demonstrated an irresponsible medical manufacturing company, her case was really based on what she did not find. She did not find the testing of the polyurethane, which proved that it was safe to implant in a human body. PSS just assumed it was safe because it was secured by a manufacturer who supplied it for "clean rooms" for the military. FDA approval was piggybacked as an amendment to the approved application for the PSS silicone gel breast implant. It was a semi-legal loophole to get it on the market, but it did not prove that implanted polyurethane was safe. Jean Sonier's studies proved it was not safe. The labeling focused on the improvement which prevented capsular contracture with their silicone implant inside.

"Clever," she thought. "Only Jennifer Fordham could have come up with this. I am amazed that the FDA would be so brain-dead as to allow this! What would I do without Jean Sonier."

The major defense of PSS was, of course, that the Mammselle had been approved by the FDA. The FDA had accepted the amended application of an approved silicone implant without looking any further.

Tomorrow, Janet would have to defeat Napoli's motion to take away her most convincing evidence, Sonier's rat studies, and convince the judge that she should be allowed to add Raoul Lecroix as a rebuttal witness, even though the time had passed for naming ordinary witnesses. She really hoped that she would not have to call Lecroix as a witness because she hadn't thought his testimony through. Janet Stephenson prepared for trials as though she were writing a script for a play. She had to know exactly what every witness was going to say. Nothing was worse than to have a trial go sideways because a witness suddenly said something new, and worse, unforeseen.

More important, Janet now had the secret documents that Sherrie Barker had delivered to Dr. Dan MacNamara, but in order to get them into evidence, she would have to lay a foundation proving that they were authentic PSS business documents. The two witnesses who could do that were not available. Sherrie Barker was dead and Dr. Dan MacNamara was still in the hospital. Sherrie's secretary never saw the documents, although she suspected that they were the reason for Sherrie's visit to Dr. MacNamara before the trial. Now Janet Stephenson had no choice but to call Jennifer Fordham as an adverse witness and use the documents as cross-examination documents in order to get them admitted in the case. It was critical to her case and her success in getting the documents admitted would insure that Rick Plume, the district attorney, could use the documents in his criminal case against Lecroix and whomever else at PSS was involved in Sherrie Barker's murder.

"Ahha," Janet said out loud to herself. "I just have to find out if Lecroix knew about the animal study documents. I'll bet that he did!" She knew that he knew about Dr. Jean Sonier's similar studies that were exposed on the television special. She had to talk to Amy Larabee and Joel Steiner. She needed a backup verification that the documents were business records of PSS because there was not a chance that Napoli would stipulate to that, even though the cover letters were on letterhead of the company and Jennifer Fordham was the person to whom they were addressed. If Lecroix could verify Fordham's position and signature and identify the letterhead, she just might be able to get them admitted even if Jennifer Fordham lied on the stand. She needed that insurance. At least she knew now how she could use Lecroix and that would make her identification of him as a rebuttal witness necessary and relevant.

Janet left her office and went in search of James and Adam. She found them in the "war room," which is what they called the file room or copier room when they were in trial. They were looking at the yellow pages trying to decide on which pizza delivery company to call for supper at the office.

"Hey, guys, after you order the pizza, I need you to go in search of a document on our PSS document database."

"Sure, thing," responded Adam, sliding off the table and handing the phone book to James.

"What document are we looking for?"

"I need any document that mentions Raoul Lecroix. He was the guy who had the exclusive distributorship for Mammselle implants for Canada."

"Canada?" James looked quizzical. "Is the Mammselle available in Canada?"

"Not anymore. Thanks to Dr. Sonier and Dr. Guilliot. But, before it was banned, he had the distributorship for the entire country in his pocket. There must be some correspondence, or a contract or something in all of the documents we have from PSS. Is it possible to find it from our data base, or do we have to start searching through the documents." Janet asked.

"Let's give it a try. I'll bet we can find something." Adam said. "What kind of pizza?"

"You choose, just order me a salad," Janet laughed. "Diet drinks, or we'll all be two ton tessies by the time this trial is over."

James was on the phone, choosing the pizza and Adam immediately went to the computer on their shared desk to begin his search.

The pizza arrived and James brought Janet's salad and diet Pepsi to her office.

An hour later Adam went to Janet's office with four documents. He smiled at her and said, "Bingo, as Dr. Sonier would say. Here is the rest of the story."

Janet took the documents. One was a memorandum from Jennifer Fordham to Jerry Carson advising him that they would be approving a contract with Raoul Lecroix. The second was the contract itself. The third was a letter from Jennifer Fordham to Raoul Lecroix, on PSS letterhead, returning a copy of the fully signed contract to Lecroix. The fourth was a letter from Lecroix asking about the possibility of another distributorship other than Canada.

Janet smiled at Adam, who had reclined on her couch while she read the documents. "Bravo, Adam," she said to him "These are perfect and exactly what we need. I don't even remember selecting them when I was in Santa Barbara. I guess I have very vigilant angels."

"Hey, what about me?" James appeared in her door. "Adam just found hints of them on our data base. I'm the one who actually dug the documents out of about a million pages of paper!"

"Good job, both of you. I love you!!!" Janet said enthusiastically. "Now, all I need you to do is make all the requisite 5 copies of each so that we can take them to Court in the morning. Then we're done and we can go home to bed."

"Sounds good to me," yawned Adam. James was already on his way to the war room, with the documents in hand.

The next morning, Janet Stephenson, Adam, and James were at the courtroom by eight ten in the morning. Terry Napoli and Rex Montague arrived with their army of black and navy blue suited attorneys and paralegals at eight twenty. Judge Parsons was announced by the bailiff's "All Rise!" at eight forty in the morning.

"Sorry for the delay, counsel," he said, "I had a brief telephone status conference to get out of the way."

Janet Stephenson and Terry Napoli were standing behind their respective tables as he spoke.

"Well, let's clear up these motions, so we can get started with jury selection. Ms. Stephenson, you have a motion to add a rebuttal witness, and Mr. Napoli, you have a motion to preclude the admission of some animal studies done by one of the Plaintiff's experts, Dr. Sonier."

"Yes, your honor," Napoli and Stephenson responded in unison.

The judge looked down at them over his reading glasses. Then he smiled.

"We are going to do this the easiest way. I have read both of the motions and the accompanying briefs carefully. There is no need for argument now because I intend to rule on each of these motions when the issue comes up at trial. Mrs. Stephenson, as I understand it, you may or may not need this rebuttal witness, is that correct?"

Janet saw where he was going and she was greatly relieved, "That's right, Your Honor," she replied.

"Then there is no need to rule on a hypothetical witness at this point. Mr. Napoli, you want to preclude the evidence of Dr. Sonier's studies, which I presume are the ones which were shown to the world in the television special the other night, right?"

"Yes, Your Honor, the studies are prejudicial to the Defendant and they have no place in a trial where they have to pass Daubert muster."

"I understand that you think that the studies should be precluded under the Daubert test as junk science, but I do not see any indication in the motions or the briefs that these studies were done at the request of any plaintiff in any litigation against a manufacturer of breast implants. As I understand the motions and briefs, including the portions of Dr. Sonier's deposition, which Ms. Stephenson attached to her Response to your motion, these rat and rabbit studies were done under the direction of the Canadian government and have been published in two peer reviewed journals as well as by the Canadian version of the American Food and Drug Administration. Am I correct?"

Napoli's neck was turning red as he stood stiffly behind the podium. "But, Your Honor, Dr. Sonier is not an independent expert. He testifies only for plaintiffs against silicone breast implant manufacturers. He is never a defense expert and he is biased."

"Well, Mr. Napoli, that may be true, but it is your job to bring out any prejudicial bias for the jury to consider. That's the stuff of cross-examination, don't you agree? And I am sure that you are more than up to the task. If not, I am certain that Mr. Montague is. He has appeared in this Court many times and demonstrated his skill in that arena." Judge Parsons smiled at Montague.

"Your honor, the photographs and videos which are a part of Dr. Sonier's report in this case will likely outweigh any cross."

"Then you must put on your pictures of healthy rats and rabbits if there are any, to contradict him. Trial strategy 101. I think the studies pass the Daubert test and your motion to preclude them is denied. Anything further, before we start with jury selection?"

Janet was so happy that she could hardly speak. "Not for us, Your Honor," she said quietly.

"Mr. Napoli?"

"Your Honor, the Defendant would like a few hours to determine if we need to file an interlocutory appeal on the matter of Dr. Sonier's studies before we begin jury selection," Napoli said.

"We'll begin jury selection at one thirty in the afternoon." The judge frowned. "We'll be in recess. See you all fifteen minutes after one in the afternoon, ready to proceed." Judge Parsons stood up and disappeared through the door behind the bench.

Napoli, by pressing the judge, had been rewarded by a pretrial denial of his motion to preclude the Sonier animal studies. If he had waited, he could have argued their admissibility before the jury and possibly created confusion in their minds. Now, the judge had ruled that the studies and the videos were admissible. There could be no argument at the time of Dr. Jean Sonier's testimony. Further, Janet would not have to tip her hand about Raoul Lecroix until after the presentation of the Defendant's case, or at least after the testimony of Jennifer Fordham as an adverse witness, in the event that she lied about the PSS animal study documents, which Sherrie Barker had given to Dr. Dan MacNamara. Janet felt completely joyous. "I may enjoy this trial, after all," she thought to herself.

Janet Stephenson always felt comfortable in the courtroom, once she got there. There was something about going through those little swinging gates in the bar that calmed her and brought her confidence. But, often as she drove to court, unloaded her briefcases, paid for parking, and went through security at the courthouse doors, she felt completely nauseous and afraid. It was during those moments, prior to actually sitting down at the counsel table that she promised herself that she was getting out of the trial lawyer business. She never told anyone, except Brad. They laughed together about her first case, representing her sister in her divorce in Weld County District Court when she had to stop at every gas station and fast food establishment between Denver and Greeley because of her upset stomach. Once she was actually in the courtroom, and finally, in the judge's chambers, she felt confident and at ease. It was just the getting there that was so stressful and she had never gotten over it. Today, after trying scores of cases of every kind, she still suffered pretrial anxiety.

"I wonder how Napoli feels," she thought to herself as she watched him from the corner of her eye as she packed up her briefcase, with her jury selection information. "He doesn't look as though anything phases him" Little did she know that Terry Napoli was stricken with anxiety and only wanted to go to his hotel room and have a glass of scotch. Napoli suddenly realized that he should not be trying this case. The judge liked and respected Rex Montague, but Judge Parsons had now ruled against him in two critical motions. "I should be giving Montague this mess," he thought. But Terry Napoli needed the big paycheck that came from working for Forrest Winchester and Conway Chemical. Montague's fees were chump change compared to the retainer his firm was being paid for this trial. Conway Chemical and PSS needed to win this case and he had been chosen out of all the defense counsel in the United States to do the job. Besides, this small firm woman lawyer was not in his league. He had gone to Yale Law and been co-editor of the Yale Law Review. He knew that Janet Stephenson was a graduate of the University of Colorado School of Law. No comparison. Except that Janet Stephenson and Rex Montague knew Judge Parsons. "I'm being home towned." he thought. "We've got to get some good press to overshadow the TV coverage of O'Brien's special." He said out loud to Montague.

"Judge Parsons is not influenced much by the media," Rex Montague said. "He watches sports and PBS."

"I'm not thinking about him," Napoli said impatiently, "It's the jury pool who needs something to remember besides Sonier's sick rats."

"What did you have in mind," Rex Montague asked.

"I don't know yet. Do we have any poll results from our survey about the TV special yet?"

"Our office staff will let us know as soon as it is available. What about this interlocutory appeal business? You know our Supreme

Court has hardly ever intervened in a trial at this stage. What do you propose to appeal?"

"I just want this whole trial to slow down and be continued to give us some time and space from the TV special." Napoli replied.

"Not likely to happen. The Judge has already denied our motion to continue. We'll start picking the jury this afternoon unless you have filed the interlocutory appeal and the Supreme Court thinks there is real prejudice. Given Judge Parson's findings, I doubt that will happen. It may be just a big waste of money and time."

"What do you care, Montague? You're getting paid."

"Then file away," said Rex Montague, shrugging his shoulders in resignation. "But I don't know how to write an appeal about nothing. Do you?"

"The studies are biased and prejudicial."

"Yes, but they are peer-reviewed and they were commissioned by the Canadian government. He's right. They do pass the Daubert test. He's going to allow them into evidence. We just have to find a way to convince the jury that they are biased or tainted in some way. Which they probably are not."

"I can handle that sneaky little Sonier," snarled Napoli.

"Then just do it," Montague said. "We have nothing to appeal at this point. Let's just bite the bullet, choose a jury and get this trial over with."

"Let's go back to your office and order some lunch," said Napoli, suddenly very subdued and thoughtful. "I need a glass of wine."

"Then we should go to your hotel. We don't allow liquor in the office," smiled Montague.

"Okay, let's go." Napoli picked up his briefcase and headed for the courtroom door. The legion of lawyers quickly followed.

Janet, Adam, and James met Pam and Larry Lawson across the street from the Denver City and County Building for brunch at the restaurant in the Art Museum. Pam and Larry were nervous and excited when James related the events of the morning.

"Is it going well?" Pam asked

"It's fine," Janet smiled. "But we haven't even selected one juror yet. The proof will still be in the pudding."

"What do you mean," asked Larry. "The animal studies will get into evidence. That proves our case, doesn't it."

"I never give predictions about what will happen in a jury trial," Janet cautioned. "You can't see into their minds or know their prejudices. We will just have to do our best to choose honest and sympathetic people. The defense attorneys will try to get those we like dismissed, so it is definitely not a sure thing."

"Well, I'm ready," said Pam "I'm ready to tell them my story, whatever happens."

Janet Stephenson reached across the table and patted her hand. "And a great story it is, Pam, my dear." She said softly, smiling at her frail client, whose blue eyes were bright and filled with hope.

Ten minutes after one in the evening, Janet, Adam, James, and the Lawsons arrived in Courtroom 1. Napoli and Montague were already at their table, pouring over the printouts of basic information about the jurors.

"Well, do we have an appeal?" Janet asked brightly.

"No appeal, Janet," answered Rex Montague. "It's full steam ahead."

"Did you advise the judge?" she asked him.

"Yes. We told his clerk that we were ready to proceed in selecting a jury."

Janet, Pam and Larry sat down at the counsel table for the Plaintiff, nearest the jury box. James and Adam were placing all of the jury selection materials on the table for Janet. Then they sat down right behind her, with notepads and pens, against the bar. They would be taking notes about the jurors as well.

The clerk came into the courtroom with two stacks to paper

"Here are the completed jury questionnaires for each of you," she said. "The judge would like you to be ready to begin voir dire in about half an hour. Will that give you enough time to review at least the first fourteen questionnaires or so?"

"I think so," said Janet.

"Should be fine, Amelia," said Montague, enforcing again his familiarity with the court.

Amelia smiled, "Let me know if you need a little more time, "she said "But the judge doesn't like to keep the jurors cooped up too long." She disappeared into the chambers behind the bench.

Janet took the questionnaires for jurors one through fifteen and divided the stack between herself, Larry and Pam. "You might find their responses to our questions interesting," said Pam. She read her stack, then traded with Pam and Larry. James and Adam were reading the next fifteen questionnaires and making notes on the jury selection charts. The jurors were seated in the jury box according to their numbers. James and Adam had prepared charts of the jury box on sheets and on a white erasable board, so that Janet could read their notes and write notes on the erasable board as jurors were chosen or dismissed. Pam and Larry had sheets of charts to note their comments as well.

Thirty five minutes later, jurors numbered one through thirteen filed in and took their respective seats in the jury box. The process had begun.

Janet Stephenson and Terry Napoli questioned the jurors about their medical histories, any legal matters in which they had been involved. They also asked each one about their knowledge of the case and whether they had any previous information about silicone gel breast implants. Surprisingly, only two of the first fourteen jurors admitted to having seen the television program about the PSS implants. After all, the special did air in the midst of both the baseball and football seasons. Janet wondered how truthful they actually were about that. If a juror would lie to get on a jury, that juror was a danger because he or she was a person who did not value truth over the opportunity to be a juror on a high profile case. Such a juror could be a dangerous juror for either side. The fact that there were five or six television trucks parked outside the courthouse and several TV crews in the hall outside the courtroom was not lost on the members of the jury panel. Everyone loves to have the fifteen minutes of fame which comes from appearing on the evening news, even if you can't say anything. Judge Parsons had issued instructions to the jurors that they were to be escorted out of the courtroom through a secluded back door and that they were to have no contact with the press, upon penalty of being dismissed from the jury if they were selected. He encouraged them to tell on each other if they had knowledge of infractions by fellow jurors.

To Napoli's continuing dismay, Judge Parsons also ordered that none of the parties or their counsel could speak to the press or the media until the verdict was in. He promised to issue sanctions and contempt orders if his rule was violated in any way. He also barred cameras and recording devices from the courtroom and placed a deputy at the door to enforce his order. Part of Napoli's strategy was to do press releases and to give interviews during any trial. However, Judge Parsons had decided long ago that this case would not be tried in the court of public opinion before there was a verdict in the actual case.

By the end of the day, they had seated four jurors: a man who was a physician's assistant, a house wife, a UPS delivery woman, and a waitress at IHOP. Napoli had used all but one of his preemptory challenges and Janet Stephenson still had two preemptory challenges left by the time Judge Parsons charged and excused the jury panel and the prospective jurors seated in the courtroom. He advised them that they must avoid all reports from any media source and that they could not discuss the case with anyone, including their spouses or significant others. Judge Parsons told all of the jurors to return to the jury assembly room by nine o'clock the next day. They filed out as Janet, James, Adam and the Lawsons stood. On the other side of the courtroom, only Terry Napoli and Rex Montague and two paralegals or attorneys remained. All of the additional cast of thousands had to vacate the courtroom to make room for the prospective jurors.

"Counsel, you may report at nine o'clock in the morning as well. We deserve a little later start tomorrow, and I have several matters that I need to deal with in other cases before we proceed with jury selection. See you tomorrow. We will be in recess." Judge Parson, in his customary style, left the courtroom through the door behind the bench.

Janet sent James out of the courtroom to survey the situation in the hall. Television crews were waiting for them to exit the courtroom and had their lights and cameras trained on the door.

"Pam and Larry, let me ask the judge's clerk if we can sneak out the private entrance," Janet said, after James reported the scene. Napoli and Montague were already outside, putting on a silent show for the press. "Adam, you and James should go out and see what Napoli is up to. I'll meet you at the car." They smiled and hurried out of the courtroom to tail Napoli and Montague, making sure they followed Judge Parson's order.

Janet, Larry and Pam were escorted by Amelia to the hall and private exit, used by the judges from Courtrooms One, Two and Three. They emerged from a door to the courtyard by Cherokee Street, on the west side of the building. No reporters were in sight. All of the television vans were in the front and on the south side of the City and County Building. They crossed the street quickly and made it to the parking lot without being discovered. Pam and Larry said goodbye and Janet waited for her paralegals. James and Adam soon appeared with the briefcases and other trial materials.

"It's a zoo!" Adam exclaimed.

"I can tell that Napoli is dying to talk to the reporters. He was taking a lot of time to say that he couldn't say anything. "James laughed.

"Montague looks like he could bite nails, but even he was smiling for the camera," said Adam.

"Well, at least Pam and Larry missed the chaos. I am a little worried about Pam having enough stamina to make it through this trial. She looked beat by the time they left." Janet said.

"Can we eat?" asked James.

"Sure," Janet laughed. "What did you have in mind? I'll call and see if Brad is home and if he can meet us somewhere."

"North Woods Inn or Macaroni Grill," suggested Adam.

"I'm happy with anything," James said. "I'm just starving."

"Brad likes the North Woods, Inn and we won't need reservations." Janet was waiting for Brad to answer his cell phone. "Hi, honey, so you are home! "she said brightly, "Want to meet us for dinner and debrief our day?"

"Sure, where?" answered her husband.

"North Woods Inn?"

"Sounds good. How far away are you?"

"We're thirty minutes away, just getting on Santa Fe."

"See you there," Brad said.

"We're ready for tomorrow," Janet said, "So, let's just relax tonight. All in all, it was a very good day."

Adam and James agreed.

Dr. Jean Sonier and Dr. Richard Guilliot had spent the day in making plans with Amy Larabee, Joel Steiner and Rick Plume to entice Forrest Winchester into their web. They had already arranged for Winchester to drop off money for Lecroix, presumably to finish the job of doing away with Dr. Jean Sonier before he could testify. As the day passed, several plans had been floated as trial balloons and discarded. All of the communications had to be by email because Jean Sonier was not about to reveal his whereabouts or meet with Amy Larabee and the Denver law enforcement people in person. Dr. Sonier did not trust anyone, and his portly French-Canadian friend only trusted Jean Sonier.

"Richard, the bottom line is that we have to be there to testify whenever Janet Stephenson needs us. The rest of this is cream on the pudding, as you might say." Sonier said to Guilliot.

"I agree, so you must just tell me what it is we must do or must not do, Jean, as I lead a very sheltered life at the University and in my lab. I have no knowledge of these, how do you say, intrigues." Guilliot smiled at the worried face of Sonier. "But I do request," he continued, "that we should travel together because I do not know how to get from anywhere to anywhere in this city. I know not even where we are, for sure."

Sonier and Guilliot had dinner at the Bennigan's restaurant on Wadsworth, near their hotel. They had also spent some time at

Janet Stephenson's office which was up the street on Wadsworth, from the restaurant. Janet had given Sonier a key to her offices at his request months earlier. When he was in Denver, he used the office as a secret headquarters, often coming there late at night when he arrived in Denver and sleeping on the couch in Janet's office. Because the offices were a converted ranch style mansion, there were several complete bathrooms with tubs and showers and other amenities. Jean Sonier even had a closet where the law office staff collected the umbrellas, jackets, toiletries and other items that he often left behind, and where he often stowed his suitcase. Janet had come to her office several times and found Dr. Sonier, en route to somewhere, enjoying a cup of tea on the office patio or working on his laptop in the kitchen area. As far as either of them knew, no one else knew that he used the offices as his own.

That night, after dinner, Dr. Sonier and Dr. Guilliot went to Janet's office, while Janet, Brad, James and Adam were at the Northwoods Inn, and shared a bottle of wine, listening to the night birds on the patio of Janet Stephenson's office. Then they returned to the hotel, for a good night's sleep.

In the morning, just as he had finished shaving, Jean Sonier's cell phone rang.

"Dr. Sonier?" asked Amy Larabee.

"Yes," he replied curtly.

"I wanted to call, rather than email our latest plan. I think this one will work."

"What do you propose?" asked Sonier.

"We would like to have Lecroix make a call to Winchester and ask him to call you to come and meet him for lunch or coffee in a crowded spot, such as Larimer Square, to make you a proposition. Lecroix will then advise Winchester that he will arrange a fatal accident for you. We need to tie Winchester to the act of an attempt on your life as well as the money drop."

"Lorna, my wife, would never approve of such a scheme. So much can go wrong."

"But, you will be safe because Lecroix will be with us and he has no actual plan to do you harm. It is all needed so that we can have Winchester arrested for participation in the plan to murder you."

"What about Guilliot? He must be with me as he is not comfortable staying here alone."

"That's fine. You can both have a nice lunch in Larimer Square after we arrest Winchester."

"How will it be reasonable for Lecroix or Winchester to have my cell phone number, Isn't that a flaw in your plan?"

"Expert witness lists must include telephone numbers. Lecroix can tell Winchester that he got your number from the PSS witness list at their offices in Santa Barbara. I don't think that Winchester will know that only your office number must be listed. What do you think?"

"I think that Winchester will smell the rat in the cupboard and will not do it. That is what I think, but perhaps he is not so bright as I give him credit for being. Will Lecroix do what you say?"

"That part is a given," Amy Larabee laughed. "He's trying to get out of this with his skin and it is touch and go?"

"When would you propose this should take place?" asked the skeptical scientist.

"Today if possible. We don't want to give him too much time to think about it. We'd like to get him to call you this morning. What do you think?"

"Well, it is worth a try, I suppose."

Dr. Sonier shut his cell phone and went to knock on Guilloit's door, between their rooms. Guilliot was ready for breakfast and was reading the USA Today, which appeared each morning outside their doors.

"Richard, I have something to discuss with you," Sonier said.

Just as Jean Sonier finished telling Guilloit about the plan, Sonier's telephone rang.

"Hello," he said, looking very serious.

"Dr. Sonier?" Winchester asked.

"This is Jean Sonier. Who's calling?"

"Dr. Sonier, this is Forrest Winchester. I don't think we have actually spoken face to face, although I was present at your deposition in a case in Chicago. Do you recall?"

"I know who you are, Mr. Winchester," Dr. Sonier replied. "How did you get my number? I think we are not on the same team and I am not so sure we should be speaking at all."

"Your phone number is on the expert witness list for the Pamela Lawson trial. Are you in Denver?"

"Why should I reveal my whereabouts to you, sir?" Dr. Sonier was firm.

"Well, I am calling you in hopes that you will be in Denver soon and that we could have lunch or coffee to discuss some important matters. I thought you were on the witness list to testify soon."

"What sort of matters could I possibly be interested in discussing with you, Mr. Winchester?"

"I would feel more comfortable discussing them in person, Dr. Sonier.

"And I am not so certain I would be at all comfortable to meet you in person, Mr. Winchester."

"Would you agree to have coffee with me or lunch in the Larimer Square downtown?" There are a lot of people there and it would seem a casual meeting."

"When?"

"If you are in town, I would suggest meeting you at the Starbucks coffee shop in Larimer Square, say, ten thirty this morning?"

"I am as curious as a cat, you might say, sir, and I will agree to come only because of that. I cannot imagine that there is anything that you could properly propose to me. I will be coming into the downtown area with Dr. Guilliot, and I suppose that I could divert into the Starbucks at about ten thirty. If you are there at that time, perhaps we could have a brief word in passing."

"Super! I'll see you then."

"Goodbye, Mr. Winchester."

Forrest Winchester hung up the phone and said to himself, "Yes!" Then he quickly dialed Lecroix's cell phone. It rang.

"Lecroix here."

"Raoul, he's coming to the Starbucks in Larimer Square at ten thirty. I know he will not be late if anything he'll be early."

"That works. I will take it from here. You just be there at a table."

"What are you going to do?"

"I think you ordered an accident, preferably fatal if I recall."

"Yes, yes, don't tell me anything more. I'll be there. Guilliot will be coming downtown with him, but only Sonier is coming to Starbucks."

"You've only paid for one accident."

"I know, I know—just FYI."

"Goodbye," Raoul hung up and handed the telephone to Amy Larabee.

At ten thirty in the morning, Jean Sonier approached the Starbucks coffee shop on Larimer Street. Through the glass storefront he could see Forrest Winchester sitting at a table by the wall. Dr. Sonier did not see that Raoul Lecroix was at the counter, acting as though he was trying to decide what to order. Sonier felt a bit dizzy with anxiety as he pushed open the door. Winchester saw him and beckoned to him. Just as Dr. Sonier started for the table, Joel Steiner appeared from nowhere, wearing a Starbucks apron. Winchester ignored him and smiled at Sonier, "Sit down, Dr. Sonier," he said.

Jean Sonier stood frozen and silent as Joel Steiner took off his apron and walked swiftly to Winchester's table. Suddenly Winchester stood up and pulled a gun from his jacket pocket. Dr. Jean Sonier threw himself on the floor and slithered under a table. Joel Steiner grabbed Winchester's arm and the gun discharged, hitting the light fixture in the middle of the room. Glass rained around the table under which Sonier was lying face down.

From behind the counter, two undercover police officers grabbed Raoul Lecroix and two more customers jumped up from the next table and grabbed Winchester. They showed him their badges,

"Forrest Winchester, you are under arrest for conspiracy to commit murder and for the attempted murder of Dr. Jean Sonier. You have the right to remain silent. Anything you say can and will be used against you. You have the right to an attorney. If you cannot afford an attorney, one will be appointed for you."

Winchester struggled for a moment, then collapsed into a chair.

"I had a feeling that something was up. I should have trusted my gut and not this gun. I only brought it just in case . . . I don't know what happened . . . Damn you, Raoul."

Amy Larabee and Richard Guilliot waited outside the window, where a curious crowd had gathered, until Winchester was taken away in a police car. Then they both came inside to rescue the frazzled little scientist. Dr. Jean Sonier was sitting at a table, with a glass of water belonging to a former patron, in front of him. The police were directing traffic and pedestrians away from the front door. A real Starbucks employee was sweeping up the glass from the light fixture.

"I shall have to explain this to Lorna." Sonier said glumly. "She is not going to be, as you say, a happy camper. But at least I got away with all my skin intact."

"You were fabulous, Dr. Sonier," said Amy Larabee. "Dr. Guilliot, let's get the two of you to someplace where you can relax a bit."

"Nothing ever goes as planned when PSS is involved," said Sonier.

"It is good, my friend." Richard Guilliot was patting his friend on the shoulder. "You were a regular cowboy, ducking under a barroom table!"

"Enough, Richard." Sonier was not amused. "This is more excitement than I bargained for."

Joel Steiner joined them after he had sent the police cars on their way.

"I was afraid that he had a gun, that's why I intervened," Joel told Jean Sonier.

"A very perceptive move, I might add," Jean Sonier was wiping his brow with his handkerchief. "I did not see the gun until he pulled it from his pocket."

"We are trained to look for those things, Dr. Sonier. Don't feel bad."

"I thought for a moment that I was a goner, as you say, since I did not realize that you were a policeman, with the apron on. A clever, though obvious, decoy. I must humbly thank you for saving my life. My Lorna will be most appreciative. But wasn't Winchester supposed to be relying on Raoul to do the dirty business?"

Amy smiled at him. "The best-laid plans . . . Dr. Sonier. But I do apologize to you. If we had noticed sooner that he might be carrying a gun, we would have called it all off. I would have called you on your cell phone to divert you from showing up."

"Well, all's well that ends well if we are going to persist in quoting English and Scottish poets." Dr. Sonier offered his first smile of the morning.

"On another topic," said Richard Guilliot, "Has anyone had information about how the Pamela Lawson trial is progressing? Jean and I are to be among the first witnesses, and I would have to say that we have been on a detour and not precisely attending to the business of preparing our testimony."

"Perhaps having Raoul Lecroix and Forrest Winchester in custody will give you some peace of mind!' Joel Steiner said. "I will give Janet Stephenson a call and leave her a voice mail to fill her in. I dare say she may know about what is happening with Winchester before his attorneys know. It all depends on which counsel he calls after booking and processing. In any case, it's all going to take a very interesting turn, I'd wager."

"Dr. Sonier, could I give you and Dr. Guilliot a lift? It's the least I can do after all that you have done for us today." Amy Larabee looked at the two men, who were obviously totally out of their element. "We could stop for some lunch at a more secluded place if you like…. It's on the U.S. Government."

"How could we refuse?" Sonier smiled at her. "Then let's be off, my friend, we have our work to do." He patted Dr. Guilliot on the back. Guilliot smiled at his colleague, who seemed more like himself.

But there was nothing on the television news about the incident and nothing in the Rocky Mountain News or Denver Post. Rick Plume, the district attorney, needed as little publicity as possible if he wanted a successful grand jury proceeding. It was just a crazy tourist who had accidentally discharged his gun in Starbucks and no one knew he was the CEO of Conway Chemical. Even Terry Napoli and Rex Montague did not know that their boss was in jail, as they continued picking a jury for the trial in Judge Parsons courtroom, less than a mile away. Jennifer Fordham and Jerry Carson were in the courtroom, representing PSS. Jennifer had called Winchester's cell phone several times, but there was no answer.

"He'll surely call me tonight." She thought to herself.

Winchester did not call Jennifer. Instead, he called Terry Napoli from the police station and left a message on his cell phone voice mail.

"Napoli, I am in the Denver County Jail. I need you, or some attorney, immediately. I have to get out of here," he said.

But, Napoli's telephone remained off until he returned to his hotel room that night. He turned on his telephone to call his wife and the message waiting alarm beeped loudly. He listened to the message twice to make sure he understood it. Then, feeling somewhat nauseous, he sat down on his bed. "What the hell is going on!" he said out loud to no one. Then he dialed Rex Montague's cell phone. Montague didn't answer, so Napoli called his home.

Montague answered the phone. "Rex Montague."

"Rex, I just had a disturbing message on my cell phone from Mr. Winchester. He's in the Denver Jail. He needs someone to bail him out"

"What? What for?"

"He didn't say. Do you have any criminal lawyers in your firm?"

"A few," Montague answered. "I'll call Lance Rivera, he's new, but he used to be with the D.A.'s office. I'll arrange to meet him at the City jail? Do you want to come?"

"God, no!" Napoli replied. "I don't know what I could possibly do."

"He called you, Terry, perhaps he needs to talk to you."

Napoli felt sick.

"Just call me on my cell if you need me. I need to get ready for tomorrow. That's what he's paying me for and that trial is going forward, regardless of what is happening to Forrest Winchester."

Montague called his colleague, Lance Rivera, on his cell phone. Lance was just finishing dinner at a Lodo restaurant and he agreed to go straight to the Denver City and County jail, which was just behind the Courthouse on Cherokee Street. When Rex Montague got to the jail, Rivera was in the lobby talking to Rick Plume, his old boss, and detective, Joel Steiner.

"Hey, Rex," Lance greeted Montague. "Seems we have a bit of a situation on our hands."

"Hello, Rick," Montague shook his hand.

"Detective Joel Steiner, Investigations DPD," Rick introduced Steiner.

"Glad to meet you," Rex Montague offered his hand and notice the firm confidence of the shake he received from the detective in return.

"What's up?" Montague tried to appear calm and confident.

Rick Plume looked at the obviously tired Rex Montague and said "It appears that your client, Mr. Winchester, took a shot at Dr. Jean Sonier, Janet Stephenson's star witness in the Larimer Square Starbucks today, but that's not all. Now that he is in custody, we also have a subpoena for him to appear before the Grand Jury."

Rex Montague looked at him in stunned surprise. "What on earth do you mean, Rick?"

"It's true. Winchester took out a gun and shot at Dr. Sonier, after inviting him to meet with him at Starbucks. Sonier dived under a table and was not hurt, but Winchester is in jail." Rick then continued, "I have a subpoena for him to testify before a secret Grand Jury in the morning, or sometime tomorrow, so he's not going anywhere. Besides, he must be arraigned before bail can be set because we are going to ask for remand because he is an obvious flight risk. He'd be out of our jurisdiction like a flash if we let him out of jail."

Montague looked as though he had seen a ghost. He was stunned.

"I don't know what to say because we are not his personal attorneys. We only represent PSS, purchased by his company Conway Chemical, in the case brought by Pamela Lawson. I think we need to get him in touch with his personal attorneys."

"Who might that be?" asked Rick Plume.

"I don't have a clue. I'll give Terry Napoli a call because it might be his firm."

Rex Montague walked across the lobby and sat down on a bench. He took out his cell phone and pushed the speed dial 6 for Terry Napoli.

"Napoli, here," he answered

"Terry, we've got a big problem here. Winchester is in jail for trying to shoot Dr. Jean Sonier at a downtown Starbucks, after enticing him there. Moreover, Rick Plume has served him with a subpoena to testify before a secret Grand Jury. What the hell is going on here?" Montague's voice was incredulous.

It took Terry Napoli several minutes to get his bearings. Then he responded, "Rex, I don't have any idea. Can you get him out of jail so that we can talk to him?"

"Doesn't seem possible tonight. The D.A., Rick Plume, is here himself, so this must be a pretty big deal. Plume is going to ask that Winchester be held in custody because he considers him to be a flight risk. I guess I would have to agree, wouldn't you? I certainly wouldn't like to be charged with keeping him in Colorado."

"Can you talk to him there?'

"Not unless we enter an appearance as his attorneys. We are not his personal counsel. Do you know who is?"

"I suppose that would be our firm. Is this Lance Rivera any good? Could he handle this?"

"Yes, he is top-notch. However, not to be crass, but our firm would need a substantial retainer given the scope of what appears to be going on."

"Of course. Why don't you go ahead there and see if you and your associate can talk to Winchester and figure out what is happening."

"All right. At least we can withdraw if it appears that there is a conflict of some kind with the Lawson case, or anything else, for that matter."

"Call me back later and let me know what's going on."

"I will. This certainly is not going to help our case if it gets out."

"It will get out. Let's just hope that we have a jury picked first. We still have three more to seat, so I hope you can keep the press out of it for one more day."

"Plume said it was a secret grand jury, so that may mean that he will be interested in squelching any publicity as well."

"Secret, eh? Well, that could be good for the short term and bad in the long run. Just let me know."

Montague walked back across the lobby. "Well, Lance, it looks as though we represent Mr. Winchester for the present. Rick, can you arrange for us to talk to him in private?"

"Sure thing, Rex. He's in a holding area right now. Detective Steiner, can you show them to an interview room and arrange for them to meet with Winchester?"

"Yep, come with me." Rex Montague and Lance Rivera followed Joel Steiner through the security and disappeared down the hall. Rick Plume sat down on a chair next to the wall and took his cell phone out of his pocket. After scrolling down his directory, he dialed Janet Stephenson's number.

"Janet, Rick Plume, here. Just thought you might like to know that Montague and his associate, Lance Rivera, have just asked to meet with Winchester as his counsel and that I am going to arrange to have an arraignment in the morning."

"Hey, Rick. Wow, that's interesting. Will he be free after the arraignment? I know he is on the witness list for PSS, but not for a while - and we haven't even finished jury selection, although we should have a jury by early afternoon tomorrow."

"I'm asking that he be kept in custody, without bail, until we finish at the Grand Jury. I wouldn't give a wooden nickel for the chances that he wouldn't be gone out of the country, even if we get his passport, which he likely doesn't even have here."

"Did he really try to kill Dr. Sonier?"

"If he were a better shot, he would have. Steiner was there undercover and grabbed Winchester, gun and all. Dr. Sonier disappeared immediately under a table. I guess it was like a movie."

"I just spoke to Dr. Sonier. He seems to have regained his composure and his perspective. I was afraid he might get on the next plane to Ottowa and be done with this, but it looks as though he's going to come through, true to form. He really is an amazing man."

"We need more people like Dr. Sonier. Well, Jan, good luck. I'll keep you up on what happens or Amy Larabee will."

"Thanks, Rick. Talk to you soon."

Janet Stephenson hung up the phone and turned to Brad, who was reading the newspaper in a chair across the room.

"Let's turn on the news and see if there is any mention of all of this." She suggested.

Janet got up and went into the TV room, as they called it and turned on Channel 7 news. She repeatedly clicked through all of the local channels, surveying all of the stories and found no mention except a cell phone photo of the front of Starbucks and a brief mention that a tourist had discharged a firearm there and had been taken away by police, on Channel 9.

"If only they knew who this "tourist" really is!" she mused out loud to no one. Brad had fallen asleep in the living room.

"Tomorrow is another day," she thought to herself and went to wake her sleeping husband and propel him up the stairs to bed.

Leslie Winchester hung up the phone, after speaking to her husband who called her from the Denver City and County jail and fixed herself a martini.

"Forrest, Forrest." she said quietly. "What have you gotten yourself into now?"

Leslie Winchester was having her second martini when she got the call she was expecting from Terry Napoli.

"Hello, Mrs. Winchester. I apologize for calling you at this late hour, but I was certain that you would like to have an update on the situation with Mr. Winchester and he had advised us that he had made his one allotted call to you already."

"I heard from Forrest, but he didn't tell me much, Mr. Napoli. Exactly what is going on?"

"I understand this is very upsetting to you…"

"Never mind that, just tell me what's happening. What did Forrest do?"

"He called Dr. Sonier, the Canadian scientist to ask him to a meeting and when Dr. Sonier came to the coffee shop, Mr. Winchester apparently took a gun out of his pocket and fired. He didn't hit Dr. Sonier, but the police have arrested him for conspiracy and attempted murder."

"Merciful God! Why did he do that? Are you sure it was him?"

"The Starbucks was full of undercover police officers. It appears to have been some sort of sting operation set up by the Denver police, using Raoul Lecroix."

"Who is Raoul Lecroix?" Leslie Winchester asked impatiently.

"He is a Canadian, who was extradited from Chicago to Denver. Although we don't have the complete story yet. It appears that he worked or works for PSS, the Company that makes the polyurethane implants, recently acquired by your company."

"Yes, yes, "Leslie said "The Pamela Lawson trial. Isn't Dr. Sonier that scientist with the rats who was on the Emily O'Brien TV special?"

"Yes, and he is one of the first witnesses that will be called in the trial, which is why he is in Denver. But there's more. It seems that after he was arrested, your husband was served with a subpoena to testify before a secret Denver grand jury. Do you have any idea what that might be about?"

"I have no earthly idea. I don't think Forrest has hardly ever been to Denver, except on the way to Vail or Aspen for ski vacations. Whatever could that be about? When is that going to happen? Where is Forrest?"

"He's still in jail. The District Attorney will not agree to bail until after the grand jury testimony because he is afraid that Forrest will leave the jurisdiction and not come back. He apparently is not essential to the Lawson case and he has been deleted from the witness list."

"Can't you get him out of jail? Is that Constitutional?"

"We are trying. Rex Montague has a young criminal attorney in his firm, Lance Rivera, who used to be at the district attorney's office and knows Rick Plume, the D.A., and most of the people there. He is handling Forrest's case. I'm having a criminal attorney from our firm come out to Denver, but criminal law is state-specific, so a Chicago criminal lawyer is not of much use here."

"But isn't there habeas corpus, or something so he doesn't have to be there with common criminals?"

"Under the law, he is treated as everyone else. Rick Plume will likely be able to keep him in jail until he is required to appear at the grand jury—for whatever reason they have."

"I suppose that means that I must come immediately to Denver." Leslie sighed.

"I'm afraid that I agree. We need you here for moral support for him, but also as the corporate representative in the Lawson trial."

"Don't you have Jennifer Fordham and her assistant there?"

"Yes, but it is good PR to have someone from Conway. Do you have someone else that you could send?"

"Not that I would trust in this mess!" Leslie sighed again. "But, I warn you that I am not much 'moral support' for Forrest. What could he be thinking? What is going on?"

"I'm trying to find out. I am just as blindsided by this as you. When do you think you can be here?"

"I will look into getting a flight sometime tomorrow and I will let you know. Give me your cell phone number, Mr. Napoli."

"It is 312-833-7878, but it will be off all the time I am in court tomorrow. You should call Teresa, Mr. Montague's secretary and she will get a message to me. That number is 303-733-6000."

"What's happening in the trial? Forrest didn't know or couldn't talk about it."

"We are finishing jury selection and opening statements may begin tomorrow. We are just hoping that none of this gets in the news. So far, it has not been covered. There was just a brief note about a tourist firing a gun randomly at Starbucks. But eventually it will be a huge story, so be prepared."

"All right, thank you, Mr. Napoli. I'll call you tomorrow. Can Montague's office send a car to the airport for me?"

"Just call Teresa in the morning and tell her what arrangements you need. She'll take care of you. You will like her."

"Thanks, Mr. Napoli. Good night"

Leslie Winchester fixed a third martini, and went upstairs to her suite. She curled up on the plum colored velvet couch in her sitting room and thought about Forrest, and what had become of their marriage. What had become of the handsome, funny and intelligent young man she had married? Now he was distant and obsessed by making money. He rarely talked to her about anything he was doing and rarely invited her to travel with him anymore. When she met him, she was public relations director for Conway Chemical and he was the new marketing manager. As he moved up in the ranks, he encouraged her to "retire" from going to the office everyday and finally, someone replaced her and she became a woman of leisure taking care of the 'home'—only it was an empty shell because they had no children. And over time, she realized she also had no husband.

"It's a beautiful house," she said to herself, "but it is not, by any stretch of the imagination, a home."

The next morning, Leslie called Teresa, and arranged to fly to Denver, arriving at six o'clock in the evening Teresa arranged a suite for her at the Brown Palace Hotel and arranged for her to be picked up and served by a limousine service while she was in Denver. That kept her at a safe distance from the hotel where all of the Lawson trial lawyers were staying, and out of the restaurants and bars being frequented by the many young lawyers Conway Chemical was paying to try the Lawson case. It seemed better that way, to Teresa.

However, the only way for Leslie to speak with her husband was to go to the Denver City and County jail. She wisely chose to make the trip by cab, wearing jeans, a dark blue turtle neck sweater and sneakers, with a jaunty, casual navy corduroy cap covering her hair. She looked nothing like the Leslie Winchester who stepped out of first class at DIA, wearing a full length mink and a diamond bracelet, who was whisked away through a private exit to her limousine.

Her visit with Forrest was in a bleak tan interview room. She had expected to meet with him on the other side of a glass barrier, but it was better than that. Forrest was not particularly glad to see her.

"You can help me most by getting me out of here." he snarled.

"Sweetheart, it sounds as though it will be tough for anyone to do that, since you shot at someone in front of about a gazillion policemen. What possessed you to do such a thing?"

"Little bastard, Sonier. He makes me crazy. His damn rats can change our world, Leslie"

"Your world, my dear. Not necessarily mine. I didn't shoot at anyone, or even decide to buy the stupid company that makes those implants. You never even discussed the acquisition of PSS with me. All I have to do is divorce you, my pet, and our prenuptial agreement leaves you strictly to your own devices, pun intended --- polyurethane-coated though they may be."

"Ha, ha." Forrest said scornfully, but a twinge of real panic went through him. "Now, Leslie, everything I have done has been for you and for the company."

"Don't even go there, Forrest." She held up her hand in front of his face. "I'm not involved in this, except as it relates to my having to, perhaps, appear at the Lawson trial. All this cloak and dagger stuff with this Lecroix guy, whoever he is, and the shooting of witnesses, is all your bag. I, frankly, don't want any part of it --- or perhaps, of you. And, on that little matter, my love, the jury is still out."

"Leslie, just find a way to get me out on bail. That's all I need at this point. It will all work out fine, you'll see." Forrest Winchester pleaded.

"Napoli said that the lawyers are trying to get you out. But, apparently, this secret grand jury thing is the hold-up. What is that about?"

"Your guess is as good as mine. I have no idea."

"My bet is that you do, but you are just not telling me."

"Leslie, I think you are tired. Let's talk about this tomorrow."

Just then the police officer came to the door and advised Leslie that her time to visit had expired.

"Come tomorrow?"

"Probably," was all she said.

Leslie had noted in the cab that it was not far from the Brown Palace Hotel to the jail. She decided to ask for directions and walk back to the hotel. It was a nice walk, through the uptown Denver streets, which are all at a peculiar angle, she noted to herself. She stopped at a little pub called "Duffy's Tavern" and had a Guinness and fish and chips on her way back. It was a restful distraction to sit alone and listen to the lively conversations of the local patrons, many of whom seemed to be attorneys and legal office staff, who had not yet made their way home from happy hour. When she arrived at the Brown Palace, the doorman opened the door for her and smiled. She smiled back, thinking that under other circumstances she could like this city. When she got to her suite, her telephone was blinking. There were three messages from Terry Napoli. She called him back on his cell phone.

"Mrs. Winchester, I was hoping that you could have dinner with Rex Montague and me, but now it seems a little late for dinner."

"I grabbed a bite on my way back from the jail," Leslie replied.

"Would you be up for a drink? There's a great place in your hotel called Ship Tavern and Rex and I could meet you there."

"Yes, I saw it when I came in. Okay, I could do that. When will you be here?"

"Fifteen minutes, okay?"

"Yes, that will be fine. I'll meet you down at the Ship Tavern in fifteen minutes."

Leslie changed from her jeans into black slacks and a black sweater. She put on a turquoise necklace and matching earrings. As she walked into the Ships Tavern, more persons than just Terry Napoli and Rex Montague noted that she was a beautiful woman. Both men stood as she approached and Rex pulled out a chair for her.

"Good evening, gentlemen," she said, without smiling.

"How was your trip? Is everything acceptable with your room?" Rex asked her.

"Fine, fine. It's a fabulous hotel. I love it." Now she smiled. "I saw Forrest. "she continued. "What is going on?"

"We just came from the jail," said Napoli. "Shall we order first? What would you like?"

"Martini, with an olive," Leslie said. "I'd rather have a Guinness," she thought.

The waiter came and took their drink orders and left a basket of snacks.

"As I was saying, we just saw Mr. Winchester. And I smell a rat," said Napoli.

Leslie frowned, "Why? Forrest was caught pretty much red-handed shooting a gun at Dr. Sonier. Thank God he didn't hit him! What more is there than that?"

"It appears that the FBI and a Denver Police Detective set the deal up. Mr. Winchester said he had a call from Lecroix, his Canadian colleague, a product distributor, who asked him to set up a meeting with Dr. Sonier. Lecroix said he was out on bail, that is why he was free to call. We found out by accident that Lecroix is still in jail. We think the police had Lecroix call and set up the meeting. As I mentioned to you on the phone, it looks like a sting operation."

"But, even if that were true, it was Forrest who took out the gun and started shooting. How do you get him out of that? And why is Lecroix in jail? What does that have to do with anything?"

"We haven't figured it all out yet. It was clearly temporary insanity. But, the fact is that no one was hurt." added Rex Montague.

"By the grace of God alone." said Leslie "But, I think Forrest knows more than he is saying. What is the subpoena for testimony before a secret grand jury about?"

Napoli took a drink of his scotch. "We don't know, yet. But we are trying to find out."

"The problem is that we have to defend the Lawson case, which has to be our primary focus for the next few days or weeks." said Rex, "However, Lance Rivera, from our firm will be looking after Mr. Winchester's case. He would like to meet with you sometime tomorrow if that is acceptable to you."

"Sure. Whatever you need." Leslie nodded her head.

"He couldn't meet with us tonight, but he'll call you in the morning to set up a time. You don't need to be in court with us until after the jury is seated. That will be, likely, day after tomorrow. We're expecting to do opening statements then." Montague said kindly.

Suddenly Leslie was very tired and longing to go to her room and be alone.

"If that is all, gentlemen, I think I'd like to turn in. It's been a long day."

"Of course," they said in unison. Both men stood up as she gathered her bag and rose to leave.

"I'm sure I'll see both of you soon. I'll look forward to Mr. Rivera's call."

"Good night" they said and she disappeared into the lobby.

"There is a real lady," said Rex Montague.

Terry Napoli nodded. He wished that she were in charge. Perhaps now she would be.

By two thirty in the afternoon the next day, Janet Stephenson and Terry Napoli had finished picking the jury. It consisted of a man who was a physician's assistant, a female UPS driver, a waitress, a housewife, a man who owned a landscaping company, a woman who provided in-home health assistance, a woman college student, an assistant coach for the Denver Broncos, a man who was a CPA and had just been married three years with two, small children, a woman who was a personal trainer, a retired United Methodist minister, a female aerospace engineer, and a man who owned a hair and nail salon. They made up a jury of twelve with one alternate. The jury included every gender, race, ethnic group, and socio-economic class in the Denver area. By all standards, it was nearly a perfectly balanced jury, which did not appear to lean toward either party. The defendant had requested a jury of twelve and was paying the additional cost. Napoli's theory and the conventional wisdom of defendants is that it is more difficult to convince twelve people than it is to convince six. Janet Stephenson had always believed that sword cuts both ways.

Janet looked at the jury as she had begun to look at all juries. It was her opinion, based on the cases that she had tried in the past ten years, that there is no unifying ethic or moral basis for decision making remaining in our society. People lie to get on juries. People lie to get off juries and people come into jury service with private agendas and prejudices which are virtually impossible to discern in the process of jury selection. In short, juries are a crapshoot. She would rather trust the determination of any case to a reasonable, experienced judge. But PSS had made a jury demand, so it had to be a jury trial. But that only meant that you could put on a more dramatic play. Judges were often annoyed by the theatrics that trial lawyers use regularly to sway the opinions of juries. A further problem was that Janet had discovered, being a female trial attorney, that she was expected to dress, appear and act as the female attorneys on Law and Order, Boston Legal and other television courtroom dramas looked and behaved. She had a dress code and grooming standards that were set not by the court but by television. Although it annoyed her greatly, Janet Stephenson refused to do anything which would prejudice her clients. If the jury expected her to look like a television lawyer, she could do that. However, she did draw the line at high heels. Men get to wear comfortable shoes in the courtroom, and so did she. Besides, Janet loved expensive suits, pantsuits, and silk blouses, with matching accessories. Trials gave her an excuse to do serious shopping without the massive buyer's remorse, which afflicted her after every shopping trip. Brad, surprisingly, agreed and encouraged her to shop even more than she did. He did, however, complain about her overly full closets.

At two thirty in the afternoon, Judge Parsons seated all of the chosen jurors in the jury box and had them raise their right hands and take the oath to be faithful jurors and uphold the Constitution of the United States and of the State of Colorado.

"You have been chosen as jurors in this case," he then told them, "and that is one of the highest duties of a citizen in our democracy. You have been chosen as the fact finders in this very complex and important case. You will hear the testimony of witnesses, you will be shown exhibits, scientific studies and you will hear the testimony of expert witnesses. Those are the witnesses who are allowed to give you their opinions about scientific, medical, or other complicated matters. You are the ones who will make the determination as to whether testimony, exhibits, and other evidence makes sense, or is credible. You may also decide that you do not believe a witness or evidence. In other words, it is your job to decide what the facts in this case are. At the end of the case, I will instruct you on the law that you must apply to the facts in order to come up with a verdict in this case. It will require your full attention and it will require that you are honest and courageous. You must take the duty of being a juror very seriously. Finally, you may not discuss this case with each other or any other person until I give the case to you. There will be newspaper articles and television stories about this case. I ask that you do not watch or read anything about this trial or related to this trial until I give the case to you. Then you may discuss it only with each other. I have also, ladies and gentlemen, made another very difficult decision. I have decided that the jury in this case must be sequestered until the trial is over. That means that we will be putting you up at a very nice hotel and providing you with all your meals until this trial is over. I am going to allow you to have television sets, but the cable news channels will be blocked and news programs from local channels will be blocked. I know that this is a hardship for all of you, but this case is a very important case and it would be very expensive for all parties to have a mistrial and be forced to try the case again. You may go home after I release you and reassemble here at five thirty in the evening, so that you can pack your bags and get reading material and other conveniences. You will be kept and transported together, but I remind you again that you may not discuss this case during the trial. In consideration of your inconvenience, we will also arrange for entertainment for you on weekends, such as plays, baseball games, movies and the like, but again, you may not discuss this case. We will not continue the trial through the weekends because the attorneys need that time to recoup, as do I. Do you have any questions?"

The CPA, with the young wife and small children, raised his hand.

"Yes, Juror Number Six?"

"Will we be able to see our families on weekends and evenings, Your Honor? I have very small children and my wife needs my help in the evenings?"

"I will allow families to come and have dinner with you at the hotel and I will allow family members to join you for activities on weekends, at their cost. However, you may need to arrange for a mother's helper or family member to help your wife at other times. There is a hardship fund which can help defray some of that cost for you. I know it is a hardship, but you have been chosen for a very important duty as a citizen of our country. Our justice system does not work without the sacrifice of citizens as jurors."

"I understand, Your Honor. I'm sure we can work it out somehow." He smiled. That made Janet feel much better. Nothing is worse than having an angry, bitter juror in a long trial.

"I must also make it clear to you, "Judge Parsons added, "Neither of the parties in this case have requested sequestration. This is solely my action and it is based on my assessment of certain facts and other matters that I cannot share with you. Trust me, it is better this way. You must not hold this against either the Plaintiff or the Defendant in this case. If you are put out with anyone, you must direct your displeasure toward me."

Both Janet Stephenson and Terry Napoli were shocked that the judge had decided to sequester the jury. Both knew the resentment of sequestered jurors, but both of them knew that there were extenuating circumstances, namely the arrest of Forrest Winchester. The judge must know, although neither Stephenson, nor Napoli had mentioned anything about it. What else did the judge know?

The waitress raised her hand.

"Yes, Juror Number Three."

"What hotel will we be staying at?"

"The final arrangements will be made and you will be advised when you come back here at five thirty. I don't mean to be secretive, but frankly, I don't know at this point. We are still working on it. I just made the decision to sequester the jury during the lunch recess, so it is taking a bit of effort to get your arrangements made. I really don't want to make a public announcement about where you will be staying either, so that is a consideration. But, it will be a hotel that you will love, I promise." The judge smiled at her and Juror Number Three smiled back.

"Yes, Juror Number Two?"

"Can we keep our cell phones?"

"Of course. You are on your honor not to discuss the case, but you may talk to anyone when you are not in a trial about anything else at all. Cellphones off in the courtroom, however."

The judge waited a moment for more questions, then dismissed them with an admonition to "reappear, with your suitcases, in this courtroom at five thirty. We will be ready to get you to your hotel in time for a nice dinner." Judge Parsons said with a smile.

All of the attorneys and the judge stood while the jurors left the courtroom.

"I apologize for springing that on you, counsel" Judge Parsons said to the stunned attorneys. "But, I have heard some rumors that there are things going on that these jurors should not hear during this trial. I want them to concentrate on what the Plaintiffs and Defendant present in this room and not all of the potential distractions that may appear in media or through courthouse rumors. I'm sure that you all know what I mean."

"What will be the trial day schedule?" Napoli asked.

"We'll start at nine o'clock and we will have lunch from noon until one thirty. Then we will go until about four thirty or so, with the jury. If we have motions and other matters, we will deal with them before nine o'clock in the morning or after four thirty when we end. It will depend on what the matter is. You are both experienced trial lawyers and you know how these things go."

"Okay," Janet said. Napoli nodded.

"Then, we'll be in recess. I'll see you at nine o'clock in the morning for Opening Statements."

The judge left the courtroom and Janet Stephenson and Terry Napoli continued to stand looking after him for a moment or two.

"Well, I certainly didn't expect that," Janet said glumly.

"He must have been talking to the D.A., or the D.A. talked to him." Said Rex Montague.

"In any case, it will benefit us all to move the trial along as quickly as we can," added Napoli.

"Mrs. Winchester will be here representing Conway Chemical," said Napoli.

"Since Conway is not a named Defendant, you could probably only have Jennifer Fordham," Janet volunteered.

"Thank you, counsel, but we will decide who we want in the courtroom, without your input." Napoli snapped.

"As you wish," Janet replied firmly. She picked up her briefcase and left the courtroom with Adam and James following quickly behind. Pamela and Larry Lawson were outside in the hall and they followed Janet to the elevators.

"Was that necessary?" asked Montague.

"I've got to get in trial mode. That doesn't include playing patsy with Plaintiff's lawyer," Napoli replied.

"I guess 'trial mode' doesn't include being a polite human being," said Montague. "I'll see you in the morning. I'm sure you've got to put on your 'opening statement' hat, too." Napoli said nothing as his colleague went through the huge courtroom doors.

"Sometimes I hate this job." He said quietly to the courtroom walls. Then he, too, gathered his papers, put them in his briefcase, and left the room.

After Larry and Pamela Lawson said goodbye to Janet Stephenson on the sidewalk outside the Courthouse, they decided to stop on their way home for a quiet dinner without the children and Grandma Lawson. They finally agreed on Ted's Montana Grill in Bel Mar. It was on their way home and they could get a quiet table on the patio at this early hour. Pamela was very tired, but she tried to keep up the energy she knew that Larry wanted her to have. She felt only anxiety about the trial, while Larry was enthusiastic and interested in everything that happened every day.

"You know, Larry," Pamela said to him as she stirred her lemonade and ice, "You should have been a lawyer. You really love this whole process and I think you would be great at it."

"Maybe I could have," Larry smiled. "But I just want this case to be over."

"It's only really beginning tomorrow," Pam said, sounding a bit weary.

"I know, sweetheart, how do you feel about it?"

"I feel great. I think we have a good jury and I think Janet thinks so too. It's just that I know the testimony of the witnesses will be more stressful, worrying that they will do well. But, you know, I am really looking forward to testifying, myself. I thought I would hate it, but I go over important things to say in my mind, every night in bed. And I know I can do it, now."

"Janet said that we will be the last witnesses when we were first thinking about the trial, but she hasn't talked about that since we went through our initial preparation session for testifying. I wonder what she is thinking now, and I wonder who her surprise, but optional, rebuttal witness is."

"Isn't it interesting to watch Janet in the courtroom? She's so different than when she is chatting with us in her office, or laughing about something with James and Adam."

Larry couldn't hide his admiration. "She's fabulous," he said. "She always knows exactly what to say and says it without hesitation. Have you noticed how her voice sounds in the courtroom microphone? She could be on the stage, with the mellow voice she has. It makes me feel so glad that she is talking because her voice puts everyone at ease. I think the jurors like her, too."

Pam was smiling. "I just get this great peace in my heart when she starts to talk or answer questions because I know that she knows what she is talking about and has the situation totally under control. She never seems nervous or frustrated—even when Napoli looks and sounds as though he will jump out of his skin."

"I wonder if Napoli will show himself to be the great Chicago trial lawyer he is supposed to be when we start actually hearing the testimony of witnesses and he gets to cross-examine?" Larry was pensive as he spoke.

"Janet puts on our witnesses first, right?"

"Yep."

"Then we get to see him do cross-examination of Dr. Sonier and Dr. Guilliot before the end of the week, don't you think?" Janet had explained her trial strategy to them and Pam had taken notes. She took her little notebook out of her purse and began studying the trial outline she had written down in her notes. She was interrupted by the waiter, who brought them their salads.

"I am ready to get to the evidence, especially since the judge has already ruled that Dr. Sonier's animal studies and those great pictures of the sick rats get into evidence," Larry said.

"I just hope that I don't turn out to be one of those sick rats," Pamela was not eating her salad.

Larry looked at her with sudden great concern, "What's wrong, Pam, are you not feeling well?"

"I just can't put my finger on it," Pam said pensively, "But, I just don't feel right and I have absolutely no appetite."

"I think it is stress from the trial. I think we should just go home so you can rest."

"No, no. I'm enjoying just relaxing here with you. Let's finish before we go home and take on our busy house." Pam smiled reassuringly and patted his hand. "I'm good." She said.

They finished their meals, lapsing into happy small talk about their children. When they left the restaurant, Pam held Larry's hand. He notice that her palm was moist and her hand a bit limp. Larry put his arm around his fragile little wife as they walked to the parking lot and their car.

Janet Stephenson went back to her office to review her notes for her opening statement. She had written it many weeks before, but she wanted to make it fresh and relevant. She also needed to be prepared to begin the testimony of Dr. Sonier, her first witness. They had agreed that James and Adam would pick up Chinese food from the Mu Lan Landing and bring it to the office about 7:30 in the evening and that Brad would stop by and join them for a quick meal in the conference room. She didn't want to waste time going to a restaurant.

"Hello, there," it was Jean Sonier standing in the door of her office.

"Hi," Janet said. "Are you ready to get after it?"

"I feel that we are really quite prepared, don't you Janet? After all we have put on this same 'dog and pony show' as you say, in many depositions. This is no different, really."

"That's right. I just want to review the order in which we will introduce the exhibits. I want to make sure that we get all of those rat pictures in front of the jury."

"I saw the trial notebook of the exhibits for my testimony," Sonier replied "And I think that it is a very impressive presentation of what I might have to say."

Just then James and Brad came down the hall. "Food's here!" James called.

"Well, let's eat, then." Janet laughed. "I guess we are ready for tomorrow."

They all went into the conference room where Adam had set out paper plates, napkins, and two liters of ice tea and diet Pepsi. All of the paper containers of the Chinese food and rice were lined up in the middle of the glass-topped mahogany table. Brad, Janet, Adam, James, Jean Sonier, and Robert Guilliot sat down and started passing the containers, chatting and laughing. Janet Stephenson suddenly felt at ease and ready for the days ahead. She was always anxious for a trial to actually start because all of the tension and stress for her came in the days before the trial. The preparation of the Exhibits and juror notebooks and the interminable deadlines were the most difficult part of any trial. The juror notebooks were neatly placed in banker's boxes and stacked by the front door. Her trial notebooks were in her briefcase. She was starting the trial with her best witness, Dr. Jean Sonier. He would be followed by Dr. Richard Guilliot. By then, the jury would know all of the problems with the PSS implant. Then, she would introduce them to Pamela Lawson, first through the testimony of her physicians, minus Dr. Dan MacNamara, absent a miracle. Dr. MacNamara was still in the hospital, and it was likely that he could not testify - unless PSS still insisted on calling him, since he was still on their witness list. She could not imagine how he could testify since the time for taking depositions to preserve testimony was long past and there did not appear to be a way for Dr. MacNamara to come to court.

After they finished eating, however, Janet spent half an hour reviewing the highlights of Dr. Sonier's testimony with him. Meanwhile, James and Adam cleaned up the conference room and disappeared. Brad waited for Janet and they locked the office and walked to their cars in the darkened parking lot.

"Are you ready?" he asked her.

"I guess I have to be." Janet hugged him. "See you at home."

＊

Terry Napoli and Rex Montague had dinner with Leslie Winchester, Jennifer Fordham, and Jerry Carson at the restaurant in the Brown Palace Hotel. Forrest Winchester had dinner in his cell at the Denver County Jail. It was not quite what he had planned. He had planned to have Leslie tucked away at home and he planned to be having dinner with his lawyers and Jennifer instead of his wife.

"Does your associate, Mr. Rivera, have a plan for getting Forrest out on bail?" Leslie Winchester asked, sipping her martini.

"It doesn't appear that we are going to be able to get him released until he testifies before the Grand Jury. "said Montague. "He was arraigned this morning in a private hearing, and the judge denied bail. Rick Plume, the District Attorney, argued that he was sure that Mr. Winchester would leave the jurisdiction if he was not remanded. He made it sound as though he had committed the murder of Sherrie Barker, which is, of course, nonsense."

"Who do you think murdered her?" Leslie Winchester asked.

"I haven't the faintest idea, but it was likely this guy, Slade, who is also dead," Montague said.

"Why would Slade want to kill a woman from California with a car bomb?" Leslie persisted. She noticed that Jennifer Fordham seemed uncomfortably silent as she sipped her wine.

"Didn't you know Sherrie Barker, Jennifer?"

"Uh, yes, I did. She was one of our sales staff, a detail person, who made sales calls to doctors."

"I know what they do," Leslie Winchester said "Have the police questioned you about her death." She asked looking straight into Jennifer Fordham's eyes.

"Yes," Jerry Carson responded. "The police and FBI both came to our offices and asked all of us questions the day that Sherrie Barker's body was identified. They were there the better part of the day. But that was the end of it."

"Have the police or the D.A. contacted you since you have been here for the trial," Leslie was not letting the subject go.

"No," answered Jennifer. "Why would they?"

"Why would they subpoena Forrest to testify before the Grand Jury and not you? She worked for you if the investigation is really about Sherrie Barker."

"Perhaps that is not the topic of the Grand Jury." Terry Napoli asked.

"Well, we shall see what we shall see." Leslie Winchester turned to her menu. "Shall we order?"

Later, as Jennifer Fordham and Jerry Carson entered the lobby of the Hyatt Regency Hotel, they were met by a process server, who delivered a subpoena to each of them, to testify before the Grand Jury.

"Damn," said Jerry Carson. Jennifer just looked coolly at him and took the elevator to her room. Carson started to follow her, then went into the lobby bar instead. There was nothing he really wanted to talk to Jennifer about just now. She needed brooding time and he needed a drink.

Janet Stephenson heard the alarm at four forty-five in the morning because she had been awake for forty-five minutes, going over her opening statement in her mind. Brad turned over and slapped the snooze button. Janet got up and went into the bathroom to take a shower. In the shower, she continued her mental review of the case. She felt a little nauseous, as she always did before she had to go to court.

'*Why do I do this*,' she thought to herself. '*Why did I give up teaching?*'

Then her mind reverted to the testimony of Dr. Sonier. She was still going through the checklist of his testimony in her mind when Brad poked his head in the bathroom and asked, "Hey, are you okay in here?"

Janet noticed that the water was cooling and she turned off the shower and grabbed her fluffy towel.

"Sorry, I was thinking," she said loudly at the door.

"I thought maybe you had washed down the drain," Brad laughed from outside. He was shaving at his sink in the dressing room, squinting at the mirror. Janet pulled on her terry cloth robe and began brushing her teeth at the other sink.

"You'll do just fine, you know." Brad said softly, "You always do. You're the best."

"Thank you, my most objective fan," Janet laughed.

"I don't fly out until four o'clock, so I thought I might come for part of the trial today. Would that bother you?"

"Not at all. Please come. Maybe be there for lunch, but I don't promise to be good company."

"I don't mean to intrude on lunch."

"It's no intrusion, please come."

"Well, you just do your thing and I'll slip in and out. If I'm there at lunchtime, we'll see what's going on."

Janet Stephenson chose a navy pantsuit and plain white blouse from her closet. She was deep in thought throughout the process of putting on her makeup and plain silver hoop earrings. She decided against wearing a necklace. Instead, she put on the Chinese pendant she usually wore. Brad bought it for her in Japan when Hannah was born. He had been deployed on a secret mission to Korea and Janet had their baby girl alone at the Seymour Johnson base hospital. Her friend, Cathy, took her to the hospital at eleven o'clock and left her there. Janet was only in the labor room for about thirty minutes before Hannah suddenly arrived, delivered by a surprised pediatrician, who was the only physician on duty. When he came home four months later, Brad brought her the silver pendant, which said, "I love you, you love me" in Chinese letters—and a string of pearls. She saved the pearls for special occasions, but she had worn the pendant nearly every day since.

James and Adam were waiting for her when she arrived at the office at six o'clock. They had the remaining exhibit boxes stacked outside the door. She knew they were hoping for a quick trip through the Starbucks drive-through on the way downtown. "The least I can do," she thought to herself smiling at the loyalty of her two assistants.

"June Pettigrew has called three times since midnight," James told her as he picked up the first box. "She knows you are on trial, but she was really upset and said that she just needs to talk to you for a moment, as soon as you have time. She had some bad news from her doctor, she said."

"Oh, dear," Janet furrowed her brow as she thought about her client. "June has been having some very serious problems. I hope she doesn't have something new!"

"I think she does," Adam said grimly. "She hinted that it was cancer, although she didn't say that in so many words."

"Her trial is coming up next, isn't it," James asked. "I know that we just finished scheduling the depositions of all of her treating doctors for the second week after this trial is finished."

"Yes," Janet said, "But I can't think about June right this minute. I have my hands and my brain full of Pam's case. I'll try and call her sometime after court today if it works out. James, perhaps you can call her and tell her that. She just needs a listening ear because she isn't at all close to her family. Her daughter has all but abandoned her to that assisted living home in Minnesota."

James nodded, not looking happy. "It's just that I don't know what to say when she tells me all of that embarrassing medical stuff. I can read the medical records, but it all seems too personal when a client wants to tell me about her intimate physical problems. I'm just a gofer and clerk! What do I know? Why does she always want to tell me?"

"Because she doesn't have anyone else. I'm sorry, James, maybe Adam will volunteer to call her." She looked at Adam, who was appearing to be very busy loading the boxes and organizing the car.

"Not me. James is way better at listening. I just get too grossed out and I can't even feel sympathetic because I just don't relate." Adam said, hardly looking up from his work.

"Good thing you aren't on the jury, dude." James laughed. "Okay, I'll call her later this morning when we have a break. Is that okay?"

"That's fine," Janet smiled at her willing assistant. "Let's get going. I'm sure you guys want to stop at Starbucks—or at least drive through."

"You know it!" said Adam, now with a smile.

Jennifer Fordham and Jerry Carson met for breakfast in the Hyatt coffee shop. Jennifer was as glum and preoccupied as she had been the night before when they were served with the Grand Jury subpoenas. Jerry Carson felt a rock in the pit of his stomach, though he was attempting to appear cheerful and to smile.

"I think we need lawyers," Jerry began.

"You *think*, we need lawyers? I say we *definitely* need lawyers, pal!" Jennifer said sarcastically, with emphasis on "lawyers."

"What do you mean?" Carson asked, furrowing his brow.

"They are going to try and pin this on us, either jointly or individually. Winchester is not our friend here, Jerry. Do you get that?"

"He's the one in jail," Jerry said quizzically.

"That's because he shot at Sonier, not because of anything to do with the bombing—I'd bet on it." Jennifer was stirring her coffee vigorously, unaware that it was swirling out of the cup. "And just keep your voice down. We shouldn't be discussing these things in a public place."

"Jen, just settle down. I can't believe this has you so rattled. We will be fine. Nothing ties us to this."

"And what about Raoul? I'm sure he's behind this. What has he got to lose?"

Jerry Carson was silent for a long time. Then he said quietly, "I'll call my attorney and ask him to get on a plane and come here. Meanwhile, our day is pretty full."

Jennifer Fordham was staring at her coffee cup. Finally, she looked up at Jerry Carson and smiled her best smile. "You're right. One day at a time. Let's get to court."

Carson was relieved at her changed demeanor and said "I'm ready." He planned to call his attorney at the first break in the trial. His anxiety level was increasing with each passing moment and he began to worry, for the first time, that matters were slipping out of his control. Jennifer was a mystery, but for now, he had to keep a calm front and watch his back.

Terry Napoli and Rex Montague arrived at the courthouse at the same time as Janet Stephenson, with Adam and James. They were polite to each other as they waited in the security line, but they all took separate elevators to the second floor, where the courtroom was located.

Pam and Larry Lawson were already in the courtroom when Janet arrived. They were sitting tensely on the front row. Both of them smiled and stood up to greet Janet, and James, and Adam, who smiled as they unloaded their boxes.

"Come on up to the table, "Janet said, holding the little gate to the area in front of the bar open for them. She showed them where to sit, next to her at the table. Janet, of course, was seated nearest to the center and the podium. Janet placed only her white trial notebook on the table. All of the other exhibits and charts were neatly stowed away in banker's boxes, under the careful eyes of James and Adam, who knew exactly where every document and demonstrative exhibit was located.

Jennifer Fordham and Jerry Carson were the next to arrive. Jerry Carson sat on the front row in the gallery and Jennifer Fordham joined Rex Montague and Terry Napoli at the Defendants' table. Jennifer sat down without speaking to the attorneys. She had a notepad and pen and she placed her purse under the table by her feet. Montague and Napoli were having a conference near the back of the courtroom with two associate attorneys. The conversation was animated but hushed. Finally, they came through the gate at the bar and sat down. Each of them had a large black notebook in front of them on the table.

Suddenly, the doors to the courtroom opened and the bailiff allowed the spectators to enter and fill up the remaining seats in the gallery. Janet recognized most of them as Silicone Sisters, many of whom were her clients, as well as newspaper reporters and television reporters, sans cameras and crew. At least half of the seats were already occupied by associate attorneys and paralegals for Montague and Napoli. When the seats were filled, the bailiff closed the doors amid noisy protests from spectators who were not allowed to enter. A security guard entered and stood in front of the doors, and the bailiff took his seat at the small desk in the enclosure by the door.

Judge Parson's secretary entered the courtroom from a door in the front. She smiled at the crowded courtroom and the waiting attorneys and asked, "Counsel, are you ready to proceed?"

"Yes," they all answered in unison, and she disappeared through the door.

A few moments later, the bailiff announced loudly, "All rise! This court is now in session. The Honorable Judge Parsons now presiding." Judge Parsons entered from the door behind the bench. He, too, smiled at the crowded courtroom and said "Be seated."

"Counsel are you ready to proceed with opening statements and testimony of witnesses?"

"The Plaintiffs are ready, Your Honor," Janet said.

"The Defendant is ready," said Rex Montague.

"Fine. I don't think there are any preliminary matters that I am aware of. Does either Plaintiff or Defendant know of anything that we must address before we bring in the jury?"

"We have nothing, Your Honor," Janet responded.

"Nor do we," answered Montague.

"Very well then, let's call in the jury. Will the Bailiff please get the jury? By the way, for all of our visitors in the gallery, it is customary for everyone to stand in respect when the jury enters and leaves the courtroom throughout the trial, including me. Please stand."

As the door opened to the jury room, everyone in the courtroom stood up. The startled members of the jury filed out and were guided by the bailiff to the jury box, where he opened the gate and ushered them in, in the order of their juror numbers.

"Good Morning, ladies and gentlemen. Let me be the first to thank you for your jury service in this case. Look at the juror on either side of you. You will occupy the same seat in which you are now sitting throughout this trial. If you enter in the order of your seats, it will expedite the going and coming which you will have to do. The first order of business is the oath, which you are required to take as jurors. Do any of you have any objection for religious or other reasons to taking this oath?" They all shook their heads and Judge Parsons then had them raise their right hands and affirm the oath of a faithful juror. After some further brief instructions about morning and afternoon breaks and the lunch period, Judge Parsons said, "We will begin with the opening statement of the Plaintiff. Mrs. Stephenson if you will proceed, please."

Janet Stephenson stepped to the podium, with her white notebook and smiled at the jury. James and Adam had placed her white flip chart, on which she had already listed all of the witnesses, in front of the jury.

Janet loved the opening statement. It was her opportunity to teach the jury, in a very conversational and informal way, all of the evidence which would be presented by scientific and medical experts. Janet Stephenson was a born teacher, and so she began. She introduced herself and then, she introduced Pamela and Larry Lawson, who stood and smiled at the jury.

"This is Pam Lawson's story," Janet told the jury.

"You will see and hear her story unfold through the testimony of a number of witnesses, and you will hear the testimony of Pamela Lawson, herself. You will also hear the testimony of her husband, Larry. They will tell you how they agreed that Pam should have the Mammselle implants after the implants were recommended by a prominent Denver plastic surgeon, Dr. Dan MacNamara, who prescribed the implants to correct the deformity in Pam's breasts, which occurred following the birth of her last child. Dr. MacNamara may or may not be able to testify here because he is still in the hospital following a tragic injury, which he suffered, but you will hear from other medical and scientific witnesses." Janet stepped in front of the jury to her flip chart and flipped over the blank front page to reveal her witness list to the jury. As she stepped beside the chart and flipped the page, she noted that a number of the jurors leaned forward in their seats.

"Our first witness will be Dr. Jean Sonier. Dr. Sonier is a biomaterials scientist with a PhD in Chemistry. Dr. Sonier was the director of the biomaterials section of the Canadian agency which is the equivalent of the American Food and Drug Administration, or FDA. Dr. Sonier will tell you about his education and experience with silicone gel implants, particularly the Mammselle implant, which Pam had. He will explain the chemical makeup of the implant to you and he will explain that this implant is particularly harmful in the human body because the coating, made of polyurethane foam, disintegrates in the body into a carcinogen, or cancer-producing chemical, called TDA. That stands for toluline diamine. Dr. Sonier will explain to you that he tested this foam covering in rats and rabbits. He will show you that in those animal studies, 100% of all of the animals developed tumors, and more importantly, in this case, each and every animal developed liver cancer.

Pamela Lawson's treating physicians, will also tell you in their testimony, that after Pam had the Mammselle implants placed in her body, she too, developed liver cancer. Pam and her doctors will also testify about the serious and fatal nature of liver cancer and they will explain that if Pam had not been fortunate enough to receive a liver transplant very recently, her liver cancer would have been fatal."

Janet then briefly listed and summarized the expected testimony of each of Pam's treating physicians and her psychological counselor. After the summaries, she closed her flip chart, and quietly looked at the jury for a moment or two, with a gentle smile. Then she told them,

"At the end of this trial, I will be asking you to award damages to Pamela and her husband, Larry, for the injuries that they have suffered and the damages which they have incurred. In addition to compensatory damages and pain and suffering, we will be asking you to consider exemplary or punitive damages because the evidence will demonstrate that PolySurgical Specialties knew, or should have known and deliberately ignored the dangers to women, who were implanted with the Mammselle implant, in order to gain a significant market share of the silicone gel breast implant market. The evidence will show that the Defendant had a willful, wanton, and reckless disregard for the life, health, and feelings of Pamela Lawson, Larry Lawson, and other users of their product and their families because there is no mention of any of the dangers or risks associated with the foam coating on the implant to warn either the plastic surgeons who insert the implants or the women into whom the implants are surgically placed. The information about the implant, called the package insert or labeling of the product, is required by the FDA and it is intended to disclose all of the risks of using a prescribed implant so that the patient's doctor and the patient can make an informed decision about whether or not the benefits of the implant are outweighed by the risks of using it. The evidence will show that there is no mention of the known disintegration of the foam covering in any of the product information regarding the Mammselle implant. The evidence will show that the surgeons, including Dr. MacNamara, did not know that the foam disappeared or became another substance until the surgery to remove Pam Lawson's Mammselle implants."

Janet Stephenson paused briefly and look calmly at the jurors before she smiled. Then she concluded,

"Thank you for your kind attention. I will not be able to address you directly again during this trial until I make my closing argument to you after the conclusion of all of the testimony and evidence. I would also ask you for your understanding if Pamela Lawson is not physically able to be present through all of the trial. You will hear from the testimony that she recently had a liver transplant and her health is very frail just now. Thank you again for your kind attention and your service as jurors in this very important case."

Janet Stephenson retrieved her white notebook from the podium, then returned to her seat at the Plaintiff's table and Judge Parsons said,

"Thank you, Mrs. Stephenson. I think that it would be appropriate to take our morning break at this time. That will allow the Defendants to make whatever adjustments are needed before we proceed with Defendant's opening statement. Mr. bailiff, will you escort the jury?"

The bailiff came and opened the jury box, and Judge Parsons rose to his feet along with everyone in the courtroom. The members of the jury filed out and followed each other to the jury room door in the far corner of the courtroom. As the door to the jury room closed, the judge said "We will be in recess for 20 minutes," and he left the bench.

Janet watched the members of the jury carefully while she was talking to them. She had been schooled in the concepts of neurolinguistic programming and the various methods by which people process information. She could tell if persons were visual, auditory or kinesthetic learners by observing them and by talking with them. But, she honestly had no idea what the jurors were thinking or how they were perceiving her opening statement. Janet had come to believe that she was missing the chip in her brain that allowed others to interpret what jurors were thinking by observing body language and eye movements or even "gut feelings." She had intuitions about people, but her impressions were intangible and not easily expressed in words. However, it was her secret belief that her impressions were as accurate as those of jury consultants who claimed to be jury selection experts, with practically psychic powers. In past trials when she had been convinced by co-counsel, she had agreed to use expensive jury consultants, with virtually no definable benefits and a lot more complication to trial preparation, which she found to be ponderous and difficult under any circumstances. But, all in all, Janet was happy with this jury. They appeared to be interested and appropriately responsive or non-responsive to her opening comments. She was interested to observe them during Napoli's opening.

During the break, Janet turned her attention to Pam.

"Do you need to take a break and get something to drink or go to the ladies room?" she asked? Pam nodded. "Let's go. It's quite a walk to the ladies room at the other end of the hall. One word of caution, don't talk to any of the reporters we are going to see on the way." Pam smiled and just nodded again.

"I'll go too," Larry said. "I need a break. By the way, Janet, after hearing your opening, I don't see how we can lose. I think some people on the jury have already made up their minds."

"Don't be too sure," Janet laughed. "You are not an objective listener to Pam's story. Wait until you hear Napoli and you will be boiling, I can promise. There is another side which he will present very well."

"You were very good." Pam said. "But I understand not to get our hopes up."

"Anything can happen in a trial. Just be patient." Janet said.

During the break, Napoli and Montague replaced Janet's flip chart with an easel and a series of laminated color posters and demonstrative exhibits. It was obvious that Napoli's opening statement was well rehearsed and expensive to produce. Their theory was the same as Madison Avenue advertising firms—professionally produced marketing pays off with the average American. The Defendants were banking on the jurors being average Americans. The information from the secret focus groups which were used to produce the visual aids had also been used by Napoli and Montague in jury selection. They didn't have to rely on attorney intuition.

In twenty-three minutes, Judge Parsons entered the courtroom. "Are we ready to proceed?" he asked Napoli and Montague.

"Yes, Your Honor," Napoli responded.

"Then Mr. Bailiff, please bring in the jury."

When the jurors were all properly in their places, the judge said "We will continue with the opening statement for the Defendant. Mr. Napoli, you may proceed."

Terry Napoli went to the podium with a slim black notebook, which he opened slowly and then he turned to the jury box.

"Ladies and Gentlemen, I am Terry Napoli, one of the attorneys for PolySurgical Specialties, the Defendant in this case. You have met me and my co-counsel, Rex Montague, during the jury selection process. It is my privilege to address you at this time and to outline for you how PSS, as our client is known, will defend itself in this trial against the claims of the plaintiff and her husband. By the end of the trial, the evidence will clearly demonstrate to you that these claims are groundless and frivolous and that PSS is not liable for any damages or injuries suffered by the plaintiff.

The evidence will likely show that the plaintiff had liver cancer and that she has had a liver transplant. However, the evidence will NOT show that there is any relationship between the Mammselle implant and her liver cancer. The evidence will show that the testimony of Dr. Sonier is not applicable to this case. You will hear the testimony of Dr. Hans Brickner, from the University of Colorado School of Medicine. His evidence will show that there is not a causal connection between the Mammselle implant and the plaintiff's cancer. The judge will instruct you at the end of the case that you are the sole finders of fact in this case. That means that you, as members of the jury must carefully consider the testimony and the credibility and the bias of each witness before you decide how much weight to give the testimony and evidence of each witness.

The evidence will clearly show that the Mammselle implant is safe and effective and that it was approved by the Food and Drug Administration of the United States of America for use as a breast implant. The evidence will show that Canada and the United States have different views regarding implants, but in the United States, approval by the FDA is all that is required for PSS to provide the Mammselle implant as a safe and effective medical product. Let me demonstrate to you what the evidence will show about the extensive process that was required for PSS to secure FDA approval of this implant."

Napoli took a laser pen out of his pocket and went through the first three charts on the easel, which demonstrated the product approval process, with every significant and insignificant step and sub-step listed in detail. According to Janet's watch, the explanation took fifteen minutes, and she could see that he was losing the interest of the jury. However, she knew that his intent was to do just that because he was trying to mitigate the expected impact of the Sonier animal studies, which were next on the agenda. Napoli continued:

"PSS cannot be held liable for injuries when it did what was required and achieved approval by the FDA. However, ladies and gentlemen, the evidence that we will present to you will make it clear that the Mammselle implant is not only safe and effective, but also that it is a revolutionary improvement in silicone gel breast implants because it prevents a terrible complication called capsular contracture. You will hear the testimony of Dr. Dan MacNamara, the plaintiffs plastic surgeon, who will testify about the many medical journal articles and speeches he has given about the problem of capsular contracture, or the hardening of the breast after implantation of silicone gel implants. Dr. MacNamara will tell you that the Mammselle implant prevents capsular contracture and is the state of the art in breast implants."

Napoli took out his laser pen again and went through four more charts, showing pictures of Dr. MacNamara at various meetings giving speeches about the Mammselle and capsular contracture. Each chart had a set of bullet points about the amazing Mammselle and Napoli read them all. Napoli paused, looked carefully at the jury, smiled and continued:

"The plaintiff's own medical records will make it clear that she, too, was the beneficiary of this improvement and that she never suffered from capsular contracture. The evidence will show that the plaintiff's risk of developing liver cancer, after having Mammselle implants, was no greater than the risk of the general population without implants to develop liver cancer. Statistically, she had no risk of developing liver cancer with Mammselle implants. That is not a risk PSS was required to disclose in its package inserts or in any other marketing or labeling material."

Napoli took out his laser pen for a third time. The last charts illustrations of epidemiological studies about liver cancer and the general population and liver cancer reported in patients with breast implants. Napoli went through them all and pointed to and used every epidemiological term on each chart. The jurors were looking at the charts, but Janet was not sure if any of them noticed that there was not a chart illustrating any study of liver cancer patients who also had Mammselle implants. She knew that no such study had been done and was somewhat surprised that Napoli would venture into the epidemiological quagmire in opening statement. Napoli was winding up:

"In short, ladies and gentlemen, the evidence will exonerate PSS from any liability to the plaintiff. We are very sorry that she has had to battle liver cancer and undergo a liver transplant. However, the evidence will show that the plaintiff has no claim against PSS for her injuries and at the end of this trial, we will be asking you to dismiss her case, without damages of any kind. Jurors are special citizens and you are very important to us. I would ask that you not be driven by sympathy or sentiment and that you keep open minds until all of the evidence is in. PSS doesn't get to put on any evidence until the plaintiff has completed her case. I ask you to wait until you hear our evidence and witnesses before you make up your mind about anything. When I speak to you again in closing argument, I will ask you to carefully consider all the evidence and to dismiss the plaintiff's case. Thank you for your patience and for your service."

"You're right, Janet, he makes me furious!" Larry whispered to Janet.

"It will be fine. It was what we expected." Pamela whispered to him.

Janet smiled at them, but was watching the jury as Napoli gathered his materials and returned to his table. The jury watched him carefully, but their faces did not disclose anything about what they might be thinking.

Judge Parsons was looking at the clock. "Well, it is 12:15. Pretty good timing, counsel. I'll tell you what, let's take a little extra time for lunch. I'll see you back here at 2:15 this afternoon. That will give you all plenty of time to eat. Mrs. Stephenson, will you be prepared to call your first witness when we return at 2:15?"

"Yes, Your Honor." Janet said.

"All right. Enjoy your lunch ladies and gentlemen. Bailiff?" The bailiff was already ushering the jury out. Everyone stood quickly and watched them go.

"We will be in recess until 2:15" Judge Parsons said, and he disappeared into his chambers.

James was at the table, "I have Dr. Sonier on the phone. Do you want him to meet us for lunch?"

"Let's go across the street to the Art Museum café. Ask him to meet us there. He and I can grab a bite and spend a little time preparing a bit and all of you can have a more leisurely lunch."

Janet looked up and saw Brad standing in the courtroom behind their table.

"Hi." She smiled at him. "Want to come to lunch?"

"Sure," he said. "Can I carry anything for you?"

"I'm just taking my trial notebook for Dr. Sonier, so I'm good. How long have you been here?" she asked.

"I heard the whole thing. You were just great, as usual. You couldn't have painted a more poignant picture. Napoli was a demonstration of glitzy overkill, but I can't tell how it played with the jury."

"We'll see." Janet said. "Ready, everyone?"

Dr. Sonier was waiting inside the café when they all arrived. Janet and Brad and Dr. Sonier sat at one table and James, Adam, Pam and Larry at another. While Brad was glad to see Jean Sonier and to renew some old jokes with him, he realized that Janet and her prime witness needed some brief time to prepare for his testimony, so he ate silently, listening to them talk, while Janet and Dr. Sonier reviewed the order of his questions and the presentation of his exhibits. Janet ate half of a grilled cheese sandwich and drank a diet Coke. Dr. Sonier, however, managed to put away the lunch special of grilled salmon alfredo and a cup of cheese and broccoli soup. Brad was amazed at how much the slight little man could eat and he had remarked about it to Janet when they had eaten dinner with Dr. Sonier in the past.

"He has to burn it off in nervous energy," Brad thought to himself, noticing that the shirt to his airline captain's uniform felt a little snug around the middle. He made a mental note to hit the hotel workout room at his upcoming layover in New York City.

Before they realized it, Dr. Sonier's watch announced that it was 1:30. He had set the alarm, as he always did, being the personification of the absent minded professor.

Adam paid the tab with the firm's credit card and they left the café and headed back to court. Brad kissed Janet on the top of her head at the Art Museum entrance and headed for the parking lot to retrieve his car.

"Call me tonight, sweets, and give me the report on how Jean does on the stand." Brad winked at Dr. Sonier who playfully waved him off with his hand.

"We shall cover the bases," he said with mock solemnity "at least the bases."

When they returned to the courtroom, Napoli and his cast of thousands were already there.

James got the first exhibit notebooks out of the boxes for distribution to the jury. They were prepared with all of Dr. Sonier's animal studies and photos because Judge Parsons had already ruled that the report and the photographs were admissible.

The judge entered and sent for the jury and the trial was truly underway.

"Mrs. Stephenson, please call your first witness." Judge Parsons said.

"We call Dr. Jean Sonier." She replied and the bailiff opened the courtroom door and called, "Dr. Jean Sonier" Just outside the door, Dr. Sonier entered and walked through the gate to the witness box. He looked completely academic in his brownish English tweed jacket, mustard yellow bow tie and round tortoise shell glasses. His medium brown hair was brushed but ever so slightly disheveled, a slightly middle aged Harry Potter.

"Please raise your right hand and be sworn," the bailiff said. Then he intoned the oath for witnesses, Dr. Sonier stated "I do." Then he sat down and pulled the witness microphone toward his face. He appeared to be completely at ease. His friendly and gentle manner put everyone in the courtroom at ease. Janet knew that juries loved Dr. Jean Sonier. What was there not to love?

"Will you please state your name and your business address for the record?" Janet began as all testimony begins.

"I am Jean Sonier. My business address is 45 Rayford Place, Montreal, Canada"

"Dr. Sonier, can you tell us how you are employed at this time?"

"I am the principal in a biomaterials consulting firm, called Andromeda, LLC"

"Could you please tell us about your educational background?"

"I have a bachelors degree in biology and a masters degree in biomaterials engineering from Case Western Reserve University and a PhD in chemistry from Oxford University. I also have a certification in biomaterials from the International Association of Biomaterials Scientists, which is headquartered in Atlanta, GA. That certification requires a post graduate degree in biomaterials from a medical school. My post graduate work in the medical field was done at Emory University Medical School in Atlanta, Georgia."

"Do you belong to any professional societies and organizations?"

"Yes, all of those, in addition to the one I mentioned are listed in my vitae. There are quite a number in the US and internationally."

"Have you published any articles or books in the fields of your study, particularly biomaterials science?"

"Yes, indeed. Those are also listed in my curriculum vitae."

Janet Stephenson turned to address Judge Parsons, who was looking with rapt attention at Dr. Sonier.

"Your Honor if we may, we would like to distribute the first set of the Plaintiff's Exhibits in their notebooks, to the jury. Dr. Sonier's CV is the first exhibit, and it would expedite my questioning of him."

"Is there a stipulation regarding the exhibits in this notebook, Mr. Montague?"

Rex Montague looked surprised. "Your Honor, we objected to Dr. Sonier's publications and illustrations, but the Court did rule that those were admissible in a pretrial hearing on our motion in limine. We would still enter our objection to those documents for the record."

"Other than that objection, counsel? Are there other objections?" the Judge asked.

Napoli and Montague were whispering furiously at counsel table when the judge said,

"Well, Mr. Napoli, then. Further objections?"

"No, Your Honor," Rex Montague replied, cutting off his colleague's whispering with a raised palm.

"Very well, the exhibits in the first notebook are admitted. You may distribute the notebooks to the jury."

James and Adam divided the stacks between them and passed out the large white exhibit notebooks to the jurors. When they had finished the task, Janet Stephenson continued.

"Dr. Sonier, I would ask that you turn to Exhibit number one. Can you identify that document for us?'

"Yes, Mrs. Stephenson, it is my curriculmlum vitae, or CV or resume as it is more commonly called."

"Under the category of ' professional organizations', are these all organizations to which you now or have previously belonged that relate to your profession as a biomaterials scientist?"

"Yes, they are."

"And, now directing your attention to the section of your CV titled 'publications,' is this a current list of all of your professional publications?"

"Yes, it is."

"Drawing your attention to the last publication in the Journal of Biomaterials, which is listed near the end of your publications, could you tell us what that published article is about?"

"That article is a publication of the report which I prepared for the Canadian government, Department of Health and Human Services, relating to my biomaterials analysis, using animal studies with rabbits and laboratory rats, of the polyurethane coating material on the Mammselle breast implant, manufactured by PolySurgical Specialties."

"Is that the same PolySurgical Specialties, which is the defendant in this litigation"

"As far as I know, it is."

"We will discuss that study in more detail later, Dr. Sonier. But first, is Exhibit One your most current curriculum vitae?"

"Yes, it is"

"Your Honor, we would move for the admission of Exhibit #1 and all of the Exihibits, numbered 1- 56, which are included in Plaintiffs' Exhibit Notebook #1."

Judge Parson looked up from the notebook and said, "Well, counsel, as I understand it, all of the exhibits for both the plaintiffs and defendant have been either stipulated by counsel or admitted by the court in pretrial hearings, so all of the exhibits contained in those notebooks will be admitted. However, there may be rebuttal exhibits which do not fall into those categories, so we will deal with any exhibits in that category as they come up."

"Thank you, Your Honor. I just wanted to make the issue of exhibits clear on the record from the outset," said Janet Stephenson.

"Well, I think it is clear. We don't need to plow all of that ground again." Judge Parsons was not smiling. He hoped this was not going to be the kind of trial where the attorneys constantly stopped the flow of the proceedings to "make things clear, for the record." To him, that meant a long and tedious trial because one or both of the parties intended to appeal from the outset and they wanted all errors of law clear on the transcript of the trial. He, as most judges, just liked trials to come to a quick and fair resolution or settlement that did not require an analysis of his decisions and actions by the Court of Appeals.

Janet Stephenson looked briefly at the jurors. They were all looking at Exhibit 1 in their trial notebooks. She smiled slightly to herself. Dr. Sonier's CV was thirty-five pages long and aptly demonstrated what a brilliant scholar and scientist he was.

"Dr. Sonier," she continued, "have you testified as an expert witness in the area of biomaterials and medical biomaterials prior to this trial?"

"Yes, many times. Again all of those cases are listed in my CV."

"What is the difference between a biomaterials scientist and a medical biomaterials scientist?"

"A biomaterials scientist determines whether a given material is safe for use in a biological system. A medical biomaterials scientist determines whether a given material is safe and effective for use as a medical implant in humans. It is a refinement if you will, of the area of biomaterials science, which coordinates closely with the medical community and medical applications for implants." Dr. Sonier explained, looking at Janet, but also talking to the jury."

"Dr. Sonier, are you certified as a medical biomaterials scientist?"

"Yes, as I explained, the medical portion of the requirements for that designation were completed in my post graduate studies at Emory University Medical School in Atlanta, Georgia, which has the most famous program for those studies in the world."

"Your Honor, we would offer Dr. Jean Sonier as a medical biomaterials expert."

"Any objection from the defendants?" Judge Parsons was looking at Terry Napoli and Rex Montague over his reading glasses.

"May we voir dire?" asked Napoli.

"Of course." said Judge Parsons. "It is going to be that kind of a trial," he thought to himself as Janet Stephenson sat down and Terry Napoli strode across the courtroom to the podium.

"Dr. Sonier, isn't it true that your actual PhD degree is in Chemistry?"

"Yes, that true. I received it in my studies as a Rhodes Scholar at Oxford University in England."

"And isn't it also true that you haven't really focused on biology since you were an undergraduate many years ago."

"No, that is not correct, Mr. Napoli. As I explained, my postgraduate work at Emory was all about biology and how certain materials react in a human biological environment."

"Looking at all of your cases, Dr. Sonier, isn't it true that you have only been hired as an expert witness by plaintiffs in every one of these cases."

"Yes, for the most part, that is true."

"And isn't it also true, that you are determined to get the implants manufactured by PSS off of the market in the United States."

"It is true that it is my professional opinion that the Mammselle implant is not a safe and effective product and that if the truth were known by the FDA, it would not be marketed in the United States as it is no longer marketed in Canada."

"But isn't it true, Dr. Sonier, that the Mammselle implant is approved for sale in the United States by the United States Food and Drug Administration?"

"Yes, that is currently the case."

"Isn't it also true, Dr. Sonier, that you are not an objective witness because you are deeply biased against the Mammselle implant and my client."

At this Dr. Jean Sonier sat a bit taller and straightened his glasses. Then he said, very calmly, "Mr. Napoli, my opinions regarding the Mammselle implant are based on scientific studies, which I have conducted and which I have published and supplied to the Government of Canada. They are not the result of any sort of scientific or personal bias."

"Dr. Sonier, you are being paid by Janet Stephenson and her client to offer your opinions to this jury, aren't you?"

"It is customary for expert witnesses to be paid for their time and for their out of pocket expenses and my charges are also listed in my curriculum vitae for your scrutiny."

Terry Napoli was not going to pursue this further because he knew that Dr. Sonier's compensation was a fraction of what PSS was paying, and of that which was disclosed, according to the rules in their CV's. Instead, he said to the Court, "Your Honor, we object to the designation of Dr. Sonier as an independent expert in the area of medical biomaterials science because he is obviously biased against the defendant and is not a truly independent expert, but someone who has been on a crusade to remove the Mammselle implant from the United States market."

"Well, Mr. Napoli, it appears from his answers that Dr. Sonier's opinions are derived from his own independent and published research. If his findings only appeal to plaintiffs, that is not quite the point, is it. Dr. Sonier will be admitted as an expert in the area of medical biomaterials science."

Janet Stephenson was surprised by Napoli's voir dire. She didn't understand why he would give Dr. Sonier the opportunities to talk about his research at this stage. Maybe he just wanted to reinforce his point from opening statement that the Mammselle is on the market in the U.S because it is approved by the Food and Drug Administration. She smiled at Dr. Sonier and continued with her questions.

"Dr. Sonier, before you tell us about your studies on the Mammselle material, which you mentioned in your responses to Mr. Napoli's questions, let me ask you some questions about silicone gel breast implants in general."

"That will be fine." Dr. Sonier said.

"Can you describe for us, in layman's terms, the materials used in a making a silicone gel breast implant, and the Mammselle implant in particular?"

"I would be happy to do that. Do you mind if I use some props, which I have in my pocket and the chart paper for a little drawing?"

"Not at all. We have a portable microphone if you need to leave the witness box. Your Honor, may Dr. Sonier be permitted to address my question using the flip chart and a portable microphone?"

"Yes, yes if it works and can be done easily." Judge Parsons said, waving his hand at James and Adam.

James and Adam quickly attached the portable microphone to Dr. Sonier's lapel and plugged the long cord into the microphone jack in the witness box. Dr. Sonier went to the flip chart beside the witness box.

"Let me just put you in the picture, so to speak," Dr. Sonier began as he drew an oval on the white paper with a black marker. "This is a basic silicone gel breast implant. It is generally about this shape and it is made of silicone. Silicone is a polymer, called dimethylpolysiloxane, but we can just call it silicone. The bag, or elastomer, is a sort of balloon, made of silicone, which is processed until it holds together and can be molded into this kind of balloon container. Less processed, or cross-linked, which is the chemical term for the soupier silicone polymer, is placed inside the balloon in the manufacturing process. The silicone gel, as this soupier polymer is called, is really like a silicone sponge, filled with micro-droplets of silicone liquid, or the least cross linked polymer. The result is a soft, pliable implant, which approximates the female breast."

Janet had a Mammselle implant, which she now handed to Dr. Sonier.

"Dr. Sonier, for demonstrative purposes, can you identify the object I am handing to you?"

"Yes, this is a Mammselle implant." Dr. Sonier said.

"Are there any additional features, other than those you have described, which are unique to a Mammselle?" Janet asked.

"Yes, you will note that this implant also has a foam material on the outside. That material is polyurethane, another polymer, which is often used for many household materials."

"Your Honor, we request permission to allow the jury to pass the demonstrative exhibit among the members of the jury."

"Do you have an objection, Mr. Napoli?" Judge Parsons asked.

"No objection, Your Honor." said Napoli.

"You may pass the demonstrative exhibit to the jury." The judge said.

Janet waited a few moments, until all of the jurors had examined the Mammselle implant. The members of the jury each appeared to be very interested and they took their time, turning the implant over in their hands, some squeezing it slightly and the UPS driver actually picked at the implant with his thumb and forefinger. Dr. Sonier watched them carefully. When they were finished, Judge Parsons said, "Mrs. Stephenson, could you let me see the exhibit, as well?"

Janet took the implant to Judge Parsons, who also turned it over and over in his hands and then handed it back to her. "You may place it on the witness box, so that Dr. Sonier can refer to it during his testimony," the judge instructed.

"Now, Dr. Sonier, you stated in response to questions asked by Mr. Napoli, that you have concerns regarding the safety and effectiveness of the Mammselle as an implant for use in the human body. Can you tell us what you mean by that?" Janet was thankful to Terry Napoli for inadvertently laying all of the foundation for that question during his voir dire of Dr. Sonier.

"Yes, of course. My concerns, as a medical biomaterials scientist, about the safety and effectiveness of this implant come, primarily, in two areas; first, the use of the silicone to make and fill the underlying implant and second, the use of the polyurethane foam as a coating. Both materials are unfriendly to the human biological environment"

"Could you explain what you mean for us?" Janet asked.

"Let me draw you another picture, "he said. Dr. Sonier flipped to a fresh sheet of paper. Then he drew a series of interconnected squiggles on the paper in the shape of an oval. "These are little drawings of silicone molecules. When they are tightly stuck together like this, they make up the shell of the implant balloon. It appears to be impermeable and looks as though it will hold the contents of the implant. However, the silicone liquid molecules are in much shorter and looser chains. It is a scientific fact, that the liquid silicone molecules traverse through the silicone envelope and into the body of the woman with the implants. When the silicone liquid 'micro-droplets' get into the biological system of the woman's body, they are picked up by giant white blood cells, called microphages, and transported about the body."

Dr. Sonier, drew a pac-man kind of macrophage, with a portion of a liquid silicone molecule in it's mouth.

"Dr. Sonier, can you explain why this 'scientific fact', as you called it, is of concern to you as a medical biomaterials scientist?"

Dr. Sonier, looked up from his drawing of macrophage pac-men with silicone molecules inside them and said, "The human body cannot dispose of the silicone in organic ways. The macrophages transport and deposit the silicone in the lymphatic system, the liver, the kidneys, even the brain and there it remains. This confuses the body and its auto-immune system, which then starts developing atypical auto immune responses to the presence of the silicone. This auto immune response presents in the patient as atypical lupus, atypical scleroderma, atypical rheumatoid arthritis or a number of other difficult medical conditions. But the silicone stays in the body, once it has escaped the implant, and there is no way to remove it. Hence a serious and permanent problem."

Janet noted that the jury was looking at Dr. Sonier and his drawings with fascination. It appeared that they wanted to raise their hands and ask him questions, but that was not allowed.

"What is your concern about the use of the polyurethane foam as a coating on the implant?" Janet was trying to keep the momentum going, but the Judge interrupted her.

"Let's just digest this all for a few moments and take our afternoon break," Judge Parsons said. "We will be in recess for 15 minutes or so. Please rise for the jury."

During the break, Janet and Pam hurried to the ladies room and had a few moments to talk.

"I love Dr. Sonier. That's all I have to say." Pamela said, with tears in her eyes as they washed their hands together.

"He is so smart and such a nice man." Janet affirmed. "I can always count on him to do well on cross-examination, which is more than I can say for a lot of witnesses." Janet was thinking of her next witness, Dr. Richard Guilliot, who was a challenge and often became very red faced and difficult to understand if he got upset or flustered, partly because of his less than perfect command of the English language, but also because he took testifying very personally and wanted so much to do a good job.

After the break, Dr. Sonier took the stand again.

"Remember that you are still under oath, Dr. Sonier," the Judge reminded him. "You may proceed, Mrs. Stephenson."

"Dr. Sonier, before the break, I asked you to explain your concern about the use of the polyurethane foam on the outside of the Mammselle implant. Could you do that for us now?"

"My concern is that the polyurethane foam does not remain foam. After the implant is placed in the body of the patient, the foam begins to disintegrate. It first begins to break down as a material when the body attempts to create scar tissue around the implant. It finally transforms into an entirely different substance known, chemically, as toluline diamine. It is often known by just the letters TDA. The problems with having TDA in the human body begin with the fact that TDA is a cancer-causing substance, or carcinogen. The second problem. And perhaps, more serious problem, is that the TDA, is a semi-liquid and is easily transported around the body by our friends, the macrophages, and by the lymphatic system."

"Why is that a more serious problem, Dr. Sonier?" Janet asked.

"It is more serious because the TDA can cause cancer in places in the body which are far away from the implant. As a result, such pesky cancers are often not immediately expected or found by physicians."

"You told us, in your responses to Mr. Napoli's questions that you had done scientific studies on the polyurethane materials in the

Mammselle implant, Dr. Sonier. Could you describe and explain those studies to us?"

"Perhaps it would be easiest to refer to the article about the studies to do that.' Dr. Sonier had opened his exhibit notebook, "I believe it is Exhibit number 2."

Janet nodded, "I would ask that the jurors turn in their notebooks to the second exhibit."

"In a nutshell," Dr. Sonier began, "we took apart a Mammselle implant and implanted the bits of polyurethane foam in the bodies of rabbits and laboratory rats, which were perfectly healthy. We also implanted tiny replicas of the Mammselle implant in other rabbits and laboratory rats."

"Why did you do that?" Janet asked

"As you can see from the first page of the article, our intent was to investigate what happened to the materials in the bodies of the animals and to investigate any effects of the implants on the health of the animals."

"What were the results of the study?" Janet jumped to the conclusion.

"If you will turn to Appendix A of Exhibit 2, I will show you. If you look at the photographs there, you can observe the appearance of each of the animals before the study and the appearance of each of them after the study. It is clear that after the study, each of the animals appears to be very ill. They all lost weight and hair, all but one developed visible tumors. But even more important, each and every one of the animals, both rabbits and rats, developed liver cancer."

"Have you documented the results of your findings in this study?"

"The tables in Appendix B, C, and D demonstrate the changes in body weight and the health of the animals. Appendix D demonstrates the findings of cancerous tumors on the livers of each animal when the animals were examined in autopsy."

"As a result of your educational background and your experience, do you have an opinion as to the safety and effectiveness of the Mammselle implant?"

"Yes, I do."

"What is that opinion?"

"It is my opinion as a medical biomaterials scientist, to a reasonable degree of scientific certainty that the Mamselle implant is not safe and effective as a medical implant in the human body."

"Do you have an opinion as to whether or not the Mammselle implant has a causal relationship to the development of liver cancer in the animals that you studied?"

"Yes, I do have an opinion."

"What is that opinion?"

"It is my opinion as a medical biomaterials scientist, to a reasonable degree of scientific certainty that the degradation of the polyurethane foam into the chemical compound toluene diamine and the certain transportation of that substance throughout the bodies of the test animals, caused the TDA to lodge in the liver of the animals and that the TDA caused the liver cancer which resulted in the test animals." Dr. Jean Sonier said with quiet confidence. Terry Napoli and Rex Montague were both scribbling on their yellow pads and Napoli was staring directly at Jean Sonier, who looked both at him and at the jury.

"Dr. Sonier, are you familiar with the requirements of the United States Food and Drug Administration for the marketing approval of breast implants?"

"Yes, I am very familiar with the FDA requirements."

"How did you gain that knowledge?" Janet asked him.

"I held the position of Biomaterials Director for the comparable Canadian agency to the FDA, called the Ministry of Health and Human Services, during the time that silicone gel breast implants were being approved for marketing in the United States and Canada. I studied the American rules thoroughly and had many meetings with my American counterparts on the issue."

"Do you have an opinion as to whether or not the Mammselle implant should be marketed in the United States and approved by the Food and Drug Administration?"

"Objection!" Napoli was on his feet waiving his yellow pad.

"What is your objection to the question, Mr. Napoli?" asked the judge.

"This witness worked in Canada and not the United States. He is out of the scope of his admitted expertise."

"Overruled. He is admitted as a medical biomaterial scientist and he has testified that he has met with the US FDA on this issue. Your objection goes to the weight the jury should give the testimony. You may cross-examine the witness. Continue, sir."

"I have an opinion," Dr. Sonier said calmly and with confidence.

"What is your opinion?"

"My opinion is that the Mammselle should not be on the market under the current rules of the United States Food and Drug Administration."

"Dr. Sonier, what is the basis for that opinion?" Janet asked him.

Dr. Jean Sonier sat silently for a moment, then straightened in his chair and leaned forward just a bit. "The FDA requires that no bad results occur in any animal tests on a medical implant before allowing tests to continue on human beings. When I last checked, there were no animal tests on the polyurethane-coated silicone implants known as the Mammselle on file with the FDA at all. The FDA does not have the information about the effects of the Mammselle polyurethane on rats and rabbits. As a result, it has been released for sale and use in human patients."

Janet wanted the jury to understand the FDA issue before Napoli began confusing it. She wanted it to be explained by the world's best teacher, Jean Sonier.

"Dr. Sonier, how can that happen under the scrutiny of the FDA, in this country?"

"I will try to explain how the Mammselle slipped through the cracks, as we say, of federal regulation. PolySurgical Specialties buys all of the materials to manufacture its implant from Conway Chemical. Conway Chemical has had FDA approval for the sale of a silicone implant for years. The FDA rules allow for a purchaser of Conway Chemical MATERIALS to use the studies filed with the FDA on silicone for their products, made of those materials. But here comes the loophole, which PSS jumped through gleefully. Silicone gel implants cause a hardening of the breast sometimes, called capsular contracture. That is an adverse effect listed on the warnings about the use of silicone gel implants. PolySurgical Specialties knew that polyurethane on the outside of the implant prevented this adverse consequence, so they submitted their application for approval as a piggyback improvement of an existing approved product. The FDA allows such an application. The application was approved as an improvement of an existing product. It's as simple as that. No animal studies required in the loophole."

Janet looked at the jury. They seemed to understand and a couple of them were almost nodding their heads.

"What happens after FDA approval, Dr. Sonier?" Janet continued.

"The manufacturer can market the implant to physicians and directly to the public now that the learned intermediary rule has disappeared in the U.S. In short, PSS is free to market the Mammselle on the open market in the United States."

"Is PSS free to market the implant anywhere?"

"In any country which does not ban it, such as Canada," he said simply.

"Objection! Irrelevant," Napoli was almost shouting.

"Overruled," said Judge Parsons calmly.

"Why can't the defendant market the implant in Canada?" Janet asked him.

"Because when I was Minister of Biomaterials, we conducted the studies which are reported and published as your Exhibit 2, and the implant was banned. The Canadian government commissioned the animal studies and banned the implant because of the results which found that every animal developed liver cancer and other health problems."

"Dr. Sonier," Janet asked "Have you had an opportunity to review the medical records of Pamela Lawson in this case?"

"Yes, I always ask to review the medical records before I agree to testify in any case." He replied.

"Have you had an opportunity to meet Pamela Lawson and talk with her?"

"Yes, I have done that as well, on more than one occasion and I have also reviewed her deposition testimony."

"In your medical education at the Emory University Medical School, did you study the causal connection between various implanted materials and the health consequences on the patients?"

"Yes, that was the very purpose of the program and the medical biomaterials certification." Jean Sonier answered.

"Dr. Sonier, in light of your review of the medical records and other knowledge of Pamela Lawson, together with your education, background and experience do you have an opinion as to whether Pamela Lawson's Mammselle implants caused the liver cancer from which she suffered?"

This was the big question and of course, Napoli objected again, springing to his feet.

"Overruled" was all the judge said. He would take it as an error of law to be appealed if it came to that.

"Yes, I have an opinion."

"What is that opinion?"

"It is my opinion as a medical biomaterials scientist, to a reasonable degree of scientific and medical certainty that the implantation and subsequent disintegration of the polyurethane implants were the cause of Pamela Lawson developing liver cancer. I noted from the operative report when her implants were removed by Dr. Dan MacNamara, that the implants were smooth and had no coating. I also noted when the implants were received and tested by Dr. Richard Guilliot at LaVeer University, that there were traces of TDA remaining on the implants after explantation or removal. I reviewed the pathological reports of the implants and of the liver, after it was removed, and found that the tissues were remarkably like those of my rats and rabbits in the effects of the carcinogen in causing the tumors to develop. It is my opinion that the Mammselle implants were the cause of Pamela Lawson's liver cancer."

"Thank you, Dr. Sonier. I have no further questions at this time."

Judge Parsons waited until Janet sat down and Napoli stood to go to the podium before he spoke.

"Well, I think we've had enough to mull over for one day. We will take up with the defendant's cross-examination in the morning. Ladies and Gentlemen of the jury, how are you doing at your hotel? Are the accommodations satisfactory and are they feeding you enough?"

The jurors all murmured and nodded at the judge. They suddenly looked very tired as a group and started gathering their notebooks and things.

"Leave your juror notebooks. They will be safe on your chairs until tomorrow. Remember my admonition to you. No talking about the case to anyone. Family may come for dinner, and so forth, but you may not discuss the case. Your bus is waiting and we'll see you at nine o'clock in the morning. Have a restful evening. All rise for the jury."

The jurors left the heavy notebooks behind and filed out to the jury room. They were already talking and laughing in relief before the door to the jury room was closed by the bailiff.

"We'll be in recess until eight thirty tomorrow morning. We'll plan to start the cross-examination of Dr. Sonier at nine o'clock in the morning Dr. Sonier, you are in the middle of testimony and remain under oath."

"Yes, Your Honor," Jean Sonier respectfully nodded to the judge.

"Good. See you all tomorrow." Judge Parsons disappeared through the door to his chambers.

Pamela and Larry Lawson appeared to be in a trance. Pamela was obviously tired and had deep circles under her eyes. Larry was just looking at Dr. Sonier as he left the witness stand and went to confer with James and Adam, who were organizing the materials and boxes for tomorrow. Janet Stephenson, who was sitting next to Pam, took her hand.

"Pam, you need to rest. Whatever you can do to relax, you and Larry need to do."

Pamela turned to her attorney and smiled wanly. "I know, Janet," was all she said.

"Janet, that was just fabulous." Larry finally said. "The man is a genius. How could we possibly lose after his testimony? The jury has to have decided after that."

"Larry, remember when I told you that you would hate Napoli after his opening? Well, trust me, you will be just as furious with him after he cross-examines Dr. Sonier. It isn't over. Not by a long shot and anything can happen. However, we did end the day on a good note. We can only hope that the jurors hold that moment in their minds. Dr. Sonier did a great job with them today."

Larry wasn't letting go. He thought that Napoli and the cast of thousands should just surrender.

"I don't get it. What more has to be said?" he furrowed his brow.

"Their entire case has to be said." Janet laughed. "Believe me, you will see why the PSS attorneys get the big bucks when Napoli takes over tomorrow."

Janet noticed that Pam was still sitting limply in her seat and she sat down beside her again.

"Pam, my suggestion is that you do not come tomorrow. The cross-examination can go on just as well without you. You will be testifying in a few days and I need you to be up to it. The jurors are prepared for you not to be in the courtroom every day."

"Do you really think so, Janet? I don't want to hurt our case."

"It won't hurt a thing. Just think about it. Larry can call me on my cell and let me know how you are doing in the morning. But, tomorrow might be a good day to miss. You've been here every minute so far. Just think how far we have to go down these long halls just to the ladies' room and you may change your mind." Janet smiled gently at her frail client.

Pam got up slowly and nodded. "Now that sounds good." She said. "We'll call." Larry steadied her as they left the courtroom and the chaos of tomorrow's preparation behind.

Napoli, Montague, and their retinue were caucusing in the far back corner of the courtroom. Several paralegals were gathering and boxing the notebooks that the attorneys had been using. Then, suddenly, the cast of thousands snapped their fingers at the paralegals and they were all gone in, what seemed an instant. The defendant's side of the courtroom was perfectly bare.

Adam, James, and Dr. Sonier came to the plaintiff's table, where Janet was going through her trial notebook for Dr. Sonier and Dr. Guilliot. "We're ready for tomorrow, I think," said Adam. "We've organized the next set of notebooks, but we can go all through Dr. Guilliot's testimony with Notebook #1, which they already have. Do you need other documents for redirect?"

Janet looked at her efficient paralegals, "No, guys, I think we are good. This is where all the work you have done in the last three months pays off. We don't have to scramble around for things at the last minute."

James smiled, "It's because of you Janet. Your brain is in the same league with Dr. Sonier. I can't believe that you can remember the documents by exhibit number, never mind which box they are in."

"I don't compare to our Dr. Sonier," Janet said fondly, to James and Adam and her favorite scientist. "Anybody up for a little early dinner at a restaurant rather than pizza in the conference room, for a change?"

"I'm starved," said Adam, "Sounds good to me."

"Wow, eating out twice in the same day! That's great." James said enthusiastically.

"I would like to, Janet, but I'm afraid there may be spies who would regard my eating with you as inappropriate, though it is not. And, I would rather just spend this evening gathering my thoughts. I don't mind pizza out of boxes," Jean Sonier laughed. "I also would like to take a walk in the Bear Creek Park and get some exercise, so my body does not fully atrophy."

"Whatever you like, Jean," Janet smiled at him. Dr. Sonier looked a little tired, she thought. Perhaps a peaceful walk was just what he really needed. "Well, guys, shall we just leave our car parked in the lot and walk over to the English Pub, or do you want to drive to someplace closer to the office?"

"I know," said Adam, "Let's go to The Pub in Bel Mar. It's got great fish and chips and shepherd's pie, and its closer to the office and on the way."

"And it has Guinness," added James.

"Okay," let's go. Jean, we're in the same parking lot, I think." Dr. Sonier nodded and they all left Courtroom One. The security guard locked the glass double doors behind them.

Terry Napoli and Rex Montague returned to Rex's office. The limousines were waiting at the south door of the City and County building to ferry them and the cast of thousands back to the Seventeenth Street offices of Montague's downtown law firm. The parade of defense attorneys lured off most of the members of the press who were waiting outside the door of Courtroom One and Larry and Pam Lawson were able to leave the city and county building without having to use the secret passage which opened to the west door.

Back at the offices of Montague, Smith & Reed, Rex Montague and Terry Napoli went into Montague's office and sat down in the large black leather chairs around the small oval oak conference table. His office was the corner office on the mountain-facing side of the building and the entire front range of the Rocky Mountains was visible from the wall of glass windows.

"I have to say, Rex, this is quite a view." Said Napoli, leaning back in his chair and gazing at the majesty of Mount Evans, in the middle of the spectacular panorama of foothills with snow-capped mountains behind them. "It beats my view of the other skyscrapers of Chicago."

"It's why we come home to Denver," Montague replied. "Are we ready for tomorrow?" he asked, changing the subject back to the courtroom.

"Is that the polite corporate 'we', Rex? I don't know about you, but I'm ready." Said Napoli confidently. "I took this guy's deposition and grilled the hell out of him. We just have to show the jury that all of his work is either not relevant because it is only mice and rabbits, or that Sonier is just so intent on tanking the Mammselle in the United States that he will say anything."

"I hope you can do it," replied Montague. "It's a shame that we had to end the day where we did. I would like to have ended on your making those points, rather than on Sonier's testimony that our implant caused her cancer."

Just then, Rex Montague's secretary came into the room with a document in her hand. She handed it to him, and he read it carefully.

"What's up?" asked Napoli, still leaning back in his chair, gazing at the mountains.

"It's a note from Rivera. He wants to talk to us about Winchester. Apparently, he was not successful in his attempts to get Winchester out of jail, but he is supposed to go before the grand jury tomorrow."

Napoli's cell phone rang. It was Jennifer Fordham. "Jerry Carson and I need to see you right away," she said.

"Well, we are in Rex's office. Where are you?"

"We're just in a little bar down the street," she said. "We'll come right over."

"Okay," Said Terry Napoli and snapped his phone closed.

Terry Napoli sat up in his chair and looked at his colleague. Then he rubbed his face with both his hands. Finally, he said, "Rex, we have our moments, but right now, I suggest that we present a united front. We are about to meet with Jennifer Fordham, our client, and the attorney for the one who writes our checks, Forrest Winchester, who, unfortunately, is in the slammer. I have no idea what has been going on, but I think we are about to find out. Meanwhile, we are quite busy ourselves in the middle of this trial. And, I need a scotch."

"I agree. I think we should both just listen right now. And, for once, I am sorry that we have a no drinking rule in our office," Rex Montague responded, warmly.

"Let's have a good dinner after we get through with them, what do you say?" said Napoli.

"Sounds good to me," Rex responded. He would have to have his secretary call his wife, who was going to meet him later for dinner at Racine's. "Excuse me a moment," he said to Napoli and left the office, closing the door.

He went to his secretary's desk and asked her to call his wife and explain that he was going to have to go to dinner with Napoli and that they would be working late. When he returned to his office, Napoli was pacing in front of the windows. Just as he was about to speak, his intercom announced that Jennifer Fordham and Jerry Carson, and Jerry Carson's attorney were in the reception area. Rex was going to go to meet them but decided to ask the receptionist to buzz his secretary to show them in. In a few moments, the door opened and Jennifer Fordham, Jerry Carson, and a tall, older man with gray curly hair entered the room.

"Jennifer, Jerry would you like to sit," Rex motioned to the black leather chairs around the table.

"Rex, Terry, this is my personal attorney from California, Justin Thomason," Jerry Carson said.

Terry came around the table and extended his hand to the attorney. "How do you do," he said, without smiling.

"Rex Montague," he said, shaking Thomason's hand. "Shall we sit?"

"Great view," smiled the new attorney as he sat in a chair facing the mountains.

Jennifer was already sitting at the end of the table. It was clear that she was accustomed to being in charge. She looked grim and was not participating in pleasantries about the view. "We need to discuss some things." She said without smiling.

"We are prepared for tomorrow and the cross-examination of Sonier." Napoli volunteered.

"Screw Sonier!" Jennifer said angrily. Then she slapped the subpoena she had received to testify at the grand jury on the table in front of the surprised attorneys. "Last night when we got back to the hotel, Jerry and I were both served with subpoenas to testify before the grand jury the day after tomorrow!"

"That is why I am here," Justin Thomason offered. "Although I practice now in California, I happen to also be licensed in Colorado. I used to practice here when I got out of law school at D.U."

Montague and Napoli were silent. Finally, Rex Montague said to Jennifer, "Do you have a personal attorney, or do you think that you need one?"

"I have no clue," Jennifer said. "But my guess is that I do. How does this affect the trial? What do we do?"

"Well, you clearly have to testify before the grand jury" answered Rex. "Our jury will never know why you are not in the courtroom, so that is the least of your problems. Technically, we only need one corporate representative and it can be anyone of you, Mr. or Mrs. Winchester, or you or Jerry."

Just then Montague's phone rang and he went to his desk to pick it up. It was his colleague, Jason Rivera, asking to join the meeting. "Come on down to my office," Rex Montague told him. Thirty seconds later, he entered the room and closed the door behind him.

"Rex," he said, extending his hand. Rex Montague shook his hand and then introduced him to everyone in the room whom he did not know already.

"I thought we should all have a word about what is going on with the grand jury," Rivera said, as he sat down at the other end of the oval table.

"What is going on?" asked Justin Thomason.

"Mr. Winchester has to appear tomorrow," he began. "Then, I think that he will be granted bail and let out of jail. I had a conference with the D.A. Rick Plume, who said they will no longer take the position that he is a flight risk. At that time, he will be free to attend your trial, after we get bond set and it is posted. His wife, Leslie, told me that she can arrange for the posting of bail."

"Why do we have to testify at the grand jury," asked Jennifer.

"I don't know exactly what the grand jury is investigating, but it is my assumption that it is the death of Sherrie Barker. I am sure that you were subpoenaed because she was your employee. The D.A. probably just wants to find out from you why she was in Denver and whether she was here on company or personal business."

"We answered all those questions when they came to our offices in Santa Barbara," said Jerry. His attorney held up his hand, motioning for Jerry to be silent.

"Why would the D.A. subpoena Forrest Winchester before Sherrie Barker's own employers?" asked Thomason.

"It may have just been accidental. The D.A. may have just subpoenaed him at that time because he was in custody for the Dr. Sonier incident. Then they felt insecure about Winchester staying in the jurisdiction since Conway Chemical is not a named defendant in the civil trial, being only the subsequent parent company."

"Why did Forrest Winchester go to LoDo to meet Dr. Sonier?" asked Jennifer Fordham.

"I can't tell you anything that my client has shared with me, as you know," said Jason Rivera, "but therein lies the connection between the grand jury and your trial, and I thought you might be able to help me with that."

Jennifer remembered her first thoughts, and her words to Jerry that Winchester was not their friend and said, "I think that I must have my own attorney before I say anything more to anyone."

"I will discuss all of this with Jerry," Justin Thomason finally replied, "and we will talk with you again, Mr. Rivera, after I feel that I have a better understanding of the facts."

Rex Montague, who did not want to complicate the civil trial by all of the unknown issues surrounding the grand jury, said, "Jennifer is right. I think that everyone who has a subpoena should confer with personal counsel before testifying. However, Terry and I have a civil case to try, where we are attempting to defend the company and we really can't be involved in the totally separate actions of the district attorney and the grand jury proceedings. I would suggest that we ask Leslie Winchester to be the corporate representative at our trial until the testimony of all of you before the grand jury is completed. That should only be a few days and well before the beginning of the presentation of the PSS case in our trial."

Terry Napoli had been sitting silently listening to all of the conversation. "Rex is right," he finally said. "Our trial has to be our focus and this may be just a distraction which Janet Stephenson has cooked up with her friend the D.A. Rick Plume. I wouldn't put it past her. She is known to be a pretty ruthless plaintiff's lawyer. In any case, Rex and I can't be distracted by these subpoenas, even if they are very troublesome for Jennifer, Jerry and Mr. Winchester. It is probably just a grand standing move and a fishing expedition. After you testify, it will probably just all go away."

Jason Rivera was looking very solemn. "I'm not getting the impression that Rick Plume is doing this as some sort of professional courtesy gambit," he said. "That would not be ethical and if he is anything, Plume is known to be a straight shooter. But, I do agree that everyone who has been served a subpoena should not speak about this matter until he or she confers with personal counsel. Thanks for talking to me. I'll be on my way."

Rivera shook hands all around, except with Jennifer Fordham, who did not offer hers. When he was gone, she said, "I do need to spend tomorrow finding a lawyer. Please get Leslie Winchester to sit in court and take notes. Sorry I'll miss your cross-examination of Sonier, Terry," and she left the room, closing the door with a bang behind her.

"We will be on our way, as well," said Justin Thomason. He and Jerry Carson rose to go.

"Will you be in the courtroom tomorrow, Jerry?" asked Napoli.

"I think we will also do some other work tomorrow," his attorney answered. "Shall we go, Jerry?"

Jerry Carson silently shook hands and left with his attorney. He was not looking as though he felt all that confident about the state of affairs in which he found himself, Montague thought as they left the room.

After they were gone, Napoli and Montague sat silently looking at the mountains for a while. Then Montague broke the silence.

"Terry, you said in your opening statement that we are going to present the testimony of Dr. Dan MacNamara. There is no doubt that we need him to testify for us, but the last I heard, he was still in the hospital, squirreled away from public contact or view, and more important, we have not presented him for an expert deposition, even though we have listed him as a witness and designated all of his medical records, articles and speech transcripts as exhibits. Do you know something that I don't know?"

"I haven't had a chance to tell you, Rex. I had a call from Dr. MacNamara's wife, Dr. Sally MacNamara. She left a message for me sometime this morning that he would testify as scheduled. However, that was a bit serendipitous because I didn't actually get the message until after I had made our opening statement. I was really just gambling that I could convince him to testify."

Rex Montague was stunned. "Well, hallelujah," he exclaimed. "Terry, that's great news. There may be only one witness who can make the jury love him more than Sonier, and that is Dan MacNamara. We may just have a chance to win this one."

Terry Napoli was suddenly furious. "Montague, we aren't even close to losing. Just wait until I take that little monkey Sonier apart tomorrow."

Rex Montague, just smiled. He wondered who was calling whom a little monkey.

D r. Sally MacNamara called Terry Napoli at his hotel room and left a message from her husband's suite in the hospital, telling him that Dr. Dan MacNamara would testify, as scheduled.

"There, it's done." She smiled at her husband.

Dan MacNamara was much thinner, and his face was still discolored and red from the burns and plastic surgery, but his good looks had, for the most part, been mostly restored. He no longer wore the brace to stabilize his head and his hair, though very short, had grown back to an attractive length. He wore jeans and a casual shirt and no socks with his loafers. While the hospital suite had made his recovery bearable, and perhaps possible, Dan MacNamara was anxious to go home. The intensive counseling, which had been a part of his treatment, had prepared him to face the world again. Now that he had made the decision to actually testify in Pamela Lawson's trial he wanted to be able to prepare at home. Sally was not so sure. She liked having Dan safe and protected at the hospital away from the photographers and media who had been nearly stalking her since the explosion. Also, the police guard remained outside Dan's room.

"Dan, I think you should plan to stay here until after you testify in the Lawson trial. It is really quite comfortable and the kids and I can come whenever you want." Sally pleaded.

"Well, I have to talk to the grand jury this afternoon, so we'll talk about it after that. What do you say?" Dan looked at Sally with tender eyes. She had been his strength and the real reason he had survived the past months.

"What are the plans to get you to the grand jury?" Sally asked.

"Joel Steiner is coming in an unmarked police car to take me there. Rick Plume said that I could come in casual clothes—so this is how they get me!" He spread his arms, stood up, and turned around, while Sally put her hands over her eyes and laughed at her newly whimsical husband. He had become, once again, the medical student with whom she had fallen in love so many years ago.

"Okay. I'll divert the attention of anyone watching by leaving after you go, so they will think that I am just leaving from a normal visit and that you are still here. Then after I do rounds this evening, I'll bring the kids back with me."

"You know, since I received the subpoena to testify before the grand jury, this all became very clear to me. I have to testify in Pamela Lawson's trial and it doesn't matter if I testify in her case, or when PSS is putting on witnesses. My testimony will be the same either way and I can be an honest and good doctor once again."

"You've always been a good doctor," Sally said gently.

"But not such a smart one. I should have figured all of this out long ago."

"But how? You had never seen the studies that PSS was keeping from you—and all other plastic surgeons, and the FDA, for that matter." Sally asked him.

"Sally, our patients rely on us to have all the information about what we are putting in their bodies before we put them under anesthetic and cut them open. I was just swept away by the money and the prestige of being the plastic surgeon who conquered capsular contracture - and I never stopped to ask myself, or anyone else, about the cost of that to my patients. PSS played on my professional and personal arrogance and I lapped it up like an anxious, starving puppy. There's no excuse. I should have had my brain turned on and demanded to see the safety studies on the animals—as well as the clinical studies. Turns out there weren't any to show me. I made my patients the guinea pigs for the PSS Mammselle!"

Sally looked at his anguished face and said to him, "Dan, that is 20/20 hindsight. You didn't know. That is the point. You were actively deceived. What are you going to tell the grand jury?"

"I don't know. I guess I'll just answer Rick Plume's questions as honestly as I can."

There was a knock at the door. Sally answered it and opened the door for Joel Steiner to enter. "Ready, Doc?" he asked.

"I'm as ready as I will ever be," said Dr. Dan MacNamara. He kissed Sally and said, "See you later, alligator." He winked at her and followed Joel Steiner out of the door. Sally closed the door and sat down in the easy chair again to wait for a bit to carry out her diversion for the press. After ten minutes or so she left the room, and took the elevator to her office on the fourth floor.

Leslie Winchester was sitting on the couch in her suite at the Brown Palace, sipping chamomile tea and listening to music from "Les Miserables" when she got the call from Terry Napoli asking her to be the corporate representative at the trial the next day.

"Why do I need to do that?" she asked. "I was thinking of missing the trial tomorrow, even though I imagine that you will be cross-examining Dr. Sonier. I thought I might need to be available to Forrest, who has to appear before the grand jury. I may be able to arrange to bond him out when that is finished."

"Mrs. Winchester, I hate to ask you, but both Jennifer Fordham and Jerry Carson have now been subpoenaed to testify before the grand jury as well. They have to testify the day after tomorrow and neither of them has had an opportunity to seek or confer with personal attorneys about the matter. They need to be able to do that tomorrow."

"Fine, but what about Forrest? He isn't going to be very pleased if he is not our first priority. And, he pays your bill. I'm sure that should be of some concern to you considering his propensity for firing lawyers. He is just sitting in the Denver jail stewing and seething about this whole business."

"We will be in contact with his attorney, Jason Rivera, constantly, so that we can get a message to you about those proceedings and when you might be needed regarding the bail arrangements."

"Well, I have to trust you Mr. Napoli because I frankly haven't a clue about what is going on here. I think there is a lot that I do not know and since I will ultimately be writing the checks, I want to advise you that I do not intend to continue to be in the dark. But, first things first. Your job is to win this trial and I will do my part in assisting you to do that. I'll be there tomorrow with the proverbial bells on."

"Thank you, Mrs. Winchester. We will have a limo to pick you up at 8:30 in the morning That should be plenty of time because your hotel is only a few minutes from the City and County Building."

"That will be fine. Thank you." Leslie Winchester said and she hung up the telephone. Then she picked it up again and ordered a bottle of chilled champagne from room service. "I may be the only person in this entire mess who has cause to celebrate," she said out loud to herself.

Terry Napoli and Rex Montague walked to Gallagher's Steak House at Fifteenth and Arapahoe and dined, as they had promised themselves, on filet mignon and salmon. They drank a scotch before dinner and shared a bottle of merlot with their meal. Their conversation was casual and light and they did not talk about the trial or the grand jury. They almost seemed to be friends. Afterwards, Rex Montague walked to his garage and Napoli walked a block or two to the Sixteenth Street Mall, where laughter from the sidewalk cafés and energy of the pedestrians on the mall sidewalks seemed almost surreal to him. He stuffed his hands in his pockets and slowly made his way back to his hotel, musing about the strange turn of events with the grand jury and its disruption of his case. He was relieved that all of the chaos that he had just endured since the end of the trial day with his clients would never be known to the jury and, so far, had not appeared in the media. He was thankful that grand jury proceedings are secret and he hoped that these proceedings had a long way to go. All he needed was to have some sort of indictments or other breaking news in the middle of his trial.

Back at the hotel, Terry Napoli returned calls to his wife and son and took a hot shower. Then he settled back on the couch in his room with his trial notebook and was soon totally engrossed in the review of his preparation of the cross-examination of Dr. Jean Sonier. When he next looked at the clock radio on his bedside table, it was one o'clock in the morning.

"All rise," the bailiff announced "This court is now in session the Honorable Jameson Parsons presiding."

The courtroom was full of the Silicone Sisters, other observers, the press without cameras, and Napoli's cast of thousands as Judge Parsons entered the courtroom from the door behind the bench. Pamela Lawson was not in the courtroom, but Larry Lawson sat at the Plaintiff's table.

"Be seated," he said. "Counsel, are there any preliminary matters before we call in the jury?"

"Not for the Plaintiffs, Your Honor," said Janet Stephenson.

"We would just like to introduce Mrs. Leslie Winchester, as the corporate representative today, Your Honor," said Rex Montague.

"Welcome, Mrs. Winchester. Is there anything further?" the judge asked.

"Your Honor, we would note for the record, that Mrs. Lawson is not feeling well enough to be in the courtroom today, but Mr. Lawson is present."

"Very well. Thank you, Mrs. Stephenson. Is there anything further?"

Everyone remained silent and Judge Parsons said, "Very well, let's call in the jury. Please stand for the jury." Everyone in the courtroom stood as the bailiff opened the door to the jury room and the jurors came out single file, proceeded to the jury box, and were seated in the seats, where they had left their heavy trial notebooks.

"We are ready to proceed with the cross-examination by the defendant's counsel of Dr. Jean Sonier. I would note for the jury that the defendant's representative at the counsel table is Mrs. Leslie Winchester and also, that Pamela Lawson is not well enough to be with us in court today. Is Dr. Sonier present and ready to testify?"

"He is, Your Honor," said Janet Stephenson.

The bailiff opened the door to the courtroom and summoned Dr. Sonier, who walked crisply into the room and through the swinging gate to the witness box. He wore a gray tweed jacket with dark gray trousers, a white shirt, and a dark red bow tie.

"Good morning, Dr. Sonier," said the judge, "remember that you are still under oath."

"Indeed," Jean Sonier responded with a polite nod.

"Mr. Napoli? Are you ready to proceed with cross-examination?"

Terry Napoli stood up and went to the podium. "Yes, Your Honor,' he said.

"All right then, you may proceed." Said Judge Parsons, leaning back in his giant black leather chair behind the bench.

"Good morning, Dr. Sonier. I am Terry Napoli, attorney for the defendant PolySurgical Specialties. As you will recall, we have met several times in the past."

"Yes, we have," said Dr. Sonier brightly.

"Dr. Sonier, you testified yesterday as an expert witness for the Plaintiff, Pamela Lawson, isn't that correct?"

"Yes, it is," said Sonier.

"And the fact is, Dr. Sonier, that in the past five years, you have testified for plaintiffs in silicone gel breast implant cases no less than twelve times in court and in more than thirty depositions, isn't that correct?"

"In the past five years, as my CV notes, I have testified 13 times in court and in 32 depositions, for plaintiffs. I have also testified 16 times for defendants in other kinds of cases during that time frame, as you will note on my CV."

"None of the cases in which you testified for defendants were breast implant cases were they?"

"No, those were cases involving other types of implants," Sonier replied.

"And, it is a fact, isn't it Dr. Sonier, that you made it your cause to remove the Mammselle implant from the market in Canada, even though it is approved for sale by the Food and Drug Administration in the United States." Terry Napoli asked firmly.

"It was not so much 'my cause' as you say, but a biomedical necessity to remove the Mammselle from the Canadian market," replied Sonier calmly.

"It is a fact that the FDA has approved the Mammselle implant for sale in the United States, isn't it, Dr. Sonier." Napoli was raising his voice.

"Yes," said Sonier simply.

"And the truth is, Dr. Sonier, that despite your efforts to have the Mammselle removed from the US market, you have failed to do so, isn't it?" Napoli demanded.

"I have made no efforts, as you say. I have only met with the FDA at their invitation to discuss the Canadian action. But that was in my official capacity."

"As a matter of fact, Dr. Sonier, you have no official capacity to speak for Canada or anyone else because you are no longer a part of the Canadian regulatory agency, isn't that so?"

"I do not speak for the Canadian government, I speak in my capacity as a medical biomaterials scientist, which is an international qualification, Mr. Napoli," said Sonier, looking firmly into Napoli's eyes.

"Let's talk about your animal tests, Dr. Sonier. You did those tests at your laboratory in Canada, right?"

"Yes, that is correct." Said Sonier.

"Good science requires that all scientific tests or studies be verified or duplicated, isn't that correct, Dr. Sonier?"

"That is part of the scientific method and part of the requirement of peer review of a scientist's work," replied the scientist.

"Well, your studies, implanting polyurethane into rats and rabbits, in fact, have not been duplicated by any other studies, have they, Dr. Sonier?"

"The studies have been published by the Canadian government and in two peer-reviewed journals, at this point," answered Dr. Sonier clearly.

"But, you would agree with me, wouldn't you Dr. Sonier, that without duplication and verification by other studies, there is no empirical proof that your studies are accurate, is there?" Napoli stated loudly.

"No, I would not agree," began Sonier, "because there is a great deal of empirical proof, as you say, in the published literature that polyurethane foams degrade into toluene diamine, a carcinogen, in laboratory conditions which simulate the human body. We extended those existing studies by implanting the polyurethane into actual living bodies of animals. In a word, our studies were the verifiable extension of the laboratory work already done on polyurethane."

"Very clever, Dr. Sonier," Napoli was almost sneering, "But the real fact is that your studies on the polyurethane foam in animals are really just junk science, meant to confuse the jury because they have not been duplicated and verified by other similar studies!" Napoli announced.

"Objection," Janet was on her feet. "Misleading to the jury."

"Sustained" said Judge Parsons. "Mr. Napoli, we had a Daubert hearing in which I ruled that Dr. Sonier's studies passed the Daubert test and are admissible. That means that I have ruled that they are not 'junk science' under the required legal standard."

"Let me rephrase. In any case," Napoli continued, undeterred, "Your studies have not been duplicated by any other medical biomaterials scientist, have they Dr. Sonier?"

"Objection." Janet said.

"I'll allow it, with this clarification for the jury: the studies are admissible in this case," said the judge.

"Our studies have not been duplicated, or reported in any peer-review journal, yet." Dr. Sonier said, "but that sort of work takes time and the studies have only been available to the scientific community a short while."

"Good science requires that any studies be duplicated and verified, isn't that true, Dr. Sonier?" Napoli continued.

"I am sure that will occur in the near future, but for the present, our studies verify the results of laboratory tests involving polyurethane under similar conditions to the biological environment of the living animal." Dr. Sonier said calmly and with confidence.

"Am I correct that you have only conducted animal studies on the polyurethane and that you have not done any studies on polyurethane in humans?"

"Yes, that is correct," answered Sonier.

"It is also true, is it not, Dr. Sonier, that there is not a direct correlation between what happens in an animal study and what would occur in a human being?"

"Not necessarily," Sonier replied.

"Rats and rabbits are not people, are they Dr. Sonier?"

"No, but they are mammals, with similar biological systems. Even the FDA prohibits tests of material in human subjects if there are any adverse effects in animal studies. That is the difference between Phase Two animal studies and Phase Three clinical trials, in the United States Food and Drug Administration's procedures for approving a medical product for marketing. You cannot go on to Phase Three, or testing in humans if there are any adverse effects on the animals tested in Phase Two."

"But, with the Mammselle implant, at issue in this case, it is a fact that the FDA has approved the implant for marketing and use as a breast implant, isn't it, Dr. Sonier."

"Yes, regrettably." Sonier conceded.

"Pamela Lawson had the Mammselle implant because her plastic surgeon, Dr. Dan MacNamara could legally choose it over other available implants on the market, right?"

"Yes." Dr. Sonier said.

"And when he chose it, he was doing nothing improper or wrong, isn't that correct?"

"As a medical biomaterials scientist, and not a lawyer, I must say that the use of this implant in the human body is wrong." Dr. Sonier said with some emphasis.

Janet smiled, just as she was rising to object and she sat down again.

Napoli looked briefly at his notes, then said "I have no further questions for this witness," and he sat down. Janet was stunned. She expected the cross-examination of Dr. Sonier to take a full day as it was listed on the proposed trial schedule. She had not planned to put Dr. Guilliot on the stand until tomorrow.

"Mrs. Stephenson, do you have any redirect?"

"Yes, Your Honor, I do have a few questions," she said.

"We will continue with your redirect after the morning break. We will be in recess for 20 minutes. Please rise for the jury."

During the break, Janet had James call Dr. Guilliot to ask him to come downtown and he discovered that he was, in fact, one block away at the Denver Public Library, doing some research in one of the computer rooms. He told James that he would be available to testify whenever he was summoned.

"Well, Janet, where do we go from here?" Sonier asked her at the break.

"On redirect, I am going to ask you some questions about Pam and her medical records, to lay the groundwork for Richard.," she told him

"Excellent," was all Sonier said as he left the courtroom for "a few moments of peace," as he put it.

After the break, Dr. Sonier took the stand again.

Janet went to the podium and began her redirect examination, "Dr. Sonier, you told us in your earlier testimony that you are qualified to look at medical records and to form medical opinions about the effect of implants, correct?"

"Yes," he responded, "That was part of the training at Emory University and I have always looked at the medical records of the patients into whom implants have been placed."

"Did you review Pamela Lawson's records, which are contained in Exhibit Notebook One?"

"Yes, I did," he said.

"You also stated in response to questions asked by Mr. Napoli, that you believe that the placement of a Mammselle implant in a patient is wrong, from your perspective as a medical biomaterials scientist, did I quote you correctly?"

"Yes, I said that." Dr. Sonier was nodding his head.

"Have you also examined any other medical evidence related to Pamela Lawson?"

"Yes, in cooperation with Dr. Richard Guilliot of LaVeer University, I examined both the implants which were removed from Pamela Lawson and her liver, after it was removed and examined by the pathologist at St. Anthony hospital here in Denver."

"What observations did you make when you examined the explanted Mammselle implant?"

"We observed that there was no semblance of the polyurethane coating remaining on the implant when it was removed. We also found residual traces of toluene diamine on the surface of the implant and in the surrounding breast tissue, which accompanied the removed implant."

"Did you draw any conclusions or form any opinions as a result of your examination of the implants?"

"Yes, I did."

"What were those conclusions and opinions?"

"I concluded to a reasonable degree of scientific certainty that the polyurethane coating on Mrs. Lawson's Mammselle implant had disintegrated and that the chemical toluene diamine had been the result of the chemical interaction between the polyurethane foam and the patient's breast tissue."

"What observations did you make when you examined the liver which was removed from Mrs. Lawson?"

"I should also state that along with the liver, we received the report of the pathologist at St. Anthony hospital. What we observed confirmed his findings that Mrs. Lawson's liver was filled with many malignant lesions and tumors. It was deformed and discolored. The malignancy was confirmed by the microscopic analysis of the liver tissue and the tumors, themselves."

"Did you draw any further conclusions or form any further opinions relating to a causal relationship between the disintegrated polyurethane foam and the malignancy that you observed in Mrs. Lawson's liver specimen?"

"Objection! Foundation! Beyond the scope of cross-examination." Shouted Napoli, who was so upset that he even was holding his fist in the air.

"Well, Mrs. Stephenson, repeat the foundation questions for the record, once again," said Judge Parsons.

"Dr. Sonier, will please explain to the jury what a medical biomaterials scientist does?"

"Yes, of course. It is the job of the medical biomaterials scientist to study the relationship between all different kinds of implanted materials and the effect of that material on the biological environment into which it is implanted and upon the health of the patient who has the implant."

"Were you applying these principles when you reviewed Mrs. Lawson's explanted Mammselle implants and the liver which was removed from her body?"

"Yes"

The judge interjected, "The objection is overruled. You may answer the question."

"Dr. Sonier," Janet repeated, "Did you draw any further conclusions or form any further opinions relating to a causal relationship between the disintegrated polyurethane foam and the malignancy that you observed in Mrs. Lawson's liver specimen?"

"Yes, I did."

"What were those conclusions and opinions?"

"It is my opinion, as a medical biomaterials scientist, based upon my training, experience and the conduct of my own original research, to a reasonable degree of scientific certainty that the degradation or disintegration of the polyurethane, resulting in the production of tolulene diamine, in the body of Pamela Lawson was the proximate cause of her liver cancer."

"I have no further questions at this time," said Janet.

"Mr. Napoli, any re-cross?" asked Judge Jameson Parsons.

Terry Napoli was already on his feet. "Yes, Your Honor," he said as he stepped to the podium.

"Dr. Sonier, let's be honest here," he began, "You do not have one single peer reviewed study from anywhere in the world which demonstrates a connection of any kind between the Mammselle implant and liver cancer in any human patient, do you."

"No, the study has not yet been done," said Dr. Sonier.

"Science is based on being able to prove causation and there is not one iota of proof for the opinions that you have stated to this jury, is there Dr. Sonier."

"All of the opinions I have are based on sound science, sir," said Sonier confidently.

"Your opinions are based on your science and yours alone, aren't they doctor." Napoli was fuming.

"My opinions are based on a lifetime of study and research. Research that your client should have done, but did not do," Sonier responded.

"You are being paid to testify for the plaintiff in this case, aren't you Dr. Sonier?"

"I am only being reimbursed for my expenses. I am not charging an expert witness fee, which experts customarily charge in these cases," he said.

Napoli stopped. He decided not to pursue this line of questioning, just in case Jean Sonier was, in fact, the virtuous man that he appeared to be. He knew that his own witnesses would not fare so well should Janet Stephenson return the favor of questioning about fees.

"I have no further questions, at this time." Terry Napoli said. He sat down, totally unsure about how Dr. Sonier's testimony was received by the jury.

"Great timing, once again, Mr. Napoli. Let's all have lunch," said Judge Parsons. "We will be in recess until two thirty. I must attend a luncheon meeting. The bus will be available to return the jury to your hotel, where you lunch is waiting for you. You may rest and refresh yourselves before we resume, sometime between two thirty and three o'clock this afternoon or whenever you are returned to us. Today we will wait on the jury. Please stand for the jury. We will be in recess."

Larry Lawson was sitting at counsel table looking anxiously at Janet. "How did that go?" he asked. "I can never tell how the jury looks at it because I know that I am not objective and because I feel so angry when Napoli asks questions."

"It was just fine," Janet said, patting him on the shoulder, "Just fine. Dr. Sonier made every point that he needed to make and he was confident and secure in his answers."

Dr. Sonier, James and Adam came over and James, always thinking of eating said, "I assume that you want to meet Dr. Guilliot at the art museum café. Shall I give him a call?"

"Yes," Janet said. "He's right next door at the library, so that is a good place to meet."

While Judge Parsons was at his meeting with the other district judges, Janet met with her next witness and Terry Napoli and Rex Montague had lunch with Leslie Winchester at the Ship Tavern in the Brown Palace hotel. They were also waiting to hear from Jason Rivera about the progress of Forrest Winchester's testimony before the grand jury. But, they heard nothing. If Janet Stephenson had any notion about what was going on at the grand jury, she was not letting on.

At 2:30 when court reconvened, Janet Stephenson called Dr. Richard Guilliot as her next witness. She carefully qualified him as a biomaterials and pathology expert, taking him through his curriculum vitae in the Exhibit Notebook. Napoli and Montague did not challenge his admission as an expert.

Using her Exhibit Notebook One, Janet Stephenson then took Dr. Guilliot through all of the pathology reports and biomaterials analysis of Pamela Lawson's implant, his laboratory procedures in identifying the TDA on the implant and the surrounding tissues, and his analysis of the cancer in the tissues of the liver, which was removed from Pamela Lawson when she received her transplanted liver. Janet had carefully introduced all of this testimony with the testimony of Dr. Sonier because she knew that the jury would have difficulty understanding the French laden English of Dr. Guilliot. Janet carefully referred the juror's to their notebooks and the many colored photos from Dr. Guilliot's electromicrograph laboratory cameras. Dr. Guilliot explained the photos from large poster sized reproductions with a pointer. He was much more comfortable standing in front of the jury with a pointer than in the cramped witness box, which was uncomfortable for his portly, though meticulously well dressed frame. After about a half an hour, the jury seemed to enjoy Dr. Guilliot's teaching style and his charming, though heavy, accent. They followed instructions carefully and some were making notes in their exhibit notebooks.

At the end of his testimony about his examination of the explanted implants and Pamela Lawson's liver, Dr. Guilliot offered the same opinion that the Mammselle implant was the cause of Pamela Lawson's liver cancer.

After the afternoon break, Napoli undertook the cross-examination of Dr. Guilliot, by asking him all of the same questions that he asked Dr. Sonier. Dr. Guilliot clearly was flustered by the confrontational questions and his face turned red. However, he carefully and calmly attempted to find all of the correct English words to explain again and again what he found as a biomaterials scientist and as a pathologist when he examined the specimens that came from Pamela Lawson.

Napoli attempted to keep Dr. Guilliot from returning to the photos and reports in the Exhibit Notebook One in responding, but when Janet objected, he finally was resigned to the fact that Dr. Guilliot was going to continue to refer to the documents in the notebook, where he could read the English words, in response to Napoli's questions. Finally at four forty in the afternoon, he concluded his cross-examination. Janet decided not to ask any questions on redirect.

"Very well, ladies and gentlemen of the jury, we will be in recess until tomorrow at nine o'clock in the morning Have a nice evening and again, you may leave your notebooks in the courtroom. Please rise for the jury." The jury filed out quietly. "Anything further counsel?" the judge asked.

"Not for the plaintiff," said Janet.

"Nor the defendant," said Napoli.

"We will begin with the next witness tomorrow, Mrs. Stephenson." Janet nodded and the judge said "Have a nice evening, then," and he was gone.

Janet had planned to put all of Pamela's physicians on the stand and finish up with all of the medical testimony before she put Pamela Lawson on the stand. Now she was not so sure that was a good idea. Pamela was not holding up as well as she had hoped that she would. Janet was really glad that Pam had missed the cross-examination of Dr. Sonier, which was sure to cause her a great deal of stress, just as it had for Larry. Perhaps she should put Pamela on the stand tomorrow, since she had just had a day to rest. Having Pam testify now might be a better plan. She sat down beside Larry at the table. "Have you talked to Pam today, "she asked him.

"Yes, I called her at the afternoon break." Larry said, "She slept most of the day, so she said that she was feeling a lot better and much stronger this afternoon. She was glad that she stayed at home today."

"How do you think she would feel about testifying tomorrow, rather than later in the trial?"

Larry looked very surprised, "Why, Janet, is there a problem?"

"Not at all," Janet began. "But sometimes it is good to be attentive to the dynamic of a trial and build on the emotional momentum that develops as the trial goes along. It just seems to me that we might want to put Pamela on next, to just tie the story about the damages to the story about the science. Then the doctors and other witnesses will just fill in the gaps."

"That makes sense, I guess." Larry said. He was worried about Pam testifying because not even Janet knew how very fragile she really was. "Let's see what Pam thinks."

"Why don't I meet you both someplace for an early dinner to discuss it?" Janet said. "If she's not up to it, we will call her treating physicians."

"That's a good idea. I'll go home and get her. Where would you like us to meet you?"

"How about Pasta's? Does Pam like Italian food?"

"That's a great place. About six o'clock?"

"Yes, that will be just about right. If I'm late, just get a table because I need to go back to the office first."

Janet spoke briefly with Dr. Richard Guilliot, who was being picked up outside the courthouse by Jean Sonier. The two scientists were heading to Denver International Airport and a flight to Montreal. Dr. Guilliot was cheerful and confident as he gave Janet a hug as Sonier pulled up to the curb in his rental car. Sonier waved at her and opened the door for Guilliot, impatiently.

"At the end of the day," Guilliot told her as he climbed into the car "truth will prevail. Truth will prevail."

Janet watched them drive away. "He has to be right!" she thought to herself.

Amy Larabee and Joel Steiner had planned to meet Rick Plume at the Hofbrau for a beer at 5:45. They were anxious to find out what they could about the grand jury, even though they knew that all of the proceedings were secret. Rick was late.

Rick Plume was in the courtroom of Judge Lucas Lee, battling with Jason Rivera about allowing Forrest Winchester to be released on bail. Winchester had finished his testimony before the grand jury and he wanted out of jail. He was very impatient and almost rude to his attorney and to the judge. It was not a good plan. The judge denied bail until Rick Plume was sure that Winchester would not have to testify further and would not be charged.

When Leslie Winchester called Jason Rivera to find out what she would need to do about paying the bail for her husband, he told her it would not be necessary because Forrest Winchester was to remain in jail, for now.

Rick Plume finally called Joel Steiner's cell phone and said he couldn't meet him and Amy Larabee, as planned. The district attorney knew that all of his decisions at this delicate point in the grand jury proceedings had to be above reproach. He could not afford to be seen with Steiner and Larabee in a public place until the grand jury had finished its work.

Leslie Winchester went to Montague & Smith to meet with Jason Rivera. She was very concerned about the turn of events at the closed hearing and Judge Lee's continued denial of bond for her husband.

"What is going on here," she asked Rivera in the glass walled conference room, where he met with her.

"I don't know, exactly," said Rivera. "I was only allowed to be present during the interrogation of your husband. But, the district attorney seems very sure that he knows what he is doing and I am concerned that he is now opposing bail, after virtually assuring me a few days ago that Mr. Winchester would be out of jail after his testimony."

"What shall I do?" she asked the young attorney.

"Nothing, for now," was his response. "I suggest that you continue to appear at the civil trial and not give the press any reason to question what is going on. I think that it is to our benefit that the only concern is the question of whether the PSS implant caused Pamela Lawson's cancer."

"Right now," Leslie Lawson said, "I need a massage and a drink."

"Sounds like a good plan, to me," said Rivera, smiling at her. "I do suggest that you do not contact your husband until we talk again."

"No worries, there," said Leslie Lawson, "because I don't have the slightest idea about what to say to him. I certainly don't want to have the press follow me to the jail, while I am my company's representative in this trial. Could you have your secretary call a cab for me? Denver is not New York, where you can hail a cab anywhere."

"If you just go downstairs, Mrs. Winchester, I'll have one of the limos take you to your hotel. The limo is still downstairs and on duty."

"Thanks," she said, holding out her hand. "Be in touch with me tomorrow. You can text or leave a message on my cell phone. I'm counting on you to take care of Forrest if that is possible."

At Pasta's, a small Italian restaurant by the Southwest Plaza Mall, Larry and Pamela Lawson had dinner with Janet Stephenson. Pamela was dressed in jeans and a light blue suede jacket. She looked rested and much healthier than the last time Janet Stephenson saw her.

"How do you feel about testifying tomorrow?" Janet asked her.

"Have you changed your mind about putting our testimony at the end of the trial," Pam asked her attorney.

"I'd like to build on the testimony of Sonier and Guilliot. It is my impression that the jury is very interested in the animal studies and they were practically taking notes when Dr. G testified about the microscopic studies on tissues surrounding the implants and your liver. Having you testify now might make that testimony more real and attachable to you as a person." Janet explained.

"Whatever you think is best, Janet." Pamela said. "You know what is best and I barely understand what is going on. Do you want Larry to testify now, too?"

Janet shook her head. "No," she said "I'd like to still have Larry testify at the end, to remind the jury, at the very end of our case, that this about your personal damages and pain."

"Okay. I'm ready. I think tomorrow is as good as any day. I feel better tonight than I have for several days and if I get a good night's sleep, I should be good to go, tomorrow."

"Great. I need to get back to my office and send a fax to Montague and Napoli about the change in witnesses. I also think that I will schedule Dr. Simon and Dr. Emmanuel for tomorrow afternoon, so I need to give them a call."

An hour later, Terry Napoli received a call at his hotel from Montague's office advising him that Pamela Lawson would testify as the next witness.

"I wonder what Janet Stephenson is up to now?" he thought to himself. Meanwhile, the cast of thousands at Montague's office were busily organizing his notebooks for the cross-examination of Pamela Lawson, Dr. Simon and Dr. Levi Emmanuel.

At the Hyatt, Jennifer Fordham and Jerry Carson were having dinner with their attorneys, discussing their testimony before the grand jury the next day. Jennifer had just retained Harley Stenmann, Esq. a well respected Colorado criminal attorney, who had gone to law school with her personal attorney in California. Jennifer had to pay him a non-refundable $25,000 retainer to convince him to clear his calendar and take her case. She had been in meetings with him since ten thirty in the morning. It was Stenmann's suggestion that they have dinner with Justin Thomason and Jerry Carson. It became clear at dinner that they would continue their meeting until late into the night.

The next morning, Pamela and Larry Lawson arrived at the City and County Building just as the bus carrying the jurors arrived from their hotel. They waited in the first floor hall by the coffee kiosk until all of the jurors had disappeared into the elevators. Several of the jurors saw them and smiled and nodded at Pam and Larry before they got on the elevators. Pam smiled back. Larry felt somewhat relieved by the slight gestures. As they were waiting, Janet Stephenson, with Adam and James came through the nearby security gate and joined them in the hall.

"Good morning. How are you feeling?" Janet asked with a smile.

"Good. I'm feeling really good." Pamela said.

They all got on the next elevator and went to the courtroom, where a full gallery was already waiting. Napoli, Montague and the cast of thousands were also there. Janet, Larry and Pamela went to the Plaintiff's table, nearest the jury, and Pamela and Larry sat down. Janet, Adam and James organized the exhibits that they would be using for the day's testimony. Napoli and Janet Stephenson exchanged nods, but neither had anything to say to the other. They were in the middle of the trial, where most of the careful work of getting all of the evidence in place for Janet and carefully rebutted, for Terry Napoli, was the order of business.

After the usual and expected pleasantries after Judge Parsons arrived, the jury came in and Janet Stephenson called Pamela Lawson to the stand. Pamela stood, and straightened the skirt of her periwinkle blue suit, then proceeded to the witness box, where she was sworn by the bailiff. Janet's blue eyes matched her suit and her short honey blond hair framed her face. Janet was glad that her hair had grown out enough so that she did not have to wear a wig. She looked innocent and frail behind the microphone. She had a tissue in her hand and Janet had placed a box of tissues on the shelf inside the witness box.

"Will you please state your name and address for the record, Mrs. Lawson?"

"Pamela Lawson, 2924 So Ingersoll Way, Denver, Colorado," she said, after clearing her throat.

Janet Stephenson carefully took Janet through the story of her life and her marriage to Larry Lawson and the birth of her children. She described how she felt that she was very deformed when her breasts sagged into limp sacks after the birth of their second child. She explained how she met with Dr. MacNamara and how she felt such hope when she heard his explanation of the repair that could be accomplished with the Mammselle implant. She identified that before and after pictures from the medical records, which were in Exhibit Notebook One. She explained that she was very happy with the result and how her breasts looked after the surgery.

The jury followed her testimony carefully and looked carefully at the photographs, which were included in their notebooks. Their faces remained interested but it was impossible to discern what any of the jurors were really thinking about Pamela Lawson.

Then, Janet took Pamela through the story of the deterioration of her health. Pamela explained her loss of energy and her gradual inability to accomplish her daily activities in caring for her family. She explained how she sought an explanation from her family doctor, Dr. Simon and how she had been referred to Dr. Hans Bricker at the University of Colorado Medical School. Finally, she explained how she was diagnosed with liver cancer and how the decision was made to remove the implants. Pamela explained that she was not a physician, but she understood that her implants were changed and no longer had the polyurethane coating when they were removed.

Pamela also testified in detail about the treatments that she received for the cancer, including the radiation and chemotherapy, which caused her to lose her hair and to have unbearable nausea and fatigue. Finally, she testified about the revelation that she would not recover unless she had a liver transplant.

Pam Lawson became very emotional in explaining how the gradual, but complete, deterioration of her health affected her family. Several members of the jury had furrowed brows and were obviously empathetic, yet most of them remained fairly stoic, while she explained that she could not pick up her children or bathe them. Pamela also explained that she had not been able to cook, do laundry or shop for groceries or do errands for months. At the end of her testimony, she explained the miracle of being able to receive a liver transplant. However, Janet was careful to leave her testimony with the present picture that her health was extremely frail and that she was still taking strong medication in the continuing attempt to prevent a rejection of the transplanted liver by her body.

Finally, Pamela explained that the problem of possible rejection of the transplanted liver was even more serious for her because her autoimmune system was highly compromised and that her ANA titers, the markers in her blood for autoimmune problems, were extremely high and not diminishing. Pamela explained that ANA titers were a measure of how many abnormal cells, ANA or antinuclear antibodies, she had. These antibodies caused her immune system to be confused, she explained Pamela also stated that it was her understanding of her medical condition, that her autoimmune system had also been compromised and that she had high levels of anti-nuclear antibodies in her system because of her being implanted with the Mammselle implants.

Napoli objected several times to the hearsay nature of Pamela's testimony about what her physicians stated. Janet rephrased to questions to ask Pamela to explain her knowledge and understanding of her condition. It was clear to Napoli that Pamela had been carefully prepared to testify and that it was better to save his energy for cross-examination.

Pamela's direct testimony took the entire morning and Napoli began his cross-examination at 1:30 after the lunch recess.

"Mrs. Lawson, as you know, I am Terry Napoli and I represent the manufacturer of your Mammselle implants, PolySurgical Specialties."

"Yes, I know, Mr. Napoli. I met you when you took my depostition."

"I have a few questions for you, based upon your testimony."

"Okay." Pamela sat up straight in the witness box, clutching her tissue. Her eyes were serious.

"Before you had your Mammselle implants, Mrs. Lawson, it is your testimony that you were perfectly healthy, is that correct?"

"Yes, I was just fine."

"The fact is, that there was no medical reason for you to have breast augmentation surgery, was there?"

"I felt that I needed to repair the deformity of my breasts."

"But that was a cosmetic reason, not a medical one, wasn't it, madam?"

"Yes, I suppose so."

"And you would agree with me that you assumed all of the risks that were associated with this personal decision to improve your looks, wouldn't you."

"I didn't assume the risk of liver cancer."

"But you would have to agree with me, that as you sit in the witness box today, you do not know of one single peer reviewed study that states that Mammselle implants cause liver cancer, right?"

"I am not a doctor, so I don't really know about those kinds of studies."

"No physician has ever told you that there was such a study, have they?"

"No."

"And the fact is that you never asked for any such information from Dr. MacNamara or any other doctor before you got the implants, did you?"

"No, I didn't"

"The fact is that you knew, from Dr. MacNamara, that the Mammselle implant was approved for use as an implant by the United States Food and Drug Administration, right?"

"Yes, I think that Dr. MacNamara told me it was approved by the FDA."

"That approval means that the implant is safe and effective for Dr. MacNamara to use in your voluntary cosmetic surgery, doesn't it."

"I guess so." Pamela answered, obviously subdued.

"The fact is that the only person who ever told you that you could sue my client for your liver cancer was not a physician, but your lawyer, Janet Stephenson, isn't that correct."

"Objection, privileged," said Janet, standing up at her table.

"Sustained," answered Judge Parsons immediately.

"Well, Mrs. Lawson, it was your lawyer, not your physicians, who found Dr. Sonier and Dr. Guilliot to testify in your case, isn't that true?"

"I don't know," Pamela Lawson answered hesitantly.

"Well, you never saw or talked to Dr. Sonier or Dr. Guilliot until you had hired Mrs. Stephenson as your lawyer did you?"

"No, I didn't."

"And, it was your attorney who had your implants and your removed liver sent to the Canadian laboratory of Dr. Guilliot, isn't that true?"

"I don't know that. They were both sent from the hospital, as I understand it."

"At the instruction of releases you signed after they were prepared by your attorney, isn't that correct?"

"I did sign releases, I know. I don't know who prepared them."

"Come on, Mrs. Lawson, you knew that your explanted Mammselle and your liver were going to be sent to Dr. Guilliot's lab, didn't you?"

"Objection," Janet said "Attorney client privilege"

"Well, the question only asks what she knew. It doesn't ask about conversations with counsel." Judge Parsons said, "Overruled"

Napoli persisted, "You may answer my question, Mrs. Lawson"

Pamela looked apprehensively at Janet, who nodded at her slightly. "I knew they were to be sent to the lab." she answered.

"And, as far as you knew, the implants were removed only to help your lawsuit against my client, isn't that true." Napoli continued confidently raising his voice a little.

"No, my implants were removed because I was ill and because there was some question about whether they were leaking silicone into my body, after I became ill and Dr. Bricker found that I had elevated ANA and other autoimmune problems."

"Dr. Bricker did not tell you to have your implants removed, did he, Mrs. Lawson."

"No, my primary care doctor, Dr. Simon, suggested that removal might be a good idea."

"Your plastic surgeon, Dr. MacNamara didn't suggest the implants should be removed did he?"

"He did the surgery, with Dr. Emanuel."

"My question was not who removed the implants, but who wanted it done."

"I wanted it done." said Pam, rather loudly, "I wanted them out," now she was crying openly. "My health was going down the tubes. I wanted them out."

"But you are not a physician are you, Mrs. Lawson."

"No, I'm not." She was still sobbing.

"The fact is, that you had your implants removed because your lawyer told you to have them out. Isn't it, Mrs. Lawson." Napoli said with disdain.

"Objection. Privilege" Janet said, on her feet.

"Now I will sustain the objection, Mr. Napoli. Please move on," said the judge.

"You would have to agree with me, wouldn't you, Mrs. Lawson, you wouldn't have had your implants removed or be here today, asking my client for these damages as a result of your decision to have cosmetic breast surgery if you hadn't met Janet Stephenson?"

"No, I don't agree with you," Pamela said, regaining her composure.

"It is true, is it not that you are asking my client, PolySurgical Specialties, to pay you damages for your voluntary use of cosmetic breast implants which are fully approved for that use by the federal Food and Drug Administration?"

"Yes, I am asking PSS to pay." Pamela said "You are not telling all of the story."

Napoli looked at her for a long moment, as she looked straight into his eyes. Then he said.

"I have no more questions, at this time, for the plaintiff."

Janet really didn't want to ask Pamela further questions because it was clear to her that Pam was wilting and that the cross-examination had caused her great stress. Stress was Pam's greatest enemy right now in her all important fight against rejection of her transplanted liver. Janet sat silently looking at her notes for several moments.

"Any redirect for the plaintiff, Mrs. Stephenson?"

Janet stood up and smiled at the judge and Pam. "I have no further questions at this time, Your Honor. We reserve the right to recall the Plaintiff as might be necessary for rebuttal."

"Very well, Mrs. Lawson, you may step down. We will take our fifteen minute afternnon break at this time. Please rise for the jury."

The jury and the judge left the room. Pam came back to the table, obviously shaken. "Did I do okay, Janet?" she asked wrinkling her brow?

"You were fabulous! "assured Janet. "Now you can just relax because you have this behind you."

"I think I'll go out for a bit. Want to come, Larry?" Her husband nodded and quickly got up and followed Pamela out of the courtroom. All of the Silicone Sisters in the gallery stood and smiled at her as she left. Pam smiled and waved her hand at them slightly.

During the break, Janet went into the hall where Dr. Simon and Dr. Levi Emanuel were waiting. "Well, you guys are next," she said with a smile. "With any luck I can get both of you on and off the stand yet this afternoon."

"I'm ready," said Dr. Carol Simon. "Which of us will go first?"

"I will put you on first, Dr. Simon, just to keep the facts in chronological order for the jury. Will that work for you Dr. Emanuel?"

"That will be fine, "the elderly physician said with a smile. "I've set aside as much time as you need. Just have your assistants keep me up on how things are going. I'll just camp out here with my book and watch the press come and go."

"Great." Janet said. "Thank you for bearing with me. I'll have James and Adam come out regularly and let you know where we are and what is happening."

Janet went back to the courtroom to organize the necessary exhibits with her assistants, who already had her trial notebooks for the two physicians on her table.

Pamela and Larry returned just before the judge and jury. Then Janet called Dr. Carol Simon to the stand. After being sworn, Dr. Simon took the stand and testified that she was Pamela's primary care physician and had been since the early days of her marriage. Janet then referred the jury and Dr. Simon to the trial notebooks, and using Dr. Simon's medical records as the point of reference for the jury, Janet asked Dr. Simon to explain all of the significant events in Pamela's medical history, including the birth of her children, her decision to have breast implants, the subsequent decline of her health and finally the cancer diagnosis, treatment and Pam's liver transplant. She did not, however, offer an opinion regarding the cause of Pamela's liver cancer, stating that the question was beyond the scope of her medical expertise.

On cross-examination, she admitted that she and other physicians rely on the approval of drugs by the FDA as the beginning basis for using drugs and implants in their patients. On being asked redirect questions by Janet Stephenson, Dr. Simon also testified that it is her opinion that physicians must continue to balance all kinds of scientific information and ongoing testing information with the needs and medical conditions of their patients. On balance, she said, she would likely not prescribe a Mammselle implant.

In responding to re-cross questions from Terry Napoli, Dr. Simon admitted that she was not a plastic surgeon and likely would not be likely to be prescribing breast implants for any patient, including Pamela Lawson.

Then Janet called Dr. Levi Emanuel to the stand. She wanted very much to end the day with Dr. Emanuel and his testimony about removing the Mammselle implant and finding that all of the polyurethane foam covering the implant was missing when he and Dr. Dan MacNamara removed the implant. She referred the jury to the photographs taken by the St. Anthony hospital pathology department, showing that the implants were smooth and devoid of foam covering. Dr. Emanuel also testified about the removal of Pamela's liver and the liver transplant. He testified about the malignant condition of Pamela's liver and again referred the jury to the grotesque laboratory photographs of the diseased organ.

On cross-examination, Terry Napoli tried to get Dr. Emanuel to say that there was no medical evidence that the missing polyurethane foam was in any was related to the development of cancer. Dr. Emanuel said, "Well, you know Mr. Napoli, it is the job of physicians to keep an alert and inquiring mind. I also do not have any proof that the disappearing polyurethane foam covering was not the cause of her cancer. I know it is ' hard to prove a negative' as you lawyers say. What I will say is that there is a question here that requires serious investigation and some answers."

"But you would agree with me, Dr. Emanuel, that as you sit here today, you can't say one way or another whether the disappearance of the foam had anything at all to do with causing Pamela Lawson's liver cancer, isn't that correct?"

"I believe there is connection, but there are no definitive studies at this point."

"You also are not an expert in oncology or cancer, are you doctor?"

"No, I am not. I am a surgeon," he said calmly.

"I have no further questions."

Janet Stephenson suddenly realized that she may have a problem. She had listed Dr. Barber, Pamela's oncologist, as a witness, but James and Adam had not been able to connect with him or to schedule a time to prepare his testimony. Janet hadn't been really concerned because she always had to meet with and prepare witnesses to testify in the evening or on weekends. She had believed his staff's representations that he was unavailable because he was busy. Now she was filled with a new and very serious concern. The force with which Terry Napoli asked his last question of Dr. Emanuel gave Janet an epiphany—they had been unable to get in touch with Dr. Barber because he did not intend to testify in Pamela's case. He was going to testify for Napoli and PSS!

Janet was deep in thought as she heard Judge Parsons, "Mrs. Stephenson, are you with us?"

"I'm sorry Your Honor. I have no further questions for Dr. Emanuel."

"Thank you, Dr. Emanuel. May this witness be excused?"

"Yes," Napoli and Stephenson said in unison.

"You are excused, Doctor. Thank you for your testimony."

Dr. Emanuel nodded at the judge and the jury and left the courtroom.

"Well, ladies and gentlemen, it has been a full day for you. We will be in recess now until ten o'clock in the morning. I have a number of hearings in the morning, so we will be starting a bit later. Have a nice evening. Please stand for the jury"

The jury left the courtroom, and Judge Parsons said "Anything further for today, counsel?"

Both attorneys shook their heads. "Then I will see you at ten o'clock in the morning. We may actually start a little later than ten o'clock and not have a morning recess. We will be in recess."

Janet looked at Pamela, who was sitting at the table. She did not rise for the judge's departure. "Are you okay, Pam," she asked. Pamela nodded. "I'm just beat," she said quietly.

"Tomorrow might be another vacation day for you, my dear," Janet said kindly to her frail client. "Whatever is happening tomorrow will go on without you, and the jury will not be surprised if you are not here."

"We'll plan on that, Janet," said Larry. "But I'll be here at ten o'clock no matter what. Who's on for tomorrow?"

"I planned on Dr. Barber, but I'll work that all out when I get back to my office and have a chance to think about it a little. But, you just get Pam home and have a restful evening."

Janet sent James to make sure the press had cleared the hallway, then asked Amelia if they could use the Judge's entrance because the members of the press, anxious for an interview with their cameras, were still filling the hall outside the courtroom. James stood outside the courtroom door, as if they were preparing to leave until Pam and Larry were safely down the private elevator.

Janet and her assistants made it through the crowd with an uninteresting "no comment" Napoli and Montague were still in the courtroom, organizing their boxes when Janet left.

Back at their offices, Adam tried again to reach Dr. Barber, but he had left his office, according to the secretary. Adam left an emergency call back on his service, but Janet doubted that he would call. She knew in her heart what had happened. Dr. Barber, Pamela's cancer doctor was going to testify as a witness for PolySurgical Specialties if he testified at all.

"Napoli is behind this, "Janet said to James and Adam. "Dr. Barber knows that it is too late for us to subpoena him to testify in our case. He surely got that information from PSS lawyers. Let's just hope that he has decided not to testify for either the plaintiff or the defendant."

"Fat chance," said Adam. "I thought there was something weird about how his office staff was treating us, kind of stringing us along and now going incommunicado. You can bet that he's up to no good."

"You know what, guys, tomorrow just might be the day for our big bomb. Maybe we should call Jennifer Fordham as an adverse witness tomorrow and get the secret PSS documents from Sherrie Barker into evidence."

"Problem. Problem," said James wagging his finger at Janet. "Jennifer Fordham hasn't been in court for the past two days. We've had Mrs. Winchester over there as the corporate representative of PSS. How are you going to make sure that Jennifer Fordham is even in the courtroom?"

"That is a problem," said Janet. "How can we find out where she is and what can we do to make sure that she is there? She's not a listed witness. She comes under our designation of 'any witness listed by the defendants' and PSS has listed her as a witness and as a representative of the defendant PSS, whom we certainly have a right to call."

"If she is in the courtroom," said Adam, "right?"

"Right," said Janet, deep in thought. "I think I need to give Joel Steiner a call."

Just then Janet's cell phone rang. It was Rick Plume, the district attorney. Janet could hardly contain her surprise.

"Hey, Rick," she said. "What's up?"

"Hi," he said, "I was just hoping for a little update from you about the progress of the trial. I've been buried in the grand jury proceedings over the Sherrie Barker bombing and I haven't kept up on what's going on. I thought I'd get it from the horse's mouth, so to speak."

"Very cute," Janet laughed. "What would you like to know? We've been just chugging along. Sonier, Dr. G, Pamela Lawson and the treating physicians, Dr. Simon and Dr. Emanuel have testified, so far. I'm just trying to decide about tomorrow. Funny you should call."

"Why?"

"I was wondering where Jennifer Fordham has been. She hasn't been in trial for two days and Leslie Winchester has been the corporate rep. Do you have any idea what's up with Fordham?"

"I may have, which brings me to the reason for my call. Any luck in getting the Barker documents into evidence yet?"

"No, that's next, perhaps. I can only get them into evidence by calling Jennifer Fordham as a hostile witness because she is the corporate representative and on the PSS witness list. I have cross designated all of the listed witnesses for PSS. But I need her in the courtroom to call her."

"Well, she's been in my courtroom," Rick Plume said.

Janet was silent. "Oh," was all she said. Then, "Is she coming back to my courtroom? I need her tomorrow."

"Janet, I need those documents or I'm not going to be able to clinch this grand jury thing. MacNamara testified, but he never looked at the documents before the bombing and what Sherrie Barker told him is inadmissible hearsay. I need you to get them in evidence in your trial, so that they will be a matter of public record. Otherwise, this may all be for naught." There was fatigue and a little desperation in the voice of the district attorney.

"My problem is that I need to have Jennifer Fordham in the courtroom to call her as an adverse witness tomorrow. Otherwise, I will have to subpoena her and I won't be able to put her on for two days, which puts my case into next week. I can only get the documents into evidence through her."

"Perhaps I'll have Leslie Winchester served with a subpoena to appear tomorrow before the grand jury. That will insure that someone else has to be there and the only person left is Jennifer Fordham because Forrest Winchester is still in jail. Maybe that will work."

"Can you subpoena her for tomorrow. It's nearly six now?"

"We don't operate on government time here, Janet," he laughed. "We're a 24/7 operation. And there are no time requirements for emergency grand jury subpoenas. I can do it."

"Great. Then I will plan to put Jennifer Fordham on tomorrow. Can you call me when you have served her, so that I will know for sure?"

"It's the least I can do. Thanks, Janet." Rick Plume said, suddenly very serious.

"Thanks, Rick. We'll get through this and it will be good." Janet said.

"I hope so. Talk to you soon. Shall I call this number?"

"Yep, it's my cell and it's always with me. Bye."

"Well, let's make sure that we have the notebooks with the PSS documents ready for the jury." she said to her assistants. "I hope Rick can serve Leslie Winchester because we don't have Dr. Barber and that means that I would have to put Larry on the stand tomorrow. I wanted him to be last."

"They're all ready to go," said James, pointing at the banker's boxes stacked by the front door.

"Your trial notebook for Jennifer Fordham is on your desk," Adam reminded her.

"Good" Janet said. "Well if you guys aren't tired of me, we could go over to Old Chicago and have a little dinner, or anywhere else you'd like to go. I'm ready for Jennifer Fordham."

"How about Red Lobster," said Adam. "I'd love to have some crab legs. And, it is a quieter place, just in case Mr. Plume calls you while we are there."

"Great. Let's lock up and I'll meet you there."

Rick Plume called Janet less than an hour later and confirmed that Leslie Winchester would be testifying before the grand jury in the morning. Janet decided to just assume that Napoli and Montague would make sure Jennifer Fordham was in the courtroom. She didn't want her actions to look coincidental with the service of the grand jury subpoena on Leslie Winchester. After dinner at the Red Lobster, Janet returned to her office to review her trial notebooks and her plans for tomorrow. No need to hurry home because Brad was somewhere between Paris and Vienna as far as she knew. She didn't expect him for two more days.

Leslie Winchester was just getting ready to leave her room at the Brown Palace and go for a walk on the Sixteenth Street Mall when there was a knock on her door. When she opened it, she was served with the subpoena to appear before the grand jury by a polite young man, who was dressed in a suit and tie. She opened the envelope, read the contents, and took her cell phone out of her purse.

"Mr. Napoli? You'll never guess what I just received by personal delivery," she said crossly.

"Mrs Winchester? I was just going to give you a call to see if you would like to join us for a drink and dinner. No. What did you receive?"

"A subpoena to appear before the grand jury."

"Why on earth??" he sounded stunned. "What do you know about those matters?"

"Absolutely nothing. However, it is for tomorrow, so it appears you'll have to get Miss Fordham to be your table mate at trial. I assume she testified today and is now free to do what she is supposed to be doing in our trial."

"I think you are right. I don't think she has to go back. I'll give her a call right now, and call you back."

Terry Napoli was just preparing to leave Rex Montague's office and go to dinner with two of his associates when he got Leslie Winchester's call.

"What's up?" asked Montague, pausing as he was going out the door.

"They've subpoenaed Leslie Winchester to the grand jury tomorrow. She's pissed as all get out. I wonder what they could possibly want from her."

"She is the major owner of Conway Chemical, which owns the company Sherrie Barker worked for. So there is a slight connection," answered Rex Montague. "Does she need a lawyer before tomorrow?"

"Do you have someone? I don't think there would be a conflict with Rivera because Leslie and Forrest Winchester should have the same interests in this matter."

"Perhaps, but she might want a Chicago lawyer, too," said Montague, putting down his briefcase. He clearly was not going to be able to go home early, as he had hoped.

"Could you check? I have to call Jennifer Fordham and make sure she's free to come to trial tomorrow. Even if Leslie doesn't have to testify, she will have to appear and we will need Jennifer in our courtroom with us." Napoli was searching his cell phone for Jennifer Fordham's number.

"Jennifer? "Napoli tried to sound cheerful when she answered her phone. "How's it going? Are you finished with the grand jury?"

"It was a crappy day and I am thinking of going out drinking." Jennifer responded.

"Why don't you let us take you to dinner instead?" Napoli said.

"Why?'

"I just thought you could give us your thoughts about what is going on. Also, I just found out that the D.A. has subpoenaed Leslie Winchester to the grand jury tomorrow, so we really need you to be in the courtroom with us tomorrow." Napoli was trying to seem matter of fact, even though he was finding himself at his wits end in having to deal with both of his female clients.

"Well, isn't that interesting," Jennifer snarled. "Sound like we need a little company strategy session over dinner, actually."

"If you like, we could meet in the dining room at the Brown Palace. I'll see if Mrs. Winchester will join us."

"Sound as though I really have no choice," said Jennifer. "I'll be there in an hour," and she hung up.

Napoli sighed and dialed Leslie Winchester. "Hi, Terry Napoli, here," he said. "I spoke to Jennifer and she's done with testifying. Would you be free to have dinner with us in the dining room at your hotel in about an hour?" he asked.

Leslie Winchester had planned to walk on the Mall and have a salad somewhere, enjoying her solitude, but she responded, "All right. It seems that we must stay on track here."

"Mrs. Winchester, about tomorrow. Do you want to have an attorney with you or meet with an attorney before you go to the grand jury?"

"I hadn't thought a thing about that," she said puzzled. "Why do I need an attorney? I don't know anything and I have absolutely nothing to say."

"Why don't we discuss it at dinner. Can you meet us in your hotel dining room in about an hour?"

"All right. That wasn't my plan for the evening, but I'll see you downstairs in about an hour." Leslie Winchester said.

Rex Montague called his wife and once again explained that he had to work late. "I'll call Justin Rivera and see if he can meet us for dinner or after, so that we can get an update on the situation with Forrest Winchester. I know Mrs. Winchester is probably totally frustrated by our not being able to get him out of jail."

"Can you line up someone to talk to Leslie Winchester if we need them?"

"I had my secretary call Joyce Symes and ask if she could meet us for dinner. She is the only criminal attorney we have, who I think can deal with Leslie Winchester. She'll call me back on my cell."

"What do you think that the district attorney is up to? He really seems to be grasping at straws in dragging all of our clients in front of the grand jury, regardless of what contact they might or might not have had with their victim." Napoli was too engrossed in the trial with Janet Stephenson to have given any real thought to the relationships between all of his clients. Montague was not so puzzled. He feared that there was some connection between the Sherrie Barker bomb killing and their case. It was just too coincidental that Dr. Dan MacNamara just happened to be in the parking lot at the same time, and that he was the surgeon who had implanted Pamela Lawson's Mammselle implants, which he purchased from Sherrie Barker. He also knew Janet Stephenson because he had been on the defense side of other silicone gel breast implant cases where she represented the plaintiffs. Granted all of the cases so far had settled, but the implants were made by other manufacturers who were anxious to avoid the publicity of a trial involving their products. Janet was a worthy adversary. She knew the law and she knew most of the trial lawyers in Denver. Although she often seemed gentle and unassuming, he had been in enough depositions and hearings with her to know that she was single-minded and sure of herself and her clients by the time she got to trial.

"Well, I hope we can find out something about what is going on from Jennifer Fordham. However, I am guessing that she has been well briefed by her attorney and that she isn't going to be telling us much," Montague said to Terry Napoli, who was sitting in one of the big leather chairs in Montague's office, deep in thought.

An hour later, the two attorneys met Jennifer Fordham, Justin Thomason, Leslie Winchester, and Joyce Symes for dinner. As Montague feared, Jennifer was not willing to say anything about the grand jury proceedings. Leslie Winchester was very quiet during most of the dinner and at the end, asked Joyce Symes to meet with her and prepare her for the grand jury appearance the next morning. Montague was deeply relieved and Terry Napoli ordered a second scotch after they retired to the Ship Tavern pub to take stock of the evening. Jennifer Fordham left with her attorney, sullen and appearing very depressed.

Janet Stephenson was very relieved to receive the phone call at dinned from Rick Plume, telling her that Leslie Winchester had been served. Now, she just had to have faith that Jennifer Fordham would be the corporate representative appearing in court the next morning. Janet was still at her office reviewing the documents, including the animal studies, which had been commissioned by PSS and then buried deep in their vaults. What a miracle that Sherrie Barker got her hands on them, Janet mused. She was still deep in thought at her desk when Brad called her on her cell phone.

"Hi, hon, are you coming home soon? The morning comes really early," he said.

"Are you home?" she asked excitedly. "I thought you were still in Europe somewhere, so I wasn't hurrying."

"No, I'm home. Are you about finished there?"

"I am now. See you in a bit." Janet hung up her phone. She put her trial notebook for Jennifer Fordham in her briefcase and checked the juror notebooks once more. Then, she locked the office and hurried to her car. She was anxious to see her husband and to hug him. It seemed as though he had been gone forever.

When she got home, Brad was waiting with a glass of red wine and some cheese and crackers in their library. He was listening to ABBA and humming along.

"What a great welcome," Janet said. She gave him a kiss and kicked off her shoes. "It feels so good to be home when you are here," she smiled at her handsome husband.

"How's the trial going?" he asked her as she sat down and reclined in her big red leather chair. He was sitting near the fireplace in his identical red leather recliner.

"It's going," Janet said somberly. "Tomorrow is the big day. I'm calling Jennifer Fordham as an adverse witness and I am going to try to get in all of Sherrie Barker's secret documents into evidence through her, by using them as cross-examination documents. They haven't been disclosed in discovery, you know. So they are not on the exhibit list. It is a really risky thing to do, but I have absolutely no choice and Rick Plume can't use them in his criminal case unless they are made public documents by introducing them as evidence in our civil case."

"Oh, my word." Brad said. "Do you think you will be able to do it?"

"It totally depends on the judge. Parsons is a brainy and thoughtful judge. He usually is really fair, but sometimes he is unpredictable. If he follows the rules to a T, I'm good. If he listens to all the BS that Napoli will surely throw out there when he discovers what I am doing, it maybe a tough sell. Under the rules, the documents should go in. She has to identify them as business documents."

"What if she doesn't identify them? You've had witnesses lie before. She may just say that she has never seen them before. If I were her, that's what I would do," Brad said.

"Then it gets more complicated. I will have to call Raoul Lecroix as a rebuttal witness, but I may not be able to do that until after the defendants put on their case. So, the documents won't technically get admitted until the end of the trial. But, the jury will have heard about them and will have the lingering questions about them all through the defendant's case. "Janet sipped her wine and wiggled her toes as she lounged in her comfortable recliner.

"It sounds as though tomorrow is going to be an exciting day. I was going to offer you another glass of wine, but I think you need a good night's sleep more."

"I'll have both," Janet laughed "at least another half glass of wine. I am as prepared as I can be. The rest is up to angels and Judge Parsons."

A Bob Dylan CD began to play on their stereo and Janet and Brad sang along softly, just enjoying the time together. Brad poured them each a little more wine then corked the bottle. When the album was over, they turned out the lights in their library and went to bed.

orrest Winchester could stand his isolation no longer. He waited until after 8:30 in the evening and when it was clear that Leslie was not coming to visit him, he asked for permission to make a phone call. He dialed Leslie's cell phone and waited for an answer.

"Hello" she said. Leslie had just finished her meeting with Joyce Symes and was not in a particularly good mood. She felt overwhelmed and blindsided by all that was happening to her.

"Why don't you come down to this god forsaken place and see me," he demanded.

"And why should I?" his wife responded, petulantly.

"If for no other reason, to see if I am alive," he practically shouted at her.

"Oh, Forrest, I'm sure that someone would tell me if anything happened to you," she said sarcastically.

"I need to know what is going on! No one is telling me anything. What is going on in the trial?"

"What is going on in the grand jury? You know that I have been subpoenaed to testify tomorrow and Jennifer Fordham and Jerry Carson have also testified. Why is that?"

"What? I didn't know that. What the hell is happening?" Forrest Winchester was becoming increasingly afraid. His attorney, Justin Rivera, was not in frequent contact with him and Winchester was deeply frustrated and felt abandoned by all those who had the job of caring about him. "Don't you care about me, Leslie?" he asked almost frantic.

"Care about you, Forrest? Funny, I don't think you have ever asked me that question," his wife mused. "Usually it is I, who am trying to figure out if you care about me. Strange isn't it. Guess what, Forrest, maybe it isn't about you."

"Leslie, I'm so sorry," he said, almost weeping, "but I really need you. I need to see you. Will you come tomorrow? I have to get out of here. There must be something you can do. Can't you talk to that worthless lawyer that Montague stuck me with?"

"I have to go now, Forrest. I'll see what I can do about getting you bail tomorrow. I've been a little tied up because I have had to sit in the Lawson trial all day every day because your sidekick at PSS, sweet Jennifer, has been out taking care of herself."

"I'm sorry, Leslie. Of course, just do what you can do," he said, suddenly realizing that if he didn't have Leslie, he would be totally lost. It was an epiphany for the self confident Forrest Winchester. "Talk to you tomorrow?" he asked.

"I'll call you or come there. Good Night, Forrest."

Forrest Winchester followed the guard from the phone room to his cell and Leslie Winchester called room service and ordered champagne.

Terry Napoli and Rex Montague seem somewhat surprised when Adam and James brought in more banker's boxes of trial exhibit notebooks the next day. Jennifer Fordham was in court at counsel table in the place of the defendant's corporate representative. Janet Stephenson breathed a slight sigh of relief when she saw her. Pamela Lawson and Larry Lawson were at her table and Larry was holding Pam's hand. Pamela was not looking well. Her eyes were sunken and dark and her hair looked thinner than usual. She was obviously losing even more weight and her clothes seemed especially large for her today. She wore a navy blue dress with a white lace collar and cuffs. Larry Lawson's face reflected the concern he obviously felt for his wife. Janet spoke to them reassuringly and patted Pamela's hand.

"Remember, you may leave the courtroom anytime you don't feel well enough to stay,' she told her frail client.

Judge Parsons entered and took the bench. "Are we ready for the jury, counsel?" he asked.

Both counsel nodded and the jury was summoned by the bailiff, who led them to the jury box. When they were all seated, the judge said, "We are ready for the plaintiff's next witness, Mrs. Stephenson."

"Thank you, Your Honor," Janet responded. "The plaintiff calls the defendant's corporate representative, Jennifer Fordham, as a hostile or adverse witness, Your Honor."

"Very well. Come forward, Ms. Fordham."

Napoli sprang to his feet as Jennifer Fordham looked at him in dismay. "Your Honor, this is most irregular. She can't do that!" he fumed.

"Why not, Mr. Napoli? Either party may call the other as a witness in any trial. When the party is a corporation, the other side may call the corporate representative."

"We were not advised. We didn't know she was going to call Ms. Fordham and we object because we have had no preparation time."

"You've had all the months that this case has been pending, sir. I'm sure your client is well prepared after having been deposed and participating in the preparation for this trial. Come forward, Ms. Fordham, and be sworn."

"I'm not prepared, Your Honor," said Fordham.

"You must address the Court through your counsel, ma'm," frowned the judge.

"We must adhere to the witness list. She is not on the Plaintiff's list," urged Napoli.

"We have listed the representative of the defendant, as well as, any witness listed by the defendant and Ms. Fordham is listed as a witness for the defendant, Your Honor," said Janet Stephenson.

"That is standard practice, you would agree, wouldn't you, Mr. Napoli," inquired the judge.

"Well, yes, but it's boilerplate, so to speak. No one actually does that." Napoli offered.

"Well, apparently the Plaintiff in this case is doing it. Please come forward, Ms. Fordham. We are wasting the jury's time here," said the judge impatiently.

Jennifer Fordham looked helplessly at Napoli, who just nodded at her to go forward. Then she stepped from behind the table and took the witness stand. The bailiff came forward from his cubicle by the door and administered the oath of truth to the surprised witness.

"Please state your name and office address for the Court." Janet began.

"Jennifer Fordham, 21626 Pacific View Circle, Santa Barbara, California," the witness said.

"Please tell us how you are employed, as well as your title and area of responsibility."

"I am the President and CEO of PolySurgical Specialties. In that position, I am in charge of running the company." Jennifer responded curtly.

"Are you in charge of the manufacturing and marketing of the Mammselle implant?"

"Ultimately, I guess you could say I'm in charge of everything the company does and the Mammselle is one of our products."

"Did your company develop the Mammselle implant, Ms. Fordham?"

"Yes, we did. It is made of materials, which were primarily secured from Conway Chemical. To be accurate, the underlying implant is a Conway Chemical implant, for which PSS designed a polyurethane foam coating."

"Isn't it true that in order to market the Mammselle implant, you relied on all of the testing and materials science Conway Chemical submitted to the FDA, for the marketing approval of their silicone gel breast implant?"

"Yes, that is a perfectly acceptable procedure in seeking FDA approval."

"But, Conway Chemical did not submit any testing data for polyurethane, did it, Ms. Fordham?" Janet queried.

"Conway Chemical does not market a polyurethane-coated implant, so that was not necessary," Fordham countered.

"And it is also true that PSS did not submit any testing data for polyurethane in seeking your approval for the marketing of the Mammselle, did you?"

"Our approval by the FDA was based on our implant being an improved version of the Conway Chemical implant because the

Mammselle prevents capsular contracture, which is a major medical problem for silicone gel breast implant patients."

"You did not answer my question, with all due respect," Janet Stephenson insisted, "My question was, isn't it true that PSS did not submit any testing data to the FDA for polyurethane."

"No, it was not required."

"But if you had submitted the testing data that you had, it is a fact, isn't it Ms. Fordham, that it is likely that the FDA would not have approved the Mammselle for marketing in the United States?" asked Janet calmly and directly.

"I don't know what you are talking about." Fordham said emphatically.

"Ms Fordham, I would like to direct your attention to the exhibit notebook in front of you. Would you please turn to the document identified as Exhibit AA? Can you identify this document?"

Jennifer Fordham opened the notebook slowly. Adam and James had placed a notebook on defendant's table and Napoli and Montague opened their notebook as well. The jury was looking on with rapt attention.

Jennifer Fordham's face blanched and her cheeks turned red, "Where did you get this?" she said without thinking.

Napoli was on his feet. "Objection, Your Honor. These documents have never been supplied to the defendant. We object to any use of the documents in this notebook."

Judge Parsons was looking with great interest at the notebook that James had provided the bailiff for the judge. "Well, this is cross-examination of a hostile or adverse witness. Under the rules, you would agree, would you not, Mr. Napoli, that documents used for cross-examination do not have to be disclosed as exhibits prior to the actual cross-examination."

"These documents were not provided in discovery. We continue to object!" he said loudly, peaking the interest of the jury even more.

"Well, why don't you lay a little foundation for these documents, Mrs. Stephenson," said Judge Parsons calmly.

"Ms Fordham," said Janet Stephenson, "Let me direct your attention to the first page of Exhibit AA. This document appears to be a letter addressed to you, Jennifer Fordham, at the address that you have given the court as your office address, wouldn't you agree."

"That's what it says," said Jennifer sullenly.

"And you would agree that the letter is on the letterhead of Sprightly Laboratories, 23977 Hawthorne, Santa Barbara, California?"

"So it appears," she responded.

"And would you also agree that Jonathan Sprightly, M.D., PhD, has signed the letter?"

"Yes"

"And, Ms. Fordham, the letter states, in its pertinent part, 'enclosed you will find the results and conclusions related to our testing of the polyurethane material covering a standard Mammselle implant, size C, on laboratory rats and rabbits,' do you see that sentence?"

"Yes," Jennifer Fordham said mechanically.

"Would you also agree that attached to this letter is a formal report and laboratory findings of Sprightly laboratories, including graphs, test data and photographs of the laboratory animals, he mentions in the letter?"

"I see the attachment," was all she said.

"Isn't it a fact, Ms. Fordham that you received this letter and its attachment at PolySurgical Specialties in the ordinary course of business and that it was retained as a business record?"

"I can't say that. I don't know if I have ever seen this before. I don't recall it." Jennifer Fordham sat up straight in the chair and her voice was firm and strong.

"Let me draw your attention to the attachment, do you see the photographs there?"

"Yes," she said

"The captions under the photographs read, "Number one, subject rat ID 721, exhibiting tumor, Number two, subject rat ID

700, exhibiting tumor, Number Three, subject rabbit, exhibiting tumor, and so on. Do you see those photos?"

"Yes"

"Isn't it true, Ms. Fordham that this report shows that every test animal developed tumors?"

"I don't know, I haven't reviewed the whole report," she replied.

"Please, take as long as you need to review the photographs, so that you can respond accurately," Janet said calmly. The courtroom was absolutely silent as Jennifer Fordham looked at the photographs, one by one, then she looked up at Janet with fire in her eyes.

"Do you need me to repeat the question," Janet asked.

"No. These are all photographs of animals with tumors. But that doesn't mean that there weren't animals without tumors, does it?"

"Let's move on to page 10 of the report, entitled 'Autopsy findings', do you see that?"

"Yes," Jennifer said.

"Reading the paragraph after the heading 'Conclusions' would you agree with me that the report states as follows: 'in conclusion, each and every animal in the study was subjected to euthanasia and autopsy. The autopsy results demonstrated a malignant tumor of substantial size on or in the liver tissue of each animal.' Do you see that?"

"Yes, I can read also."

"Isn't it true, Ms. Fordham, that this study makes it clear that you knew, prior to receiving FDA approval to market the Mammselle, that the animals implanted with the implant's polyurethane foam coating all developed liver cancer?"

"No, it is not true. I haven't seen this before," Jennifer Fordham's eyes were steel.

"Let me draw your attention to the page labeled Exhibit BB. Do you see that page?"

"Yes."

"This Exhibit BB appears to be a memorandum on PSS letterhead, from you, Jennifer Fordham to Jerry Carson, stating that the results of the Sprightly Laboratory study must not be released to anyone until they are verified by another independent lab. Do you see that?"

"I see that, but I don't remember this memo"

"Look at the signature at the bottom, is that your signature, Ms. Fordham?"

"I don't know, I can't be sure. Lots of people wrote memos for me."

"But, you testified that you are in charge of running the company, isn't that correct."

"Yes, I am."

"So you are responsible for any memo, even if someone else has the authority to write it for you, isn't that so."

"I don't remember this memo."

Janet had laid the foundation, so she said, "Your Honor, we would ask for the admission of all of Exhibit AA and Exhibit BB."

"Any objection, Mr. Napoli," asked the judge.

"Yes, Your Honor. We object on the basis of authenticity, relevance, and violation of the discovery rules."

"Mrs. Stephenson, your response?"

"Your Honor, the foundation for admission has been laid. The letter, to which the report is attached was written to this witness, Jennifer Fordham, at PSS headquarters. The memorandum, Exhibit BB, which makes up the remainder of the notebook, was written by the witness, on PSS letterhead and signed by her or by her surrogate. It is admissible as a business record because she discusses the disposition of Exhibit AA in her memo, Exhibit BB. The documents are relevant because they clearly show that PSS had animal studies, in its possession, which demonstrated the same results as those of Dr. Sonier. In fact, Dr. Sonier's studies are the confirming independent studies that the witness says in her memo that she is waiting for."

"Well, the documents are clearly relevant and they appear to be on letterhead and they reference that the study will be kept in the ordinary course of business, so to speak. Ms. Fordham will not admit to her signature and we do not have any other comparisons or witness to identify it as hers, or in essence to authenticate the documents. Mr. Napoli has made it clear that the documents were not produced by PSS in the discovery process as business records. I am going to reserve my ruling on admissibility for the moment."

"May we show the documents to the jury, Your Honor" Janet asked hopefully.

"Not until I rule on admissibility, Mrs. Stephenson," the judge said, raising his eyebrows at her.

Napoli smiled triumphantly and sat down. Janet noticed that several jurors, who had been leaning forward, sat back in their chairs and crossed their arms. They wanted to see the documents and she was hoping that they did not consider that she had failed in getting them important evidence.

"Ms. Fordham, did you ever request any animal studies on the polyurethane foam which covers the implant." Janet persisted, knowing now that Fordham would lie, as Brad said.

"The studies were not required by the FDA for approval, why would I?"

"My question was, did you?"

"No" Jennifer Fordham lied confidently, crossing her arms.

"I have no further questions at this time, but I reserve the right to recall Ms. Fordham, Your Honor." Janet said, noting that Jennifer was smiling slightly. She hoped the jury noticed.

"No questions." said Napoli.

"We will be in recess until two o'clock," said Judge Parsons. "The jury may return to the hotel, bailiff, as I have some matters to attend to. Please rise for the jury."

Everyone stood. Janet looked at Pamela, who had her head in her hands. '*Oh no,*' thought Janet, '*She doesn't understand what I am doing and that the documents will get in.*'

"Are we losing?" asked Larry, "what happens if the documents are not admitted?"

"No worries," Janet said with a smile. "The documents will be admitted. This is all a part of the game. Remember, I read the documents to the jury. They know what they say, they just couldn't see the pictures. I have the testimony to get them admitted all taken care of. I just had to lay the foundation with Jennifer Fordham now, so that the jury will be thinking about it in the defendant's case."

"I don't really understand any of this Janet," said Pamela weakly. "We just have to trust you."

"Who's next?" asked Larry.

"You are," Janet said. "I would suggest that you take Janet home, so that she can rest. Then you come back about one forty-five in the afternoon. We've gone over your testimony and I think that you can be a lot more candid with the jury if Pam is not in the courtroom. She's had enough for today." Janet said kindly.

"Okay. You're right. Pam is done in. Let's go, sweetheart," said Larry. He seemed relieved that he would not have to testify with Pamela looking at him. He couldn't talk about the despair he was feeling if she were in the courtroom.

Adam and James were very quiet as they left the courtroom. "Let's go over to the English Pub," Janet said. Then, noting their serious expressions said, "Come on, guys, it's all good. I have a plan."

"I hope so," Adam said. "The jury really wanted to see those notebooks. I think they were pissed."

"They'll see them," Janet promised. "Just wait, this isn't over yet!"

When they all returned at two o'clock, the atmosphere in the courtroom was obviously more somber. In the middle of Larry Lawson's testimony, it began to rain. Lightning and thunder crackled outside the huge courtroom windows and added a dramatic backdrop to Larry Lawson's sad story of the destruction of Pamela's health and the damage to his family caused by her cancer, liver transplant and continued inability to participate as a wife and mother. He told sadly, with tears in his eyes how their children, David and Sarah, had gradually turned to their grandmother for most of their mothering since Pamela's illness. He was so profoundly sad and his testimony was so touching that Montague persuaded Napoli not to cross-examine him. The day ended with the jury going back to their hotel in the pouring rain and Napoli and Montague feeling that they had won a slight victory in the battle of the cancer ridden rats and rabbits. Janet knew it was only round one.

Now, Janet had to decide when to put on the testimony of Raoul Lecroix. As she drove back to her office, she was deep in thought about whether to call Raoul Lecroix as her last witnesss, now, and rest, or wait until after Napoli and Montague had put on the case for the defendant. She had planned to wait until after the defendant's case. But, it would seem that a more consistent and powerful move would be to ask Judge Parsons to put on her rebuttal witness to the testimony of Jennifer Fordham now. Then her entire case would be before the jury and Napoli and Montague would have to refute it all in their case.

"Hey, Janet, you missed our turn," James said to her.

Janet came out of her reverie just as she drove past the driveway into their office complex. She laughed.

"Well guys, I guess I am finally losing it." She turned around at next stoplight and went back to the office.

"What do we need for tomorrow," Adam asked her as they unloaded the car.

"Tomorrow, I think I will put on Raoul Lecroix, our rebuttal witness."

"I thought he would be at the very end," said James, confused.

"I need to call Rick Plume, but if he will bring him to the courthouse, I think it is better to put him on before we end our case. Then, I will rest our case tomorrow."

"Cool," said Adam "Half our work will be done."

Janet went to her office and called Rick Plume. "Hey, Rick" she said. "How's it going with you?"

"Okay, but I need those documents," he said glumly. "Parson's clerk told me that they were not admitted today."

"If you will bring Raoul Lecroix to court for me tomorrow, I think I will be able to get you the documents by the afternoon."

"Done," the district attorney said, suddenly cheerful. "What time do you want him there?"

"Bring him to the witness room at about 8:15. I'll prep him a little and then ask Judge Parsons to allow me to put on our rebuttal witness now. If he agrees, he will be finished by the morning recess and the documents should be in evidence before noon."

"You do good work, my friend," Rick Plume sounded almost jubilant.

"Thanks," Janet said "See you tomorrow."

Adam and James had the Raoul Lecroix contracts and memos from Jennifer Fordham already printed and were putting them into separate little notebooks for the jury in the conference room. "We're ready, boss!" James said, holding one of the notebooks up for her to see.

"Good work, guys. Now go have a nice evening and I'll see you back here at 6:45 in the morning for a final check on what we have to take."

When she pulled into her garage, Janet suddenly felt completely exhausted. She was sitting in her red leather chair in the library when Brad came in the back door with the mail.

"Hi, sweets," he smiled at her. "How's it going?"

"I'm glad you're home, Brad. I'm just really tired tonight. I put Jennifer Fordham on today and she refused to identify her signature or admit that she knew about the PSS animal studies that I got from Dr. Sally MacNamara and Amy Larabee, the FBI agent. I was amazed that she was able to be so cool and lie so easily." Janet said.

"What will you do now?" he asked still holding the mail.

"Put on the suspected murderer, Raoul Lecroix." Janet said. "The D.A. promises that he will be truthful on the stand and identify Fordham's signature on the memo. We will also have the bonus of getting in the fact, through him, that he lost the PSS sole distributorship in Canada due to the work of Jean Sonier and Dr. G. That is if Judge Parsons allows any of it."

"He'll allow it, don't you think?" Brad asked.

"You'd think so, but I gave up long ago on predicting what judges will do in any case. You can have a slam dunk case and have it all slide sideways into the trash, just because a judge is having a bad morning." Janet said softly.

"I'll tell you what, let's go down to Ted's and have some comfort food and a glass of wine. Then you just need a good night's sleep. We're both too tired to cook tonight."

"Sounds great," said Janet. "Just let me put on some jeans."

When Larry Lawson got home from Court, Grandmother Lawson had dinner waiting for him. She was just putting the children in the bath tub and Pamela was sleeping in the master bedroom. Larry peeked in at her and then went to have some of the tuna casserole and green beans, with fresh baked rolls which were in the oven. He ate alone in the kitchen, enjoying the happy sounds of his children splashing in the tub and laughing with their grandma in the bathroom down the hall. Suddenly Pam appeared in the doorway in her robe.

"Hi, "she said. "How was it?"

"Okay. It's always hard to talk about our very personal lives in front of strangers," Larry said. "You always wonder if they really give a damn."

"It seems like a good jury, Larry. I'm sure you were wonderful. You are wonderful, you know." Pam hugged him, then sat down at the table.

"How are you feeling, honey? You were dead to the world when I looked in on you before."

"I am not feeling very good. I am so nauseous and light headed. I can't keep anything down—even tea or toast. I think I should go back to the doctor, perhaps tomorrow."

Larry nodded. "You can't go on like this. This trial is just horrible for you, Pam." Larry took her hand and noted that he could feel every bone. "I think you should not go to the trial tomorrow."

"What's happening tomorrow?" she asked

"I'm not sure. Janet didn't say, but I know that she is planning something dramatic."

"I just hate to not be there. What will the jury think of me?'

"What they should think—that you are sick and that they are the only ones who can help you after all that PSS has done to you."

Pam laughed. "Now you sound like a lawyer, Larry"

Just then Sarah and David came running into the kitchen with freshly combed damp heads and fresh clean pajamas asking to be kissed and tucked into bed. Both Pam and Larry followed them down the hall to their rooms and tucked them into bed. Grandmother Lawson sat down in the living room and smiled to herself. "Such a precious family," she thought.

Terry Napoli and Rex Montague left the courthouse after Jennifer Fordham's testimony feeling jubilant. Jennifer Fordham didn't feel so jubilant. The experience in front of the grand jury was troubling, although she gave all of the same answers that she had given to the investigators who came to her office weeks before. She joined Terry, Rex and Jerry Carson at the Ship Tavern in the Brown Palace after the trial for a strategy session. None of them had heard from Leslie Winchester, after her grand jury testimony.

"Why don't you try Leslie's room once more," Montague suggested to Terry Napoli. "We really need to know what's going on with that grand jury."

"Why?" asked Napoli. "We've got plenty to do in preparation for the beginning of our case. My guess is that Janet Stephenson is going to rest her case tomorrow and that the judge will want us to start putting on witnesses."

"We are ready. Although it will seem somewhat redundant, perhaps because Jennifer is our first witness." Rex Montague smiled at her. "You were dynamite today, Jennifer. Janet Stephenson was stopped in her tracks."

"Don't underestimate her, Rex," Terry Napoli replied with a slight frown. "She didn't seem that worried that the judge didn't let the documents in. And, she will get another shot at Jennifer on cross-examination when we put her on. Jennifer, what are those studies? Are they really bogus? Why haven't we known about them before?"

Jennifer looked at him and lied. "I think that was some work that was done while my father was still alive. I haven't seen them."

Montague was suddenly alert. "Then where did those memos with your signature come from?"

"I don't know," she said.

Just then, Leslie Winchester entered the Ship Tavern and stood briefly at the door looking for them before Rex Montague stood up and waved at her. She came to their table as Napoli quickly added another chair.

"Mrs. Winchester. How are you? How did it go today?" Terry Napoli asked gently.

"I'm not my best. It certainly was not an experience that I'd like to repeat. Frankly, I didn't know how to answer a single question the district attorney asked me. It made it clear to me that I have no idea about what is really going on here." Leslie Winchester's face was pale and drawn.

Jennifer Fordham looked down at her drink and did not respond.

"I know you can't discuss the questions or the proceedings, but the district attorney say anything to you or to Joyce Symes about letting Mr. Winchester out on bond?"

"He said that they would be speaking to Jason Rivera about Forrest. That's all. Please order a martini for me." Leslie Winchester said.

Jerry Carson, who had been totally silent, quickly went to the bar to place the order. Then he returned to the table and sat down.

"What happened in the trial today?" Leslie Winchester asked.

They all looked at each other and Terry Napoli said, "Janet Stephenson called Jennifer as an adverse witness and tried to get some documents into evidence. The judge has not admitted the documents and has taken the issue under advisement, so far."

"What documents?" Leslie asked.

"The documents appear to be old animal studies ordered by Jennifer's father, before his death. We don't know how Janet Stephenson got them or where they came from." Napoli said.

"Why were they so important?" Leslie asked, taking a sip of her martini.

"They are studies of implantation of polyurethane into animals, which show that the animals developed tumors and cancer." Napoli said flatly.

Leslie Winchester stared at him. "Oh my god. Are they studies that we knew about?"

Jerry Carson was shaking his head. "Nobody could have known about them. Nobody!" he said.

"Jerry!" Jennifer said sternly under her breath.

"What do you mean?" Leslie Winchester demanded.

"It's nothing," was all Jerry Carson would say. "I'm going to my hotel. I don't feel very well." He got up abruptly and hurried out of the bar.

"What's going on, Jennifer?" Leslie Winchester asked sternly.

"Nothing that I know of. At least we are all finished with the grand jury. They will surely let Forrest out tomorrow because this is all just bogus. They are chasing shadows here. The judge has even refused to admit the bogus documents into evidence, to Janet Stephenson's dismay."

"Shall we have some dinner and go over the beginning of our case?" Montague said brightly, taking a cue from Jennifer's confidence. "I agree with Jennifer. At least the grand jury subpoenas are done with and we can focus on our case."

"Let's." said Napoli. "I made reservations in the dining room. We can go over as soon as we finish our drinks."

At the Denver City and County jail, Forrest Winchester was having beef stew and coffee in his cell. He was beginning to be very concerned that no one seemed to be able to get him out of jail and, moreover no one really seemed to care.

The next morning, Janet Stephenson met with Raoul LeCroix in a witness preparation room, down the hall from the courtroom. She showed him the memos and the contracts and he scowled at her. A deputy district attorney and a sheriff's deputy were also in the room.

"Can you identify the signature on these letters and the memo, Mr. LeCroix?"

LeCroix put on his reading glasses and looked at the documents carefully. "Yeah, that's Jennifer Fordham's signature," he said pushing the documents back across the table to Janet.

Then Janet showed him the memo which had the animal studies attached. "Can you identify this signature?"

LeCroix put his glasses on again and looked at the exhibit. "It's the same. It's Jennifer Fordham's signature."

"Mr. LeCroix, I would ask you to look at the attachment to this memo. Have you ever seen those documents before?" Janet asked as she placed the animal studies exhibit in front of him.

"Where did you get this?" LeCroix demanded. "Where in the hell did you get this report?"

Janet Stephenson was totally surprised at his reaction, but she remained perfectly calm.

"Have you seen this before?"

"Hell, yes," he said angrily. "These documents were in Jennifer's old man's safe in her office in Santa Barbara. I didn't know there was a copy!"

Janet was elated, but she remained completely composed as she said "When did you see them?"

"You ask me the right question, lady, and I will say." LeCroix snarled. He had to cooperate in her trial, or the district attorney would not follow through as he promised.

"What is the right question?" Janet asked, puzzled by the game he was playing.

"You'll know when it's time. You'll know."

There was no more time to talk to LeCroix. Janet Stephenson was due in court and she had to convince the judge to allow her rebuttal witness now.

Janet arrived in the courtroom just as Judge Parson's clerk was asking James and Adam about her. "Are you ready to proceed," Amelia asked.

"Yes," Janet said, just as Judge Parsons entered through the door behind his bench.

"Shall we bring the jury in?" he asked.

Janet nodded, as did Napoli.

When the jury had taken their places, Judge Parsons said, "Mrs. Stephenson, please call your next witness."

"Your Honor, I call our rebuttal witness, Raoul LeCroix."

Napoli was on his feet. "I object Your Honor. This is not the time for rebuttal. Rebuttal comes after the defendant has had an opportunity to put on its case!"

Judge Parsons also looked at Janet quizzically. "Mrs. Stephenson, your response?"

"Your Honor, Mr. LeCroix is called as a rebuttal witness to the testimony of the adverse witness, Jennifer Fordham, who testified yesterday. He is being called to rebut her testimony because it is an important part of the case of the Plaintiff. The defendant is not prejudiced by calling the rebuttal witness immediately after Ms.

Fordham, whose testimony he is rebutting. The defendant will have ample opportunity to respond in its case. Calling the rebuttal witness now just makes more sense to the presentation of the evidence for the jury."

"Mrs. Stephenson's point is well taken. Ms. Fordham was an adverse witness, and a representative of the defendant. She is entitled to call a rebuttal witness to address the testimony of Ms. Fordham. I will allow it."

"But Your Honor, we had no notice of this witness." Napoli said angrily.

"We discussed her rebuttal witness by name in our pretrial hearing, according to my notes, Mr. Napoli," the judge said. "That is adequate notice for a rebuttal witness."

Janet nodded to the bailiff, who opened the door and called for Raoul Lecroix. Lecroix entered the courtroom. He was dressed in a navy blue suit and red tie and he was accompanied by a sheriff's deputy, who was also in civilian clothes. The deputy stood by the door as Lecroix approached the witness box.

"Please swear the witness," Judge Parsons said to the bailiff.

Raoul Lecroix was sworn and Janet Stephenson took her place behind the podium. Adam and James had the jury notebooks ready for distribution to the curious jurors.

"Please state your name and your address for the record," Janet began.

Lecroix spelled his name and gave an address in Chicago as his residence.

"How are you employed?" she asked.

"Currently unemployed. My last employment was as a consultant for PolySurgical Specialties. Prior to that I had the exclusive distributorship for the Mammselle implant in Canada."

"Are you acquainted with Jennifer Fordham?"

"Yes, she is the boss lady at PSS and she was my boss, as well." LeCroix sounded surly.

"Are you familiar with her signature?"

"Yes," he said.

"How did you become familiar with her signature?" Janet Stephenson asked.

"She wrote me letters and I received and saw memos with her signature, during my time at PSS." LeCroix explained.

"I am handing you a small notebook of documents, Mr. Lecroix. Can you identify these documents?"

Lecroix opened the notebook and put on his glasses. Then he looked carefully at each document. Finally, he responded, "Yes, I can identify these documents. The first and last are letters to me from Jennifer Fordham and the other document is the contract for my distributorship of the Mammselle implant in Canada, signed by both Jennifer Fordham and myself."

"Do you recognize the signature on those documents as that of Jennifer Fordham?"

"Yes, I am very familiar with her signature." Lecroix said.

"Now, Mr. Lecroix, I would ask that you look at the documents in another notebook." Janet handed him the notebook with the memos and the animals studies from PSS. "Can you identify these documents?"

Lecroix smiled slightly at Janet. Janet realized that she had asked the question he wanted.

"Yes, I can identify these documents. The memos are memos from Jennifer Fordham, with her signature and the other document is a copy of the report of animal studies done on the foam material that covers the Mammselle implant, which were generally kept in the safe in Jennifer Fordham's office."

"How do you know that?" Janet continued the inquiry.

"Because I saw her put those documents into the safe. I was watching from the office door after one of her detail persons, Sherrie Barker and I, had accidentally seen them on the table in Jennifer's office. I asked her about them and she told me they were old studies that her father had done by an outside lab."

"Your Honor, we would move for the admission of the documents in the notebook, which the Court has under advisement and the documents in the notebook, which Mr. Lecroix has just identified today. Exhibits 25, 26, 27."

"Any objection, Mr. Napoli?"

"Yes," Napoli responded. "We object to 25-27 on the grounds of relevance and we continue our objections as previously stated to those exhibits under advisement."

"Well, I think the foundation and authenticity issues have been adequately addressed by the testimony of this witness. All of the documents relate to the Mammselle implant. They will all be admitted. You may proceed."

"May we distribute both exhibit notebooks to the jury, you Honor?" Janet asked.

"You may," said the judge.

Adam and James quickly gathered up their exhibit notebooks and passed them out to the jury, who immediately opened them and began looking at the pictures of the rats and rabbits, just as Janet hoped they would.

"No further questions at this time," said Janet, "Your witness."

Napoli stood up. "Mr. Lecroix, where are you currently staying?"

"I am a guest of the City and County of Denver," Lecroix said matter of factly.

"You're in jail, aren't you?"

"Yes."

"Why?" Napoli demanded.

"They haven't yet decided," Lecroix responded.

"Why were you arrested?" Napoli demanded, suddenly very interested.

"I can't say more. I take the fifth." Lecroix said.

"Have you been arraigned?" Napoli demanded.

"I have not been arraigned," the witness responded.

"Why should we believe you? Have you made some deal with Mrs. Stephenson?"

"No," was all he said.

"I'm finished with this witness," said Napoli in disgust, hoping that the jury would dismiss his testimony because Napoli had no more questions.

"Any questions on redirect, Mrs. Stephenson?" the judge asked

"No, Your Honor, although I reserve the right to recall this witness if needed for further rebuttal," Janet said.

"Then, this witness will be dismissed, subject to further recall." The judge nodded at the sheriff's deputy as LeCroix went through the swinging bar towards the courtroom door. "Please call your next witness, Mrs. Stephenson."

Janet went to the podium. "Your Honor, this witness concludes the Plaintiff's case, with requested leave to recall witnesses as may be required for rebuttal."

"Very well," said Judge Parsons. "Given the developments in the case this morning, I am going to allow the defendant until after lunch to begin its case. We will be in recess until two o'clock this afternoon, when we will hear the defendant's first witness. Members of the jury, the bus will be available to take you to your hotel to relax until then. I trust Mr. Napoli and Mr. Montague will be prepared to move the rest of the case along with dispatch, so that you can be released from sequestration as soon as possible. Please stand for the jury." After the jurors had left the room, Judge Parsons said to the attorneys for PolySurgical Specialites,

"Now would be the time the Court would ordinarily entertain motions for a directed verdict or dismissal, and the defendant is certainly entitled to make those arguments and to make your record. However, I will advise you that I believe that there is a considerable amount of evidence here in support of the claims that the Plaintiff has made and I am not inclined to either dismiss or direct a verdict from the jury. Let me know after lunch. If you decide to make arguments, I will hear them before we bring in the jury. We will be in recess until two o'clock," he said and left the bench.

Janet Stephenson felt incredible relief. She turned to Larry and Pamela Lawson, who were sitting, as if in shock, at the plaintiff's table. Pamela had tears streaming down her face and Larry leaned over to hug her.

"See, its all good." Janet said.

"You are amazing," Larry said. Pamela just nodded.

"I suggest you don't come back this afternoon, Pam. There is no need for you to labor through the defendant's case. It will just cause you unnecessary stress. Our case is in, and the jury has the PSS animal studies. It's all good."

"It's all good," said Pam. "I am going to go to the doctor and see if we can control this nausea. It's nearly unbearable. Larry may be late, will that be okay?"

"Of course," Pam said gently. "I'll let the judge know. Just do what you need to do. You've done your best here."

Pamela got up slowly and Larry helped her out of the courtroom. James and Adam were organizing their boxes and bringing out the cross-examination notebooks. When the Lawsons had left, James asked, tilting his head with his brown eyes sparkling, "You deserve lunch, boss. Food?"

Janet laughed at her impish clerk. "We all deserve it. My treat, as usual. Where shall we go?"

"Let's go to Gallagher's or the Broker," suggested Adam.

"Okay, which one? You know I hate to choose." Janet said, suddenly very hungry.

"The Broker," said Adam. "I love that shrimp bowl thing."

Janet put her notebook of research regarding directed verdicts in her briefcase and followed Adam and James out the door. She was already composing her responses to Napoli's inevitable arguments in her mind. She doubted that he would give up the chance for a legal argument, just in case there was a need for the defendant to appeal. But, she had been wrong about Napoli's strategy before. Before they drove to the restaurant, Janet called Rick Plume's cell phone and left a message that the documents had been admitted by the judge. She wanted to talk to him directly, but decided that it was important for him to know as soon as possible that he could access the documents. She assumed that he would have to secure certified copies from the Court files and that might take some time since the documents were actually exhibited in an ongoing trial and not already in a file in the court records office where anyone could check them out and copy them.

At lunch, she reviewed her notebook and ate a shrimp salad, while her team made the most of every luncheon course offered. They were accustomed to her being totally distracted and unresponsive to frivolous conversations when they were in trial or when she was concentrating on preparation.

Napoli and Montague returned to Montague's office where a catered lunch was waiting in the conference room. Now their portion of the trial was about to begin in earnest. The first decision was whether or not to request a directed verdict, or whether to honor the judge's request to get on with the trial. They did not agree. Rex Montague knew that Judge Parsons had already decided not to direct a verdict. If the PSS animal studies had not been admitted, they had a better chance. With the animal studies in evidence and the testimony of Jennifer Fordham virtually impeached, Rex knew that they had no chance. He believed they should just get on with their case as quickly as possible and try to end the trial before Janet Stephenson emphasized all of the plaintiffs' cases by cross-examination. Napoli was not convinced, but by the end of the lunch break, he acquiesced to the knowledge of the older local lawyer about their judge.

Janet Stephenson and her clerks were in the courtroom when they arrived, quietly pouring over the cross-examination notebooks. Janet was still reviewing her legal research on directed verdicts and her trial notebook. Both Larry and Pamela Lawson were missing.

Terry Napoli and Rex Montague noted that the gallery was full of the group of women known as the Silicone Sisters, who were anxiously awaiting the beginning of the presentation of the PSS case. Their law clerks had carefully stacked all of the defendant's exhibit notebooks on the end of their counsel table. Jennifer Fordham entered the courtroom with Jerry Carson and took her seat behind the stack of notebooks. Jerry Carson sat on the first row of benches just behind the bar. Leslie Winchester came a few moments later, dressed in a stylish crème colored silk suit, and sat beside him. They acknowledged each other but did not speak. Her face was somewhat drawn and her lipstick seemed just a little too red. Napoli and Montague both smiled at her and she nodded back, without smiling.

Amelia came in to ask if the parties were prepared to continue and a few moments later Judge Parsons opened the door and took his seat at the bench.

"Well, how shall we proceed counsel?"

Napoli stood and went to the podium. "Your Honor, the Defendant is prepared to proceed with its witnesses."

Janet was stunned and she quickly closed her legal research notebook.

"We will reserve our motions until the completion of the Defendant's case," Napoli explained.

"Well, good enough. Let's get the jury then," said the judge energetically, while the bailiff hurried to the door of the jury room to summon the members of the jury. When they were seated, the judge said, "Good afternoon, ladies and gentlemen. We are now ready to proceed with the Defendant, PolySurgical Specialties, witnesses. Mr. Napoli, please call your first witness."

"We call Jennifer Fordham," said Napoli firmly.

Jennifer Fordham got up from the counsel table and approached the witness stand.

"You have been previously placed under oath, Ms. Fordham," reminded the judge. "Please be aware that you are still under oath."

Jennifer Fordham nodded and entered the witness box. Rex Montague turned in his chair and motioned to Leslie Winchester to take Jennifer's place at the counsel table. Leslie Winchester looked at him and firmly shook her head. Rex Montague's face flushed and he turned back in his chair to face the witness. Janet Stephenson noted the unspoken hostility in Leslie Winchester's face and in her angry response to Montague. Just then her cell phone vibrated. It was Rick Plume calling her back, but now he would have to wait until the afternoon recess to talk to her.

Napoli, dapper and professional, began the long testimony of Jennifer Fordham. Slowly, question by question, he elicited the history of PolySurgical Specialties. Jennifer Fordham explained that the company had been started by her father, who was a professor of organic chemistry at California Polytechnical Institute at San Luis Obispo, California. He had been involved in a lifetime of research on medical implants and implantable materials, primarily polymers. Jennifer explained to the jury that she had spent her childhood in his laboratories and at his office at PSS because she was an only child. She teared up when she told the jury how her mother had tragically died when Jennifer was only six years old. Jennifer also modestly testified that she was an excellent student and went on, with a "full-ride scholarship," to get her degree in marketing from Stanford, although she had started out to follow her father into chemistry. After graduation, she explained that she went to work at PSS, and at her father's death, she became CEO and president of the company. She told the jury about the Mammselle implant and all of its improvements over other silicone gel breast implants. She explained also that she had continued the development of the Mammselle implant and developed the worldwide marketing plan because she wanted the benefits of avoiding capsular contracture to be available to "all women, no matter where they live." In the last year because she was made "an offer which she could not refuse," she told the jury that she sold her family's company to Conway Chemical, the major supplier of silicones to PSS. But, she explained that she had agreed to stay on for five years as the President in order to follow through with her "dream of all women everywhere having access to a Mammselle." Forrest Winchester became chairman of the board of directors. She explained to the jury that the sale was good for the company because it provided capital to PSS, which was necessary to fulfill her dream and "the dream of her father."

At that point, Judge Parsons finally said that the Court would be in a brief recess, and Janet rushed outside to return Rick Plume's call.

"Hey, Jan!" he said "Say, could I possibly get copies of the documents with Exhibit stickers from you, so that I can get them to the grand jurors? I'll substitute certified copies as soon as I can pry them out of the clerk of court."

"Sure," Janet replied. "If you can have someone stop by the courtroom, we'll give you an extra set. We always make an extra set of trial notebooks."

"They won't be able to come in the courtroom. Could you have one of your staff wait outside the courtroom with the notebooks?"

"I'll have Adam outside. He'll be holding two white notebooks. Who are you sending, so that I can tell Adam who he is looking for."

"I'll send Reggie Bates. Tall, red hair and freckles. Can't miss him, but he'll have his ID, too."

"Okay. Will it be soon? I think Napoli will wind up his questioning of Jennifer Fordham before too long."

"Ten minutes," said Plume.

Janet returned to the courtroom and gave Adam his instructions. Janet hoped there would not be press outside, but it was not likely that they would be interested in Adam and what would appear to be a friend. Adam left the courtroom just as the judge entered to complete the day.

The jury entered and Jennifer Fordham took the stand again. Napoli then began a long and detailed series of questions about other medical implants, which were manufactured by PSS. Janet objected as to relevance, but the judge overruled her objection when Napoli argued that he was laying foundation regarding the credibility and reputation of the defendant.

Within fifteen minutes, Adam came back quietly and sat down at the bar behind Janet. When she turned to look at him he gave her silent thumbs up and smiled. When Janet turned back, she noticed that Judge Parsons was looking right at her and at Adam. She smiled slightly at the judge and then returned to her copious note taking.

Forty-five minutes after five in the evening Judge Parsons interrupted Napoli, between questions with "Are you at a convenient stopping place, Mr. Napoli?"

Looking suddenly relieved, Terry Napoli replied, "Yes, Judge, this would be a good place to break off until tomorrow."

"Good. Then we will continue with Ms. Fordham's testimony tomorrow. We will begin at nine o'clock in the morning How many witnesses do you expect to call tomorrow, Mr. Napoli?"

"It is difficult to say because it depends upon the length of cross-examination," Napoli responded. "But, I hope to call at least two more witnesses tomorrow."

"All right, we will be in recess. Please stand for the jury. Have a nice evening, everyone." The jury marched out and disappeared into the jury room and Judge Parsons disappeared into his chambers.

"What witnesses are you going to call after Ms. Fordham, Terry?" Janet asked.

"We haven't yet decided the order of witnesses," Napoli responded in a frosty tone. "I'm sure you'll be at least as prepared as we have been for your surprises."

"Generally, are you calling experts, physicians or other corporate witnesses? Could I have that clue?" Janet asked firmly.

"You have the witness list, Mrs. Stephenson. They are all on it in roughly the 'will call' order." Napoli snapped and turned his back to her as he gathered the papers and notebooks from his table.

Janet did not respond or address him further. She had all of the cross-examination notebooks prepared and she could review them as each witness gave his or her direct testimony, putting sticky notes on cross-examination documents. Cross examination had always been her strongest skill. Janet Stephenson was always able to think on her feet and she knew the witnesses and their depositions as well as any attorney could. All she needed was a good night's sleep.

When Janet Stephenson and her clerks left the courtroom, they noticed that the press was energetically interviewing the Silicone Sisters. She thought that she heard Forrest Winchester's name as they hurried past the cameras, lights and reporters.

"I wonder if something is going on," she said. "Did you guys hear anything from the press this afternoon?"

"No. But, some reporter did see that guy from the D.A.'s office talking to me and seemed to notice when he flashed his ID at me. He didn't ask me any questions, though." Adam said.

"Maybe we had better watch the news tonight," James said.

As they reached the car, Rick Plume called Janet on her cell phone. "It's done, thanks to you, Janet Stephenson, lawyer extraordinaire!"

"Tell me," Janet said, excitedly.

"I can't tell you. You know that. Just know that the documents are in and you done good."

"Okay." Janet said, resigned. "But Rick, you may want to watch the news. I just thought I heard Forrest Winchester's name come up in an interview of a TV crew with a group of women who are part of the Silicone Survivor's organization. They have no real reason to be talking about Forrest Winchester, as it relates to our case. He has been absent for nearly the entire trial. Do you know if there are any leaks or rumors out there. Also, Adam said a reporter observed the handoff of the documents to your staff outside the courtroom. Perhaps we should have picked another place."

"Well, whatever comes out now is speculation. At least all of the evidence is before the grand jury and all we have to do is wait. I'm not worrying about it and you shouldn't either. I understand you've rested your case."

"Yes. Jennifer Fordham is on the stand, telling about the wonderful family business. It will take another half day. The next witness is a mystery person, somewhere on my witness list."

"It will be fine. Just do what you do." Rick said confidently.

"Keep me posted so I am forewarned of the results?" Janet pleaded.

"You've got it. Bye now. Good luck." Rick was gone - home for dinner for the first time in three weeks

J anet opted for a quiet evening by herself, with a sandwich and a glass of wine, sitting mindlessly in front of the television set in their comfy TV room. Brad was on his European loop and would be gone for two more days. She felt almost joyful that she was done with direct examination of witnesses. Cross-examination allowed creativity and a lot less methodical preparation the night before. Tonight she was zoning, except for one thing. She had to call Pamela and Larry and find out what they learned when Pam went to see her doctor. She decided to call first, before she turned on the television set and before she poured a glass of wine.

Larry answered the telephone. "Hi, Larry," the tired attorney said brightly.

"Hey, Janet. How's it going?"

"Jennifer Fordham is giving the entire history of PSS. You didn't miss a thing. How is Pam and what did her doctor say?"

"Well, we have to go back tomorrow because they have to admit her to the hospital for a couple of days of tests. Actually, it can't wait. I hope that doesn't cause us a problem. I was going to call you in a little while to discuss this because Pam is sleeping right now."

"What do they think the problem is?"

"You know, Janet. The problem is always possible rejection of her liver, even though nobody is saying it yet. But, I can tell that her team of doctors is concerned. That's what the tests are for, I'm sure." Larry sounded exhausted.

"Well, don't worry about the trial. I'll explain it all to the judge. You just take care of Pam and I will keep you posted. You can always call me on my cell and I'll call you back at a break."

"Okay. Will do. We may know more tomorrow or the next day."

"Bye, Larry. Give Pam my love. I'm sending you angels." Janet could hear the children laughing and singing a silly song with Grandma Lawson in the background as she hung up the phone.

Janet went to her room to put on her pajamas and a robe and then to the kitchen, where she fixed a ham and cheese sandwich and a glass of wine. Then she curled up on the comfy couch in the TV room and switched on the set with the remote. LA Law was on and she laughed out loud at the unbelievable courtroom antics of the attorneys in the show. Judge Parsons would never allow such behavior in his courtroom, nor would any judge before whom she had ever appeared. There is no striding around in front of the jury in a real courtroom. Attorneys question witnesses and make arguments only from behind the podium. A real trial lawyer must ask for permission to approach the witness or the judge's bench. The LA Law attorneys would be held in contempt on their first day in the Denver District Court or the United States District Court for the District of Colorado—and in most jurisdictions, even Los Angeles. Maybe that is why it was so much fun for Janet to watch what might be in a mythical land of law and order. Tonight it was lots of fun.

After LA Law the local news came on Channel 7. Janet immediately recognized the lead in as a story about her trial as she saw the Silicone Sisters in front of the camera. She turned up the volume. The reporter was asking one of the ladies about PolySurgical Specialties and the Mammselle implant. After her response about the implant allegedly causing cancer, the reporter asked the well dressed lady if she knew that the chairman of the board of PSS, Forrest Winchester was in the Denver jail. The woman looked smug. "I've only heard a rumor of that," was all she said. "I can't say more."

Another woman, dressed in black from head to toe, was quizzed about the testimony of LeCroix, and the fact that he, too, was in jail. "I'm sure they are all in this together and they all belong in jail," was her response.

The reporter then stated that there is no comment from the district attorney and that Judge Parsons is not allowing any media in the courtroom. The anchor also added that the jury in the Lawson v. PSS case was sequestered, but that their investigative reporters would be following this developing story. However, Janet was sure that it was only a matter of time before the entire story of Sherrie Barker's murder and Dr. Dan MacNamara's involvement with her case would be in the news. She just hoped that their trial would be completed first and she hoped that Napoli would not drag it out past next week. Tomorrow would be Wednesday. If only he would finish up by the weekend!

Janet didn't know that Terry Napoli was watching the same newscast in his hotel room. "I've got to get this trial finished before all hell breaks loose," he thought to himself.

Terry Napoli had a big surprise planned for Janet Stephenson tomorrow. He poured himself another scotch and sat down in the lounge chair in his room, smiling to himself.

The next morning, Janet and her clerks arrived at the courthouse at 8:15 in the morning In the parking lot, they ran into Dr. Sally MacNamara parking her car, so Terry Napoli's secret cat was out of the proverbial bag. Sally MacNamara had dropped Dr. Dan MacNamara off at the west entrance to the courthouse, where he was met by one of Terry Napoli's paralegals and whisked up the back stairway to the witness room, where Janet had met with Raoul LeCroix.

Sally MacNamara was anxious to talk to Janet Stephenson because she had heard from Amy Larabee and Rick Plume that Janet had succeeded in getting Sherrie Barker's documents into evidence and that Rick Plume had successfully added them to the evidence before the grand jury.

"Good job, Mrs. Stephenson," she said.

"Oh, call me Janet, please," began Janet, "I'm guessing that seeing you here this morning is not a coincidental parking lot meeting to talk about the documents, is it."

"Didn't you know that Dan agreed to testify?" Sally asked, stunned.

"No, I didn't know. Napoli is giving me some of my own medicine because I didn't disclose that I was calling Raoul Lecroix yesterday. I was relying on the witness list and the hearing about the rebuttal witnesses, to request that the judge allow me to call him. Otherwise the documents would not have been admitted until after PSS finished with all of their witnesses. That is when rebuttal witnesses are generally called. But I knew that the district attorney needed the documents to be admitted because he was nearly finished with witnesses for the grand jury, so I decided to take the chance that logic would prevail. Happily the judge saw it our way."

"Well, I don't know what Dan is thinking, exactly, but I can't believe that he is not going to support his patient, Pamela Lawson." Sally said.

"He has a lot at stake because he based his professional reputation on the benefits of the Mammselle implant in preventing capsular contracture," Janet said.

"He doesn't seem to think much about himself these days," Sally said quietly. "He has had a lot of time to think in his hospital room. He was all alone most of the time these last months."

Adam and James reminded Janet of the time and they rushed off to the courtroom with Janet in tow. Dr. Sally MacNamara paid for her parking and slowly followed. When she entered the courtroom, it was nearly full of spectators and Napoli's cast of thousands. Sally found a place to sit on the back row, near a window. There was no sign of her husband or the attorneys for PSS. Janet Stephenson and her clerks were busily pouring over notebooks at their table. Pamela Lawson and her husband were also missing. Suddenly, Terry Napoli and Rex Montague burst through the courtroom doors carrying notebooks. They sat down at their counsel table just as Amelia entered the courtroom to ask if they were ready to proceed. Both attorneys nodded.

"All rise," the bailiff nearly shouted.

Judge Parsons entered from behind his bench and said, "Please be seated. Counsel, are we ready to resume and call in the jury?"

Janet stood and said, "Judge Parsons, I regret to inform the Court that Mrs. Lawson is very ill and is going to have to be hospitalized for a few days for some necessary tests. Neither she nor her husband will be able to be with us in court today, but we request that the trial continue as though she were present."

"That's fine, Mrs. Stephenson, we understand. I will advise the jury. Now, are we ready to proceed?"

"Yes, Judge," Napoli said brightly. Janet nodded.

"Very well, Bailiff, will you please get the jury? All rise for the jury."

The audience and the attorneys all stood up as the jury filed in and took their places in the jury box. The judge motioned for everyone to be seated and he sat down behind the bench

"Ladies and gentlemen, I must explain to you that the Plaintiff, Pamela Lawson, has taken ill and must be hospitalized for a few days for some tests. She and her counsel have requested that we go forward with the trial in her absence. You are instructed not to hold her absence against her in any way as you consider your verdict in this case later on. Do you understand?"

The members of the jury all nodded.

The judge continued, "Mr. Napoli, do you have a new witness for us this morning?"

"Yes, Your Honor. We would call Dr. Daniel MacNamara to the stand." Terry Napoli turned and looked at Janet Stephenson directly. Janet smiled and turned back to her notebook. The bailiff called for Dr. MacNamara and in a moment, he entered the courtroom. Janet did not flinch or act the least bit surprised. Terry Napoli was very troubled by her failure to object. He expected her to be totally unprepared to see Dr. MacNamara take the stand, but she was acting as though she had known all along that he would be the next witness.

Dr. Dan MacNamara was wearing a navy blazer with gold buttons and tan trousers. He had on a white shirt, but without a tie and loafers. Although he looked well dressed, he certainly did not look formal or stiff. Despite the obvious scars on his face from multiple reconstructive surgeries and his very short hair, he was still a handsome man who looked as though he would be more comfortable sailing or playing golf than entering a courtroom to be a witness. He approached the witness box, walking very confidently and was sworn by the bailiff.

"Dr. MacNamara, will you please state your name and your office address for the record?" Napoli began. Dr. MacNamara complied.

"Dr. MacNamara, could you tell us how you are employed?"

"I am a plastic and reconstructive surgeon."

"Could you tell us a little about your educational and professional background?"

Dan MacNamara then explained that he had graduated from New York University with a degree in Chemistry and then went on to the NYU medical school. He explained his residencies in general practice at the Cleveland Clinic and his residency at the University of Colorado Health Sciences Center, including his specialization in plastic and reconstructive surgery there. He told the jury that he fell in love with his wife at the CU Health Sciences Center and in love with Colorado at the same time and decided to settle in Denver where he joined a practice or plastic and reconstructive surgeons who office near St. Anthony Central hospital.

"Are you board certified in plastic and reconstructive surgery, Doctor?"

"Yes, I am."

"Are you acquainted with the Plaintiff, Pamela Lawson?"

"Yes, I am. Mrs. Lawson is my patient. I performed reconstructive surgery fitting her with the Mammselle implant and I also performed the explant surgery to remove those implants a few years later."

"During your private practice as a plastic and reconstructive surgeon, did you become familiar with the Mammselle breast implant?"

"Yes, I did."

"Could you tell us about that?"

"One of the complications of silicone gel implants is that the breast tissue begins to form scar tissue around the implant making it hard and painful to the patient. I became interested in the

Mammselle implant because it appeared to solve that problem for patients. Patients who were implanted with the Mammselle implant did not develop capsular contracture. I found it amazing."

"Did you begin to use the implant in your practice."

"Yes"

"Did you ever have occasion to tell other physicians such as yourself about the implant?"

"Yes, I wrote several articles about the problem of capsular contracture that were published in medical journals. After I was introduced to the Mammselle implant, I actually made many presentations at medical meetings about the Mammselle and how it appeared to solve this problem for plastic and reconstructive surgeons and their patients."

"At this time, did you consider the implant to be safe and effective?"

"Yes, I did or I would not have implanted it into the breasts of my patients."

Napoli smiled, almost gleefully.

"Did you recommend the Mammselle implant to Pamela Lawson?"

"Yes, I did."

"Did you believe, as a board certified plastic and reconstructive surgeon that it was safe and effective for Pamela Lawson?"

"At the time I performed her reconstructive breast surgery with the Mammselle implant, I believed it was."

Janet's ears perked up at this answer. She had been listening intently trying to develop her cross-examination because she had not been able to depose Dr. MacNamara because of his injuries. Could she afford to take the chance that he had changed his mind about the implant? His answer to this question gave her a bit of hope.

"Dr. MacNamara, was the Mammselle implant approved by the FDA for use in patients such as Pamela Lawson."

"Yes, it was."

"What does FDA approval mean to a physician?"

"Well, FDA approval is supposed to mean that the government has approved the medical device or drug for use in humans. It also allows the drug or medical implant manufacturer to market its product to physicians and now, to the general public."

"Have you relied on FDA approval throughout your practice?"

"Yes, I have."

"Are you aware of any studies, whatsoever, in peer reviewed medical journals which prove that there is any relationship between use of the Mammselle implant and the development of liver cancer in any human being."

"Not in any human being," said Dr. MacNamara simply, looking directly at Janet Stephenson.

Napoli thought, "Wow, he's really sticking it to her. He's looking right at Janet Stephenson."

Janet looked back, right into his eyes. Her heart almost stopped. Now she understood why Dr. Dan MacNamara had agreed to testify for Napoli. He was actually waiting for her cross-examination.

"At the time that you performed reconstructive surgery using the Mammselle implant to reconstruct Pamela Lawson's breasts, were you relying on the FDA approval of this implant."

"I relied on the FDA approval and my own clinical experience that patients with the Mammselle implant did not develop capsular contracture," he said.

"At the time that you performed Mrs. Lawson's implant surgery did you have any reason to believe that the implant would do any kind of physical or medical harm to your patient."

"I thought I was doing the best I could possibly do for my patient," Dr. MacNamara said calmly.

"Thank you, Dr. MacNamara. I have no further questions at this time." Napoli said confidently.

"Thank you, Mr. Napoli," said the judge. "Let's take our morning break and then we will resume with cross-examination. All rise for the jury."

Janet spent the morning recess quickly outlining her cross-examination. When the trial resumed, she stepped calmly to the podium.

"Dr. MacNamara, I am Janet Stephenson. I represent Pamela and Larry Lawson in this matter. I have a few questions to ask you."

Daniel MacNamara just nodded.

"You stated that you performed both the surgery, placing the Mammselle implants into Pamela Lawson and the surgery to remove them, is that correct."

"Yes, it is correct. In the second, or explantation surgery, I was assisted by Dr. Levi Emanuel."

"When you placed the Mammselle implants, would it be fair to say that they looked pretty much like our demonstrative exhibit here?" Janet handed him the foam covered Mammselle implant.

"Yes, the implants were silicone gel filled implants with a polyurethane foam covering, just like this one."

"When you removed the Mammselle implants, what did you find?"

"We found that the implants were completely smooth and that there were no traces of the polyurethane foam on the implant or in the tissue surrounding the implant. The tissue surrounding the implant was stringy and watery, and there was no scar tissue."

"Where did the foam on the implant go?"

"It had obviously disintegrated in the body or had changed into some other substance other than polyurethane foam."

"What happened to the implants after you removed them?"

"We sent them to our pathology laboratory for initial tests and then they were sent on to a biomaterials laboratory in Canada to be tested by a biomaterials scientist named Dr. Richard Guilliot."

"Did you get the results of his tests?"

"Yes"

"What information did the tests provide to you?"

Napoli had caught on "Objection," he said, jumping to his feet, "Hearsay."

"Sustained," the judge said.

Janet placed the first exhibit book with Guilliot's test results in front of Dr. MacNamara, and asked, "Would you please turn to Exhibit 7, in the notebook, all of which as been admitted into evidence?"

"I have it," said Dr. MacNamara.

"Can you identify that exhibit, Doctor?"

"Yes, it is the pathology report from Dr. Guilliot, indicating that he found tolulene diamine or TDA both on the surface of the implant and in the samples of the tissue from around the implant."

"What did this information mean to you as Pamela Lawson's physician, Dr. MacNamara?" Janet asked.

"TDA is a known carcinogen or cancer producing agent, which has been banned by the FDA in the United States from use in hair dye and any number of products used outside or externally to the human body. I was very troubled to find that there was TDA on the implant I had placed in Mrs. Lawson, as well as in her surrounding breast tissue."

"Dr. MacNamara when you were introduced to the Mammselle implant, how did that occur?"

"I was visited at my office by a representative of PolySurgical Specialties, who told me about the implant and the fact that it prevented capsular contracture, which was a special professional concern of mine. She promised me a discount if I would try the Mammselle in my patients. I took the discount and eventually took money from PSS to make speeches to my colleagues about the Mammselle at medical meetings and to write journal articles with anecdotal reports about my successful use of the implant in my patients."

"In any of the product labeling or package inserts, is there any information about the foam covering disappearing or disintegrating after the implant is placed in the patient's breast?"

"There is no information about that issue. I had no idea that the foam disintegrated until I performed the surgery to remove Pamela Lawson's implants."

"Dr. MacNamara, you said in response to Mr. Napoli's questions that you did not know of any peer reviewed study which found a relationship between polyurethane foam and cancer in human beings, do you recall that answer?"

"Yes."

"Do you know of any study, as you sit here today, that found a relationship between implanted polyurethane foam and cancer, particularly liver cancer, in animals?"

"Yes, I do. After we performed the explant surgery and I reviewed Dr. Guilliot's report, I did some further research and I found Dr. Jean Sonier and Dr. Guilliot's article in the Journal of Biomaterials about their rat and rabbit study, implanting Mammselle polyurethane foam."

"Was that study ever disclosed to you by PSS prior to your being retained to make speeches about the Mammselle to medical groups?"

"No."

"Dr. MacNamara, I would like you to open the notebook in front of you and review Exhibits 23 and 24, which are animal studies attached to a memo signed by Jennifer Fordham on PSS letterhead. Do you see those."

"Yes," Dr. MacNamara looked at the notebook pages one by one and carefully read each one. When he looked up, his eyes were brimming with tears. He did not speak.

"Dr. MacNamara, have you ever seen these documents before?"

"I think I had them in my hand, but I did not open the envelope and I have not seen them," he said huskily.

"Dr. MacNamara, those exhibits have been admitted as evidence in this trial. My question to you is if you had seen them prior to performing the surgery to place implants into Pamela Lawson, would you have placed Mammselle implants in her breasts?"

"Mrs. Stephenson, these implants are murder by another name, Mammselle. I would never have used them. God forgive me, I would never have used them." Tears were streaming down his face. In the back row of the courtroom, tears also streamed down the face of Dr. Sally MacNamara, who bowed her head and covered her face with her hands.

Janet had other notes on her pad but she said "I have no further questions for Dr. MacNamara."

The courtroom was absolutely silent.

Judge Parsons finally said, "Mr Napoli, any redirect?"

Terry Napoli stood up and went to the podium. "Dr. MacNamara, you said that you had the studies in your hand but you did not open the envelope. Isn't it a fact that PSS did supply the information to you and that you failed to fully review it by your own negligence."

Dr. Daniel MacNamara gathered his composure. He looked for a long time at Terry Napoli, then he said, "I received these documents for the first time from Sherrie Barker, the PSS sales representative, the night before Pamela Lawson's liver transplant surgery, not before I began making speeches and implanting Mammselle implants in my patients. Sherrie Barker left my office that day and was killed by a bomb in her car. I never saw the PSS studies implanting foam into animals until I came to the courtroom today. The documents were in my office and I was in the hospital because I was going to my car at the same time as the bomb exploded. But perhaps I was negligent in not asking more questions and believing what seemed too good to be true. Yes, Mr. Napoli, perhaps this is all my fault." Tears streamed down his face again.

"No more questions," said Napoli.

"Mrs Stephenson?" the judge asked. Janet shook her head.

"The witness may be excused," said the judge kindly.

Dr. Sally MacNamara met her husband at the door and they went out of the courtroom together.

"We will adjourn for lunch now," said Judge Parsons. "We will resume with the Defendant's next witness at 1:30 in the evening Please rise for the jury."

Janet looked at the jurors as they left the courtroom. They were all very somber and did not look at any of the attorneys, the spectators or each other.

Janet, Adam and James all sat in the courtroom until everyone was gone. Napoli and Montague left with their cast of thousands to waiting limousines and a catered lunch at Montague's offices. Janet wondered who they were planning to call after Dr. MacNamara. Somehow, it didn't seem to matter. She felt wounded and sad inside after watching the agony of Pamela's doctor on the stand. She was so glad that neither Larry nor Pam had been in the courtroom.

"Let's just go get some sandwiches downstairs and sit in the park," Janet suggested to her clerks. "I really need some fresh air."

That afternoon, Terry Napoli called Dr. Hans Bricker, from the University of Colorado Medical School, to testify that there is no verifiable connection between silicone implants and autoimmune disorders, such as those suffered by Pamela Lawson and other women who have silicone gel breast implants. Dr. Bricker spent a long time "educating" the jury about the medical process of autoimmune reactions and the human immune system.

Janet asked him only a few questions about the large numbers of silicone gel breast implant patients who had sought testing from his laboratory and his professional knowledge that most of the women had elevated antinuclearantibodies or ANA. He was firm in the testimony that he couldn't come to any conclusions with any degree of medical certainty until there was more data collected and it was all analyzed in an epidemiologically correct study. He did say that immune deficiencies and disorders make it more difficult for a transplant patient to retain an implanted organ without rejection. Janet led him through Pamela's medical records to the testing which showed that she had exactly the immune disorder which poses a problem for transplant patients.

On redirect, he reaffirmed that there is no verifiable connection between silicone implants and autoimmune disorders. He did not mention polyurethane foam.

At the end of his testimony, Judge Parsons called it a day and told them that court would reconvene at ten o'clock the next morning so he could take care of some other pending matters. The jury looked exhausted as they left the courtroom.

Napoli and Montague sat talking quietly at their table after the jury left. Janet Stephenson and her clerks were reorganizing their notebooks and deciding what to take back to the office when Montague said to Janet.

"Janet, any word about how Mrs. Lawson is doing?"

"I haven't heard anything today, Rex," she replied.

"What would you think if we made a settlement proposal, just to make it easier for her?"

Janet smiled and said, "Rex, you know I will always recommend settlement if the price is right."

Napoli stood up and reached out to shake her hand. "How about we get back to you later this evening? Can you be reached?"

"Rex has my cell phone number," Janet replied. "I'll listen to whatever you have to say."

After they had left the courtroom, Adam said, "Whooa, Janet. I think you have them on the run. Do you think they will really settle?"

"Don't count on it, Adam. But, I will listen to them. It is never that easy, especially in the middle of their case."

"But they aren't doing so well, are they?" James asked.

"James, you never know how a jury is interpreting the evidence. After today, they may think that the really negligent one is Dr. MacNamara. He was Pam's last line of defense."

"No way," said James.

"We'll see." Janet said. "Let's just get out of here. Tomorrow is another day."

At about eight o'clock that night, Montague called Janet and offered six hundred thousand dollars to settle the case. She called Larry Lawson and left a message on his cell phone for him to call her, no matter the time. Janet also called their home and left a message with Grandma Lawson. Ten minutes after ten o'clock, Larry Lawson returned her call.

"How is Pam doing?" Janet asked.

"We really don't know yet," Larry responded. "She's still in the hospital and will be probably until the weekend, to finish all of the tests they are putting her through. She's really tired, so I hope that they will let her sleep at night."

"Well, we have an interesting development," Janet began.

"What's up, Janet?"

"PSS has made a settlement offer of six hundred thousand dollars —in the middle of their case."

"Why? I don't understand why they would do that now. Did something happen today?" Larry asked.

"Yes. Dr. MacNamara testified for them on direct examination, but may have been our very best witness when I cross-examined him. He even broke down in tears on the stand and said that he would never have put the Mammselle implants in Pamela, or any patient if he had known that the foam disintegrated or if he had known about the animal studies."

"Six hundred thousand dollars hardly seems fair, does it? Pamela is expecting something in the millions."

"We can make a counter offer and we should," Janet responded.

"Six million," said Larry. "I think they are off by a factor of ten." His voice was firm.

"Six million dollars, it is," Janet replied. "I'll call Montague and leave him a message."

"Great. Also, I won't be in court tomorrow. It will be the worst day for Pamela because the tests they are doing will likely make her sick. I think I need to be there with her."

"That's fine, "Janet said kindly. "The judge understands and he gave a nice speech to the jury, about why Pamela was not in the courtroom. If PSS wants to continue to negotiate, I'll leave you a message on your cell phone."

Janet hung up and dialed Montague. She left the message of the $6,000,000 counteroffer on his cell phone and then went into the kitchen to get a glass of milk.

She had just settled on her comfy couch when her cell phone rang. It was Brad.

"Hey, what's up?" he said brightly.

"Hey. Well, we just got a settlement offer in the case - $600,000."

"Wow! Does that surprise you?" Brad asked.

"Yes and No. Dan MacNamara testified today for them, but his intent was to really testify for Pam on cross-examination. It was pretty amazing. He was so emotional that he even cried. I have to confess that I was really touched and nearly everyone had tears in their eyes. But, I think that they planned to make the offer before the surprise of his testimony. I just don't know exactly what is going on."

"What did you say to them?"

"I talked it over with Larry Lawson and left Montague a message with a six million dollar counter offer." Janet summarized.

"That will probably end the discussion," Brad said, somewhat glumly. "Your share of $600,000 would really come in handy right now."

"What do you mean?" Janet asked "Has something happened?"

"Just before I left on this trip, I had a call from Mr. Sunman, the IRS guy I have been working about the audit of our taxes and your firm. They are about to make an assessment and it is going to be in the hundreds of thousands because the IRS is not going allow a business deduction for all of the money that was advanced for client costs in the IUD cases."

"What does that mean?" Janet asked, suddenly sick at her stomach.

"It means that all of the money that your S corporation borrowed to pay the hundreds of thousands of dollars in costs in those cases will be treated as income and we will be taxed on it because the cases are locked up in the bankruptcy and appeals and are not 'concluded', in his terms. So, the costs cannot be written off as bad debt until they are 'concluded' according to the IRS definition. That means a big tax bill for us because all of the tax consequences flow through to our individual tax return." Brad explained.

"Oh, brother!" Janet said. "I can't believe this is happening! Sometimes I wonder why I am working so hard anyhow."

"You are suing huge corporations, Janet. What you have to understand is that this audit and all of these problems are not coincidences. They want you out of this litigation game. You are such a small firm, they know that they can pull strings to ruin you financially, so that you cannot afford to take on any more contingent fee cases. They also know that ordinary people can't afford to sue them if they cannot retain attorneys on a contingent fee. Could Larry and Pamela pay your hourly rate of $300 per hour, win, lose or draw? No ordinary person could. You have hundreds of thousands of dollars worth of attorney and paralegal time in this case already."

"You're right." Janet said glumly. "But, I can't think about this now. I have to finish this trial. I just hope that Pam makes it. She is back in the hospital for tests, and I think there is a distinct possibility that her body is rejecting her new liver."

"Oh, dear!" said Brad. "Well, sweetie, I'm sorry. I should have waited until I was home to talk about this IRS thing. Just put it all out of your mind and give them hell. Don't give away the case for a paltry settlement. There is too much at stake for your clients."

"I won't," Janet assured him, "It's just that $600,000 is a lot of money and you never know what a jury is thinking or what they are going to do. I really can't read this jury, but that is not news. It is frustrating to never have an inkling or idea of what a jury is thinking. I'm missing that chip in my brain that makes me intuitive in that way. You are much better at reading minds and people than I am."

"Oh, right! That's why I'm a pilot and you are the trial lawyer," Brad teased.

"When will you be home?" Janet asked.

"Friday night or Saturday morning," Brad promised. "I have to get a hop from New York after the last leg. They have added an internal trip through Amsterdam to my schedule."

"I just really miss you!" Janet said sadly. "Please leave me a voice mail on my cell and let me know where you are and what's happening, okay?"

"Will do, sweetie. Go to bed. I love you."

"You too," she said.

Rex Montague listened to Janet Stephenson's voice mail message as he was driving to his office the next morning. "Six million dollars. PSS will have to have a jury come up with that kind of verdict before they'll pay anything close," he thought to himself.

"Did you hear from Janet Stephenson," Terry Napoli asked him the moment he walked into Montague's office twenty minutes later.

"Yep. She made a six million dollar counteroffer," he said flatly.

"She's crazy. She needs that money and so do her clients." Napoli said. "I know that she's got huge tax problems and other cash flow issues. Our people are totally on top of it and she's in a financial pit."

"You don't know Janet Stephenson," Montague replied. "I truly don't know if she cares about money."

"What?" said Napoli "She's a plaintiff's trial lawyer. They are all money grubbing bastards who will sell their souls and their clients for a good settlement. What makes her different?"

"I don't know," Montague mused. "I just get the feeling that she is. Maybe her husband is independently wealthy or something. She didn't seem enticed by six hundred thousand dollars."

"Well, I think we just let it go to verdict. It can't be worse than six million and the jury may just blame Dr. MacNamara for his participation in marketing the implant. They may have been put off by his schmaltzy act on cross-examination. I was. I think the injury made him mentally unstable."

"That's one way to spin it." Montague said. "We've got to get to court."

Janet and her clerks and Napoli, Montague and the cast of thousands all arrived at the courthouse a little after eight o'clock in the morning Janet nodded to them as they unloaded their trial notebooks and materials from their limousine at the curb. Inside the courtroom, the settlement offer was not mentioned by any of them.

Leslie Winchester, Jerry Carson and Jennifer Fordham all entered the courtroom at the same time. Leslie Winchester and Jerry Carson sat in their usual places in the front row of the gallery and Jennifer Fordham took her place at the defendant's table with Rex Montague and Terry Napoli. Leslie Winchester's face was flushed and stern and she appeared to be deliberately ignoring Jerry Carson, sitting next to her. Leslie Winchester was dressed in a stylish apricot colored coat dress accented by a matching coral and turquoise necklace and earrings. Jennifer Fordham was dressed in a white suit, with a red blouse and red pumps. She appeared confident and smiled broadly at Rex Montague as he pulled the chair out for her to be seated. She sat down and pushed her hair back from her face, looking straight at Janet and her team. She even smiled at James, who did not smile back. Janet took no notice of any of them. When she was in court, all of the other parties and the spectators were invisible to her. She was hardly aware of anyone other than the judge, the witness and the other attorney. James and Adam had learned to write her notes and never to attempt to whisper or speak to her after the judge entered the room. She would not hear them.

All of the Silicone Survivors who had attended every day of the trial had arrived in the courtroom and claimed their seats in the gallery before any of the attorneys or parties arrived. Many of them had notebooks and had been taking notes during the trial. They whispered and talked softly to each other, waiting for the trial to begin again.

"Is Mrs. Lawson still in the hospital?" Judge Parsons asked Janet when he entered the courtroom a few minutes later.

"Yes, Your Honor," Janet responded. "She has further difficult tests today and Mr. Lawson felt that he needed to be with her. I hope that you will excuse their absence."

"Of course," he said kindly. "I will further advise the jury. Are we ready to continue, Mr. Napoli?"

"Yes, Judge," Napoli responded. "We have two further experts. Dr. Lyndon Sloan, a former member of the Food and Drug Administration and Dr. Betsy Cooper, a biomaterials scientist."

"How much longer do you anticipate your case will take?" asked the judge.

"Depending on cross-examination, we should be able to finish both of these witnesses today." Said Napoli.

"Any further rebuttal witnesses, Mrs. Stephenson," the judge inquired.

"At this time, we would not have further rebuttal. However, I have not heard the testimony of Dr. Sloan and Dr. Cooper, so I reserve the right for rebuttal depending on how cross-examination goes." Janet said.

"Good. In the event that there are no rebuttal witnesses, we can conclude tomorrow with closing arguments, jury instructions and the jury will have the case by tomorrow afternoon. That will be good. I will have them deliberate over the weekend because they are sequestered and I'm sure they would rather finish this up so they can get home."

"That's fine," said Janet. Napoli nodded in agreement.

The judge called in the jury and he told them that Pamela and Larry Lawson were still to be excused for their absence from the courtroom. He also gave them an outline of the remaining parts of the trial and advised them that they might get the case as early as Friday afternoon, so that they could then deliberate through the weekend. There was obvious relief on the faces of the jurors when they were advised that the end of the trial was near.

Napoli called Dr. Lyndon Sloan to the stand and the bailiff retrieved him from the bench in the hall outside the door. Dr. Sloan was a tall, thin, balding man in his sixties, with frameless glasses, who was dressed in a shiny gray suit with a bright red tie. He walked quickly to the witness box and was sworn by the bailiff.

Dr. Lyndon Sloan testified that he held a PhD in epidemiology from Emory University and that he had worked at the Food and Drug Administration for thirty years before retiring last June. He now owned a consulting firm and had testified in six trials, on behalf of drug and medical manufacturers since retiring. In the FDA, he was in the compliance and auditing division. He was admitted as an expert on the FDA approval process and procedures.

"Dr. Sloan, what is the purpose of FDA approval of medical implants?" Napoli continued.

"FDA approval means that the FDA has determined that a medical implant is safe and effective and that it may be marketed to the medical community." Dr. Sloan replied.

"Were you at the FDA when the Mammselle implant was approved for marketing?" Napoli asked.

"Yes, I was. I was on the team that reviewed the final approval of that product."

"Dr. Sloan, did the Mammselle implant meet all of the requirements of the FDA?"

"As I recall, yes, it did. It was approved as safe and effective for marketing."

"At any time since the Mammselle was approved, has that approval ever been rescinded or removed?"

"Not to my knowledge." Dr. Sloan said confidently.

"Do you have an opinion, Dr. Sloan, as to whether physicians and patients can rely on FDA approval as proof that an medical implant is safe and effective for surgical implantation in patients?"

"Yes, it is my opinion that physicians and patients can rely on FDA approval as an indication that and FDA approved medical implant is safe and effective." Dr. Sloan said.

"Dr. Sloan, do you have an opinion as to whether or not Dr. MacNamara could rely on the FDA approval of the Mammselle implant in making the decision prescribe and use it in the reconstructive surgery he performed on the Plaintiff, Pamela Lawson?"

"Yes, it is my opinion that Dr. MacNamara could rely on FDA approval of the Mammselle," Dr. Sloan stated confidently nodding his head.

"I have no further questions at this time," Napoli said.

Dr. Sloan smiled and waited for Janet Stephenson to come to the podium. Janet opened her notebook and smiled at Dr. Sloan.

"Good morning, Dr. Sloan. I am Janet Stephenson, the attorney for Pamela Lawson. We met at your deposition, and I have a few questions for you based on your answer to the questions posed by Mr. Napoli.'

"Good morning. I remember you, Mrs. Stephenson," Dr. Sloan said pleasantly.

"Dr. Sloan, as I understand the process, the Mammselle implant was approved by piggy-backing if you will, on the prior testing done on the silicone gel breast implants manufactured by Conway Chemical. Is that correct?"

"Yes, I think that the Mammselle was approved as an improvement of the Conway Chemical implants because the Mammselle prevented the objectionable adverse consequence of capsular contracture."

"So, it would be fair to say that PSS did not have to submit new animal studies or clinical studies in humans to secure approval to market the Mammselle, right?"

"Yes, that is the process for this kind of application," he said, looking quizzical.

"Did you review any animal studies done by Conway Chemical or any other source in the process of approving the Mammselle?"

"That review was not necessary because we had the certification from Conway Chemical that PSS could rely on their studies because the base implant of the Mammselle is actually a Conway Chemical implant. In other words, PSS purchases the basic implant from Conway."

"So it would be fair to say that you did not review any animal or clinical studies on the polyurethane foam covering that PSS placed on the implant to achieve this 'improvement.' Correct?"

"Yes, this is correct. Such a review is not required to process the kind of application for approval filed by PolySurgical Specialties."

"Have you ever reviewed any of the animal studies on the polyurethane foam used on the Mammselle which were conducted by Dr. Jean Sonier and Dr. Richard Guilliot from Canada?"

Janet asked.

"Objection, irrelevant." Napoli said emphatically.

"Overruled," said the judge simply. "Please answer the question."

"I have heard about Dr. Sonier, who is no longer with the Canadian agency, but I have not reviewed his studies. You showed them to me at the deposition, but I never reviewed them at the FDA."

"Dr. Sloan, I would like to show you them again today. Please open the Exhibit Notebook one, at look at the first few exhibits if you will."

Dr. Sloan complied. Then he looked up and straight at Janet.

"Dr. Sloan, would it have made any difference in the FDA approval of the Mammselle if you had reviewed these studies, which demonstrate ubiquitous formation of malignant tumors on the livers of the animals, before the approval of the Mammselle?"

"No, I don't think it would have made a difference. These studies were done in Canada, by another agency. Also, you cannot translate adverse effects in animal subjects directly to adverse effects in humans. There is not a one to one correlation."

"Dr. Sloan, I would now like you to look at the small exhibit notebook in front of you. Please review the exhibits in that notebook, which are animal studies on the foam commissioned by PSS."

Dr. Sloan complied. As he looked at the exhibits, his face became noticeably flushed. Finally, he looked up and pushed up his glasses from where they had slipped down on his nose.

"Dr. Sloan, would it have made any difference in the FDA approval of the Mammselle if you had reviewed these studies, which also demonstrate a malignant tumor in the liver of each animal, before approval of the Mammselle?"

Dr. Sloan cleared his throat and sat up straighter in his chair, then he replied "Mrs. Stephenson, I have to say that it would not have made a difference because animal studies were not required for the kind of application PSS filed, and further because there is no direct correlation, as I said between what happens in animals and what happens in humans."

"So, what you are saying, Doctor, is that the FDA truly does not protect patients such as Pamela Lawson, isn't it." Janet said calmly, looking at him.

"We do our best," he said quietly.

"No more questions," Janet said, closing her notebook and looking at Dr. Sloan.

Napoli stayed in his seat and said, "No more questions."

"Dr. Sloan, you are excused," said Judge Parsons. "Although it is a little early, let's take our lunch break, now. I will see you all at 1:30. Please rise for the jury."

Leslie Winchester left the courtroom as soon as the judge stood up from the bench. Napoli and Montague, who turned and saw her abruptly leave, looked at Jerry Carson, who shrugged his shoulders in dismay.

"I thought we would all have lunch," said Jennifer Fordham. "We have over two hours and I think we all need to talk."

"Can you give Mrs. Winchester a call on her cell?" Montague asked her.

"I think that you and Terry are the ones with the power to summon Leslie Winchester, not me." Jennifer laughed.

Napoli used his speed dial. "She's not picking up. Shall I leave her a message to meet us at the office?" Montague nodded.

"Let's go. The cars should be waiting. She'll either show or she won't." Montague said.

"Dr. Cooper will join us for lunch. My paralegal called her, "said Napoli.

Janet, James and Adam watched the cast of thousands flow out of the courtroom. Then they decided to go to their favorite restaurant at the Art Museum across the street. Janet took only one notebook. She was ready to be done. Her closing argument had been written for weeks.

Just after they were seated, Larry Lawson called and asked if he could join them. He arrived just after they got their drinks. Janet had ordered him ice tea and a tuna salad sandwich.

"Hi, Larry. How's Pam." Janet asked.

"Not good. She's sleeping for the first time since the middle of last night. I thought I needed to come and touch base with you. We don't have all the tests back, but it is looking more and more as though her body is rejecting the liver. They have her on some powerful IV's now, trying to deal with it and reverse the process. They are also concerned about infection somewhere else because her immune system is so dramatically repressed."

Janet's heart sank. She was hoping that good news was the reason he was coming to meet them for lunch. "I'm so sorry to hear that." She said, patting his arm. "What can I do?"

"Janet, just finish this trial. We have to be done." Larry said urgently.

"We're on the last witness, so we'll be finished with testimony today. Closing arguments and jury instructions will be tomorrow morning. The jury should have the case before noon tomorrow and the judge is not giving them any breaks. They have to deliberate straight through to a verdict. The jury looks content with that, at least when he gave them an overview this morning." Janet explained.

"Any response to our counteroffer?" Larry asked.

"No one has even mentioned the settlement," Janet said. "I think it's going to verdict."

"Do you think we should have accepted that settlement, Janet?" Larry asked.

"Well, you never know what a jury is going to do, but I really believe that they could award you more than $600,000. I have to tell you, however, the decision is completely yours. I can tell them that you will accept it if you want." Janet said softly.

"Damn, I don't know what is best. Can't you tell me?" Larry said, almost frantically.

"I think you should talk to Pamela about it and let me know. I can't decide for you. At this stage in any trial I am too much of an advocate. I believe in our cause and I think the testimony has gone in very well. But, I will not make any prediction about what this jury, or any jury, will ultimately decide." Janet said firmly, but gently.

"All right. I'm going back to the hospital. I'll talk to Pam as soon as she wakes up. Please call me when trial is finished, or at the break." Larry wiped his brow with his napkin and rushed out of the restaurant.

Janet Stephenson felt a lump in her throat and a strange foreboding. She hated these feelings of free floating anxiety that accompanied trying cases. This anxiety was soon to escalate into almost unbearable proportions as soon as the jury began deliberating. But first, there was one more witness to finish.

The afternoon went quickly. Dr. Betsy Cooper was a pudgy middle aged biomaterials scientist who worked at a private laboratory near Stanford in Palo Alto, California. Her specialty was animal testing of implanted materials and the major point of her testimony and her unshakable opinion was that no matter what adverse effects were evident in tests on animals, those tests did not mean that the material could not be implanted in humans. It was her opinion, and she stuck to it, that it was more likely than not that Pamela Lawson's liver cancer was not caused by the implants and that it had nothing whatever to do with the disintegration of polyurethane foam.

Despite Janet's attempts to shake her opinion, she stated it over and over. She did not see a correlation between the TDA found on the removed implant and Pamela's breast tissue and cancer far away from the site in Pamela's liver. She said over and over that any animal tests to the contrary had to be inconclusive as a matter of biomaterials science.

Janet ceased her cross-examination when it became apparent that Dr. Cooper would use any cross-examination question as an opportunity to restate her firm opinion, without regard to whether the opinion was responsive to the cross-examination question.

At the end of her testimony, Judge Parsons dismissed the jury and instructed Janet Stephenson and Terry Napoli to be prepared to begin with their closing arguments in the morning. The judge limited the closing argument to one hour for each of them. He advised the jury that he expected them to be able to begin deliberations before noon. He advised them that all deliberations would be in the jury room and that they were not to discuss the case with anyone, even each other outside the jury room. At their hotel they were to rest, eat and refresh themselves, but not deliberate or consider the case. The jurors all agreed that they understood and would follow the judge's instructions. All of the attorneys doubted that jurors ever follow that instruction completely.

James, Adam and Janet Stephenson packed up the remaining exhibit boxes, leaving only the demonstrative exhibits that were going to be used in their closing argument. Janet drove her car to the south door of the City and County Building so that they could remove everything easily. She waited behind the limousine into which Napoli and Montague's cast of thousands were loading the defendants extraneous boxes and trial materials. As she waited to pull her car up before the door, Janet saw Leslie Winchester and Terry Napoli talking together on the sidewalk. She saw Leslie pull her arm away from Napoli, who was attempting to assist her into the waiting limousine in front of the limousine into which their boxes were being loaded. Leslie Winchester turned abruptly and walked to the corner where a number of cabs were waiting for customers. Napoli looked after her for a moment, then disappeared into the limousine with Rex Montague and their paralegal staff members.

"I wonder what that is about," Janet thought to herself.

Leslie Winchester went directly to the Denver City and County jail and asked to see her husband, Forrest Winchester. She was told that he was in a conference room meeting with his attorney, Mr. Rivera.

"Please tell them that I am here and that I would like to join them," Leslie asked graciously, but firmly.

In a moment, Jason Rivera came out to meet her and she followed him through the security to the conference room without windows, where her husband sat in an orange jail jumpsuit.

"Well, as I live and breathe, she does exist," Forrest Winchester said, without standing.

"Hello, Forrest. How are you?" Leslie said, without smiling.

"Rotten as hell. How are you? You don't look any the worse for wear." Winchester said eyeing her impeccable dress and makeup.

"Mr. Rivera. Can we get Forrest out of here? I would really like him to be in the courtroom tomorrow for the closing arguments in our case." Leslie Winchester asked the attorney.

"We were just discussing all of our possibilities for bail." Jason Rivera said.

"And?" Leslie asked.

"No way." Forrest sneered. "I'm likely to rot here."

"We've requested another bail hearing, but the district attorney has convinced our judge to wait until the grand jury proceedings are completed."

"I thought they were finished days ago," Leslie said, confused. "That man, LeCroix, came to testify from jail."

"I'm not coming to testify." Forrest said flatly. "Frankly, my dear, even though you don't give a damn, it is my opinion that this is damn near hopeless. I assume you will get used to my less than fashionable attire after a while."

"Why are you so rude to me? I'm not an attorney and I'm not the one who shot at Dr. Sonier."

"Oh yes, good for you. I forgot. Look Leslie if you aren't going to pay to get me a lawyer who can figure out a way to spring me, why don't you just go back to the Brown Palace and have a cucumber facial and a massage. I'm sure just seeing me is stressing you out."

Leslie Winchester looked at him for a long time, and then said. "You're right, Forrest. I am stressed out. I'm sure you'll figure this one out on your own, just as you figured out how to get yourself into this mess. A massage sounds great." She turned to leave and started for the door.

"Wait, Leslie. I'm sorry," Winchester began, "I don't blame you and I need you, honey. I have no hope of ever getting out of here unless you will arrange bail for me."

"And then what?" she said without turning around.

"Then we can figure out together how to solve all of these problems. I really can't do it without you, you know." Forrest Winchester stood up and touched her arm. She turned around.

Jason Rivera stood up and walked to the corner of the room where he sat down on a chair.

"I don't know what to do. I don't think our part of this Lawson trial is going very well and the plaintiffs turned down our settlement offer, demanding six million dollars to settle. It will go to the jury tomorrow. Jennifer Fordham just smiles and struts around as though everything is hunky dory. I have no idea what is going on with this grand jury thing, but I have the feeling that it is all bad." Leslie Winchester had tears streaming down her face. Suddenly she began sobbing.

Forrest Winchester took her in his arms and cradled her head against him. "I know. I know. But, I can't do anything stuck in here, without even a cell phone. I need you to see if there is some other way that Napoli can help us. He's from a high powered firm, no offense

Mr. Rivera. Please talk to him. I know his partners have strings they can pull, probably even in this hick town of Denver."

"Terry Napoli? He's not a criminal lawyer," Leslie said confused.

"Not Napoli, someone else in his firm in Chicago. He'll know. Just ask him—tell him—that he has to get me out of here." Forrest Winchester was holding Leslie by the arms at arms length practically screaming at his wife.

Suddenly Leslie Winchester shook off his hands and looked at him. "I'll talk to him. I have to go now. I'll be in touch," she said and quickly left the room.

Forrest Winchester was still shaking with frustration and fury as the door closed behind her. Jason Rivera sat in the corner with his head in his hands.

T he next morning, everyone was at the courtroom before eight o'clock in the morning including the press. Janet Stephenson, Adam and James came especially early so that they could have breakfast at Dozens before going to court. Janet found it relaxing to have a cup of tea and a scone and review her closing argument notes, while James and Adam just loved the huge country breakfasts, with waffles and fat English sausages. Brad had left a voice mail on her cell phone telling her that he hoped to be home by six that evening. Janet felt a certain peace and relief that the long trial was nearly finished. At this point in the trial, she was happy to just accept whatever the jury decided.

Terry Napoli ordered eggs benedict from room service and ate in the hotel's terry cloth robe so that he would not dribble eggs on the front of his white shirt. He only had one white shirt left and he hoped he would not have to send his shirts to the laundry again. He just wanted to pack up the dirty ones and go home to Chicago. He had nearly forgotten what his little boy looked like and his conversations with his wife had disintegrated to three minute exchanges, once a day.

Rex Montague and his wife went to the 6:30 a.m buffet at the Columbine Country Club. On Fridays, the Columbine Rotary Club met there, so the kitchen opened a buffet for all other members as well. Mary Montague was coming to hear the closing arguments.

She left her car at the Mineral Street light rail station, so that she could shop downtown and then take the light rail home, while Rex began the long vigil which accompanies waiting for a jury to return a verdict.

Leslie Winchester scheduled a six o'clock a.m, massage and had tea and crumpets in the Brown Palace Spa. She did not call Terry Napoli as she had promised her husband. She decided that Napoli needed to be able to focus on his closing argument and that Forrest would have to wait until the jury was deliberating for Napoli's attention.

Jennifer Fordham and Jerry Carson had renewed their affair after Jennifer's fit of pique after receiving the grand jury subpoena. They spent the night together, but met as friends in the hotel coffee shop for breakfast, before taking a cab to the Denver City and County Building. Both of them had taken care to dress particularly well because Jennifer was sure that there would be a lot of media coverage of this final day of the trial. Although they had been ordered by the judge to avoid the press and television cameras during the trial, she hoped that ruling would not apply when the case was safely in the hands of the jury. Jennifer wore navy blue suit with burgundy silk trim and matching burgundy heels. Her skirt was slightly shorter than the skirts she had worn throughout the trial and tighter.

Forrest Winchester remained in his orange jail jumpsuit and gloomily ate his oatmeal and cold wheat toast in his cell. Raoul LeCroix refused the oatmeal when it was brought to his cell and had to be content with coffee and toast.

Amy Larabee, Rick Plume, Joel Steiner and Ben Smith all met at the Starbucks across from the courthouse that morning because the grand jury had indicated that it might have further questions before they made their final determination. The grand jury had been deliberating for nearly a week and they did not believe that it could go on much longer, but they had no way of knowing.

At precisely nine o'clock in the morning, Amelia entered the courtroom and noted that it might be impossible to fit one more body in the benches in the gallery. The attorneys were present and Jennifer Fordham was seated at the defendants table, but Larry and Pamela Lawson were not at their table. Janet Stephenson told her that Pamela was still in the hospital receiving intravenous medication. At 9:04, Judge Parsons took the bench.

"Counsel, are we ready to proceed with closing arguments?"

"Plaintiffs are ready, Your Honor."

"Mrs. Stephenson, my clerk has advised me that Mrs. Lawson remains hospitalized, is that correct?"

"Yes, Your Honor," Janet responded.

"Very well. I will further advise the jury about that. Mr. Napoli, are you ready to proceed?"

"Yes, Judge, we are ready." Terry Napoli said.

"Please stand for the jury. Mr. bailiff if you will please get the members of the jury."

The members of the jury followed the bailiff into the courtroom and took their places in the jury box. They all looked as though they were ready to hear the arguments and begin their deliberations. Several of the men were dressed in suits, even though they had dressed casually throughout the trial.

"Ladies and gentlemen, today we will hear the closing arguments of the plaintiff and the defendant. After that I will advise you on the law and instruct you to retire to the jury room with all of your notebooks and begin your deliberations. Mr. and Mrs. Lawson remain unable to be with us today. Mrs. Lawson is receiving some necessary intravenous medication in the hospital and Mr. Lawson felt he should remain with her. Again I advise you that you may not hold their absence against them in your deliberations because it involves a serious health matter beyond their control. Mrs. Stephenson will begin with the closing argument for the Plaintiffs. Mr. Napoli will then give the closing argument for the Defendants and Mrs. Stephenson is allowed a brief rebuttal argument after that. Mrs. Stephenson, you may begin."

Janet Stephenson went to the flip chart and easels which James had place in front of the jury. Leaning against the flip chart were blown up photographs of the rats and rabbits with tumors and a timeline, which Janet had professionally prepared. Janet felt relaxed and happy as she began to speak.

"Ladies and gentlemen, I am so pleased to finally have this second and last opportunity to talk to you directly. Throughout the trial, I have been able to only question witnesses and speak to Judge Parsons in the courtroom. Now I have the opportunity to speak directly to you and to ask you for your verdict. First of all, I want to thank you for your kind attention throughout the trial and for your service on this jury. You have fulfilled one of the most sacred responsibilities in our society by sacrificing your personal lives to sit here day after day. You have sacrificed even more by being separated from your families and your lives in being sequestered. Pamela and Larry Lawson want me to be sure to tell you that they will be eternally grateful to you. I am grateful as well. Thank you so much.

In this trial you have heard a lot of testimony from many witnesses. I just want to summarize some of that testimony for you in these closing moments. I told you in my opening statement that this case is the story of Pamela Lawson, but this is also a case about corporate irresponsibility, recklessness, indifference, and greed.

PolySurgical Specialties made an implant which Dr. Dan MacNamara called 'murder by another name,' Mammselle. Those are not my words, those are the words of the plastic surgeon who was deceived by this company into thinking that this polyurethane-coated implant was the panacea he had been searching for. It prevented painful capsular contracture in his patients. It was approved by the FDA. It was perfect. He did not know that after he put the implant into Pamela Lawson's breasts that the foam would disintegrate into a known carcinogen, TDA. He did not know, what PSS knew, that they had animal studies in their possession where every single animal developed tumors and liver cancer. He told you that if he had known those terrible facts, he would never, never have used the Mammselle implant to reconstruct the breast of Pamela Lawson, or any other patient. Dr. MacNamara never knew that the foam totally disintegrated until he performed the surgery to remove the Mammselle implants from Pamela Lawson's body, after she had become desperately ill.

Dr. Jean Sonier and Dr. Guilliot told you about their animal studies on the Mammselle foam, where every rat and rabbit also developed liver cancer. They used those studies to make sure that no woman in Canada would ever have a Mammselle and they took those studies to the FDA in the United States."

Here, Janet lined the blown up photos of the grotesque tumors on the rats and rabbits on the easels in front of the jury box. The jurors looked at them transfixed, even though they had seen them before.

"But our FDA ignored the studies. Our FDA allowed the marketing of the dangerous implant, without requiring any testing of the foam. All PolySurgical Specialties had to do was file an application for approval of the Mammselle as an 'improvement' over the already approved Conway Chemical silicone gel breast implant. That's a loophole you could drive a truck through and PSS drove the Mammselle to market through that loophole, with the blessing of the FDA. All the while, this corporate defendant knew that it had studies in Jennifer Fordham's safe, in the CEO's safe, which proved the same medical facts which Dr. Sonier proved. Those cancerous rats and rabbits saved the women of Canada from the Mammselle, but because Jennifer Fordham buried those tests in her safe, Pamela Lawson was not saved. She developed liver cancer. She had to have a liver transplant to stay alive.

The medical records that you have before you in your notebooks, demonstrate the gradual and steady decline of Pamela Lawson's health after she had the implants. Pamela and her husband, Larry, both told you, tearfully, how their beautiful lives have been totally destroyed as her health was destroyed and she faced death."

Janet placed the charts with the timelines, showing the decline of Pamela's health on top of the animal study charts before the jury. She carefully and methodically reviewed the decline of Pamela's health using the summarized medical records on the charts. Then she stepped back and looked at the members of the jury for a moment in silence. They continued to look at the charts.

Janet continued, "You, ladies and gentlemen, are the only ones who can decide which witnesses were credible and which were less than truthful. That is your job. You are the fact finders here and no one can change your collective decisions about the true facts in this case. Judge Parsons will advise you on the law you must apply, but you decide the facts.

The facts have been proven by the evidence you have in your notebooks and the testimony you have heard from all of these witnesses. Pamela Lawson's life, as she knew it, was taken from her by PolySurgical Specialties, a company which put an implant on the market which causes cancer. PSS knew. In addition, PSS deceived a good and kind physician, so that he would agree to help them market the implant and put it in his patients. That is willful, wanton and reckless behavior on the part of this very wealthy corporate defendant, which is now owned by the fabulously wealthy Conway Chemical. It is conduct which is in complete and total disregard of the life, the feelings and the rights of Pamela and Larry Lawson and their two precious little children, David and Sarah.

I am asking you to consider all you have heard and award compensatory and punitive damages to Pamela and Larry Lawson in the amount of at least ten million dollars. That is the only gesture you can make to repair the destruction of these lives. The rest is in the hands of God and his angels."

Janet removed the charts and easels and handed them to James and Adam, who removed them and placed them behind the plaintiff's table. Then Janet sat down.

"Let's take a short break, ladies and gentlemen, to allow Mr. Napoli to prepare his materials. We will be in recess for fifteen minutes. All rise for the jury."

Judge Parsons and the jury left the room. Janet, too, went down the long hall to the bathroom. She didn't want to speak to anyone, even though several of the Silicone Survivors followed her and wanted to talk in the ladies room. She smiled and deflected their questions. The media filled all the halls, but did not approach her.

When Janet returned to the courtroom, Napoli had all of his charts in place and he was scurrying around them making a final review. Amelia entered and asked if he was ready and he nodded. A moment later, the judge appeared and summoned the jury. When everyone was in place, the judge said. "Mr. Napoli, you may proceed."

Terry Napoli went to his line of easels and charts in front of the jury.

"Ladies and gentlemen, I, too, would like to thank you for serving on this jury and for the inconvenience and sacrifice that you and your families have made to participate in this civic process. Although I represent PolySurgical Specialties, you must remember that corporate parties are also just made up of people like you. Corporations are a part of all Americans and are not indifferent or unfeeling money machines, as Mrs. Stephenson would have you believe. PSS is a family company, started by Jennifer Fordham's father, a professor at a respected college. He was a scientist who held a dream and a passion for using his knowledge to manufacture implants, which would improve the lives of real people. The first thing that I want you to remember in considering the evidence and the testimony you have heard is that PolySurgical Specialties followed the rules. PSS sought and secured the approval of the FDA before they ever sold one single Mammselle implant. The marketing of the Mammselle implant was perfectly legal. Dr. Lyndon Sloan told you that it was perfectly legal. Dr. Lyndon Sloan also told you that the application for FDA approval would have been granted, EVEN IF the FDA had seen the rat and rabbit studies that Mrs. Stephenson has made such a production about. Why? Because the rat and rabbit tests are irrelevant.

Ladies and Gentlemen, all of the fuss that the Canadian researchers made is just an attempt to mislead you into thinking that if something bad happens to a rat, it will happen to a human. Dr. Betsy Connor and Dr. Lyndon Sloan told you that is not true. There is not one shred of truth in it. The fact is that Mrs. Stephenson and her parade of Canadian experts did not AND can not produce one single peer reviewed medical journal article which says that the foam on the Mammselle implant causes liver cancer in humans. Mrs. Stephenson is asking you to compare apples and oranges.

The fact of this case is that the Mammselle implant is a huge improvement over other silicone gel breast implants because it does prevent capsular contracture - a terribly painful complication of breast implants."

Terry Napoli then removed the coverings from the photos he had on easels in front of the jury.

"I have here, for demonstrative purposes, some photographs of the breasts of women who suffer from this condition. I want you to see how serious and obviously painful a condition capsular contracture is. As you can see, the condition causes terrible disfigurement and the resulting pain and when the Mammselle came on the market, it was a major medical improvement in plastic surgery for women. Dr. MacNamara recognized that it was a huge improvement over the implants he and other plastic surgeons had to use."

Napoli then removed two of the photos, revealing blown up photographs of Dr. Dan MacNamara giving speeches and demonstrating the use of the Mammselle at several medical conventions. He was even shown holding up a Mammselle implant and smiling broadly. Then Terry Napoli removed a new Mammselle implant, in its packaging from a box in front of the jury.

"Ladies and gentlemen, this is the Mammselle in its package. It is sterile and carefully manufactured to be a blessing and not the curse that Mrs. Stephenson has described to you. Let's open it up."

Napoli took off the plastic seal, removed the package insert brochure, and held the implant in his hand.

"Pass this around among you, ladies and gentlemen. You can see that it is soft, pliable and pristine. The Mammselle is not the murderous monster Mrs. Stephenson described to you. It is a blessing to thousands of women, who chose not to suffer as these women, in these photos before you have suffered. The Mammselle prevents this suffering because it prevents capsular contracture. It does everything it promises in this brochure, which is packaged with the implant. It is an improvement over every other silicone gel implant on the market. That is why PSS was acquired by Conway Chemical. Conway Chemical wants only the best for the patients it serves.

Now, I do not mean to seem insensitive to the fact that Pamela Lawson is very ill. She has had cancer and she has endured a liver transplant. But there is not one shred of evidence that her cancer was caused by the Mammselle implant—not one shred. There has been no evidence presented in this trial—and there is no evidence in all of the medical journals published in the United States AND Canada that the Mammselle implant, or any of its materials, caused liver cancer in humans. People are diagnosed with liver cancer every day in this country, with or without a breast implant. You cannot, in good conscience, hold PolySurgical Specialties responsible for the coincidence that Mrs. Lawson had a Mammselle implant and also developed liver cancer. There has been no proof of any kind that Mrs. Lawson's cancer was caused by her implant - none!

I ask you to dismiss the claims against PolySurgical Specialties in this case. PolySurgical Specialties followed the law, the rules of the FDA, and of medical science. PSS developed an implant which prevented a terrible condition, properly sought FDA approval, and marketed it through the efforts of a nationally respected plastic surgeon. The Mammselle has not been taken off the market or limited by the FDA in any way. The Mammselle is innocent of these charges. While I feel very sorry for Mr. and Mrs. Lawson, we ask that you dismiss their claims. Thank you again for your careful and kind attention in this trial."

Terry Napoli and his paralegals removed the charts and photos and Napoli sat down, then he smiled at the jury.

"Mrs. Stephenson, do you have remarks in rebuttal?" Judge Parsons asked.

"Yes, Your Honor, I do." Janet said. She rose from her chair and walked confidently in front of the jury.

"Members of the jury, my grandmother used to warn me about half truths—telling me that a half truth is often a more dangerous lie than an outright lie because people rely on what you say and can be grievously injured. Dr. Dan MacNamara sat in front of you and emotionally told you that if he had known about the effects of the Mammselle implant's implanted foam on the animals he would never have used it. If I remember his words he said, "God forgive me."

FDA approval in this case is a joke. The silicone in the implant was tested on animals and then in humans by Conway Chemical, but the foam was not. The killer here is the foam. PSS knew that the foam caused serious adverse effects in animals, but PSS could not test the foam in humans. Why, you may ask."

Janet placed a chart on the easel, and said, "these are the phases of FDA testing for a new drug or implanted material. Phase I—testing in the laboratory. In our case, Dr. Sonier and Guilliot told you that in contact with organic or biological substances, polyurethane foam breaks down into TDA, a known and published carcinogen. The testing should stop there and FDA approval should be impossible. But let's assume that the foam gets to the next phase, Phase II, animal testing. The implanted material must have NO adverse effects in animals or it cannot go on to Phase III testing, which is clinical studies of the implanted foam in human beings. The plain fact is that when ALL of the animal subjects develop liver cancer, the foam would never have been approved for testing in humans, let alone put on the medical market.

"In this case, Jennifer Fordham knew that the foam caused liver cancer in laboratory animals. But, she hid those animal studies away in the safe in her office. Then, she and others at PSS deliberately searched for and found the regulatory loophole which allowed them to file an application for approval as a 'piggy back' on the Conway Chemical approved implant. As a result, no testing in humans was ever required or done. But you, members of the jury, know the truth. You know that PolySurgical Specialties deliberately put a product on the market which they knew, from their own contracted animal studies, would NEVER have been allowed to go on to Phase III studies in humans. Instead, PSS forced patients, including Pamela Lawson to be the human test subjects. That is why Pamela Lawson developed liver cancer after being implanted with the Mammselle. She was forced to be a human guinea pig by the greed of PolySurgical Specialties. They made a fortune preventing capsular contracture with this implant. But you know the rest of the story. PSS took the life blood of Pamela and her family. You must make them pay for their willful, wanton, reckless and greedy conduct. Thanks so much for your attention and concern."

Janet removed her chart and smiled gently at the jury. Then she returned to her chair. The room was absolutely silent.

Judge Parsons cleared his throat, then said," Members of the jury, I will now instruct you on the law. My bailiff will distribute to you the jury instructions and verdict forms for you to use in your deliberations in this case. When you have reached a verdict, you must complete the verdict form and give it to the bailiff. I will now go over all of the jury instructions with you. You may refer to the packet which I am having the bailiff distribute to you."

Judge Parsons went over all of the jury instructions one by one and then gave the oath to the bailiff to keep the jury. The jury members took their instructions and their exhibit notebooks and went silently to the jury room.

"Counsel, you may return to your offices, or wherever, but please advise my clerk about where you will be and make sure that she has your cell phone number. When we get a verdict, we will call you. As I advised the jury, they may work as late as they choose and begin no later than nine o'clock tomorrow morning. We will bring in their meals, except for breakfast, until they have a verdict. We will be in recess awaiting the jury."

Adam and James gathered their charts and remaining exhibits and Janet Stephenson went to the defendant's table and shook hands with Terry Napoli and Rex Montague. "Good job, counsel," she said with a smile.

"You are a worthy adversary, Janet" said Terry Napoli.

"And so are the both of you," she replied smiling at Rex Montague, who smiled wanly and nodded at her.

Just then, Janet felt her cell phone vibrating in her jacket pocket. It was Larry Lawson.

"Excuse me," she said to the attorneys as she opened her telephone. "Larry?" she said.

"Janet, can you talk? I was just going to leave a message that we have a meeting with the oncologist team in an hour. What's going on there?"

"Finished. The jury has the case and have just gone to the jury room. We are in recess, subject to recall by the judge's clerk." Janet said as she walked to a quiet corner of the courtroom.

"I'll give you a call after this meeting. They should have the test results compiled to share with us then. I won't kid you, I'm very worried. Pamela seems to just sleep and doesn't really care if I am here or not here." Larry Lawson sounded frantic.

"She's probably sedated, isn't she, Larry?" Janet asked.

"Yes, somewhat. Perhaps that is all that it is," he replied.

"We must pack up here and get this stuff to the office. Then I'll come over to the hospital," Janet said. "I'll give you a call, so that you can meet me downstairs in the coffee shop or somewhere so that we can talk."

Terry Napoli and Rex Montague had already left the courtroom with all of their paralegals, attorneys and clerks. Only a few of the faithful audience of Silicone Survivors remained, waiting to talk to Janet. Several of the ladies gave her hugs and told her that she did a good job. Janet was superstitious about ever discussing a case when a jury was deliberating, but she was gracious and then escaped with James and Adam, out the secret judge's staircase, into the west courtyard of the City and County Building. They hurried to the parking lot and loaded what was left of their trial exhibits and charts for the last time.

Janet sighed deeply as she sat quietly for a moment behind the steering wheel.

"I just don't see how the jury won't rule for us," James said.

"It's easy, "Janet said. "They decide to believe Napoli instead of us. It happens all the time and it's impossible to know what a jury is thinking. Want some lunch?"

"I'm not hungry, "said Adam. "My stomach is in knots. I can barely stand this."

"Okay. Let's just go back to the office and chill a bit. We have plenty to do there with three more cases going to trial in the next six months. I haven't focused on them at all and I'm sure I have a huge stack of messages," said Janet.

"I'd wait until this is done to return calls," offered James. "I can't even think right now."

Terry Napoli, Rex Montague, Jennifer Fordham, Jerry Carson and Leslie Winchester all met at the restaurant in the Brown Palace Hotel for lunch. Everyone was subdued and thoughtful.

"We just might win, Terry," said Rex Montague. "That was a hell of a closing."

"Thanks," said Napoli. "I think we have a decent shot. I just can't read this jury though."

"I know we'll win," Jennifer said brightly, "Your closing was fabulous, Terry."

Leslie Winchester silently sipped her glass of white wine. She thought it could go either way. Janet Stephenson's closing argument taught her some things that she didn't know.

"What is going on with Forrest?" asked Jerry Carson, as if he had just thought of Forrest Winchester for the first time in months.

"We need to get him out," said Leslie flatly. "Terry, Forrest told me that your firm would be able to send a crack criminal attorney from Chicago to help out. He doesn't think that Jason Rivera has what it takes. Is that true? Could your firm send someone who could be successful in getting him out of there? He said you would know what he was talking about. I sure don't."

Terry Napoli looked confused. He hadn't been thinking about Forrest Winchester at all.

"I can talk to the head of our criminal department. But, I think he would have to be licensed in Colorado or just come in as 'of counsel'. But I will give him a call right now. Perhaps they can get someone on a plane to help Jason Rivera. What do you think, Rex?" Napoli had suddenly become much more cordial, now that the trial was finished. He realized that he actually liked Rex Montague.

"I don't know. I know that Jason Rivera is as good a criminal attorney as there is. He has a lot of experience and he knows the district attorney, Rick Plume. I don't know what another attorney can add, but it is certainly your call. I'm sure Jason will welcome any help he can get. I think he is very frustrated about Plume's delay of a new bail hearing. But he can do that, since Forrest was arrested with a gun and actually shot at someone. I still don't get the grand jury proceedings and how they could involve Forrest." Montague added.

Terry Napoli left the table with his cell phone and when he returned, he reported that the head of the criminal department, itself, was getting on the next plane to Denver. Both he and Leslie Winchester were amazed and wondered if they should have called him much sooner.

Larry Lawson met with the physicians alone. Pamela had drifted into a semi-conscious state and her condition was deteriorating noticeably. They told him that the situation was grave and that Pamela's body was rejecting the transplanted liver. She had been placed on the transplant list for another liver last night, but they advised him that, unless it came very soon, Pamela would be too weak and too critical to survive another transplant surgery.

Larry called Janet Stephenson and asked her to meet him as soon as she could in the coffee shop at the hospital. Meanwhile, Pamela Lawson was moved from her room into isolated intensive care. Larry was sitting at a table with his head in his hands when Janet arrived.

"She's going to die," he said openly weeping. "It's just a matter of time and she probably will not regain consciousness. I have kissed her and talked to her for the last time," he sobbed.

"Are you sure?" Janet tried to sound reassuring.

"Yes, they have just moved her into isolated intensive care. She can't even have visitors, except me, covered with hospital gowns and masks. She wouldn't even know me if she did wake up," the devastated young man cried.

"Can I call someone to be with you?" Janet asked.

"There is no body, except you, Janet. My mother needs to stay with David and Sarah, who don't know and can't know what is happening."

Just then, a nurse came into the coffee shop and told Larry that he needed to come with her. He motioned for Janet to follow. They went on the staff elevator to the ICU floor and through the double doors into the circular room with patient rooms all around a central nurses station. A physician was waiting for Larry and he was quickly gowned and whisked into Pamela's room, tying on a mask. Janet sat down in a chair by the door. Her heart was in her mouth and she felt as though she could scream with anxiety. The sounds of all of the equipment in the unit suddenly seemed very loud, although all of the nurses and other personnel seemed to be speaking in whispers. Janet sat unmoving in the chair for what seemed like a very long time. Then Larry and the physician emerged from Pamela's room. Tears were streaming down Larry's face and the mask hung around his neck. "She's gone," was all he said. Janet stood up and hugged him close. Larry Lawson's boyish body was racked with sobs and she moved him gently toward the chair where she had been sitting. She knelt down beside him and patted his head. A gowned nurse appeared with a glass of water, which she handed to Janet.

"Here, Larry, have a drink of water," Janet said helplessly. He took it as an obedient child might and took a drink. Then he handed it to her.

"You may go to the family lounge just outside the ICU doors to talk if you like," suggested a kind nurse. Larry nodded and he and Janet left the ICU. Fortunately no one was in the lounge, so they could talk.

"What happens to the case, Janet," Larry asked frantically.

"I hope that nothing will happen. It was submitted to the jury while Pamela was alive. It should just go on as though she is still alive."

"Do we have to tell them?" Larry asked.

"Yes, I suppose we do have to advise the judge, but I don't know when"

Suddenly Janet's cell phone began to vibrate. She looked at it. It was the Court.

"Janet Stephenson," she answered.

"The jury is back," said Amelia. "How long will it take you to get to the courthouse?"

Janet looked at her watch. It was fifteen minutes before eight. The jury had been out since eleven o'clock in the morning They had been deliberating nearly eight hours.

"It will take me about forty minutes," she replied.

"The judge wants to take the verdict tonight, even though it is late, so that he can release the jury before the weekend. So come as promptly as you can," Amelia told her.

"I'll be right there." Janet said.

Larry looked at her stunned. "What shall I do?" he asked.

"Just stay here. There are matters for you to attend to and as of this moment, Pamela is still in ICU. I'll be back as soon as I can make it and then we will decide what to do. Don't talk to anyone. If you can, stay in the ICU unit. They will keep her there for a while." Pamela said, thinking as fast as she could.

Janet called Adam and James and told them that the jury was in and that she was on her way to the courthouse. They told her that they would meet her there. Janet found a parking place on the street right by the night entrance to the City and County Building. She hurried through security and up back stairs to the courtroom, carrying only a legal pad and her purse. James and Adam entered the courtroom a moment after she did.

Terry Napoli, Rex Montague, Jennifer Fordham were at the defendant's table and Leslie Winchester was sitting in the front row. There were no spectators. Because it was after hours, there were no television cameras inside the courthouse or in the halls.

Amelia came in to check on who was present and a moment later Judge Parsons entered the courtroom. "Counsel, as you know, we have a verdict. Bailiff will you bring in the jury,"

The members of the tired looking jury filed in and took their places in the jury box. Some of them looked around the uncommonly deserted courtroom.

"Mr. Foreman, have you reached a verdict?" the judge asked.

"Yes, Judge, we have." The foreman said and handed the bailiff the verdict form.

The bailiff took it to the judge, who silently read it and returned it to the bailiff.

"Mr. Foreman, you may read your verdict."

"We find for the Plaintiffs and against the Defendant. We award compensatory damages in the amount of five million dollars and punitive damages in the amount of five million dollars. The total verdict is ten million dollars."

Janet's heart was pounding and she felt as though she would faint. James and Adam stood motionless.

"Members of the jury, thank you for your service. You are dismissed. You have all been advised to call your family members to pick you up at the hotel. The bus is waiting to transport you immediately back to the hotel to retrieve your belongings. Again thank you for your attention during this difficult and long trial. Please rise for the jury."

Janet smiled at the jury, with tears streaming down her face. Several of them smiled back at her. Many of the members of the jury also had tears in their eyes.

Terry Napoli, Rex Montague and their clients immediately left the courtroom and did not speak further to Janet. Janet thanked Amelia, who came in to make sure that everyone was clearing out of the room. The clerk looked very tired. "I'm so glad I can sleep in tomorrow," she laughed.

Janet hugged both of her clerks and told them. "I'm going back to the hospital. I'll call you both later on. Have a great weekend."

"Nothing is ever easy," Janet thought to herself as she drove back to the hospital. Her cell phone rang.

"Hi, honey, I'm home, "Brad said cheerfully. "Well almost home. We just landed."

"Brad, I'm so glad you called. It's all over!"

"What? What happened."

"The jury just came back after eight hours and awarded ten million dollars!"

"Wow, that's terrific! "Brad said.

"It's not that easy," Janet told him. "I just came from the hospital. Pamela passed away at almost exactly the same time as the jury decided on its verdict. I am going back to the hospital now to tell Larry and decide what to do next."

"Why, what's the problem? The jury has decided haven't they."

"Yes, they have decided, but I am sure that as soon as Napoli and Montague find out that Pamela has died, they will file a motion to have the verdict reduced to the statutory limits for a wrongful death. That makes a ten million dollar verdict possibly as low as $250,000.”

“Damn, I can't believe that!” Brad exclaimed.

“Well it hasn't happened yet and it is only a possibility that the defendants will ask for a judgment notwithstanding the verdict. I just have to explain all of these possibilities to Larry Lawson. When will you be home?”

“A couple of hours, by the time I finish all my paperwork at DIA,” Brad said.

“Okay. See you then.”

Janet found Larry in the coffee shop. He was sitting motionless in front of a cup of coffee.

“What happened?” he asked Janet.

“They awarded you and Pam ten million dollars.” Janet said.

Larry Lawson started to cry. “And Pam couldn't hold on to find out that she had won,” he moaned. He was rocking back and forth in his chair, hugging his ribs.

“Larry, I just want you to know that there is a possibility that the defendants will file a motion to reduce the verdict when they find out about Pam's death. They will argue that they are only liable for damages for her wrongful death.”

“What does that mean,” Larry asked.

“It could mean that they will ask for the verdict to be reduced to $250,000, which is the statutory limit for wrongful death damages in this state.” Janet told him.

“My God, we turned down a settlement offer for $600,000. Could that happen?”

“Anything could happen. I just have to do the research and be prepared if PSS does file such a motion.”

“Oh, they will file it. You can be sure of that, the heartless bastards.” Larry was crying again.

Just then a tall older man walked into the coffee shop and came over to Larry.

"Larry, I am so sorry." He said. Larry stood up and hugged the man.

"Janet, this is Pastor Hughes, our minister. I called and asked him to come." Larry explained.

"Nice to meet you," Janet smiled and felt relieved that someone had come to comfort her client. "Larry, just don't think about our issues now. I'll take care of them. You just take care of yourself and your children. Pastor Hughes, here is my card. Please call me if I can do anything at all. I have some matters to conclude with our trial."

"Is it over, Larry?" the pastor asked.

"Just now. We got a ten million dollar verdict, but it isn't collected until all the legal wranglings are over." Larry said. He smiled at Janet and gave her a hug. "You're terrific," he said to her with tears in his eyes.

"Call me, "Janet said "And I'll keep you completely posted."

Janet Stephenson was exhausted. Her day had been a roller coaster from beginning to end. She was glad the Brad would be waiting at home with a smile and possibly a glass of wine, but her heart felt like a stone inside her chest. Poor Pam if only she could have known. Tears were still running down Janet's cheeks as she pulled into her garage. "What is this all about, anyway?" she thought to herself.

The grand jury concluded its deliberations and issued its indictments of Forrest Winchester, Raoul LeCroix, Jennifer Fordham, and Jerry Carson for the murders of Sherrie Barker and Tom Slade and the attempted murder of Dr. Dan MacNamara, at six o'clock in the evening on Friday, while the Lawson v. PSS jury was still deliberating. Rick Plume spun his staff into high gear, even though it was Friday, to get arrest warrants issued for Jennifer Fordham, Jerry Carson, Forrest Winchester, and Raoul Lecroix.

Forrest Winchester and Raoul Lecroix were easy to find. A sheriff's deputy served them in their jail cells. Jennifer Fordham and Jerry Carson were arrested at eight thirty in the Ship Tavern at the Brown Palace Hotel, where they were having a drink in commiseration of the Lawson verdict with Terry Napoli, Rex Montague and Leslie Winchester.

Jennifer Fordham was still dressed in the suit she had chosen that morning in case the television reporters would be covering the last day of trial. Her burgundy stilettos were causing her pain and she had kicked them off under the table in the bar. When she put her shoes on again, she was taller than the Denver police officer who arrested her and took her away in handcuffs.

Leslie Winchester and the two attorneys watched Fordham and Carson's arrest in shock and disbelief. Leslie Winchester ordered another martini. "What could possibly happen now," she asked the stunned attorneys.

"I'm not sure exactly what happened here," said Rex Montague.

"That's why grand juries are secret, Rex," said a subdued Terry Napoli. Not only had he lost the case, but most of his clients were taken away in handcuffs or were already in jail.

"This has not been a good day, all around," said Leslie Winchester. "Appears I am your only client left standing." She was getting a little tipsy, but somehow, she didn't care.

"I was planning to leave in the morning on a seven o'clock flight," Napoli began. "Should I stay?"

"For what?" Leslie asked. "You said yourself that you aren't a criminal lawyer. Those people all need criminal lawyers, I would guess." She gestured toward the door where Jennifer and Jerry had been removed by the police. "I have to stay. My beloved is still in the slammer. Besides I'm getting attached to the massages in this hotel's spa!"

"Well, as for me, I'm of no use to anyone tonight," said Rex Montague. "I need to go home. I think I still know the way. Good night all." Montague left, anxious to feel the fresh Colorado night air on his face and anxious for the comfort of Mary and his bed.

Leslie Winchester looked at Napoli and said, "Mr. Napoli, what happens now? Appeal, more motions or what?"

"Well, we would normally file motions for a new trial and if it is not granted, we would appeal the case. We will have to post an appeal bond of at least fifteen million dollars with the notice of appeal. An appeal will take a minimum of two years to complete," he said somewhat mechanically.

"And if we don't appeal?" she asked.

"We pay the ten million dollars, plus costs, plus interest from the date the case was filed," he said.

"Why can't we settle. Is there any chance that the Plaintiff will settle for less?"

"Why would they. The plaintiffs have a verdict and Conway Chemical has the wherewithal to pay it. Would you settle?" Terry sneered, also feeling a little tipsy from his three scotches and no dinner.

"Mr. Napoli, please stay in town so that we can talk again tomorrow. I would like to meet you for breakfast around nine o'clock if I could."

"Okay," he said. "But let's make it ten o'clock. I'd like to sleep in a little if you don't mind."

"That's fine. I'll see you in the coffee shop at ten o'clock."

Leslie Winchester finished her martini and left the bar, waving at Napoli. Terry Napoli had another scotch and then had the bellman call him a cab to take him to his hotel. He undressed and climbed into bed, exhausted. He was asleep in ten seconds.

At the Hofbrau Steak house, Rick Plume, Amy Larabee, Joel Steiner and Ben Smith all met at nine o'clock for drinks and a steak dinner.

"It was a long, long, long path," Rick said to the others, raising his glass. "Here's to all of you and here's to Janet Stephenson."

"I wonder if their verdict is in. Their jury was still in the jury room when we dismissed the grand jury at six o'clock. Judge Parson's bailiff told me at the coffee kiosk that the judge was hoping they would return a verdict before the weekend." Joel Steiner added.

"We should give Janet Stephenson a call. She should know about the indictments from us," Amy Larabee said to Rick Plume.

Rick flipped open his cell and scrolled to Janet Stephenson's number. "Hey, Jan. Rick Plume here. The team has gathered at the Hofbrau and we are all calling you to let you know that the grand jury indictments came in at six o'clock. Winchester, LeCroix, Fordham, and Carson are all headed to the big house, thanks to you, Ms. Super Lawyer."

Janet Stephenson was stunned. She was sitting on the TV room couch with Brad and her glass of wine, trying to recap the day. "That's great, Rick!" she said.

"Yep. And we had a call from the sheriff's office that Fordham and Carson were arrested in the Ship Tavern at the Brown where they had gone to drink with their lawyers."

"No kidding?" Janet was trying to imagine the scene. "Did you know that we got a verdict?"

"We were all wondering. We knew your jury was still in their jury room when we dismissed the grand jury. What happened?"

"Ten million dollars," was all she said.

"Fabulous!" Rick exclaimed.

"I was stunned," she said. Then she continued quietly, "Rick, thanks for the call, but I have to run now. I'll talk to you soon." Janet didn't want to answer any more questions about her case tonight. She wasn't ready to share Pam's death, especially since they were all calling her from their celebration dinner.

"Sure, Janet. I'll call you Monday." Rick hung up and said to the others, "She got a ten million dollar verdict. The jury came in tonight. I'm so glad. It would have been a bummer if it would have been anything different. But, for some reason, she didn't seem all that excited."

"I'm sure she's beat. I wonder how Pamela Lawson is holding up." Amy Larabee mused.

"It will still take time to sink in and I'm sure there will be an appeal. But today, it's all good. Salud, my friends!" Rick said, raising his glass.

The press may have been excluded from the City and County Building because the verdict came in at night, but by morning, all of the newspapers and television stations were humming with the story of the indictments of the grand jury and of the death of Pamela Lawson. Janet Stephenson was awakened at 6:30 in the morning by a call from Larry Lawson, frantically asking her what she could do about the television trucks and reporters surrounding their home. Brad was making tea in the kitchen when he noticed that their house was under a similar siege. He was surprised by a reporter dashing across their patio toward the backyard gate. Janet was still in her pajamas and robe talking to Larry Lawson on the telephone when the doorbell rang.

"Larry, I'm sorry. I guess I was tired. I should have realized that this would happen when the press found out about Pamela's death. I'm sure they've had someone keeping tabs at the hospital. Don't talk to anyone. I'll be right over," Janet said to her distraught client.

Brad answered the door and told the reporters that Janet was unavailable right now, but that she would have a statement for the press as soon as it was appropriate.

Janet rushed to her room and dressed in black pants and a black sweater and quickly put on some makeup. She was searching for a lost shoe when Brad came into their bedroom.

"Do you want me to go with you, sweetheart? Or, should I hold down the fort and protect our house, here?" he asked.

"I think you should keep these idiots from overrunning our home." She said. "Boy, I just didn't think this one through, did I. I have to get over to deal with the press before Larry Lawson has a total breakdown. He's not doing very well with this. I'll call you as soon as I get there and put out the initial media fires."

Janet found her lost shoe under the bed and put it on. Then she flew down the stairs grabbed her purse and briefcase and went into the garage. When the garage door opened and she started backing out in her black Lexus she almost ran over a television cameraman. She smiled and waved at them as she backed out of the driveway and pushed the remote to close the garage door. She did not open her window.

When she got to the Lawson home, she pulled into the driveway and hurried to the front door. Suddenly all of the reporters who were waiting around in the front yard rushed over to her.

"I would like all of you to give Mr. Lawson and his family some space and some respect. We will call and let you know when we are ready with a press release or we can arrange a press conference. We will try to do that as soon as possible, but we will call all of your stations and advise you of the details. I'm sure you can appreciate the trauma this little family has endured. Please, I ask you to just extend to them a little of the milk of human kindness." Grandma Lawson was waiting for her to step onto the porch. She quickly opened the door and let Janet inside.

Terry Napoli and Rex Montague both heard about Pamela Lawson's death as they were shaving in their respective bathrooms. Each called the other immediately. Leslie Winchester was sleepily watching the television set in the Brown Palace Spa as she waited for her seven o'clock am massage.

"Oh my God," she said out loud. She opened her purse and took out her cell phone to call Terry Napoli at his hotel, just as a therapist came into her room and said, "Ma'am there are a bunch of television cameras and reporters waiting for you to come out. What shall I do?"

"Tell them to please go away. My attorneys will contact them when we have something to say. I have nothing to say to them about anything." Leslie was shaking with anxiety as she dialed Napoli's cell phone.

"Mr. Napoli, Leslie Winchester here. Have you seen the news? Pamela Lawson died in the night. I'm in the spa and I can't leave because there are television cameras and reporters waiting outside to pounce on me. I need you to come here right now and get me out of this mess!"

"Be calm, Mrs. Winchester. I just saw the news myself, but I'm sure that they are also interested in what you have to say about the indictments as much as about Pamela Lawson dying. Just stay in the spa where you are. I will be there within half an hour."

Leslie Winchester closed her cell phone. "Can you get me a bloody mary?" she asked the attendant, who had come into the room to help her.

"Yes, ma'am."

"Good," she said. "I have to wait here for my attorney to come and save me from those crazy people outside. Please let me know when Mr. Terry Napoli arrives and I need my clothes, so I can get dressed."

"Right away, ma'am," the young woman said, and she was gone.

Terry Napoli, Rex Montague, and Leslie Winchester met at Montague's office an hour later. Montague's paralegal and secretary were both in the office, answering phone calls in their jeans. Napoli and Leslie Winchester were both glad to see the fresh coffee and rolls in Montague's office.

"Looks as though we may have lucked out, Terry," Montague said.

"What do you mean?" asked Leslie Winchester.

"Now that the plaintiff is no longer alive, we can make the argument that she cannot collect the ten-million-dollar judgment. Her husband may only be entitled to recover the limited amount available under Colorado's wrongful death statute—two hundred fifty thousand dollars. That's a lot less than ten million dollars plus costs and interest," Montague explained.

"How ever could that be done?" Leslie asked.

"We would file a motion for a JNOV, which means a judgment notwithstanding the verdict, asking the judge, as a matter of law, to reduce the verdict to the statutory maximum for wrongful death," Napoli said.

"Do you think the judge would do that? Would he take away their verdict?" Leslie Winchester asked skeptically.

"It's sure worth a try. I think we have to do it," said Rex Montague. "What's your thought Terry?"

"Absolutely. Let's get it drafted and filed."

"It's actually practically done. I had my paralegal come in as soon as I heard the story and begin the draft and pull the cases we would need to cite," Montague told him.

"Then we can file it today?" asked Leslie.

"We can file it and ask the court for a forthwith hearing on Monday or Tuesday," said Montague. "I think Judge Parsons will hear it quickly if Janet Stephenson has an opportunity to respond. I'm sure she wants a decision, but she is probably also dealing with all of the personal issues of the Lawson family, so we may not get a hearing as fast as we would like," Montague added.

"What a break!" said Napoli "What a break."

Janet Stephenson held a brief news conference at her office later that day. She told the press that the jury had awarded Pamela and Larry Lawson a ten-million-dollar verdict, but that it was totally overshadowed by the death of her client. She also said that the funeral would be only family and completely private, without press. She asked the media to please respect them in this time of unbearable sadness. She said she had no comment when asked about the indictments of Winchester, Fordham and Carson.

After all the press left, she began her research on her response to the motion for a JNOV to reduce the verdict, which she was certain was coming. She wanted to respond immediately upon receiving the motion. But, she knew precisely what the motion would say.

Monday morning, at eight o'clock in the morning Janet Stephenson received the motion by courier. At eight forty-seven in the morning she received a call from Amelia, Judge Parson's clerk, asking how quickly she could respond to the motion. She told Amelia that she would hand carry her response to the court before noon. Amelia told her, that if she could respond by two o'clock in the afternoon, the judge would like to set the motion for hearing on Tuesday, the following day at eight thirty in the morning Janet agreed to appear at that time to argue the motion. Amelia said that there might not be arguments, that the judge might just render his ruling so that the case could get on to an appeal without delay. Janet sent Adam to the court with her response and sent James to deliver a copy to Montague's office at ten thirty in the morning.

On Tuesday morning, Janet arrived at the court at eight twenty in the morning Terry Napoli and Rex Montague were already there and Leslie Winchester arrived a few moments later. She did not sit at the council table but took her usual place in the front row of the gallery.

At eight thirty in the morning, Amelia came out to check and see who was present and to advise any members of the press who might be there that the judge was closing the hearing. No one else was in the courtroom. A moment later, Judge Parsons appeared.

"Well, counsel, life is full of surprises. I never imagined that we would be seeing each other again so soon. Mrs. Stephenson, please let me extend my condolences to you and to your client's family. This is indeed a very sad turn of events and a very unfortunate one."

Janet nodded in appreciation of his kind words.

"I have considered your motions and responses very carefully. I am going to dispense with an oral argument this morning because all of this is very fresh in all our minds. I am also impressed that both sides have cited all of the law that exists in Colorado under this fact situation. I am going to give you my ruling orally, but I have also prepared a final written opinion so that the inevitable appeal of the case will not be delayed. This is one of the most difficult rulings that I have had to make in my career on the bench.

I make the following findings:

Pamela Lawson was present and participated in the full presentation of her case, even testifying to the jury at length regarding her pain and suffering and that of her family. But I will take judicial notice of the fact that St. Anthony Hospital records her time of death at 7:30 in the evening last Friday. I received the note from the bailiff that the jury had reached a verdict thirty-two minutes after seven in the evening, according to the stamp on the note. They may have actually reached a verdict a few moments before that because the note had to be carried to chambers and stamped, but the official time of the verdict is 7:32. That means, that given these 'official times' Pamela Lawson was deceased when the verdict was rendered.

The defendant argues that I must reduce her damages to the maximum under the wrongful death statute, and I must agree. I hereby reduce the damages for her death to two hundred fifty thousand dollars plus interest and costs. Larry Lawson is also a plaintiff who offered detailed explanations and testimony about his personal losses of consortium and his pain and suffering. This is a distinct and separate cause of action for which damages can be awarded. He testified about his lost work and the medical costs he had to pay because he was the sole breadwinner. He also testified about what the loss of his wife would mean to him in the future in terms of having no mother for his children and no helpmate. I am awarding Larry Lawson damages in the amount of one million two hundred fifty thousand dollars as compensatory damages, together with interest and costs.

I am sure there will be an appeal, so I have had Amelia prepare certified copies of my order so that either party can file the notice of appeal as soon as possible. I recognize that, to some degree, this is a case of first impression and that there are arguments on both sides which the Court of Appeals will have to sort out. None of the cases cited by either plaintiff or defendant cover the exact turn of events and facts in this case, so the Court of Appeals might very well have something to say on cases such as this. That will be all. We will be in recess."

Judge Parsons stood up, did not look at any of the attorneys, and left the bench.

Terry Napoli and Rex Montague were so jubilant that they could hardly contain themselves, but they both approached Janet graciously and extended their condolences. Janet Stephenson felt as though she had been punched in the stomach. She could not speak to them. She only nodded.

Leslie Winchester, however, did not seem to share her attorney's happiness. She sat still as a stone and was not even smiling. When Janet glanced at her, she thought she saw tears in her eyes.

Janet drove directly to Larry Lawson's home. The house was full of family and friends and there was the inevitable potluck buffet of food, brought in by church members and neighbors. Sarah and David were playing in the backyard with some other children and mercifully seemed not to grasp the significance of what was going on inside the house. Janet asked Larry if they could talk privately. They went into the extra bedroom, which Larry had turned into a study.

"Larry, I came straight from the hearing on the motion to reduce the verdict."

"And?" Larry asked.

"The judge reduced Pamela's damages to two hundred fifty thousand dollars and reduced your damages to a million and two hundred fifty thousand dollars. But he gave us certified final orders so that we can file an appeal immediately," Janet explained.

"So the total verdict is one million five hundred thousand dollars?" he asked.

"Yes," Janet nodded.

"Not quite ten million dollars, is it?" Larry said sarcastically.

"I think our chances on appeal are very good," Janet said. "Even Judge Parsons said that this is a case of first impression, which means that it is very likely that the Court of Appeals will want to rule on the incredible facts in this case. I think I should appeal immediately."

"Yes, immediately. How long will it take?" Larry asked.

"The Notice of Appeal can be done by tomorrow. There is really only one error of law and that is the reduction of the verdict."

"Let's do it," he said. "Before Pamela's funeral. I will feel a lot better."

"You've got it, Larry," Janet hugged him and said her goodbyes. She went to her office and began work on the Notice of Appeal and finished it by about one o'clock in the evening Again she sent Adam to the Court of Appeals and to Judge Parson's court with the pleadings and she had James deliver copies to Rex Montague's office.

Terry Napoli and Rex Montague were meeting with Leslie Winchester and Jason Rivera when Rex's secretary brought the Notice of Appeal into Montague's office.

"I thought you'd like to have this right away," she told her boss.

Montague looked at the pleadings and handed them to Napoli. "One thing you can say about Janet Stephenson is that she doesn't waste any time. Here's the Notice of Appeal of the JNOV."

"What exactly does that mean?" asked Leslie Winchester.

"It just means that Larry Lawson and his attorney, Janet Stephenson, have filed a Notice of Appeal with the Colorado Court of Appeals. Now the case will go to them for review. The process will likely take about two years, but we may win it on appeal as well."

"What do you mean 'may' win it on appeal?" Leslie demanded.

"You heard Judge Parsons say that this is a case of first impression. That means that there is no case that really acts as precedent, so the Court of Appeals can do whatever it likes in terms of interpreting the Colorado wrongful death statute," Montague replied.

"Can the ten million dollar verdict be reinstated?" she asked.

"Yes, and more. That verdict if reinstated would have 8% interest from the date of the filing of the Plaintiffs' lawsuit in the district court, so interest could be quite a chunk of money." Montague added.

"Oh, my word, this gets worse and worse. So, today's victory could be all wiped out with penalties?" she asked.

"You could look at it that way, I suppose," offered Napoli.

"And what are the attorneys' fees for the appeal?" she asked.

"Our firm would charge a beginning retainer of a hundred thousand dollars for the appeal," said Montague simply.

"But it could cost more than that?" she asked.

"Yes, it could. Depending on the amount of work that we get into." Montague added.

"I have to think about this. Don't do anything until you hear from me." Leslie Winchester gathered her things and left the room.

The attorneys all just looked at each other in silence. That was not the reaction they expected.

Leslie Winchester went to the jail to see her husband. This time she had to meet with him in a secured setting, where she spoke to him by telephone and looked at him through a glass window.

"Forrest," she began simply, "I'm going back to Chicago and I'm filing for divorce. You are on your own and I shall not pay any bail for you and I will not pay any attorneys for your defense. I wish you well, but frankly, I think that you are guilty and I don't want anything more to do with you or your friends." Then she hung up the phone and left him, motioning angrily to her through the window. She did not see them take him out of the room.

Then Leslie Winchester went back to the Brown Palace and had a martini and a massage.

Afterward, she put on jeans and a sweater and went for a walk on the Sixteenth Street Mall, stopping at a sidewalk café for a crab salad and a glass of iced tea. When she returned to her hotel room, she called Forrest's secretary and assistant at the offices of Conway Chemical and told them that Forrest had been fired. She asked them to direct an immediate memo to the members of the board of directors advising them that Forrest Winchester had no further signing authority on any bank account or document relating to Conway Chemical. She was taking over all of the positions formerly held by her husband. She also called her personal attorney and asked her to prepare the necessary documents for her to file for divorce.

Then Leslie Winchester called Rex Montague's office and asked to speak to Mr. Montague. She was advised that he was in a meeting with Jason Rivera and Terry Napoli, still. She asked that she be connected and she asked Montague to put her on speakerphone.

"Mr. Rivera, I must advise you that you may continue as Forrest Winchester's attorney if you like, but neither I nor Conway Chemical will be paying for any of his attorney's fees and costs. He has been removed from his employment at Conway Chemical and has no further access to any of its bank accounts or other assets. I have advised Mr. Winchester, in person, of my intention to file for divorce as soon as I return to Chicago.

Mr. Napoli and Mr. Montague. I do not want to go through any appeal of the Lawson case. You are directed to settle the case with Mrs. Stephenson. I understand that this total package could cost me and Conway Chemical upwards of fifteen million dollars if it goes all the way to appeal, the verdict is reinstated and we have to add on the interest and the additional attorneys' fees for the appeal. I am willing to split that with Mr. Lawson. See if he will accept seven and a half million dollars to settle. If he will, I will see that he is paid and that the two of you are paid by the end of the week."

Napoli and Montague were stunned. "Mrs. Winchester, are you sure that you don't want to think about this some more. Why don't we meet for something to eat," began Napoli.

Leslie Winchester interrupted him, "I've eaten, thank you. I just need to get this resolved and get back to running my family's business. I've had quite enough of Denver. I will be at my hotel. I'd like you to call me back within the hour." She hung up the phone.

Janet Stephenson was just pulling into her driveway when her cell phone rang.

"Janet?" It was Rex Montague.

"Yes, hello Rex," Janet answered.

"Janet, we have been discussing the state of the case with Leslie Winchester and she wants us to make you a proposal. She does not want to take her company through the publicity of an appeal, so she has authorized us to offer your client the sum of five million dollars to settle and dismiss the appeal."

Janet couldn't believe her ears. "Say that again," she said.

"Five million, Janet. Can you talk to your client and get back to me tonight. I know that is a bit irregular, but she wants to return to Chicago and wants this resolved first."

"Yes, I'll talk to Larry right away and call you back.," Janet said.

Brad came out of the house to see why she was sitting in her car in the driveway and he waved at her. Janet rolled down her window.

"Brad, why don't you come with me over to the Lawson's. I have something to talk to you about."

"Sure," her husband said and closed the door behind him. He climbed into the passenger seat and said, "What's up?"

"I just got a call from Montague saying that Leslie Winchester wants to settle the case before appeal for five million dollars. He wants to know tonight. So, I have to go to talk to Larry. I can't do this on the phone."

"Cool!" said Brad. "Why the change of heart, I wonder."

Janet called Larry and told him that they were on their way and needed to talk to him. He was waiting and very curious when they arrived. Grandma Lawson was just putting the children in their pajamas.

"Let's go in the study," Janet said.

They closed the door and Janet said, "Larry, I just got a call from Montague saying that they want to settle the case. They have offered five million dollars."

Larry Lawson's mouth dropped open and his eyes opened wide. He actually looked like a cartoon, Brad thought. "Take it!" Larry said.

"Just a minute," Janet warned. "Let's think about this. I want to make sure that we don't leave any money on the table. If Montague has offered us five million dollars, it sounds to me that there is some kind of formula. Just think about it. If the verdict were reinstated, you would get the ten million plus all of the pre- and post-judgment interest. That would make it around fifteen million. I'll bet we can get them to split that with us. Why don't we make a counteroffer and say that we will settle for seven million five hundred thousand dollars?"

"I don't know, Janet. When we dinked around with them before with the six-hundred-thousand-dollar offer, they just took it off the table," Larry said. "I'd be happy with five million."

"I think it's worth a try," Janet said.

Larry looked at her for a long moment, then at Brad sitting quietly in the corner and then he said, "Okay, let's go for it. Are you going to call him now?"

"Yes, he asked me to try and get this done tonight."

Janet dialed Montague's last number from her cell. "Montague," he answered.

"Rex, its Janet Stephenson. I discussed this with Larry and he has authorized me to tell you that he is willing to settle all claims and dismiss the appeal for seven million five hundred thousand dollars."

Montague was silent. "Rex, are you there?" Janet said.

"Yes, Janet. I'll see what I can do. Are you at this number for a while?"

"Yes, and Rex, one more thing. It has to be paid within seven days," she added.

Janet hung up the phone.

"Let's have some coffee and lemon meringue pie," Larry said. "Maybe he'll call back soon."

Janet, Brad, Larry, and Grandma Lawson all sat down around the kitchen table and Grandma Lawson served them pie and fresh coffee. They were talking about Pamela when Janet's telephone rang again. Janet answered. It was Napoli.

"Okay, Janet. You drive a hard bargain, but you have a deal. You dismiss the appeal and we will arrange to wire transfer funds to your trust account in the amount of seven million five hundred thousand dollars by noon on Friday. We will have the settlement documents and release sent over to your offices by courier tomorrow. You can give the courier a sealed envelope with the wiring instructions then"

"That sounds perfect. Thanks, Terry. Talk to you tomorrow." Janet smiled into the phone.

"What!" asked Larry.

"Seven million five hundred thousand dollars will be wire transferred to my firm's trust account by noon on Friday. Now you get your entire five million dollars. PSS is paying your attorney's fees. Maybe you and Grandma and the kids should plan a trip to Disney World." Larry Lawson burst into tears. He reached across the table and took her hands in his.

"Thank you, Janet. I don't have better words than, just thank you for everything."

Janet looked at Grandma Lawson, who also had tears streaming down her face. She was nodding silently in agreement.

Janet and Brad finished their coffee and pie and gave hugs all around before they left. Brad drove home.

"You do good work, my sweet," Brad told her in the car.

For the first time in many months, Janet's heart felt lighter. There was light at the end of her very long tunnel. Even the IRS dragons could be beaten back into their cave. She could pay a bonus to her faithful staff. James and Adam would be ecstatic. She couldn't wait to tell them. When she reached Adam, he and James were at Chili's. He grabbed James and went outside so he could hear her because he couldn't believe his ears that the case had settled without appeal.

"Brad, why don't we take a trip before I launch into my next case," she said after she talked to her clerks.

"Sounds like a terrific idea. We have a granddaughter we need to see," he said. "Let's do it."

Janet leaned over and kissed him on the cheek. "You're the very best," she said.

www.ingramcontent.com/pod-product-compliance
Lightning Source LLC
Chambersburg PA
CBHW030354200726
48286CB00014B/1406